THE SAME BREATH

THE LAMB AND THE LION
BOOK ONE

GREGORY ASHE

H&B

The Same Breath
Copyright © 2020 Gregory Ashe

Published by Hodgkin & Blount
https://www.hodgkinandblount.com/
contact@hodgkinandblount.com

Published 2020
Printed in the United States of America

Trade Paperback ISBN: 978-1-63621-001-8
eBook ISBN: 978-1-63621-000-1

For that which befalleth the sons of men befalleth beasts; even one thing befalleth them: as the one dieth, so dieth the other; yea, they have all one breath; so that a man hath no preeminence above a beast: for all is vanity.

Ecclesiastes 3:19

1

Teancum Leon had barely gotten home from the Division of Wildlife Resources when a knock came at the door. Scipio, his black Lab, was in the middle of doing a welcome / please-take-me-out-for-a-walk dance, but the Lab adjusted his priorities and began to bark.

"All right," Tean said, stroking the dog's ears as he bumped him out of the way.

Mrs. Wish, his neighbor from the end of the hall, was wearing her usual ensemble, regardless of day or night: a full-length house dress, something Tean imagined her picking from a color page in the Sears Catalogue, and a chemically pink terrycloth robe over it. Her long white hair was free of its usual bun, and her eyes were wide.

"There's an intruder," she said between gasps for breath.

"Oh my gosh. Did you call 911?"

"Not that kind," she said, and then she grabbed his arm and dragged him out of the apartment. "It's a spider."

"In that case, I've got to take Scipio for a walk," Tean said.

Mrs. Wish drew herself up, glancing back at Tean's door and then looking down the hall toward her own home. "I'll walk him," she said, like a woman offering to step in front of a firing squad. "You deal with that nasty little murderer."

Tean sighed and nodded. While Mrs. Wish hurried back to rescue Scipio, Tean made his way along the hall and pushed open her door. He had to snag the domestic short-hair that tried to slip out of the apartment—he thought this one was Senator Frank B. Bandegee, because he remembered the white patch on her chest—and then he was inside the apartment, pushing the door shut behind him.

Very little ever changed about Mrs. Wish's apartment: the smell of dander, animal and human, mixed with wet cat food and a floral scent. Collectible presidential ashtrays, holding the mounds of potpourri that provided the flowery note, were placed on occasional tables and shelves and ledges around the room. Doilies. A million doilies. A framed, larger-than-life portrait of President Woodrow Wilson, hanging where most people would have placed a television (once Mrs. Wish had sent Tean into the bedroom to examine a . . . deposit that Senator Henry Cabot Lodge had left on the carpet, and he had stumbled onto an autographed photograph of President Gerald Ford in a heart-shaped frame. President Wilson's illicit rival? Tean was dying to know). And, of course, the Irreconcilables, perched on bookshelves and the back of the sofa, crawling through their cat mansion, swishing past Tean with disdainful looks that said they would accept a display of affection, albeit unwillingly. Their numbers varied between twelve and eighteen; Tean no longer tried to keep track.

Setting down Senator Frank B. Bandegee, Tean made a quick tour of the apartment. He made the mistake of getting too close to Senator Poindexter, a vicious Siamese, and earned a nasty swipe at his ankle for his mistake. In what Mrs. Wish optimistically called the guest bedroom, which was a confection of pink, sateen, and spills of creamy lace—canopy bed included—he found the intruder. The closet doors were open, and Mrs. Wish had dragged one of her heavy dining chairs into place so she could reach the shelf at the top where the spider was hiding.

Tean climbed up onto the chair and examined the shelf: several folded blankets, a lacquered wood box, and a manila folder. On the tab of the folder, Mrs. Wish's Palmer script read: *Reagan – Shirtless.* In smaller letters below, she had added, with quotation marks included, *"The California Showboat."* Tean was reaching to open the folder when he heard the front door. He jerked his hand back.

"Oh, Dr. Leon," Mrs. Wish said, wringing her hands from the guest bedroom's doorway. "You really have to be careful."

Tean shifted his attention to the intruder: a small black spider hanging from its web in the closet's upper corner.

"He looks like a nasty customer," Tean said.

"Well," Mrs. Wish said, obviously at a loss for words. "Smash him!"

"I don't think we need to do that."

"Dr. Leon, I know a black widow spider when I see one. They can kill an adult. Think of what their poison could do to the children."

"Venom," Tean said absently. "Not poison. Do you have a pen? Never mind, I've got a Blackwing in my pocket." He drew out the pencil, got the eraser as close to the web as he could, and tapped the wall. The spider scuttled along the web, following the vibrations. Tean withdrew the pencil, watching as the spider searched for its prey.

"Perhaps my bust of the lesser Roosevelt," Mrs. Wish offered.

"I don't think that'll be necessary."

"Be honest, Dr. Leon. How much danger are the Irreconcilables in? I'll book a hotel. I assume you'll be available to help with their carriers. We can transport them in two trips—"

"I don't think that'll be necessary," Tean said hastily.

"If something happened to one of the children, I'd die. I'd just die."

"Well, we're all going to die, Mrs. Wish. And they're technically not children. They're cats."

That seemed to throw off the rhythm of Mrs. Wish's performance. She put her hands on her hips, staring up at him, and said, "I hardly think a crisis is the time to wax philosophical."

"I'm not being philosophical. I'm just pointing out that we're nothing but complex molecular chains that will eventually dissolve and be recycled into something else. A plant, maybe."

Mrs. Wish stared at him.

"Err. Like catnip. Some of the same basic building blocks that make up Mrs. Wish could one day be inside a cloth mouse, giving some lucky cat hours of entertainment. That'd be nice, right?"

For a moment, Mrs. Wish didn't seem to know what to say. She settled for: "I should think not."

Wiping sweat from his forehead, Tean said, "Right. Well, about the spider—"

"I'll get the lesser Roosevelt."

"Hold on, and then you can decide. First of all, it's not *Latrodectus hesperus*—not a black widow, I mean."

"I know what a black widow—"

"You can see for yourself." Tean offered her the chair, but she shook her head. Pointing with the Blackwing, he said, "No hourglass marking on the ventral abdomen."

"Perhaps you're confused about which side the marking should be on."

Tean tapped the wall again, and the spider scurried across its web, exposing its dorsal side, which was also dark and unmarked.

"Well," Mrs. Wish said, tugging on her terrycloth sleeves. "What is it then?"

"I think it's *Steatoda grossa*, what's called a false black widow."

"I still think a good smashing is in order."

"If you like. But just so you know, *Steatoda grossa* preys on a variety of pests, including *Latrodectus hesperus*. Real black widows, I mean."

Mrs. Wish thought about this. "It won't harm the children."

"No, it won't bother you or the cats."

"And it might even stop something from harming them."

"That's right. There's almost always one thing higher on the food chain. Predators who prey on predators, you know? All the way up to the apex."

After a moment, Mrs. Wish nodded and proclaimed, "Then it stays. If you'd please hand me that folder, though, while you're up there." She murmured something vague about "important documents" and "setting my affairs in order" and tucked the Reagan folder inside her robe like she was robbing a bank.

Tean carried the dining chair back to the front room, with Mrs. Wish dogging him.

"Violet will be very sorry to have missed you," Mrs. Wish said. "She'll be here in a couple of hours."

Tean smiled and nodded.

"I'll send her over with a plate of cookies."

"That's really not necessary."

"She's already got age lines, unfortunately," Mrs. Wish said, tracing them on her own forehead to illustrate. "But I imagine if you squint, or perhaps if you close your eyes when you kiss her, they won't bother you too much."

"Uh. Yes. Well—"

"Twenty-seven, poor dear. Practically a spinster. We tell everyone she's twenty-five because it's just too embarrassing otherwise."

Edging toward the doors, Tean nodded.

"I think she's had the one dead tooth fixed," Mrs. Wish was explaining, "so you won't be bothered by that, at least."

"I hear Scipio barking," Tean said, throwing open the door. "I've got to run."

"I don't hear —"

But he was already sprinting down the hall.

When Tean let himself into the apartment, Scipio was waiting for him, pressing a cold nose against his arm, snuffling, trying to scent out all of the Irreconcilables that had dared get too close. Tean thought of Mrs. Wish's granddaughter coming over with a plate of cookies that were the sugary equivalent of hard tack. He grabbed Scipio's harness and asked the Lab, "What do you think about another walk? A really long one, this time?" The dog park, he thought, was far enough away to be safe.

2

"People suck," Tean said, letting Scipio off the leash. The dog park was busy on Friday afternoon, and Scipio ran off to join Bear, a hundred-and-thirty-pound St. Bernard who dwarfed Tean's black Lab but had still become a regular playmate.

"Ok," Hannah said with a sigh. She was still removing the leash from her own dog, Divorcee. She worked with Tean at DWR, and she had called as he was leaving the apartment to ask if he was interested in being set up on a blind date with a guy she knew. When Tean tried to dodge by explaining he was going to the dog park, she had insisted on joining him. It was nice to have company, even if Hannah didn't realize she was helping a fugitive.

October in the Salt Lake Valley was beautiful; the underbrush on the Wasatch Mountains to the east burned red, and the sun setting over the Great Salt Lake to the west painted everything else gold. Autumn in Utah was a precarious pleasure, always ready to slip early into winter and stay there. Days like this one, with the breeze coming off the mountains and the skies perfectly clear, made sure the dog park stayed busy.

"What does that mean?" Tean asked.

"It means you're trying to get out of this date."

"Everyone's trying to set me up today. Why won't anyone let me have forty or fifty years of peace before I die?"

"Go have fun, princess." This was directed to Divorcee; the teacup Yorkie scampered five feet away, stopped, and looked back. "Go on."

"I'm not trying to get out of a date," Tean said.

"Ok."

"I'm just pointing out an incontrovertible fact."

"Here we go."

"People suck," Tean said, varying the tone a little in case she'd missed the point.

Hannah just sighed. "Can we talk about something else?"

"Miguel asked me if you were single today."

"Did you tell him I'm married?" Hannah said.

"Yes."

"Great. End of conversation."

"I saw those reports you put together on—"

"Not work."

"Well, I wanted to ask—"

"Nope. Work stays at work. I don't want to think about work. Sook's funeral is this weekend, and I don't need anything else making me think about work." Hannah studied the leash, which she wrapped around her hand as she asked, "I don't suppose you've heard anything new from the detectives."

"I don't think it's that straightforward." In fact, Tean thought, nothing had been straightforward about the case. Sook Hyeon, one of the DWR's conservation officers, had been killed the week before. She had been in a bad part of town, late at night, and nobody could explain why a nice, smart Mormon girl with a 401k and a master's degree, with a good job and a boyfriend, with overprotective parents who still called to make sure she was home safe at the end of every day—nobody could figure out why that kind of girl had been where she'd been, had died the way she had died.

Hannah nodded, tears in her eyes. "I know. It's just—she was my friend, you know? And it doesn't seem real."

"I'm sure they're doing all they can," Tean said.

Nodding, Hannah wiped her cheeks as the tears came faster.

"I'm so sorry," Tean said. He moved in for a hug, reconsidered, but was already committed. He ended up giving her an awkward, one-armed embrace from the side, and Hannah laughed brokenly and patted his arm.

"I went through her logs and reports," Tean said as he stepped back, "and I made some calls. Nobody could tell me anything out of the ordinary. And I gave all the information to the police."

"You didn't have to do that."

"I know; the detectives would have looked at it on their own eventually."

"No, I mean, you're a good guy for doing it."

"I'd be a better guy if I weren't planning how to ditch this blind date."

Hannah slapped his arm. "Sorry. I told myself I wasn't going to bring Sook up again."

Scipio and Bear had both gotten hold of a rope, and Bear was dragging Scipio around in an uneven version of tug-of-war.

"We could talk about books," Tean said.

"Pass."

"If you ever read a book . . ."

"Let's talk about the very exciting date that I'm setting you up on. Why do you think you won't like Rand?"

"Because his name's Rand. Why can't Utah people name their kids anything normal?"

"You are Utah people. And you have a weird name too. Anyway, he's a nice guy, and he's cute. I showed him your picture, and he said you were hot."

"That doesn't say much for his taste," Tean muttered.

Hannah slugged him.

Across the park, Scipio and Bear were wrestling. Bear's owner was a young guy with a lot of muscles and who apparently owned only tank tops. A couple of times he and Tean had talked. He had a faux-tribal tattoo on his shoulder. Between the tank tops and the tattoo, he was the closest thing to a bad boy Salt Lake City seemed capable of producing.

"That guy's straight," Hannah said.

"Straight's a twentieth-century term. Everybody's on a sexual spectrum now."

"Not on the Wasatch Front they aren't."

"Hence my point," Tean said. "People suck."

"Ok, sweetie, get it all out of your system."

"If you insist—"

"I was talking to Divorcee."

The Yorkie was pausing every eighteen inches to investigate another clump of grass, obviously trying to choose the best spot.

"Oh. Well, I'm going to tell you anyway."

Sighing, Hannah nodded.

"In the ocean—" Tean began.

"So help me, if you bring up the whale thing again, I will kill you, and then I will kill myself."

Divorcee trotted back toward them, steering straight for Tean. She had some sort of obsession with using his shoes as her personal potty pad, and he darted behind Hannah. "I wasn't going to bring up the whale thing."

"Uh huh."

"I wasn't."

"The ocean was just a logical place to start," Hannah said.

"Exactly. Where all life began," Tean said. "As a biologist who specializes in native aquatics, you should know that."

"Oh my gosh," Hannah said. "I might honestly have to kill you."

"Do you know how many people get murdered on first dates? Especially blind dates?"

"How many?"

"A lot," Tean said.

"Just because you saw one Lifetime movie about it doesn't mean it happens a lot."

"He might want to harvest my kidneys."

"Rand doesn't need your kidneys; his kidneys are perfectly healthy. That's the first thing I ask every guy before I set you up with him."

"He could traffic me. I could wind up in sexual slavery."

"Heaven help whoever buys you."

A breeze picked up; crabapples lined one side of the park, and the too-sweet stench of rotting fruit floated on the air. Tean decided to try a different tack. "Do you know how many bear-related fatalities occur every year? In the United States, anyway."

"On average, three," Hannah said.

"You only know that because you work at DWR too," Tean said. "Other people would be suitably shocked."

Hannah paused long enough to tuck her chestnut hair behind her ears and arrange her features in an expression of surprise.

"That's better," Tean said. "And do you know how many homicides occur every year?"

"Five."

"Don't do that."

"Do what?" Hannah asked.

"Four hundred thousand, globally. Every year. In some countries, it's the leading cause of death. People killing each other is the leading cause of death."

"Please tell me this is not what you're going to talk about with Rand."

"And do you know how many bears kill other bears?"

"It's rare," Hannah said.

"Again, insider knowledge; unfair advantage because you're a biologist. Most people wouldn't have any idea. It's so rare that the *Smithsonian* dedicated a whole article to it."

"Divorcee, sweetie, come on."

The Yorkie was investigating the shoes of an old woman perched on a bench.

"Leave her alone," Hannah said. "I'm sorry!"

The old woman waved and laughed.

Divorcee saw her moment of opportunity and struck, spraying the woman's foot.

"Oh my gosh," Hannah shouted, "I'm so sorry!" Then, to Tean, "I've got to handle this. Good luck tonight."

"People suck, that's what I'm trying to explain."

"See you at Sook's service?"

"And if you compare the number of bears—"

"Don't screw it up," Hannah called back as she ran toward the old woman, who was now trying to hop on her unsullied foot while using the back of the bench for balance.

"Animals are better than people," Tean shouted after Hannah.

"You're a wildlife vet," Hannah shouted back. "You know that's not true!"

"At least animals don't—"

"Talk about movies," Hannah shouted over him. "Rand loves movies." She turned to the old woman, apologizing. When she reached for Divorcee, the Yorkie sprinted away from her.

"The whale story is better," Tean informed Divorcee as she pranced up to him. He glanced over to check on Scipio, who was playing tag with Bear now, both dogs sprinting the length of the park. The late afternoon sunlight drew long shadows: the fence, the dogs, the guy with the tank top and tattoo.

Out of the corner of his eye, too late, Tean registered what was happening. Sniffing his shoe, Divorcee got into position and gave him the last drops in the tank.

"Damn it," Tean shouted. "Your dog, Hannah!"

"What were you saying about animals?" she called.

3

"People suck," Jem said, carrying the TV tray with a Stouffer's single-serve lasagna into the living room. He had to kick aside some of the bagged newspapers, and his foot came down on something that was soft and squishy. On his next step, he connected with a loose can of store-brand cola, and it shot out, ricocheted off the entertainment center, and hit a pyramid of root beer bottles. The bottles came tumbling down, brown glass tinkling, but at least none of them broke. "God damn it, Benny, you've got to clean this place up. You're supposed to be an adult, for Christ's sake. This place is a sty."

Benny swiped at the stringy hair hanging in front of his face, glanced up from the mess of papers in front of him as Jem set down the lasagna, and mumbled, "Doesn't matter. Nothing matters anymore. They're gonna kill me. This time I'm serious. They're really going to kill me."

"Nobody's going to kill you. People suck, sure. But nobody's going to kill you."

"Yes, they are. They are."

"Who's they?"

Benny just mumbled to himself and bent closer to examine pages filled with his scrawl.

"Hey, dummy," Jem said, rapping Benny on the head. "I'm talking to you."

"Cut it out," Benny said, swiping at Jem.

Jem was faster, though, and he rapped on Benny's head again. "Meds?" he asked.

"Doctor took me off them."

"No joke? That's great."

Benny scratched out a line on the topmost page and scribbled something in the margin.

"Don't lie to me, Benny. Where's your medicine?"

"I don't like how it makes me feel. I'm not taking it anymore."

"Not your choice."

"I flushed all the pills."

Jem had to walk into the kitchen. The apartment was a shithole in West Valley, built in the 1970s by guys who had never cared about the place looking nice or lasting long. Now, almost fifty years later, the whole complex was a shrine to greedy landlords. Ancient paint bubbled and peeled, evidence of water damage and, probably, mold. The carpet was brownish gray and matted—Jem had been shocked when he had moved Benny's bed to discover a patch of robin's egg blue that must have been the original coloring. The linoleum in the kitchen was peeling, and half of the time when Jem came over, he ended up using crazy glue to stick it back to the floor. In the bathroom, the ceiling bulged and sagged ominously, and once, Jem could have sworn he'd seen a drop of water.

He stood in the kitchen, staring at the pile of dishes in scummy gray water, at the refrigerator with the door that wouldn't close all the way, at the range with the foil-wrapped drip pans, crusted now with a layer of burnt food. At least the place smelled like lasagna, even if it was only temporary. For another minute, Jem stood there, flexing his hands. Then he did what he always did.

First, he went through the cabinets, checking cans.

"Why haven't you eaten any of the vegetables?" he shouted into the living room.

"I don't like French-cut green beans."

"These aren't French cut."

Silence for thirty seconds. Then, "They have too much sodium."

"Why didn't you eat the fruit cocktail?"

"I'm on a diet."

"You've got to eat something that didn't come in plastic wrap," Jem said. "I'll make carrots; I saw some in the freezer." He opened another cabinet. "Benny, where's that spice rack? I'll put some garlic powder in the carrots."

The only answer was papers shuffling.

"Benny?"

Next door, Mrs. Johnson was shrieking about her lying, piece-of-shit husband, and then there was a deep, gonging noise that made Jem picture a cartoon cat getting struck by a cartoon frying pan.

From the opening to the living room, Jem asked, "Benny, spices?"

Benny wouldn't look up.

"Jesus Christ, Benny," Jem said. "Again?"

"I needed cash to buy my girlfriend dinner. Elisa said she'd give me twenty bucks for the spice rack."

"Jesus fucking Christ, Benny. That shit costs me money, ok? All this costs money. I don't buy you fucking groceries so they can sit in your fucking cabinets, and I don't buy you fucking spice racks so you can sell them to fucking Elisa so you can have twenty fucking bucks to buy your fucking imaginary girlfriend a fucking hamburger."

"She's not imaginary," Benny said.

"What's her name?" Jem said, louder than he meant to. "Where'd you meet her? What's she do for work? What's her favorite fucking color, Benny?"

Flinching, Benny tried to maneuver his bulk closer to the pages, tried to make himself smaller, which was hard to do when he was over two hundred pounds.

Opening and closing his hands, Jem said, "Sorry."

Benny crossed something out; his hand was shaking.

Moving to the couch, Jem dropped down, met by the sour stink of body odor. "Benny, I'm sorry. It's just—it's a lot of stuff."

"I don't need you to buy me anything."

"I know."

"I never made up an imaginary girlfriend in my whole life."

"I know."

"I'm fine," Benny said. "I don't need you."

Jem studied the bagged newspapers, the magazine pages cut out and pasted over the windows, the greasy smears in the carpet, the handwritten manifesto spread out in front of Benny. He closed his eyes and said, "I know."

Next door, Mrs. Johnson was sobbing.

"Why did I tell you to be careful around girls?" Jem asked.

"The same reason you're careful around boys."

"Which is what?"

"You don't want your dick to do your thinking for you."

"Right. And what else?"

"It's easy to believe someone likes you because everybody wants to be liked."

"That's right," Jem said. "And people will believe anything if they want it to be true. Even you. Even me."

Benny just shrugged.

"What's her name?" Jem asked again.

"I don't want to tell you."

"For Christ's sake."

"Anyway, I won't be your problem for much longer," Benny said. "They're going to kill me."

"You're not a problem. And nobody's going to kill you, Benny."

"They are. I know too much; it's all right here. They have to get rid of me."

"Benny, I know you don't like how you feel on the meds, but you can't just go off them. We'll go see the doctor again. We'll find something that helps you and doesn't make you feel bad."

Benny shrugged.

"How's your pump?"

"Fine."

"Insulin?"

"Fine."

"Did you test your blood sugar?"

"It's fine, Jem."

"When's the last time you tested it?"

"Dunno."

"Ok, I'll get a strip."

"This morning."

"Benjamin Lindsey Guthall, if you are lying to me, I will beat your ass."

He flashed Jem a wounded look. "I checked it this morning."

After that, there wasn't much Jem could do. He conducted his final walkthrough and spotted the backpack with a pup tent strapped to the top. When he got back to the living room, he said, "Are you going to the Jenkins' place?"

"Maybe."

"No, we don't play that way."

"Yes."

"When?"

"I don't know."

"When, Benny?"

"Tonight."

"For how long? It's Friday, so when are you coming back?"

"I don't know."

"Jesus Christ," Jem said.

"I don't! I know too much, Jem. I've got to lie low for a while. I'll be up there until it's safe to come back."

"Did you tell the Jenkins you were coming?"

"Not yet."

"Fine. I'll call them. Next week, Benny, we're going to see your doctor, and we're going to try different meds."

Benny was reordering the pages in his lap.

"Tell me you heard me."

"Ok, all right, I heard you."

"What's our rule?"

"You've got a million rules."

"What's our rule, Benny?"

"Cell phone on and charged, and I answer when you call."

"Even if you're in a movie."

"Even if I'm in a movie," Benny repeated.

"Even if you're taking a dump."

"You're so gross."

"Get up and give me a hug."

"Jem," Benny whined.

"Get your fat ass up."

After some more groaning, Benny stood, and they hugged.

"Eat that before it's cold," Jem said, pointing at the lasagna, where the red sauce was already congealing.

Benny just nodded and mumbled.

Outside, at the bottom of the stairs, Tommy Johnson, twelve years old, was smoking a fatty blunt. His eyes were glazed when he looked up at Jem.

"That bad?" Jem asked.

Tommy blew a ring of smoke, his head sagging back as he stared at the October sky.

"Let me get a hit," Jem said. Tommy passed it over, and Jem took a few long drags, holding the smoke, his eyes closed, letting the world soften. When he passed it back, he said, "You eat dinner?"

Tommy shook his head like he was in slow motion.

Digging out his last ten, Jem said, "Go get something to eat."

Then Jem headed back into the city, trying to figure out the best place he could get an asshole to buy him a drink.

4

The Lagartija wasn't exactly fine dining, but it had prices in Tean's budget, friendly staff, and a killer mole sauce. It was consistently one of the top-rated places to eat in Salt Lake City, even though it didn't look like it with its yellow-and-red-brick exterior and the old-fashioned bulbs on the restaurant's sign.

Tean waited at the hostess stand, checking his phone, checking his watch, checking his eyebrows in the plate-glass window. They were bushier than ever, which made absolutely no sense at all because Tean had gone after them like a madman with a pair of nail scissors maybe a week before. He pushed his hair back a few times. He checked his glasses. They were crooked, permanently bent, but he managed to make them slightly less crooked. Somebody would go home with the guy in the glass, he figured. Not Rand. Definitely not. But maybe a cockroach would have too much to drink.

His phone buzzed. Maybe it was Rand calling to cancel. Maybe North Korea had finally launched a nuke and targeted Salt Lake City. A guy could hope. Tean didn't recognize the number.

He accepted the call and said, "Leon."

On the other end of the call, he heard nothing. Then someone started breathing heavily.

"Hello?" Tean said again.

The heavy breathing continued for a few more seconds, and then the phone clicked off.

"Tean?" a voice said behind him.

"Hi, yeah," Tean said, pocketing the phone and turning. "Rand?"

They both chuckled and did an awkward handshake that Rand turned into an even more awkward one-armed hug. Rand was, of course, another one of the all-American beauties that the Mormon families seemed to churn out: dark hair in a conservative part, blue eyes, clean-shaven, a strong jaw. He smelled a little citrusy. And maybe a little boozy, too.

"God," Rand said, "I love this place. Did you already put your name in?"

Tean had, and he waved at Esme, who had already made sure he'd be seated in her section. She led them to a two-top near the front, but Rand stopped her and asked if they could sit farther back. Esme didn't exactly grimace, but she came pretty close. She led them to another table in the back corner. Strands of lights ran overhead, but back here, they left a pleasant pool of shadow. The hub of voices was quieter too, although the noise from the kitchen compensated for it.

"More romantic," Rand said, dropping into the far seat and then leaning out to look past Tean, his vision fixed on the entrance. "Don't you think?"

"Sure."

"I've brought a lot of guys here," Rand said, still peering past Tean.

"That's nice."

"They've got great margaritas. Do you want a margarita?" Rand started snapping, trying to get Esme's attention as she passed their table again.

Tean was thinking about how many bears eat other bears. He could hear Hannah telling him, *Don't screw it up.*

"Hi, yeah," Rand said when Esme finally came over to put chips and salsa on the table. "Definitely a margarita, the bigger one, for me. And for this guy, what are you having?"

Esme's glare was hotter than the sun, and Tean ducked his head; they'd grown up together, just a few blocks apart, and Tean knew this whole story was going to be repeated for approximately the next thirty years of his life.

"A Sprite, I guess."

"Oh Christ," Rand said, laughing. "Oh Christ, don't tell me you're still hung up on all that church shit."

Grizzly bear claws were four inches long, Tean reminded himself. Long enough to get to Rand's jugular.

"How about a Corona?" Tean said.

"Better," Rand said, laughing. "But that's just a start. I'm going to get you fucking wasted and then I'm going to pound your ass like crazy."

Tean's face was burning as Esme left. He opened his mouth before he could stop himself and asked, "Do you know how many bear fatalities happen in a year?"

"Huh?" Rand pushed a chip around in the salsa. "Oh, right. You're like a vet or something, Hannah told me."

"Yep."

"What about bears?"

Hannah's voice again: *Don't screw it up.*

"Nothing," Tean said. "Just an icebreaker. Hannah said you're a lawyer."

"Oh yeah," Rand said, his shoulders back, his elbows out, taking up more space. "Lots of big cases right now. We go after the bad guys."

"That's pretty cool. Are you a prosecutor?"

"Oh no, man, they make shit money. I'm with Fransen and Wood. We're nailing the state right now, we're fucking crucifying them. You know about all the shit at the medical examiner's office?"

"Some kind of delay, right?"

"Not a delay. Those assholes are too busy stealing from the dead to do their jobs. We've got several plaintiffs who claim their loved ones' possessions were not returned, and on top of that, a criminally long backlog of autopsies they haven't completed. The state is going to pay through the fucking nose."

"Getting those bad guys," Tean said.

"Fuck yeah."

"So, you're into movies, right?"

After that, Tean didn't have to say anything except his order; Rand filled in the silences with lengthy expositions on movies — "nobody makes art anymore, you know?" — Disney — "just can't believe George Lucas sold out to them" — and actors — "Paul Walker is just so underrated that he's basically the one real tragedy of our generation." Between lengthy opinions, he guzzled the first margarita and started a second.

"What about you?" Rand finally asked. "Do you like movies?"

Tean had been trying to reproduce parts of the CDC's mortality tables in his head, and it took him a moment to realize that Rand was waiting for an answer.

"I do like movies," Tean said, "but I haven't seen many lately. I kind of liked—"

"Oh, I bet you haven't seen *Get Out*. Have you seen it? I bet you haven't seen it. It's fucking fantastic, man. It's the best thing ever. And it's really fucking empowering."

"No, I haven't seen it."

But it didn't matter because Rand was already going again, something about Key and Peele and post-racial something, finally pausing to stare at Tean over the margarita and say, "I mean, you're brown. You get it."

At which point, the volume of that little voice that sounded like Hannah got turned all the way down to a buzz, and the volume of the voice that sounded a lot more like Tean got turned all the way up.

"What's the point of this?" Tean asked, gesturing between them. "What are we even doing here?"

"Well, I thought—"

"Do you think lions have to listen to agonizing soapbox speeches about cinema just so they can have sex?"

"Hey," Rand said, "hold on."

"Did you know," Tean said, "that statistically, romantic love only lasts one year, but the average marriage lasts eight years? That's a seven-year difference. Seven years that you're miserable because you let your penis do all your thinking."

"Uh."

"What do you think about that, Rand? Seven years. Is it worth it?"

Rand took a few more gulps of his margarita and managed to say, "Yeah, totally, I mean, marriage is such a hetero concept anyway. And the church is just so fucking wack about it. I mean, you know."

Tean did know. Go on a date with any gay guy on the Wasatch Front, and you were bound to hear over and over again about the church, which meant the Mormon church. So Tean told the same lie every gay Mormon guy told.

"Yeah," Tean said. "I don't even think about church anymore."

"Totally, totally," Rand said. And then, because the church doors were now open, "I knew Hannah on my mission. Did she tell you that?"

"She mentioned it," Tean said.

"She said you went to Peru."

"That's right."

"Man, I was gay as fuck on my mission. I just wish I'd told somebody so they'd send me home."

Tean smiled and took a long drink of Corona, the bottle cool and smooth under his fingers, the light warping along the glass. He remembered lying in bed, the sea breeze rolling in across the balcony, and reaching out, his fingers trailing along Ammon's pale, perfect skin.

"Missions are a crazy time," he said.

"You like random facts," Rand announced.

"I wouldn't call them random."

"I read this study about married people. Do you know that the average married couple only has sex once a week?"

"Sounds excessive."

The confusion on Rand's face almost made him laugh.

"Did you know that the average wedding and the average divorce both cost approximately twenty thousand dollars?" Tean said. "That's twice what my car is worth, and you have to pay it twice because your penis makes you think all those hormones running through you are something significant, and then you're stuck for seven years trying to work up the courage to get out of it."

Rand stared down into his third margarita, swirling it. "Yeah," he muttered. "Yeah, fuck love. Fuck it."

"I mean, what's the whole point anyway?" Tean said. "Why are we even here? You said you're going to get me drunk and plow me? Great, sounds like a plan. Let's do that. But I mean, love, marriage, what's that all about?"

"Fuck it," Rand mumbled and then took a long drink, shooting a glare at Tean like Tean might try to stop him.

"Hooking up, great," Tean said. "But love? Marriage? Do you know how much time the average couple spends together? Do you want to guess?"

"Oh shit," Rand said, closing his eyes. "I shouldn't have gone for three of these bad boys."

"Two hours a day. Two. And statistically, they spend half that time watching TV. I mean, marriage is basically just a contract that shoves someone into your life, somebody who loses the remote and won't do the dishes, and in exchange, you get to watch some TV together and have to have sex every once in a while."

Rand's face screwed up, and he wailed, "Jesse loved to watch *The Bachelor.*" Then he started to sob.

"Not again," Tean said, staring down into his beer. Esme came toward them, a frown on her face, but Tean waved her away. He let Rand cry for a while, and then he nudged the half-eaten plate of flautas toward him and said, "Jesse's your ex?"

"He's just—" Rand's breath hitched in his chest. Another wail escaped him: "He's just so perfect!"

"Well, I'm sure he's not perfect. Maybe it'll help if you remember that he's slowly dying, like all of us, as irrevocable DNA damage accumulates in the cells."

Unfortunately, Rand seemed not to have heard this piece of advice. "No, he is. He's perfect. He teaches kindergarten, and he runs marathons, and he's nice to my parents. He never makes a mess in the kitchen. He did the laundry every week. And now he's gone." Rand looked around. "Where's the girl? I need another one of these."

"I think three might be enough," Tean said, wondering if Esme would stab Rand in front of witnesses if she heard him refer to her as the girl. "What happened with Jesse?"

"I screwed it up." Swirling the remains of his margarita, Rand said, "Like I screwed this up."

"To be fair," Tean said, "I was the one who went down a black hole about love."

"Yeah, but I talked about movies. God, that was some pretentious, boring shit."

"I almost told you my whale story."

"What's the whale story? Oh, hey, can I get another?"

"No," Tean said, waving off Esme. "He's fine."

"You wanna go back to my place?" Rand said. He fumbled through his wallet for cash. "I've got a sweet townhouse. We can fuck each other like crazy."

"Thanks," Tean said. "Maybe you should text Jesse."

"No way. No way. No way."

"How long were you together?"

"Two years."

"What happened?"

"He said I didn't listen to him or respect him."

"And?"

"And we had a huge fucking fight and he left." Rand blinked. "Are you sure you don't want me to do you? I bet you get wild."

"Um, no. Did you try apologizing?"

"What?"

"Did you ever tell Jesse you were sorry?"

Rand stared at him, blinking some more. "Huh?"

"Apologizing is really important," Tean said. "At least, when it's sincere, which is probably twenty percent of the time with humans. With animals, though, it works all the time. Wolves, for example. Did you know that wolves and dogs have perfected the non-verbal apology? It's even got a name: the apology bow. You've probably seen it if you've ever yelled at a dog."

"What are we talking about?"

"Jesse. And you. And apologizing. You're going to do it like a wolf, not like a human who treated a nice guy like crap."

"Hey!"

"Do you know why wolves apologize?"

Rand was obviously still trying to decide if he was going to press the issue.

"Wolves apologize," Tean said, "because like humans, they're pack animals who crave social integration. But unlike humans, who suck and are the absolute worst, wolves have no problem expressing submissive behavior in a genuine way: I was wrong, you were right, that kind of thing."

"Holy shit," Rand said. "I am way too fucking drunk for wolves."

"Phone," Tean said, waving for Rand to pass it over. When Rand did, Tean found Jesse BOO under favorites, opened the messaging app, and typed out a few lines. He passed it back.

"No way," Rand said. "He's going to think it's a trick."

"Then you'd better mean it before you hit send."

"You really think he'll, you know," Rand swallowed and wiped his eyes, "want to talk to me?"

"Only one way to find out."

Rand's thumb hesitated over the screen, and then he tapped it.

"Sorry this was such a bad first date," Rand said.

"At least you didn't harvest my kidneys," Tean said.

"You're a really good guy," Rand said.

Tean spun his bottle and smiled. He didn't like how it felt on his face.

Rand frowned, but before he could speak again, his phone buzzed. He put it to his ear. "Hey, Jess. Yeah, now's a good time."

Waving once, Rand stumbled away from the table.

"Another resounding success," Esme said, picking up the cash.

"Ha ha."

"He didn't leave crying. The last guy was bawling so hard he couldn't walk in a straight line."

"How was I supposed to know his grandmother had been eaten by a bear?"

Sighing, Esme grabbed Rand's plate. "You are a real treat."

"If it's any consolation, I'm statistically likely to die choking on popcorn in my apartment, and it'll probably take days before anyone finds the body."

"You know what?" Esme said. "It is."

5

Jem went to the bar in the Apollonia, one of the most expensive hotels in Salt Lake City, situated between Temple Square and the Salt Palace Convention Center—in other words, the perfect place to stumble across closeted gay Mormon businessmen who had some extra cash to burn. He timed his entrance so that he collided with a stout, middle-aged guy in a Jazz jersey. They exchanged apologies, and Jem made his way to the bar. He ignored Stef, who was drying glasses behind the bar and rolling her eyes. Her hair was red now, and the sides of her head shaved.

It only took a moment to scan the sheep at the bar: four men, two in conversation, two sitting by themselves. Jem immediately crossed off the guy on the right; he was engaged in a loud phone call with someone he kept calling princess. The guy on the left, though, had looked over when Jem collided with the other man at the bar's entrance, and he'd already glanced at Jem a second time. He was a nice looking, blond, late thirties, probably really starting to feel the pinch of a wife and two and a half kids. Between his hands, he cupped a tumbler—so maybe he wasn't the nice Mormon daddy he looked like. Jem counted three stools over and sat.

Stef was rolling her eyes again.

Ignoring her, Jem asked about local whiskey and bourbon.

"We've got High West." Stef had her lines pretty much perfect by now. "They do a traditional, Old West blended whiskey: rye, scotch, and bourbon. Do you want to try it?"

Jem made a face.

"It's pretty good," the guy to Jem's left said. "I tried the Campfire."

"Yeah?" Jem said. "Honestly, I have no idea what I'm doing." He laughed. "I'm not much of a drinker, but, I don't know. Tonight I was feeling a little reckless."

"Get him a Campfire neat," the guy said, and then he swiveled on the stool, his legs spread, studying Jem openly.

Jem had never really mastered blushing on demand, but he could do a pretty good job of combing his fingers through his beard, biting the corner of his mouth, looking away and looking back. The guy's grin got bigger, more confident. When Stef came back, setting a tumbler in front of him, Jem patted himself down and lurched off the stool.

"You've got to be kidding me," Jem said. "Hold on."

He made his way back to the entrance, studying the floor, squatting near the door. After about a minute, the guy from the bar came over.

"What happened?"

"Somehow I dropped my money."

"You lost your wallet?"

"No, I left my wallet in my room. I just brought cash and my ID." He flashed the Montana driver's license, one of many fakes. "Dang it. Never mind. This is like a sign, you know? I should have just watched *Rocky* and gone to bed. I cannot believe I dropped that money. It was the rest of my per diem."

"You know what?" the guy said. "I don't think you dropped it."

Jem worked on his quizzical expression; he was getting pretty good at quizzical. "What do you mean?"

"That guy who ran into you on the way out? That's a classic pickpocket move. Crash into a guy, take his wallet while he's recovering, and he doesn't realize until you're long gone. A hotel like this, with a lot of people from out of town? Perfect venue."

"Oh my gosh," Jem groaned. "Are you serious? That actually happens?"

"All the time. Don't worry; you'll learn these things."

"No way," Jem said. "I'm going back to Missoula tomorrow, and I'm not leaving again." He chuckled. "Would you believe I was so proud of myself for getting around the last few days? I thought I was street smart."

The guy laughed a little too, touched Jem's shoulder, and tugged him toward the bar. "Come on, have a drink. On me. Don't beat yourself up about it; guys like that, they prey on people who are just a little too confident."

"Gosh," Jem said, trying hard to ignore Stef pretending to stab herself in the ear. "That's crazy."

This time, they sat next to each other. The guy introduced himself as Patrick; he had a whole story about working out of San Francisco, but when he put his phone and keys on the bar, his keychain had a loyalty card for a sandwich shop that only operated in the Salt Lake Valley — Jem recognized the logo — and his ring finger showed a lighter patch of skin where he normally wore a wedding band. Jem spun him a story back, something about ranching in Montana, keeping the details light. When Patrick spread his legs, Jem spread his legs. When Patrick leaned on the bar, Jem leaned on the bar. Jem asked questions, always tagging on Patrick, Patrick, Patrick, working the name into conversation as much as he could. Nothing too personal, because he didn't want Patrick to spook and think Jem might have realized Patrick was local and not a California tycoon, but he asked business questions, then questions about whiskey, questions about life. Questions about women, Jem unspooling his doubts: why couldn't he find the one? Why didn't it feel 'right'? Anything to make Jem look naïve and inexperienced; anything to make Patrick feel worldly and sophisticated.

When Stef brought sliders, nachos, and a draft beer, Patrick's hand moved to Jem's thigh.

Deer-in-the-headlights was a Jem Berger classic, and Patrick ate it up like candy.

Patrick smiled. He was in control, the mature guy who was about to make a conquest and also provide a moment of sexual awakening. Jem focused on the sliders so he didn't throw up a little inside his mouth.

"I think maybe you want to keep talking," Patrick said. "Do you want to go back to your room?"

Jem gulped. It might have been a little over the top, based on the face Stef made, but it worked a surprising amount of the time. "My buddy's here with me."

"Oh."

"But we could go to your room," Jem said, and then he played with his beard and stared at the food, mumbling, "If, you know, if you want to."

"Yeah," Patrick said. "I definitely want to." He laughed, squeezed Jem's leg, and excused himself to go to the bathroom.

"You are a bad man," Stef said.

"Fuck that," Jem said. "This asshole probably lives fifteen minutes from here," the words emerged between bites as he shoveled the remaining food into his mouth, "and he's going to get a room right now because he thinks he's going to get his dick wet. My bet is that he'll try to get me to leave right after, and if I won't, then he'll make up an excuse and jet. The little wifey will miss him if he's gone too late."

"You are a very bad man," Stef said, and then she drifted away as Patrick came back.

"Hey, cowboy," Patrick said, his hand light on Jem's shoulder. Jem tried, again, not to throw up a little. "Ready?"

Jem licked the last of the nacho cheese off his finger, grinned, and nodded.

A nice-looking guy, the first good meal all week, some decent whiskey, a soft bed, and a room that had honest-to-God heat. Jem whistled "Home, Home on the Range," while Patrick groped him in the elevator.

6

Utah's Division of Wildlife Resources had their main offices in Salt Lake City, on North Temple, west of downtown proper. Tean's office was on the ground floor, with a huge window that took up most of one wall and looked out on the scenic DWR parking lot. With the exception of the lab and the necropsy area, the building tended to smell like any other government structure, with the chemical perfume of industrial cleaner. Hannah had tried to improve that by adding an essential oil diffuser to his room, which was currently spreading the scent of lemon and quince—also Hannah's choice. Across from the desk, Tean had hung some of his favorite posters—front and center, a rendering of the earth and the sun hanging in space, and in a cheery font, SMILE! IT TAKES EIGHT MINUTES FOR LIGHT FROM THE SUN TO REACH EARTH, SO FOR ALL WE KNOW, IT'S ALREADY EXPLODED!

On Monday, Tean was reviewing numbers on this year's mule deer population when the phone rang.

"Leon," he answered.

Heavy breathing.

"Who is this?" Tean said.

More heavy breathing.

"I'm going to report you to the police," Tean said, which was a bluff.

An electronically distorted voice said: "Leave it alone."

The call disconnected.

Tean was still staring at the phone, trying to figure out what was happening, when Hannah came into the room and shut the door.

"What's wrong?" she said.

"Nothing. Just a weird call."

"Oh, gosh. Don't get me started. I had some woman on the phone asking me if I could criminalize fishing statewide. She said she used to be a cutthroat trout and then her consciousness metempsycho-something and now she's a real estate agent."

"If this is about adding another conservation officer to native aquatics," Tean said, "I can't do anything for you until we hire someone into Sook's job."

Tucking her hair behind her ears, Hannah said, "Have you heard anything else?"

"I made a few more calls this morning," Tean said. Then his eyes went to the phone, and he thought of the call he'd just received. He shook his head. "I didn't get anywhere. Sook was out in Tooele most of last week, but nobody will say more than ten words to me. I might have to drive out there."

"And what's your detective going to say about that?"

"Ammon isn't my detective, Hannah." She opened her mouth, and he held up a finger. "What do you want?"

"I'm not always trying to get something from you, Tean."

"Uh huh."

"Sometimes I just want to check in on you as a person."

"That's even worse," Tean said.

"How was your weekend?"

"I got a sunburn on my neck. I probably have skin cancer. I'll be dead by the end of the year."

"Uh huh, uh huh, and how was your date?"

"I think it's a second-degree burn."

"For freak's sake," Hannah muttered and darted out of the office.

That had been easier than Tean expected.

Two minutes later, though, Hannah was back, and she slapped a flattened tube of diaper cream on the desk.

"Uh."

"For your neck, dummy. It works great on sunburns."

"Ok, but, like. You've already used that one on butts."

"Use it. Don't use it. Die from skin cancer. I don't care. How was your date?"

"Fine."

"No. No, it wasn't fine because Rand told me he's back together with Jesse. Really? That's how your first date ended, and you want to tell me it was fine?"

"He said Jesse was perfect."

"Jesse is acceptable," Hannah said, dropping into the chair and propping her Merrells on the desk. "Jesse's the human equivalent of a water cracker. I wanted you and Rand to get together."

"I don't think he was my type."

"What is your type?"

"What is a nice Mormon girl like you doing setting gay guys up?"

"I like gay guys. What's your type?"

"Blue eyes," Tean said. "Wavy dark hair. Great body. Looks good in tights."

Letting her head flop back, Hannah said, "You're describing Superman."

"You didn't let me finish: can fly, heat vision, stops to help old ladies cross the street—"

"Ok, you're definitely describing Superman."

" —draws strength from the yellow sun—"

"Teancum Mahonri Leon," she began.

"God, it sounds so Mormon when you string it all together like that."

"What is your type of non-flying, non-laser-eyes, human male?"

"Pass."

Shoving her chestnut hair back, Hannah brought her head up to glare at him.

"Regular human males are a pass," Tean said. "People are the worst. Do you know—"

"Don't start with the bears again."

" —in the ocean—"

"Or that goddamn whale."

Tean grimaced. "What's the upside if I get a boyfriend? Mediocre sex and someone who wants to talk to me all the time?"

"You like talking to people."

"No, I don't."

"You like talking to me."

"Debatable. And what's the downside? The downside is that I have to cook for two people, clean up after two people, pay for two people to go to the movies, worry about two sets of problems, and seven years later, he's going to finally work up the courage to end things, and he'll take all my mother's jewelry and run off with the pool boy."

"That took a turn, but not as bad as I expected."

"If he doesn't kill me and Scipio in our sleep and bury us in the desert."

"There it is. Maybe you should see a shrink."

"What about you?" Tean asked. "Let's talk about you. Are you ok? You left pretty fast after the funeral."

Tean hadn't blamed her; the funeral had been bleak and poorly attended. Much of it had been conducted in Korean, but the service itself had been Mormon—at least, the parts Tean had understood. Sook's parents had been quiet and reserved, and although they had seemed grateful that Tean and other co-workers had come to pay their respects, they had been grieving their daughter, with no energy or attention to spare for people they didn't know. Worse, a pair of plainclothes detectives had sat at the back of the service, obviously hoping Sook's killer would make a dramatic gesture or announcement.

"I just keep thinking I don't know why someone would have done that," Hannah said, her voice thin, her eyes wet. "Sook was kind to everyone."

"She was in a bad part of town," Tean said. "She got out of her car."

"What's that supposed to mean?"

"It doesn't mean anything."

"You can't blame the victim."

"I'm not blaming her," Tean said. "I'm just saying it's not exactly impossible if you think about where she was in the middle of the night."

"It doesn't make any sense," Hannah said, and then she did start to cry.

"Let me get you a cup of water," Tean said.

Nodding, Hannah said, "And we're changing you off lemon and quince. It's overstimulating you."

With a sigh, Tean grabbed a cleanish mug from the desk and headed for the hall.

"Maybe lavender," Hannah said.

"Sure."

"Something that won't rile you up."

Tean closed the door and headed for the water fountain. He was halfway there when Benny Guthall came around the corner, and Tean had to struggle to suppress a sigh. Benny was in his usual infiltration gear, which meant the poor kid, who had to weigh over two hundred pounds, was dressed head to toe in black, with black engineer boots and a pseudo-military black rucksack with a pup tent lashed to the top. His long, stringy blond hair was held back by a black-and-white bandana—Tean had seen the bandana plenty of times before, and he knew it was printed with skulls. In spite of his appearance, though, Benny was a solid outdoorsman. The kid had hiked back to some pretty remote places. Tean knew; he'd had to hear all about it.

Trying to hold back a sigh, Tean waved.

"Mr. Leon," Benny said, stomping toward him. "I'm not leaving until I get justice. Your stormtroopers will have to drag me out of here. Or you can just have them execute me on the spot, if that's what you want. But that's the only way you can get rid of me unless you're willing to stand up, be a man, and do what's right."

"Hi, Benny," Tean said. "How'd you get past Antonia?"

"Your fascist guards can't stop the course of righteousness, Mr. Leon—"

"Dr. Leon."

"Your fascist guards can't stop the course of righteousness, Dr. Leon—"

"Benny, hell's bells, what are you doing back here?" Antonia was the closest thing the DWR had to a stormtrooper: she was fifty-two, black, and had her hand on her radio as she came galloping around the corner. "Come on, get back to the lobby."

"Get your stormtrooper off me," Benny screamed when she touched his arm.

"Ok," Tean said. "It's ok, Antonia. I'll talk to him and walk him out."

"I'm sorry, Dr. Leon. Dr. Redfoot needed me to hold the door for her, and Benny snuck off while I was distracted."

"It's ok," Tean said again.

Behind him, the door opened, and Hannah stuck her head out into the hall. "Hey, what happened—oh, hi, Benny."

"Come on, Benny," Tean said. "I've got five minutes."

"You'll have to have your goons put a bullet—"

"Clock's ticking," Tean said, as he passed Hannah the water.

"Somebody's murdering all the birds at the Great Salt Lake," Benny said. He dragged a ream of papers out of his ruck, struggling for a moment when they got caught on something inside, and then shoved them at Tean. "That's the main problem. But I've also compiled a list of everyone who is guilty of any sort of environmental damage this week."

Paging through the stack of handwritten papers, Tean said, "This is very thorough, Benny."

"That's just this week?" Hannah asked.

"Those people must be held accountable for their actions. I will be conducting a water strike beginning immediately." Benny snapped one end of a pair of handcuffs around his wrist; he closed the other around the handle of the closest door. "You have three days before I die of dehydration to arrest and prosecute—"

Tean bumped the cuff, and it slid free from the open end of the handle. Then, taking Benny's arm, he steered the kid back toward the lobby.

"—and appropriately punish those people for, hey, wait—"

"Benny, you know I appreciate how much you care about the environment."

"Mr. Leon, hold on, hey!"

"What kind of birds did you see dead at the lake?"

"California gulls," Benny said, "northern shovelers, ruddy ducks, eared grebes, and ring-billed gulls."

"Ok," Tean said. "You didn't touch any, did you?"

"I had my hazmat suit on."

"Benny, we talked about this: no touching dead animals. You could get sick."

"I'll be fine. I'm a warrior for justice. I'm a berserker for Mother Nature. You're just a shill for the corporate puppeteers; you wouldn't understand."

"Well, please remember that you need to make an appointment if you want to talk to me. Or you can ask Antonia to see if I'm busy."

"You're always busy."

"Well, I do have a job."

"And I can't make an appointment." As they stepped into the lobby, Benny twisted free, facing Tean as he backed toward the door.

"I can't leave a paper trail. I can't leave a record of any kind. Otherwise, they'll know."

"Nobody's going to stop you from coming to see me," Tean said.

"Yes, they will. They'll know, and they'll have to step up their plans to eliminate me."

Shaking his head, Tean said, "Nobody's trying to hurt you, Benny. We're all happy to see you when you come."

"Not you. Them. They're going to have to kill me. It's the only way they can stop me." Benny was breathing faster, his cheeks purple as he hyperventilated. "But I'm not going to let them."

"Benny, hold on. You're upset. Sit down. Let me call someone—"

Benny stumbled toward the door, shaking his head. He shot out into the parking lot. Tean watched him go.

"I'm sorry, Dr. Leon," Antonia said again.

"No, it's fine. Nobody's ever been able to stop him; he's been sneaking in to see me since my first week."

"But I've got my eye on him now."

"It's really ok, Antonia."

"What was that all about?" Hannah asked from the hall, still sipping water from Tean's mug.

"Birds?" Tean said, offering the sheaf of pages for inspection. "And a million other things, apparently. Who knows?"

"Huh. Well, now that I've got your attention," Hannah said, "I do actually want to talk to you about moving another conservation officer to native aquatics."

7

City Creek Mall was a beautiful, open-air commercial center in the heart of Salt Lake City. True to its name, a creek ran through the center of the mall: a miracle of water in the high desert. Sunlight played on the water, reflected light dancing on the pale granite and glass. The stores were all the kind that Jem had shoplifted from but where he had never been able to afford a legitimate purchase. The mall had been built in 2012, literally across the street from the Salt Lake City Temple, the Mormon equivalent of Mecca. It had required tearing down blocks of old buildings. The Mormon Church had invested close to a billion dollars to create a shrine to capitalism, mostly in hopes of slowing urban decay and keeping the wrong types of people from clogging the streets on their way to worship. Jem was fairly sure irony didn't rank high on the list of Mormon tenets, but maybe they could at least taste the hypocrisy.

He sat on a bench in City Creek; the water babbled a complement to the piped-in top-twenty pop songs, and behind him, the shop that sold fifty-dollar candles made the air smell like campfire, cinnamon, and anise. The day was warm enough that Jem wasn't quite comfortable under his windbreaker, but he didn't take it off. He liked the 90s geometry of turquoise and pink on the polyester. And it helped him keep a few tricks up his sleeve.

Two benches down, on the other side of the creek, a Tongan girl who might have passed for twelve was playing with a badly scorched Barbie. Jem was careful not to look at her.

Huffing breaths and shuffling steps announced Myers Bruce. The man hadn't given Jem his name, but Jem had found it out after their first interaction, which had been a conversation in a sex-toy shop just outside the city limits. Bruce had paid with a credit card; he probably hadn't expected Jem to shell out twenty dollars to the clerk just to get his name off the transaction receipt. Jem had asked a friend to run the name, just to make sure this wasn't a sting, and after that, it had been smooth sailing.

Bruce dropped onto the other end of the bench. He wasn't wearing a trench coat and a fedora, but he still managed to make himself look like a guy in a bad spy movie: huge sunglasses, a khaki jacket with the collar turned up, a newspaper tucked under his arm. The only thing left was for Bruce to whisper a coded message into his watch or something like that. Sheep like Bruce made Jem exhausted.

A pair of women emerged from the candle shop behind them, one of them gushing about the clearance sale on watermelon-scented products, and Bruce tensed like he had a knife to his throat. As the women's conversation faded, Bruce sagged, wiped sweat from his forehead, and then slid a page of loose-leaf out of the newspaper. He slid it over to Jem. Jem glanced at the scribbles, crumpled the paper, and shoved it into a pocket.

Bruce expelled a sharp breath.

"I told you we do all this quiet and casual and talking," Jem said. "Nothing dumb that's going to draw attention."

"You didn't answer my texts."

"I told you the rules. Phone calls only, nothing in writing, no dumb shit that's going to draw attention. I think we're done here," Jem said, standing. "I don't have time for amateur hour."

"No, no, please. Please!" The words emerged in a fierce whisper.

Jem hesitated.

"An extra ten bucks," Bruce said.

"An extra fifty because you're pissing me off and because you were late."

Indecision scrawled its way across Bruce's features. Then he nodded.

As Jem sat again, he worked the first manila envelope free and passed it over, saying, "Here's your selection. Two hundred per kid. Stills only."

"You said you had video!"

"Sure," Jem said. "I do. We do this, and I know you're not a cop, and then next time, we talk about videos."

Bruce licked his lips. He had his hair buzzed short, and he was young, probably early thirties. Something about him screamed mom's basement at Jem. "In the pictures, they're — well, you know. You can see?"

"Everything," Jem said. "Stuff you've never even thought of. We're not talking one or two still shots, buddy. Fifty pictures per kid."

Bruce licked his lips again. He worked open the clasp on the envelope, drawing out the pictures one by one. They were stock photos that Jem had gotten online and printed. In one of the pictures, a boy with tousled hair was driving a go-kart. In another, a blond girl was fishing. They were bullshit — anybody looking at them could tell they were staged and photoshopped. But by the time a guy like Bruce got to this part of the deal, he was at the point where desire overrode all the red flags. That was how just about every con worked: desire bulldozing common sense. It didn't matter what the person desired, but Jem liked to stick to the holy trinity: sex, drugs, and money.

"Her," Bruce said, picking out a black girl doing math on a slate. Honestly, Jem wondered how the guy rationalized the bizarreness of the picture. "And . . . her." The blond girl who was fishing.

"Read me the description on the bottom," Jem said, pretending to dig through his backpack. "So I know which ones you want."

"Out loud?"

"Quietly, if that's not too fucking hard, but yes, out loud. I'm not a fucking mind reader."

"Blond girl," Bruce whispered, "six years old, includes physical violence."

"Ok." Jem twisted at the waist, trying to get the pocket of his windbreaker closer to Bruce.

"Black girl, seven years old, cutting."

"Four hundred dollars," Jem said. "Plus fifty for acting like a fucking rookie."

While Bruce counted out the cash, Jem shoved the selection photos back into the envelope, slid it back inside his jacket, and took out a stack of identical envelopes that he had differentiated with a six-digit, bullshit code on the top right corner. Each one was full of clippings from *Mother Earth News* and *Green Living*. He picked two at random, pretended to inspect the codes, and then nodded and put everything else back into his backpack. Benny had told Jem, while he was cutting up the magazines, that one of the articles was about elm seed bug infestations. Jem wondered if Bruce liked reading about pests.

Jem made Bruce count out the cash again, watching this time, looking for the tricks that he would have tried himself if he were on the other side of the table. When Jem was sure the count was good, he slid the envelopes across the bench, took the cash, and stuffed it into a pocket.

Bruce reached for the clasp on the first envelope, and Jem grabbed his wrist and hissed.

"Are you fucking kidding me?" Jem said. "Are you out of your goddamn mind?"

"I wanted to—"

"I know what you wanted to do. You want to take those out right here and get both our asses in jail? Jesus Christ, you stupid asshole. So fucking desperate to go rub one out. Get a fucking clue."

Pink-faced, Bruce shoved the envelopes under his arm without examining their contents. "I hope this doesn't mean—I mean, I'll still be interested in those videos—"

"Get the fuck out of here," Jem said. "I'll call you when I'm not so fucking pissed at you."

Bruce took a huge breath and tottered away. As soon as his back was to Jem, Jem grabbed his phone. He ended the audio recording, opened the camera app, and snapped pictures of Bruce walking away. He was snapping pictures as the Tongan girl clutched her Barbie to her chest. He was snapping pictures as Bruce and the Tongan girl collided, and for a moment, his hand was on the back of her head and her body was pressed against his leg. The girl, Sammi, was a pro, and that last picture was just about perfect, so he shoved the phone back in his pocket and enjoyed the sunny day.

When Bruce had vanished from sight, Sammi came up behind Jem and punched him in the shoulder. She and her family lived in the same building as Jem, although they actually paid rent and had light and heat. Her long dark hair was pulled across one shoulder now, and she had her hands planted on her hips.

"Ouch," Jem said.

"He smelled like mothballs and butterscotch candy."

Jem made a face.

"Yeah, it was gross. That's an extra ten."

"Not part of the deal, sister."

"And you didn't say he was going to touch my hair. That's an extra twenty."

"Not a chance."

"And he had a boner. That's an extra twenty."

"Sammi, your mom will wash your mouth if she hears you saying boner."

"I'm sixteen," she said, twisting the head of the Barbie savagely. "I'm not even a virgin anymore."

"Because that's the sign of adulthood."

"You're so old it's gross sometimes."

"Thank you. I'll spot you an extra thirty."

Her dark eyes flashed, but she nodded. "Cheapskate motherfucker."

"Sammi! Watch your language!"

She grinned.

He counted out eighty dollars and handed them over. "Shouldn't you be in school?"

"And miss out on easy money?"

"No more sloughing school."

She made a face that only teenage girls are capable of making.

"Do you want to end up like me?" Jem said.

"You're smart. You've always got money. You wear nice clothes except when you have gross old stuff like that jacket. And you do what you want." She shrugged. "Seems like you're doing pretty well to me."

"Yeah, well, I have a very glamorous life that involves begging your parents to plug in an extension cord for me every morning. No more sloughing."

She made that face again.

"I'll tell your mom."

"God, shut up, fine."

"Now be a good little girl and go play with your dolls."

She gave him a three-minute-long suggestion about the various ways he should violently finger himself and then jogged off, the scorched Barbie cradled in the crook of her arm.

8

Tean still prayed in the mornings. He didn't touch his scriptures anymore — they were in a shoebox, along with a rubber banded stack of forty-seven Magic: The Gathering cards, third edition, including the Shivan Dragon he had won from Rafa, Esme's brother, in sixth grade. He didn't kneel or bow his head or fold his arms. Much of the year, he sat for a few minutes on the small balcony outside his second-story apartment and watched the mountains. They were a presence in his mind, and his thoughts stretched out to them, to whatever might be immanent in them. They hid the dawn. If something in the bones of the world heard him, it gave back only shadow and silence.

When light dusted the aspens, he went inside. He made peppermint tea and ate a banana, listening to the news on his phone, just the top five today: a man and woman living in Texas had been traced back to their former life in one of the Bible-belt states, where authorities had discovered an abandoned home with six children chained to their beds; another teenage boy had taken his mom's handgun to school and killed three classmates; a man was accused of keeping his daughter as a sex slave in a basement for twenty-nine years; bees were still dying out all over the world, and nobody could figure out why, threatening an environmental collapse; and hey, great news for everybody, researchers had found that shopping could both help the economy and actually boost your mood, so spend a few bucks for Uncle Sam and save yourself the Prozac scrip. Tean finished his tea, took Scipio on a nice, long walk, and left for work.

The valley was slowly coming awake: minivans and SUVs crammed with children, trucks bearing construction equipment to job sites, tech yuppies zipping along in their Teslas. Utah had been the Mormon motherland for over a hundred years, a bastion of conservativism, but the times were changing. Tech companies were invading the so-called Silicon Slopes; Californians had realized they could buy much larger homes and enjoy a relatively similar climate — lots of sun, low humidity, easy access to nature — without paying a small fortune; new home construction soared, and the accompanying jobs spurred immigration in a state that already had a high immigrant population. And, of course, every Mormon born in Utah inevitably came back; Tean wasn't sure any Mormon born there had really, truly left. They might play expat for a while in another state, but eventually, the motherland called them home. Wasn't he a shining example of that?

His apartment was in Central City, a neighborhood in, well, the center of the city: brick bungalows with young families, apartment buildings from the 80s, easy walking to corner markets. It would have been easy walking, too, to the Marmalade District and Capitol Hill — Salt Lake City's gayborhoods — if Tean had been interested. He wasn't interested, though; he was there for the low rent. New money was changing everything, though. A lot of the older buildings were gone. A lot of the homes had been demolished, with more expensive condominiums and townhouses in their place. The city had a new class to cater to, and Tean figured his days in Central City were numbered. He'd end up somewhere else in the valley; he always did.

Normally, his commute west across the city took ten minutes; today, though, he drove north until he hit I-80 and followed it out of the city. Ahead of him, the Great Salt Lake had already caught the morning light; where the wind stirred the water, the sun cut gleaming crescents on the crests of waves. He followed the interstate out to the Great Salt Lake State Park — like Central City or the Marmalade District, where marmalade had been made for decades, another example of Utah's creative nomenclature — and found a spot to park. The park had a small harbor with floating wooden piers and boat slips. It was another perfect day in October, crisply cool that would warm to the mid-70s, the sky pale blue, the briny, fishy smell of the lake whipping away on the breeze. A few people were already getting out their boats, ready to enjoy the day — never mind that it was a Tuesday.

With the engine off, he tried following up on Sook's final reports. He placed a few calls to people Sook had visited or contacted in the week before her death. This time, nobody even answered. He figured they were starting to recognize his number. Next, he called the Salt Lake City homicide detective handling the investigation into Sook's death.

"Young," the detective said.

"Hi, Ammon. I just wanted to check in and see if you had any updates."

Silence.

"Maybe we could —"

"It's an ongoing investigation; I can't comment on it."

"Ok," Tean said, taking a deep breath before the plunge. "Do you want to come over tonight? I know Tuesdays aren't always good for you, but it's been a long time —"

This time, the silence was punctuated by the sounds of movement: irregular breaths, the click of a door closing.

"Are you kidding me right now?" Ammon asked.

"I just —"

"Do you have any common sense? Any at all?"

"I'm sorry, I thought —"

"No, Tean. You didn't think. I'm at work. My job. What if I'd been on speakerphone?"

"I'm sorry."

"Damn it. We've been over this a hundred times."

"I know. I'm sorry; I forgot."

After a slow exhalation, Ammon said, "I shouldn't have talked to you like that."

"No, you were right."

"I'm under a lot of pressure right now. Today hasn't been a good day."

Tean waited a moment and said, "I miss you."

"I miss you too. I don't know about tonight; can I call you later?"

"Of course."

The harsh rasp of breath came across the speaker, and for a moment, Tean thought Ammon might actually say it, the thing always on the verge of luminescing between them. Then Ammon said, "I've got to go," and disconnected.

Gathering his scraps of self-respect, Tean got out of the truck. He started off walking the shore, a narrow strip of sand bristling with clumps of sagebrush, and then, where the ground sloped higher and away from the concentrated salinity of the lake, sego lilies and soapweed and patchy blue grama. He found the first dead bird, a crow, crumpled behind a salt-rimed clump of greasewood; a swarm of brine flies buzzed up when Tean stepped closer, and he fanned them away as he examined the crow from a safe distance. He saw the dried strands of nasal discharge, sighed, and walked back to the truck. His Keens crunched across the sand.

Out of the back of his DWR truck—a white, ten-year-old Ford F-150 with semi-regular fuel-line problems—Tean grabbed his gear: a disposable coverall, disposable gloves, disposable plastic bags, and rubber boots. The thing about Benny, he thought as he dressed, was that Benny might get details wrong, but he was usually right about the big picture. Benny had been showing up at Tean's office on and off for years now, and while Benny's delivery had initially made Tean want to ignore him—they're out to get me, evil stormtroopers, etc., the stuff that made Hannah wrinkle her nose and say Benny was crazy—Benny had drawn Tean's attention to genuine problems with poaching, an ailing elk herd below Grandview Peak, and a sewage line break that was killing hundreds of fish. Benny usually hadn't been right about the cause of the problem—he'd insisted, for example, that extraterrestrial invaders were using the elk for target practice—but that didn't mean that a real problem didn't lie below the surface.

In this case, it looked like Benny had been right: birds around the Great Salt Lake were dying. Unfortunately—for Benny, at least—the cause didn't seem to be a genocide conducted by evil corporations. The nasal discharge was a good sign that this was a simple case of avian cholera, which ran rampant at the Great Salt Lake every few years. Tean would need to confirm the diagnosis with a necropsy and with a bacterial culture to detect *Pasteurella multocida*, the causal agent behind the disease.

Ignoring looks from the families making their way to the boats, Tean moved along the shore, taking photos of each carcass *in situ* and collecting specimens. He wanted multiples of each type of bird; although the nasal discharge was consistent, it was important to corroborate his findings and, more importantly, to check for the presence of other diseases that might be active in these populations. Benny's list was comprehensive, and Tean was able to find California gulls, northern shovelers, eared grebes, and ring-billed gulls. He couldn't find any ruddy ducks, and he found only the one crow. He also collected water samples near each cluster of carcasses. After a few trips back to the truck to transport everything, he bagged the coverall and gloves for disposal at the DWR, and then he disinfected the rubber boots before storing them again.

Heading back into the city, Tean rolled down the window, listening to the sound of the waves, the wind in the buffalo grass, the cry of a gull. The sun was hot on his arm. Ahead of him, the Mormon temple burned like a pillar of white fire; beyond, the mountains kindled their own blaze. Then the carcasses shifted in the back of the truck, and he remembered his grandfather, smelling of Al Capone cognac-dipped cigarillos, helping Tean settle the stock of a shotgun against his shoulder, Tean's first time turkey hunting. Rolling up the window, Tean tried to think about all the work Benny had dumped in his lap.

9

On Tuesday, Benny still wasn't answering his phone. Jem lay on the extra mattress in his apartment—technically not his, technically belonging to the good people at Zion Home and Family Residential Services, the company that managed the Bluebell Apartments—scrolling through pictures on his phone while he tried to figure out what to do. The day had warmed up nicely, and with the windows open, Jem could sprawl on the mattress in shorts and a t-shirt and feel pretty good. The nights were getting colder and colder, and while the apartment would never actually get freezing—the building was heated, even if Jem's unit wasn't, and some of that heat kept the apartment livable—Jem knew he had some uncomfortable months coming. Still, he had electricity (so long as Sammi's parents, the Latus, continued to accept twenty dollars a week from him and didn't forget to plug in the extension cord), and Jem had running water, hot water, so he figured this was probably the best setup he'd ever had.

The problem, Jem thought as he scrolled back through all the pictures, was that Benny wasn't actually very good at answering his phone even under normal circumstances. Now, hiding out at the Jenkins' ranch, Benny probably thought every phone call was tapped, or the FBI was tracking him by GPS, or a kill squad was just checking in to set up a fucking appointment.

Rolling onto his stomach, Jem decided four days was enough time for Benny to play *Naked and Afraid*. After a lot of talking, a shared cigarette in the parking lot, and a hundred bucks, Jem had convinced the administrative assistant at Benny's psychiatrist to squeeze Benny in for an appointment on Wednesday. Benny was on Medicaid, but after a couple of rounds of trying to find a decent doctor, trying to get an appointment, trying to get the meds, Jem had given up on that bullshit and settled for paying for everything with cash. And since the appointment was tomorrow, Jem needed to get Benny back from the Jenkins today and make sure he showered—make sure, because last time, Dr. Schnirring had politely asked Jem to step into his office with Benny at the end of the appointment and then had explained, like Jem and Benny were thirteen years old, the basics of personal hygiene.

Jem called the Jenkins' home number. He pictured the ranch: the exposed logs and the leaning chimney, the slope of scraggly pine and scrub sage climbing the backs of the Oquirrh Mountains, the only safe place he and Benny could escape to while growing up.

Dale answered, her voice soft as ever. "Hello?"

"Hi, Sister Jenkins. It's Jem. Is Benny around?"

"Well, sweetheart, it's so lovely to hear your voice. Why don't you come around anymore?"

"You know me," Jem said, staring at the bare, stained mattress underneath him, the thin carpet, the rusted fire escape beyond the window. "I'm living the high life."

Dale laughed. "Well, if you ever have five minutes, you know Elvin and I would love to see you. You could come for dinner. Why don't you do that?"

"I'd like that," Jem said.

"What about this Sunday?"

"I'll have to check my schedule at work."

"That job," Dale said. "They run you ragged. Who knew being a bigwig lawyer was such a busy job?"

"I know," Jem said. "Sorry for the rush, Sister Jenkins, but could I speak to Benny?"

"Well, he's not here, Jem."

"I know, I know. He's camping. I thought maybe he'd come up to the house for grub, though. If you see him, will you tell him I'm coming to get him?"

"Sweetheart," Dale said in that tone of mild confusion Jem had heard so many times in his life—when, for example, she and Elvin had picked him up from juvie. "He's not here. He's not camping, I mean. He left yesterday."

"Ok," Jem said. "Did he have a ride? Or did Brother Jenkins drive him?"

"Hold on a moment. Elvin? Elvin? Did you drive Benny into town? No, dear, he says those friends with the loud music picked him up."

"Oh."

"Benny said you knew he was going with them. Oh dear. You did know — I mean, we wouldn't have let him leave if we thought — "

"No, no, it's fine, Sister Jenkins. I just forgot."

"Are you sure? We really wouldn't have let him go. We know he can wander."

"Sorry to bother you."

"You're never a bother, dear. We'll see you Sunday, then. Benny too, of course."

"I've got to check with work," Jem said.

"Of course, of course."

He disconnected and stared at the phone. Then he punched the mattress twice. Moving around the apartment, Jem lost the shorts and put on a relatively clean pair of jeans and sneakers. He grabbed his wallet and his windbreaker, checked his tools: a length of paracord with a hex nut tied at one end, an empty tube sock, a barrette with one edge of the clip sharpened, a folding slim jim, and a compact, telescoping antenna he'd ripped off an RCA television. Before he left, he made sure that the deadbolt was set. Then he went down the fire escape, closing the window behind him.

Jem's motorcycle was used, a Kawasaki with way too many miles, and a bad choice for a state where snow was pretty much a certainty. But it was reliable, and it had been in Jem's price range, and he'd been able to talk a friend into registering and licensing it, so the tags were current. Jem's apartment was in West Valley, and Benny's was too, but five miles south. When he got to the building, which had sagging aluminum siding and weeds growing along the walls, he parked at the bottom of the stairs. Tommy Johnson was on his skateboard, trying to do a trick on the curb, and he waved once before turning his attention back to the board.

Jem took the steps slowly, hitting each one hard. When he got to the door, he hammered on it. He waited a few seconds, took the spare key from his wallet, and let himself inside.

Somehow, the apartment looked even worse than it had a few days before. In the front room, the couch cushions lay on the floor, one of them with the zipper half undone. The TV had been turned sideways, and the entertainment center had been pulled out from the wall; one of the glass doors hung open, and DVDs of *The Dark Knight* and *An Inconvenient Truth* had slid onto the carpet. The kitchen showed the same signs of chaos, with the cabinet doors open and the table yanked out from the wall. In Benny's bedroom, the mattress hung halfway off the box spring, and the sheets had been stripped from three corners. The mirrored cabinet in the bathroom stood open; Benny's bottle of clozapine was in the trash, empty.

But no backpack, Jem thought. No sheaf of papers covered in Benny's writing. No camping gear.

On the second walkthrough, Jem shoved his hands in the windbreaker's pockets and looked at everything more carefully. He toed over the couch cushions. He stretched up to check the top shelves of the kitchen cabinets. He tipped over the bathroom trash.

He left, locking the door behind him, and found Tommy trying to do a kickflip on the stretch of asphalt near the dumpsters.

"You seen Benny?"

Tommy shook his head without glancing over, tucking his hair behind his ears, and tried again.

"When was the last time you saw him?"

"Dunno."

"What the fuck, Tommy? I'm talking to you."

"I don't know," Tommy said, looking up this time, and then he caught the board with his foot and studied Jem. "What's up?"

"I don't know."

"You wanna toke? I just rolled a nice one upstairs. You look like Mr. Spacely, you know, right before he's gonna blow?"

Grabbing a handful of Tommy's shirt, Jem propelled him toward the apartment building and pretended to try to kick his ass. Tommy looped one arm around his skateboard, grinning as he stumbled away.

With the sound of Tommy's steps ringing on the stairs, Jem took out his phone. He didn't have names programmed into the speed dials—just numbers, and he matched the numbers against the list he kept in his head. He tapped thirty-seven and listened to the phone ring.

"Hello?" asked a croaking voice.

"Where the fuck is Benny?"

"Holy shit, man. What time is it? Holy shit."

"Chaquille, I'm going to come over there and beat your ass if you don't start talking. Where is Benny? I know you went up to the Jenkins' place and got him; you couldn't turn down your fucking music for five seconds. Now, where is he?"

"Chillax," Chaquille croaked.

"No," Jem said. "This is not a Lil Wayne song. I will not chillax. Where is he?"

From the other end of the call came the crinkle of aluminum blinds. "The sun is up, man. Holy shit."

"Fine. I'll come ask you in person. Just like I did when you tried to take him to Burning Man."

"Shit, man. Calm down." But Chaquille had lost some of the lazy, croaking easiness. Sometimes, when Chaquille sharpened up like this, Jem could actually believe that he was a grad student studying aerospace engineering at the U. Most of the time, though, Chaquille was just a stoner who loved conspiracy theories almost as much as Benny. "Don't need to get worked up. Yeah, I got him from that weird house. He called and asked me to pick him up."

"Is he at your place? Because I swear to Christ, if you got him high, I will—"

"Chillax. He's not here. I dropped him off someplace. That's it, just gave him a ride."

"Where'd you drop him?"

A tractor trailer roared past, kicking up a Burger King wrapper and sending a half-eaten ice cream cone rolling up against the curb.

Chaquille giggled. "Holy shit, I don't even remember, man. I am so fucking fried."

"Ok," Jem said, heading toward the curb. "Ok. You're baked. You don't remember. Ok."

"Hey, do you still talk to Sarah?"

"I need you to listen to me really carefully, Chaquille. I'm going to get on my bike." Jem stomped the half-eaten cone. "And I'm going to come pay you a visit." He stomped again. "And I'm going to help you remember where you took Benny." Scraping the smushed cone and ants from his sneaker, he added, "Go ahead and take the door off the chain so I don't have to work myself up kicking the shit out of it."

"Hold on, hold on, hold on." Chaquille's voice sharpened. "I'm kind of remembering now. It was—it was kind of out by the airport. Well, in that direction, anyway."

"A house? An apartment? An office?"

"Big building. I don't think it was an apartment."

"On North Temple?"

"Could have been."

"You are a fucking waste of a human being," Jem said, disconnecting the call. But at least he had a good idea where Chaquille had taken him.

"Yo," Tommy called. He was sprawled under one of the tiny maple trees planted along the verge, working the flame of a lighter at the end of a blunt. When it was lit, he took a long drag, head sagging back, and held out the blunt with two fingers.

Jem joined him in the shade, took a hit, held it. Then he exhaled slowly.

"You're just like fucking Spacely," Tommy said.

"No more skateboard without a helmet," Jem said.

Tommy rolled his eyes.

"No more weed," Jem said, butting out the blunt and then sticking it in his back pocket.

"Fucker," Tommy said. "That's mine."

"This shit messes with the developing brain, dumbfuck. No more weed until you're in your twenties, hear me?"

"Why are you being such an asshole?"

"Did you eat today?"

"Fuck off."

Jem passed him forty bucks; after a few angry glares, Tommy snatched it out of his hand.

"You spend that on food," Jem said. "Not on grass."

Tommy just shook his head.

"And no more fucking *Jetsons*," Jem called over his shoulder as he jogged toward the bike. "Read a fucking book."

On more than one occasion, Jem had driven Benny to the Utah Division of Wildlife Resources building on North Temple. Benny cared about the environment, and he tended to get stuck on one thing for a while. Usually that meant a slow buildup until Benny decided to take action, and sometimes that action meant going straight to the Man. In this case, the Man was a wiry guy with glasses, kind of cute if you liked sheep, whose name was Leon. From the few times Jem had stayed to make sure everything was ok, Benny usually liked to have some kind of showdown with Leon — although Benny's version of a showdown involved hunger strikes and nonviolent resistance. They were annoying, not destructive, eating up people's time and throwing their schedules out of whack. Jem kind of liked the idea of dropping Benny in with a bunch of unsuspecting sheep and letting him wreak havoc.

When Jem got to the building, which was relatively new, with lots of glass and brick and light-colored stone, he drove around the lot, checking out the place. The main entrance had a security guard just inside, and each side of the building had a secured exit that Jem imagined was probably required for safety reasons. He decided to start with the simplest option first: the main entrance.

Behind the security desk, a black woman in a guard's uniform had a folded-over newspaper, and she gave him a hard look when he came through the doors.

"I'm here to see Dr. Leon," Jem said.

"All right," she said. She picked up a phone, placed the call, and asked, "What are you here about?"

"A guy named Benny—"

"Oh no," she said, hanging up. "Not a chance."

"I just wanted to ask a couple of questions."

"Uh uh." She got up from her seat and pointed at the door. "You can just walk right on out of here."

"I'm not—"

"That young man has made me look like a fool enough times. Uh uh. You walk right on out of here."

"If I could just—"

"Don't make me use my radio."

"All right," Jem said. And he headed outside.

Outside, he examined the building again. The front doors had a lot of numbers on them; he found seven that he figured were the main phone line, and he placed a call. He got two roboticized options: enter your party's extension or speak with someone who can assist you. Jem wanted some assistance.

"Oh no," the friendly young woman said when he asked. "I can't transfer calls directly to Dr. Leon's office."

"It's just a few simple questions."

"I can give you his voicemail. He's very good about checking it; I'm sure he'll get right back to you."

"No, I need to talk to him right now. It's an emergency."

"I'm very sorry," the girl said, so chipper she sounded like she could chew her way through a log. "How about voicemail?"

Jem hung up.

He walked around the building again. He didn't see a spot that was obviously designated for smokers, which was a shame, but it came with the territory in Utah. His best shot was probably the loading docks. He moved the bike and parked right by the walk-out door to the docks, killed the engine, and rolled his shoulders. When possible, he preferred to observe, strategize, and plan his escape. But every job ultimately came down to riffing, and what he did best was riff.

He buzzed at the back door, and an old guy with bowl-cut white hair opened it.

"Courier pickup," Jem said. "Something from Dr. Leon."

Bowl-cut shook his head. "Nothing going out today."

"Really?" Jem glanced back at his bike. "I drove out here from Sugarhouse."

"Sorry. Everything went out FedEx about an hour ago."

"That's all right," Jem said with a big smile. "At least it's a beautiful day."

"Sure it is," Bowl-cut said, easing his hand off the door.

"Do you mind checking?" Jem said. "I got the call like half an hour ago. Maybe he just hasn't brought it down here yet."

Frowning, Bowl-cut gave a shrug. "Come on in."

Jem followed him inside and found himself in a large, open area that clearly doubled as both a shipping and receiving area and a warehouse: racks of metal shelving broke the cement slab into aisles, and cardboard boxes and plastic barrels filled the shelves. Bowl-cut led Jem back to a desk. He ignored the computer and picked up the handset of a phone mounted on the wall.

"Dr. Leon?" he asked Jem.

"That's right."

Bowl-cut keyed in 10117, which Jem figured was a super-complicated code that meant Dr. Leon's office was in room 117.

"Got a bathroom I can use?" Jem asked. "I've been going all day."

"That hall," Bowl-cut said.

Jem nodded. He opened a fire door, stepped into one of the hallways that was clearly part of the office space, complete with blandly inoffensive artwork and a plastic ficus. Ignoring the bathrooms on his right, he jogged down the hall. The rooms on either side of him varied: some were offices — in one, a woman with frizzy chestnut hair was doing something on her computer while rocking out to Bastille; in another, a mousy guy was looking at internet ads for nail polish — and others were obviously multipurpose rooms or meeting rooms, the kind of heavenly space where people got to listen to quarterly reports and learn teambuilding and generate departmental slogans that would inspire them to new and greater heights in the management of wildlife resources.

In a stairwell around the corner, Jem found one of the fire doors. He propped it open with a rock and jogged back.

"He doesn't have anything," Bowl-cut said.

"Ok," Jem said, smiling. "Thanks anyway."

He made a big show of starting up the Kawasaki while Bowl-cut watched, and then he drove around the building, killed the engine, and parked again. He let himself in through the fire door, kicking the rock back into the hardscape, and eased the door shut. Then he found himself in a room he decided to call Multipurpose Room B. He found the phone, pressed 10117, and imagined himself giving the semi-annual report on fish roe. He tried not to puke.

"Leon," a quiet voice answered.

"Yeah, this guy keeps insisting he's supposed to pick up something from you. He won't leave."

"Great," Leon said with a sigh. "I'll be right there."

"Thanks, boss."

"Who is this?"

Jem hung up.

He headed out of the room, checked the numbered plaques, and followed the hall. When he went around the next corner, he checked shoulders with a wiry guy. Jem made the match in an instant, and he exaggerated the stumble, giving himself the extra seconds he needed to snag the keys from the doc's pocket.

"Sorry," Leon said, righting himself and not even glancing over as he hurried on.

Jem found 117, let himself in with Dr. Leon's keys, and started searching for any sign that Benny had been there.

10

On his way back from collecting the birds at the lake, Tean considered running an errand while he was still out, and he got stuck in the perpetual morass of I-15. In *Good Omens*, Tean remembered, Neil Gaiman or Terry Pratchett or maybe both of them together had made a joke about a highway near London that was infernally designed, a kind of hell on earth. Tean had liked the book all right, but that part had really stuck with him. Hell was humans in motor vehicles.

After ten minutes of honking and merging and trying to get into a lane that didn't stop moving as soon as Tean found an opening, he realized he'd made a mistake. I-15 was a traffic jam at any time of day; it was the only major north-south highway in the state, and as the population boomed and people moved farther and farther out for affordable homes, traffic only got worse. And, of course, add in the fact that the Saints turned into raging assholes as soon as they were behind a steering wheel and you had the full experience of Utah driving.

Tean squeezed the DWR truck in front of a blue van with kids hanging out of the windows—literally. A horn blared farther back, and he glanced up to see a black SUV crowding into the same lane, maybe five cars behind him. Exhibit Z: yet another asshole. Then the lane Tean was in came to a grinding halt.

A few minutes later, he merged right, and he even managed to move a hundred yards down the interstate. Then traffic stopped again. He flopped back in his seat, glancing at the rearview mirror, and frowned. The black SUV was stuck between two lanes, obviously trying to get into the new lane Tean had chosen.

The interstate had been a bad idea, and Tean decided to take the surface streets. When his next opening appeared, he sidled right again, and after another hundred yards, he reached an off-ramp. A series of staccato blats made him glance at the mirror again.

The black SUV was bulling through traffic, coming straight for the off-ramp.

So it was a coincidence, Tean told himself. Just a coincidence.

But the SUV followed him west on 3400 South. And it followed him north on Redwood Road. Tean forgot the errand and made a course correction, heading back toward the office. And the SUV was still following him when he merged onto the I-215 beltway.

By the time Tean pulled into the DWR parking lot, his whole body was tense. But the SUV just rolled past the entrance. He tried to get a look at the driver, but the windows were tinted, and Tean could only make out the shape of a figure behind the wheel.

Letting out a breath, Tean pulled around to the back, trying to shake off the weirdness of the encounter, but his mind kept going back to Sook, about all the unanswered questions around her death. And the same morning that Tean placed a phone call to Ammon about the investigation, a black SUV started tailing him. Coincidence?

And then Tean heard his own thoughts, smacked himself on the side of a head a few times to shake the crazy loose, and got out of the truck. He got a cart from the warehouse, loaded the birds, and took them to the necropsy lab in the basement. He didn't have time to conduct full necropsies on all the specimens today, but he wanted to at least get started and, more importantly, begin the cultures.

In the locker room, he changed clothes. Then, in the lab, he added a coverall, a rubber apron, and protective gloves and boots. He got a mask and face shield, set up his digital camera, and put out his voice recorder so he could dictate the necropsy report. Then he filled in the preliminary information on the report, labeled sample containers, and wrote out cards with the same information so that he could include the card with each necropsy photograph.

The external exam with each specimen was relatively straightforward. He had already noted the nasal discharge, but now he collected samples. Then he inspected each carcass for trauma and external parasites, took pictures from various angles, and measured and weighed the carcass.

The next portion of the necropsy was the internal exam. He opened up the specimens and took samples of the hearts and livers, sealing the samples in Whirl-Pak bags he had already labeled. The visual inspection suggested that *P. multocida* was the culprit here: the hearts and livers, and in some cases the gizzards, were marked by lesions common to avian cholera, which corroborated what he had suspected from the nasal discharge. White and yellowish spots on the livers marked areas of tissue death, and in some cases, the livers were enlarged, with an unusual, coppery tone. He continued the internal exam, working carefully through the specimens. In some of the birds, he found undigested food in the upper digestive tract; in the lower digestive tract, many of the specimens had a thick, yellowish fluid. In a few cases he found parasites and worms, which he preserved as samples, and then he took samples of the intestines themselves. Finally he removed the specimens' heads and bagged them individually.

After preparing cultures to test for the presence of *P. multocida* — he used tissue from the hearts and livers — Tean stored the rest of the samples in the freezer. Then he cleaned up the necropsy lab, cleaned himself up, and headed upstairs to his office.

He was fifteen minutes into the necropsy reports when someone rapped on the door.

"Where have you been?" Hannah asked.

So he told her.

"I just figured it was a big party last night," Hannah said.

"Goodbye, Hannah."

"I just figured you were hungover."

"I have work to do."

"Or maybe you'd gone to a rave and woken up handcuffed to some visiting surfer dude's bed."

"We're in a landlocked state; there are no surfer dudes."

"People surf the lakes," Hannah said. "Kind of. And lots of surfer dudes come here to visit."

"I don't like surfer dudes. Anyway, don't you have something to do? Shouldn't you be boiling mollusks or kissing June suckers or something like that."

"If you don't like surfer dudes," Hannah said, "you can probably throw away those fifteen Hollister calendars you keep in a box in your closet."

Tean's head came up so fast he thought he'd given himself whiplash.

"I know," Hannah said, waving a goodbye as she left. "It's all that long, pretty blond hair."

"I don't like pretty hair," Tean shouted after her.

Norbert Smith, who was almost eighty and had spent most of his life trying to catch poachers in the vast emptiness of northwest Utah, stopped in the hallway and stared through the doorway.

"That was, um, relevant in context," Tean said.

Norbert sucked his teeth, nodded, and shuffled away.

Tean tried to get back to his reports, but twenty minutes later, a call interrupted him.

"Leon," he said.

It was Larry Gregorson from the dock. "I've got a courier here who says he's supposed to pick up something for you."

"No, I don't have anything going out."

"That's what I told him," Larry said before hanging up.

Tean got maybe five more minutes of work done before his phone rang again.

"Leon," Tean answered again.

"Yeah, this guy keeps insisting he's supposed to pick up something from you. He won't leave."

"Great," Leon said with a sigh. "I'll be right there."

"Thanks, boss."

Then Tean realized this wasn't Larry—Larry would probably rather have his vocal cords cut than call Tean boss.

"Who is this?" Tean asked.

But the call had already disconnected.

Sighing, Tean pushed off from his desk and headed for the dock. As he came around the corner, somebody crashed into him, both of them stumbling for a moment. Then Tean righted himself, caught a glimpse out of the corner of his eye—some guy he didn't recognize—and kept going.

When he got to the dock, Larry was sitting at his desk, reading a Book of Mormon.

"Where is he?" Tean said.

"What?"

"Where's the guy?"

Larry tweaked one of the onionskin pages. "You expecting one of your guys, Dr. Leon?"

"No," Tean said. "I'm talking about the courier."

"Oh, he's long gone."

Tean waited for an explanation, but Larry bent over the book again, his body turned just enough to wall out Tean. After a quick glance around the warehouse to make sure the courier wasn't actually still waiting, Tean headed back to his office. As he walked, he reached for his keys and swore. He must have left them on the desk. Or maybe he'd left them downstairs in the locker room. He'd have to get Antonia to let him back into the office to check.

But when he passed his office, he saw that the door was open, held by the pneumatic stop. And a man was sitting in a chair in front of Tean's desk. Blond, he'd styled his hair in a hard side part, and he was muscular in a way that had nothing to do with gyms and everything to do with hard work. While his hair was a dirty blond, his beard had flecks of gold and silver and copper in it. He was wearing jeans and a turquoise-and-pink windbreaker with a geometric pattern, and although the thing looked like it belonged in the 90s, somehow he pulled it off.

"I'm sorry," Tean said, stepping into the office. "Can I help you?"

The guy opened his mouth, and then his breath hitched and he pinched the bridge of his nose. "Sorry," he said, "God, I'm totally out of control right now. I'm really sorry. I just need some help—I just need some help—" And then he stopped again, struggling with his breathing. "I just need some help finding my brother."

11

The worst part, Jem thought as he tried to pull himself back together, was that the crying had come totally out of nowhere. The doc sprang into action, moving around the desk to open a drawer, pulling out a pack of tissues, passing them to Jem. Jem grabbed the packet and mopped at his eyes with a wad of tissues.

"Are you ok?" the doc said. He was cute: maybe ten years older than Jem, wiry, his wild dark hair brushed back, bushy eyebrows, his glasses askew. "Can I get you something? Water?"

Jem shook his head.

Behind the desk, the doc was still standing, shuffling papers, picking up pens and letting them trickle out of his hands, opening the top-right drawer and then closing it again. Jem focused on wiping his face with the tissues, part of him just trying to get himself back under control, part of him waiting to see if the doc noticed that Jem had rifled the desk. But he just kept moving things and picking up things. He still hadn't noticed his keys where Jem had left them, half-hidden behind a mug with a picture of a koala.

"I'm ok," Jem said, balling up the tissues in one hand and giving a weak smile. "I'm not really a crier, you know. I'm just overwhelmed."

"That's all right," the doc said. "I guess I'm not sure why you're here. You said something about your brother? I don't—I think you might be in the wrong place."

"You're Dr. Leon?"

Nodding, he said, "Tean is fine."

"Tean. That's a nice name. Where's it from?"

"Mr. . . ."

"Guthall. Jem."

"Mr. Guthall—"

"Jem, please."

"Jem, I think you'd better tell me what's going on. How did you get in here?"

"The door was open," Jem said.

Tean just looked at him.

"Ok," Jem said. "Your office door was open, but . . . Just don't be mad. I saw somebody leaving through the side door, and I grabbed it and came inside. But only because the guard at the front desk wouldn't let me talk to you, and then I tried calling, and they'd only give me your voicemail, and Benny's been missing for over a day. Please don't throw me out. I just want to ask you a few questions."

After a moment to line up the pens on his desk, Tean said, "Benny?"

"Yeah. He's my brother."

"I didn't know Benny had any brothers. He told me he'd been a foster child."

"Foster brother," Jem said quickly. Then, unable to help himself, he asked, "He told you that? Really?"

Another nod, and this time, a small smile. "Benny's a sharer. And pretty easy to get off track, actually. Especially once you ply him with a Coke and some Zingers."

Jem sat back and muttered, "God damn it."

"What?" Tean said.

"He's diabetic."

"Oh."

"No, it's not your fault. He knows he's not supposed to have that shit." Then, frowning, Jem said, "So that's your job? Hang out with nutters and eat junk food?"

"Um, no, not exactly. But Benny's kind of a special case. He's a regular around here—he's really persistent. Plus he's a sweet guy. And when I first started, a few years back, I don't know how to explain it. You know how when you're new, everything seems really significant? I guess I just took it really seriously, trying to make sure he felt like he'd been heard. He was always genuinely distressed." Tean shrugged and looked at the desk. "Can't keep that up in the long haul, you know. Seems kind of silly now. Mr. Guthall, why are you here?"

"Benny's missing."

"I know. You said he's been gone for a day. That's not a very long time. Are you sure he's not just out with friends?"

Jem shook his head. "Benny's not well, and it's not just the diabetes. He can't run off like this. Even if he's only with friends, I need to find him and get him home."

"Oh," Tean said. "I'm sorry."

"So am I," Jem said. "Imagine flying in from California every time your kid brother decides a road trip to Zion is a good idea."

"Do you surf?"

The question came from the hallway, where a woman with short, chestnut hair was peering into the office.

"What?" Jem asked. "Surf?"

"Ignore her," Tean said, scrambling out from behind the desk and shooting toward the door.

"Have you ever grown your hair out?" the woman asked.

"Go away," Tean growled as he tried to yank the door shut; the pneumatic door closer interfered, though, making it impossible for him to slam it.

"Do you have a boyfriend?" she called through the narrowing opening.

Then the door clicked shut, and Tean braced his body against it, spread eagle, as though the woman might knock it down.

"She's got hoof-and-mouth disease," Tean said.

"Ok."

"We're going to have to put her down soon."

"Oh, I'm sorry."

"Don't be. It's a mercy killing."

Jem grinned, and after a moment, a smile tugged at the corner of Tean's mouth. The moment dragged, and Jem waved at the cluster of posters on the wall. "I like your space posters."

Tean glanced over at the posters, frowned, and looked back at Jem. Jem realized he had made some kind of mistake.

The moment passed, though. Taking his seat behind the desk again, Tean said, "I didn't realize Benny had someone like you taking care of him." He shook his head. "That's got to be hard for you, devoting so much of your life to someone, especially at a distance." His head came up, and his dark eyes fixed on Jem in a way that was uncannily knowing. For a moment, Jem wondered if he'd somehow given himself away. "Benny's lucky to have you."

"He doesn't think so," Jem said. "Ask him about the asshole in his life sometime. But, you know: brothers. What am I supposed to do? I bet your brothers would do it for you."

He gestured to the family picture on Tean's desk, which was angled so that Jem could see it. You could tell a lot about somebody by the shit they kept, and that photograph was the only one in the office—no girlfriend, no boyfriend, no friends, no pets. Just Tean's family in a cluster of faces, some of them obviously blood, some obviously in-laws. Tean had been shunted all the way to the side.

But Tean didn't grin or nod or smile the way Jem expected. His thumbs traced the lip of the desk, and then he said, "Sure." He cleared his throat and added, "Benny was here yesterday—I guess that's what you're interested in. We talked, but just for a few minutes."

"Did he tell you why he was here?"

"Yeah," Tean said. "He thought birds were being poisoned. Benny often gets the big picture right but not the details, so I went to check it out this morning. I'm pretty sure we're seeing an outbreak of avian cholera, although I'll have to send off some samples to be tested for toxins."

Jem stretched and frowned, and then he noticed the way Tean's eyes slid across him when his shirt pulled up. Still stretching, Jem scratched his belly, his knuckles rucking up his shirt a few more inches. The doc needed to be careful or his eyes were going to fall out of his head. At least that answered one question.

"Where was that?" Jem asked.

"What?"

"The birds," Jem said, tugging his shirt into place and, when Tean flushed and brought his eyes up, catching his gaze with a smirk. Tean flushed more deeply. "Where did you say the dead birds were?"

"Why?"

"Because Benny might have gone back there."

"Oh. Oh, right. Well, I was at the Great Salt Lake State Park. I suppose he could have gone back there. We had a talk about not touching dead animals; we've had lots of talks, actually, but they don't seem to make much of an impact."

"Try getting him to eat his fucking vegetables," Jem said.

This time, the doc's smile was like a lightning strike, huge and brilliant and gone. "Do you really think the disappearance could be related to, you know, Benny's environmental concerns?"

"You mean the fact that he was nutso?" Jem shrugged. "Maybe. Probably. He's always going on and on about people trying to get him, but that's . . . that's one of the ways he's not well. But he loves to be out in nature. He could have fallen and hurt himself. He could have gone into a diabetic coma. He could have gotten lost. Or maybe he just hitched a ride to Canyonlands. I don't know; all I know is his friend dropped him off here, and that's the last anyone's seen of him."

Nodding slowly, Tean stood and snagged his keys. "Let's go see."

"What?"

"Let's see where he went when he left."

"Did you tag him?" Jem asked.

"No," Tean said with another flash of a smile. "But we've got security cameras. Come on."

He turned and hesitated, looking down at his keys, seeming to consider where they had been hiding, and moved toward the door. Jem, already standing, moved too, timing his movements to Tean's. He was riffing again, but that was what he did best. He grabbed Tean's hand the moment it closed on the door handle. Tean stiffened like an electric current was running through him, but Jem was slow to peel his hand away.

"Sorry," Jem murmured, and then he set his other hand low on Tean's back, feeling the tight muscles there. "After you?"

Jem wasn't sure if humans could really spontaneously combust, but Tean looked like he was well on his way. He dropped the keys twice, and Jem made sure that on the second time, their hands touched again. When his fingers closed around Tean's, Tean actually yelped.

"Did I hurt you?" Jem said.

Shaking his head vigorously, Tean shoved the keys in his pocket, jerked the door open, and hurried down the hall. He led Tean to the security desk at the front, where the security guard was still reading the paper

"Oh no," she said when she saw Jem. "I told you no."

"It's ok, Antonia," Tean said. "I did need to talk to him, but I hadn't told you. That was my fault."

Antonia glared at Jem; she was grinding the tip of a pencil into the half-completed crossword puzzle.

"We do need to take a look at the security footage from the other day. Do you mind if I use the security office?"

"Of course not, Dr. Leon. But I really think that young man should sit himself down right here where I can see him. You don't need him bothering you."

Jem set his hand low on Tean's back again and guided him away from the security desk. Tean squirmed away from the touch and turned to face Jem.

"I guess I could wait out here," Jem said quietly.

"That would probably be best," Tean said.

"If you don't want me in there, I understand. I know I'm not anyone special, and I don't deserve special treatment, but—but I just hate the thought that I might miss seeing something that could help me find Benny."

Indecision locked Tean's face.

"Please," Jem murmured, stepping in closer. "Then I'll be out of your hair."

"Yeah," Tean said. "Sure. Ok."

Tean led him to the next door, and they stepped into a cramped room. Lockers lined one wall; on the wall opposite, shelves and hooks held miscellaneous equipment: neon orange vests, traffic cones, portable lights, a whistle on a black shoelace. The air smelled like rubber and furtive smoke breaks. Somebody clever had hung a poster that was obviously a take on the pinup girls from another age: a grizzly bear stood, one ankle coquettishly behind the other, a pink tulle skirt immodestly raised above its knees. All Jem needed to see was a desk calendar with cat pictures and he'd go smash his head against the side of a dumpster until he lost consciousness.

Shoved up against the far wall was a desk with a Snoopy doll wearing what Jem guessed was an honorary Utah conservation officer badge. A computer monitor showed grainy color footage from an interior camera; after a moment, the image switched to another camera, and then it switched again to an exterior shot. The angle was wide, and Jem realized the cameras had been set up to give a good view of North Temple in both directions.

"We do get some pretty extreme people," Tean said, gesturing at a wide shot of North Temple as he sat at the desk. "When we upgraded security, we decided it'd be good to have an idea of how people approach the building."

"That's really smart," Jem said, moving to stand close behind Tean. Not touching—too much touching was creepy, and besides, it needed to seem natural—but close. "And you've got footage from yesterday."

"Sure," Tean said. He clicked through several options, and the image on the screen changed to color footage of North Temple going west. Tean scrubbed forward until the timestamp showed 10:01:13. "Sorry I can't be more specific than that; I don't remember exactly when he got here."

They watched the sped-up video, slowing down only when a van approached so that Jem could see if it was Chaquille's.

"There," Jem said, grabbing Tean's shoulder. "That's his friend who dropped him off. Holy shit, you're amazing."

Tean shrugged off the touch and clicked a few more times, and then a camera inside the lobby showed Benny entering, talking to Antonia, and pacing. He was lugging his backpack and pup tent after the weekend camping at the Jenkins' ranch.

"You are amazing," Jem said, squeezing Tean's shoulder again.

"Ok," Tean said, wriggling out from under Jem's hand, but Jem could tell he was trying hard not to look too pleased. "Now let's see when he leaves."

He switched back to the west-facing camera again and played the sped-up video again.

"Nothing," Jem said.

"So we'll try the other way. Maybe he went east."

But the timestamp reached 12:58:25, and there was no sign of Benny moving east on North Temple.

"Try the parking lot," Jem said.

At 11:03:42, Benny walked into the frame, moving toward the northeast corner of the lot, where several dumpsters backed up to a chain-link fence. Jem's fingers tightened, and this time, it had nothing to do with riffing, nothing to do with the game. They watched until Benny was nearing the far edge of the frame.

"Ok," Jem said. "Maybe he hopped the fence—"

He forgot what he was about to say because a black SUV drove on-screen, pulling up next to Benny, and Benny stopped walking. Tean drew in a sharp breath, and Jem could feel Tean tense under his hand. Jem barely registered those details. All he could do was stare at the video, watching as Benny climbed in the SUV and disappeared from sight.

12

Tean stared as the black SUV rolled to the edge of the frame and vanished. He tried to convince himself, again, that this was a coincidence. He scrubbed the video forward, then back, and then forward again. He switched cameras. Nothing on the westbound feed of North Temple, but eastbound, the timestamp read 11:09:19 when the SUV pulled out of the DWR parking lot and headed back toward the city.

"What the fuck?" Jem said. "Why would he get in the car? What happened in the six minutes they were sitting in the parking lot?"

His hand was still on Tean's shoulder, heavy, his grip tight enough to be painful, but Tean didn't say anything. Then Jem swore again, spinning away and ripping his hand free. The feeling of the touch lingered like a sunspot.

"Do you recognize the SUV?" Tean asked.

Jem shook his head.

"Do you know who might have picked him up? A friend—"

"No. Benny doesn't really have friends. He buys weed from Chaquille, sometimes stuff that's a little bit harder, and Chaquille kind of . . . puts up with him, I guess. Anyway, that's not Chaquille's van."

"Maybe I could call—"

"No." It was practically a shout. Then Jem just stood there, pinching the bridge of his nose, those broad shoulders bowed. "Just give me a minute."

Tean waited and said, "Why don't we go back to my office?"

Jem's eyes were closed; his fingertips were white from pressure.

Standing up, Tean touched his arm, the polyester shell of the windbreaker rustling. Jem smelled like pot and clean sweat. He flinched when Tean touched him, jerking away, and Tean thought about their hands meeting when they reached for the door at the same time; he thought about the confident, gentle pressure Jem had applied at the small of his back. Now Tean studied Jem more closely, trying to make the pieces of the puzzle fit.

"My office?" Tean asked again.

"Uh," Jem took a deep breath, his breathing ragged. "No, I'll just—I should just—"

"Come on," Tean said

Jem hammered on the poster of the bear a few times, swearing in a vicious growl, and dropped his hands to his sides. He was breathing hard.

"Come on," Tean said again.

Jem nodded.

He let Tean shepherd him back to the office; Tean got him seated, and then he fiddled with the diffuser, which now smelled like lavender. Over Jem's head, one of his demotivational posters stared back at Tean: a night sky, a shooting star, and the words IN MANY CULTURES, A SHOOTING STAR SIGNIFIES GOOD LUCK . . . STRANGELY, DINOSAURS ARE NOT ONE OF THEM. Tean carried the kettle to the water fountain, and while he filled it, Hannah poked her head out of her office.

"Don't offer him that weird grass tea," she whispered—loudly—from her doorway. Then she held up several pre-packaged bags of tea.

"Nettle tea is not—"

"Don't do it!"

With the kettle full, Tean hesitated. Then he stomped down the hall, snatched the tea, and stomped back toward his office.

"You can thank me later," Hannah whispered—loudly—after him.

With the kettle heating, Tean fiddled with the mugs, stacked the foil-wrapped tea bags and then spread them like a deck of cards, stacked them again, and wondered what in the world he was doing.

Jem coughed, cleared his throat, and dropped his hand to his side. "Ok," he said, but his eyes were a little red. "Ok, I'm fine."

"How about some tea?"

"I'm taking up way too much of your time. I'll just go. I don't— I don't know what I'm even doing." He looked so different from the guy who had been waiting in Tean's office just a half hour earlier: that guy had been smooth, smiling, somehow in control even after bursting into tears. This guy, on the other hand, had a little bit of clear snot in his beard. "Thanks for looking at the video. I really appreciate it."

Tean sat on the edge of his desk. When Jem stood, Tean asked, "Where are you going to go?"

"Fuck. I don't know."

"What are you going to do?"

"I have no idea. Benny hasn't—that's not normal, ok? I mean, sure, sometimes he's hooked up with strangers and gone somewhere. But I could always get a hold of him. Sometimes he'd tell me before he left. Sometimes I'd have to call him, and then I'd rip him a new asshole. Sometimes I'd have to go get him. But at least I'd know he was safe. This, with him disappearing, complete radio silence, this is totally new. It's weird."

"It's scary," Tean said.

Jem shook his head and then stopped and said, "Yeah." He tried to say something, and then he had to cover his eyes again. "Look, this is really embarrassing." His voice got thicker with each word. "I just need a minute, um, the bathroom, Christ, anywhere."

"Down the hall," Tean said. "Do you want me to—"

But Jem was already gone.

Tean sat at his desk, spinning the mug that said VETS DO IT WILD, and felt totally useless.

When the door opened and Jem stepped back into the room, the blond man was smiling, although his eyes were redder than ever. "Ok," he said with a slick smile. "Sorry about that. Back to normal over here."

"You don't have to be back to normal," Tean said. "You can be upset and worried and scared. Heck, you can be angry if it helps."

"I'm all right. Just needed a minute to pull it together."

"Sit down and have some tea. I've got nettle tea, and I make that myself, or I've got, um," fanning the tea selection again, "chamomile, orange blossom, oolong, and something called Morning Jazz, which sounds like a Suzanne Somers workout routine."

"Then definitely Morning Jazz."

Tean packed a mesh tea infuser with nettle leaves and set it in one mug; in the other, he set the Morning Jazz tea, with the little paper tag hanging over the rim. He poured the water, handed one mug to Jem, and was surprised when Jem accepted the mug with both hands, wrapping Tean's in one of his own and trapping it against the mug. The guy who had flinched away in the security room was gone, and the first guy was back with a weak smile, squeezing Tean's wrist as he said, "Thank you. I didn't think you'd be cute and kind."

And that did it: everything in the room was different, a new heat tangling behind Tean's breastbone, Jem's touch sending a live current up Tean's arm, Jem's eyes a blue-gray squall that warned Tean to batten the hatches. Then Tean thought of Ammon, and the little circuit breaker at the back of his brain tripped.

"It'll probably give you some sort of food poisoning because God only knows how old it is."

Jem's smile held steady, "I don't mind things—or guys—who are a little older than me." His thumb slid along the knob of Tean's wrist.

"The packet says it'll put a zing in your step, which sounds like it might have nerve toxins."

"I forgot to take my nerve toxins this morning."

"I'm sure it's not fair trade. The farmers who grew this are probably slowly dying of malnourishment."

Jem's smile burned even brighter, and Tean had the impression that this was his real smile; his two front teeth were slightly crooked, and somehow, it made him adorable. "I think it's really great that you care about social justice. A lot of the guys I date don't even want to think about that stuff."

"You have snot in your beard."

Jem's eyes got huge, and Tean suddenly heard what he'd just said. Working his hand free of Jem's, Tean stumbled back to the desk, grabbed his nettle tea, and gulped down a mouthful. It was too hot, and it burned his mouth and throat, but he swallowed it anyway and immediately started coughing.

"Are you ok?" Jem said.

"Yes. Yeah. Um, listen, I know someone. I mean, I have a friend who's a detective with the police. I'd like to put you in touch with him."

Hesitating, Jem set the mug down slowly. "I don't think the police will—"

"Just unofficially. He might be able to help."

"No," Jem said, shaking his head. "I really want to keep the police out of this. Benny has had . . . problems. Because of his mental health. I don't want this turning into something bigger than it needs to be."

Tean took another gulp of the nettle tea and said, "I think you need the police at this point. Actually, I think we both do. That SUV? It was following me earlier today. I thought maybe it had something to do with—well, something else, it doesn't matter. I was getting these weird phone calls, and then the SUV showed up. I thought maybe they were connected, but now I think maybe it's related to Benny. When he came here yesterday, he was convinced someone was trying to get him. He told me about the birds and gave me a bunch of papers, telling me he had written down all the people who needed to be punished for the different things they'd done wrong. I didn't really think anything about it until I saw that SUV in the video; I just assumed it was . . ."

"Benny being Benny," Jem said. "Yeah, I know what you mean. He gave me the same story, more or less, but I've heard it a hundred times. Why would this time be any different?"

"Because we just saw somebody pick him up in a black SUV. And a similar black SUV followed me after I went to look at those dead birds."

"But you said Benny wasn't right; you said the birds had a disease."

"That's what it looks like," Tean said, "and I still think I'm right, but I have to wait on the tox report to be sure."

"So Benny figures out somebody is poisoning birds—accidentally or not—and reports it to you. But they, whoever they are, get wind of it, and now they've picked him up to quiet him? That sounds like some paranoid shit right there."

"I know that a black SUV was following me," Tean said, "and it looked a lot like the one that took Benny. I'm not crazy."

For a moment, that other smile was back—the one with the crooked teeth on full display, the one that wasn't quite as polished but was so much better. "Did you hear yourself going on about the tea?"

"Ok," Tean said, surprising himself with a laugh. "I'm definitely crazy, but not about this."

After a moment, Jem nodded. "Let's call your friend."

Sitting at the desk, Tean placed the call.

"Young." The background noise made Tean think that Ammon was in a car.

"Hey, I've got a weird situation, and I need your help."

Muffled noises came over the line, and then, "Is this about the Hyeon shooting?"

"No. Well, I don't know, actually. It's weird, like I said, and complicated. Can we meet you somewhere?"

"Who's we?"

"A friend."

"Who is he, Tean?"

"Somebody who needs help. Do you want to do this over the phone? I guess I can just explain it now."

"No," Ammon snapped. Then, with more control, he said, "No, I can meet you after work."

"Ok. Hey, thank you, I know—"

The call disconnected.

Jem's eyes were fixed on Tean, and he found himself awkwardly finishing the sentence: "—this is inconvenient. Ok, bye."

When Tean put down the phone, Jem was still staring at him.

"He can talk after he gets off work," Tean said. "It'll probably be seven or eight, though, by the time he gets to my place."

"You have a detective who makes house calls?"

Tean felt his face heat. "He's a friend from growing up."

"A friend who hangs up on you?"

"We just got cut off," Tean said, but his face was even hotter.

Jem nodded.

"You know what I want to see?" Tean said, trying to keep his voice even. "I want to see those papers, the ones where Benny listed his alleged culprits."

"Oh," Jem said, ducking his chin. "I didn't think of that."

Tean hit speakerphone and called Hannah's office.

"Please tell me he picked the Morning Jazz tea," Hannah said. "I mean, he's hot, and he's your dream California surfer boy, even if he doesn't have long hair, but if he loves Morning Jazz tea, oh my gosh, wouldn't that just be perfect? You could both be like little old ladies drinking tea together."

"Your dream California surfer boy," Jem whispered, his eyes widening, a huge smile forming.

"Hi, Hannah," Tean said through gritted teeth. "Speakerphone."

Something clunked on the other side of the call, like Hannah might have banged her knee against the desk, and then she said, "Dang it. Um, yes, hi. Hello, Dr. Leon. How are you today?"

"Do you know when the trash gets taken out?"

"Yes, Dr. Leon. Every day, Dr. Leon. Our custodial staff—"

"I know, I know. I mean when does it get picked up. You know, the dumpster."

"Oh, of course, Dr. Leon. That's a brilliant question. Thank you for clarifying. Working under the auspices of your leadership has been a complete privilege, and any potential romantic partner ought to know—"

"Hannah!" It was half scream and half plea.

"Wednesdays and Saturdays, Dr. Leon. And, Dr. Leon, if I may be so bold, I happen to have a cousin with a condo at Bear Lake if you and a friend were looking for—"

Tean punched buttons on the phone, trying to kill the call. It only took about eight tries.

"California—"

"No," Tean said.

"—surfer boy."

"I do not like California," Tean said. "Do you know that California used to be called the Grizzly Bear State, but then they killed all the grizzly bears, so now it's the Golden State?"

Jem nodded, his expression serious. "I admire their adaptability in the face of tragedy."

"And did you know the bear that's on the state flag, he was a real bear, and his name was Monarch, and he was one of the last of his species, and he died alone in a zoo?"

"That's very sad, but look on the bright side: he was surrounded by people who loved him, and I bet he had great end-of-life care."

"And I don't know any bad facts about surfers but I'm going to find some."

Jem just nodded some more.

"I bet the board wax kills turtles," Tean said.

"Actually, they've developed some great, eco-friendly formulas."

"But I'm sure surfing itself negatively affects marine life."

"You know, surprisingly, it can actually promote positive symbiotic relationships."

Tean grabbed the desk until his knuckles turned white.

"It's ok," Jem said. "You seem really smart. I'm sure you'll find something."

Running his hands through his hair—and then grabbing his hair—Tean gave a few hard yanks.

"What about the dumpster?" Jem suggested. "You had such a great idea about the dumpster. You should be proud of that."

"Please stop trying to help," Tean said.

They went outside. The October day was pleasantly warm, the sun bright through a skein of cirrus clouds. North Temple was busy, with cars and trucks and tractor-trailers whipping past the DWR building. The smell of diesel exhaust and an occasional whiff of too-hot oil mixed with the smell of the asphalt.

When they reached the dumpsters at the back of the lot, Jem took the lead, throwing open the lids. The warm day had cooked up a powerful stench, and Tean grimaced and fanned the air. He got a grip on the dumpster, braced his foot, and readied himself to climb in.

"Hold on," Jem said, stripping off the windbreaker. He wore a gray tee that said Smith Field House, and he had excessively nice muscles. "Hold this."

"No, I'll look," Tean said. "It was my idea, and I might recognize my trash."

"We're looking for a sheaf of papers covered in Benny's handwriting," Jem said. "I don't exactly need a lot of clues." He grinned, stepping closer, and Tean caught another whiff of clean sweat and marijuana. Jem tugged on Tean's polo. "Besides, how can I let a guy wearing a khaki polo, khaki pants, and khaki boots ruin his perfect outfit?"

Tean glanced down at the three shades of khaki. "Huh?"

"Oh my God," Jem said, biting his lip. "Like a giant, khaki baby."

"Look, I should—"

But before Tean could finish, Jem was using those nicely muscled arms to drag himself up and into the dumpster.

"You guys make a lot of garbage," Jem said, toeing aside some of the bags. "The papers should be near the top of the pile, right? Would they have dumped any more already today?"

"Maybe," Tean said. "I should have asked."

"That's ok."

"It's going to be in a clear liner," Tean said, "not one of those thick black trash bags they use in the warehouse and the bathrooms."

"Check," Jem called, his back turned to Tean as he shifted more of the garbage. "Heyo," he shouted as he held up one of the smaller, transparent bags. He shook it, inspecting the contents through the bag, and then tossed it aside. He let out another cry of triumph as he surfaced with another bag. And another. But he discarded all of them.

Then: "Bingo!" He waved a transparent liner at Tean. "Damn. You drink a lot of tea."

"Well, I'm going to die no matter what. I figure maybe the tea will slow it down a little."

"Plus you like how it tastes."

"No, that's not why I—"

"Is this diaper cream?"

"Um."

Jem trampled several bags as he made his way to the dumpster's rim. He leaned over, displaying the bag. "That's diaper cream."

"It's not mine." And then, before he could stop himself: "It was an experiment."

"Uh huh."

"Give me that," Tean said, yanking the bag away. He ripped the plastic and pulled out the sheaf of pages Benny had given him. A couple of them were wet along the edges from the discarded nettle leaves, but the ink hadn't run too badly and was still legible. "Ok, we can—"

But Jem had disappeared into the dumpster again.

"Hey," Tean said. "What's going on?"

"Fuck," Jem shouted, the word so distorted by anger that Tean barely recognized it. "Fuck, fuck, fuck."

"What? Did you cut yourself? Are you ok?"

A moment later, Jem surged up from the trash bags. He was holding out a military-style black backpack with a pup tent lashed to the top.

13

For the rest of the afternoon, Jem hung around Tean's office, waiting to meet with Tean's detective friend. They checked the security video again, on the off chance that they could see who had dumped Benny's camping gear. No luck, though — the SUV blocked the dumpster from sight, and whoever had done it remained hidden from the camera.

While Jem waited out the hours, he tried to keep busy. While Tean did whatever he was doing — scribbling on papers, typing like mad, pushing his huge, crooked glasses back up his nose — Jem emptied the backpack and found two packages of Oreos (empty), two bags of beef jerky (empty), a can of asparagus (unopened), printed-out computer pictures of ladies with black leather bustiers and riding crops, a box of matches, on and on like that. Some of Benny's camping gear was missing — he always had an aluminum mess kit, for example, plus his Teenage Mutant Ninja Turtles bowl, a Hamburglar novelty canteen, cooking oil, instant hot chocolate, a change of clothes, and probably other things Jem was forgetting.

After repacking the bag, Jem stood in a stairwell and made phone calls. He called Tinajas, one of his go-to sources. They had filtered through some of the same foster homes, and the bond had lasted, although she'd built a more traditional life than Jem. When she picked up, he asked her about black SUVs.

"You're kidding, right?" she asked; he could hear typing in the background. "Do you know how many vehicles are registered in Salt Lake County?"

"A lot," Jem said. "But it's for Benny."

"A million, give or take. A million cars. And we don't record vehicle color on the title. Do you have a license plate?"

"No."

"Cariño," she said.

"Ok," Jem said. "Thanks anyway."

"Where are you living now?"

"I gotta go," Jem said and disconnected.

He tried Chaquille again, but Chaquille had wised up or was too stoned to function. He called the Latus, Sammi's parents, and asked them to keep an eye out, just in case Benny showed up. He tried the Jenkins again, but they couldn't offer anything new. When Jem thought about his next call, his stomach started churning, and he went into the bathroom and washed his face with cold water. He didn't do anything stupid like stick his hand down his shirt and trace the scar, but he thought about it. Then he thought he might throw up, but he only spat a few times into the sink and ran the back of his hand over his mouth, smelling the campfire smoke from Benny's gear. When he went back to the stairwell, he placed his last call, making sure to press *67 first to hide his number.

LouElla answered. "Hello?"

"It's me," Jem said. "Have you seen Benny?"

"Now who the fuck is me?"

"You know who it is. Have you seen Benny? Has he been around there?"

"Well, if it isn't Princess Jemma. Saints alive, Princess."

"Did he stop by? Did he call?"

"I still owe you a broken tooth, Jemma. Where are you hiding these days?"

Jem pulled the phone away from his ear; LouElla was just too loud. "If he shows up, call me."

"Why would I—"

"Because you'll get what you always fucking want," Jem said, his voice breaking into a shout. Then he jammed a finger against the screen, disconnecting the call, and took two fast steps and punched the wall.

When he looked over, Tean was standing in the doorway to the stairwell.

"What?" Jem said.

"Are you ok?"

Shaking out his hand, Jem couldn't find a word to answer him.

"Who was that?" Tean asked.

"Nobody," Jem said.

"Do you want—"

"No. I don't want to talk about it. I don't want to sit down in your office. I don't want any fucking tea."

Color darkened Tean's cheeks, and he pushed the crooked glasses back up slowly. "I was going to ask if you want me to clean up your hand."

Glancing down, Jem saw blood dripping slowly onto the vinyl. He looked up, chewing the inside of his mouth, and said nothing.

"Ok," Tean said and left.

"Fuck," Jem said. "Fuck, fuck, fuck," he shouted, the words echoing up the stairwell.

Then he got paper towels, mopped up the blood on the floor, and ran cold water over his knuckles until the bleeding was mostly stopped. When he went back to Tean's office, he clamped a wad of fresh paper towels over his hand. The room still smelled like campfire smoke, mixed with the weak lavender output from the diffuser. Tean was typing again.

"Sorry about that," Jem said. "Kind of lost it there for a minute."

Tean nodded.

"If I wasn't too much of an asshole," Jem said, "do you have a first aid kit?"

"Bring a chair over," Tean said without looking away from the screen.

After dragging one of the chairs around the desk, Jem sat. Tean typed for another minute.

"What are you working on?"

"A report."

"On what?"

"June suckers."

"Ok," Jem said, smiling. "Talk about a cliffhanger. You can't just leave me hanging like this."

When Tean looked over, his expression was flat.

"I'm sorry," Jem said. "I lost my temper."

"No need to apologize," Tean said. He opened a drawer, took out a first aid kit in a zippered, neoprene case, and pulled out disposable gloves, a tube of antibiotic ointment, gauze, and tape. "Do you think you broke any bones in your hand?"

"When I hit the wall, you mean," Jem said, "before I was a major asshole to you?"

Tean just leveled another of those flat expressions at him.

"I don't know," Jem said, letting the smile shrink a little.

Exhaling slowly, Tean took Jem's hand in both of his, palpating. "Tell me if it hurts."

Jem shook his head.

Somewhere down the hall, a phone was ringing.

Tean's hands were gentle and surprisingly callused. His movements were confident and steady, in contrast to the wild hair and his flustered speech. Jem tried to remember the last time someone, anyone, had touched him like this: not for sex, not for a fight, not part of a game. When Tean leaned in, the air brought the scent of sagebrush and timothy and pine resin.

Once, as a boy, Jem had played a game that he and Tony Poucher called hotfoot: they'd struck matches and then tossed them at each other, both of them laughing like lunatics and running away, never mind that the matches went out almost as soon as they threw them. Most of the matches. In August, with the prairie grass so dry that it was tinder, they'd started a fire that took out a WPA cabin and a few hundred acres of canyon before the blaze burned itself out in a natural fork in the river. This was a little bit like that: it had started out as a game, yanking the doc's chain as long as he was useful, and somehow it was suddenly much more serious. The dizzy recklessness of it, the stinging heat in the tips of his fingers, the first tongues of flame that came before an inferno.

With his free hand, Jem pushed the crooked glasses back up Tean's nose. Tean started and pulled back.

"I'd say you're ok," Tean said, dropping his hand, "although if you have swelling that lasts more than a day, or if you have pain besides the split knuckles, you probably need an X-ray."

Jem's mouth was too dry to answer.

"Hand here," Tean said, motioning to a spot on his desk that was covered with computer printouts. Jem laid his hand lightly on the papers, and Tean applied the ointment with a few quick brushes of his index finger before taping the gauze in place. He glanced up; his glasses were halfway down his nose again.

"Thank you," Jem said, and it didn't sound like his game voice at all, didn't sound like riffing, didn't even feel like riffing. He pushed the glasses back up, and this time, Tean didn't pull away. Jem's bandaged hand slid to Tean's knee. He let his hand ride up an inch.

"I've got to get some work done," Tean said, his voice rough.

Jem let his hand skate up another inch of ropey muscle.

Tean caught his wrist.

"Yeah," Jem said, doing some mental digging, trying to find the gameshow smile that used to be right at the top of the heap. "Of course."

14

Outside the DWR building, with the October day's warmth still leaching out of the asphalt, Jem followed Tean to his truck. It was obviously a government vehicle; Division of Wildlife Resources was painted on the white panels.

"I texted Ammon. Detective Young," Tean corrected himself. "He says he can't get there until after seven now."

"A pet detective you can text whenever you want," Jem said.

A blush moved under Tean's soft brown skin. "I can give you the address. Just come over around seven."

"Sure," Jem said. "I guess an Uber will get me out there, right?"

"Oh," Tean said. "I forgot. Dang it. You're visiting. Where's your hotel?" He frowned. "Where's your luggage?"

"Uh," Jem said. "Great question. No luggage. I rushed out of the house kind of unprepared. Where is an extremely cheap hotel that will take cash?" Tean's look was just enough of a question that Jem laughed and added, "Not everybody in California is rich, and I maxed out my card getting the plane ticket. That's just one more reason I'm going to whip Benny's ass raw when I find him."

Tean ran a hand through his brushed-back hair. His glasses almost took a dive, and he caught them at the last minute. He scrubbed a knuckle across one bushy eyebrow. Then he froze.

"I'm not really going to hit him," Jem said.

Tean shook his head. "Don't turn around, but it's back."

"The SUV?"

"Yep."

"Where?"

Straight behind you. Westbound lanes of North Temple. They're just sitting at the curb."

"Call your pet detective," Jem said.

"No, wait—"

But Jem spun and sprinted toward North Temple. Tean's description had been accurate: the black SUV was idling at the curb just outside the DWR facility. He got his hands in his pockets, pulling out the paracord in one, the hex nut tied at the end of the cord slapping against his leg as he ran, and grabbing the antenna in the other.

The SUV lurched forward, the engine roaring. It cut into traffic, and a green Geo slammed on the brakes, horn blaring as the driver tried to avoid a collision. The SUV swerved once as the driver overcorrected, and then it shot down North Temple, heading west. Inside the Geo, a middle-aged woman glanced around as though trying to figure out what had happened. Then, after a moment, she drove on.

"Fuck," Jem shouted.

Then he went back to Tean.

"Well, a little late for that," Tean was saying into the phone. "Ok. Ok. Hold on. Did you get the license plate?"

Jem shook his head. "It didn't have one."

Tean relayed this information and asked, "Could you make out anyone inside the vehicle?"

Another shake of his head. "Windows are tinted too dark."

Tean repeated this, listened, and said, "Ok. Thanks, Ammon."

"First name basis?" Jem asked as Tean disconnected.

"He said don't approach the vehicle."

"Well, it was worth a shot."

Tean chewed his lips; his glasses were inching down his nose, about to take a tumble. Then, pushing them back into place, he said, "Come on. We can stop by the store so you can pick up some clothes, and then we'll get you to a motel."

"No way. I've already taken up your whole day."

"Something weird is going on, and it seems like it involves both of us. I kind of want you to stick close until we figure that out. Unless you think that's too weird."

"It's definitely not weird," Jem said. "I mean, it's probably the safest thing we can do. But you've already spent so much time helping me, and I'm this total stranger who just dropped a mess of problems in your life, and you've probably got plans with your boyfriend."

"Yeah," Tean said with a grimace. "I wish."

Jem grinned.

"Oh my gosh," Tean said. "I can't believe I fell for that."

"Neither can I."

"Oh my gosh."

"So," Jem said. "No boyfriend."

"It's a little more complicated than that. Come on, let's go."

"Can I ask you something?" Jem said.

"Not if it's about my complicated situation."

"No." Jem could feel his control of the game slipping, and he tried to get it back, but the question broke out before he could stop it. "I don't want to be rude, but why are you helping me?"

Frowning, Tean said, "I'm worried about Benny. Sure, he's annoying, and he causes complete chaos when he shows up at work, but he's genuine, and he cares, and he's obviously had a hard life. And you're here, and you're a fish out of water. No offense, but you're definitely out of your element with this."

Jem bit the inside of his cheek. "Definitely."

"And anyway, it's Utah, so get ready for people who are so polite and friendly and eager to help that you're going to want to pull your teeth out by the time you leave."

"You know what I think?" Jem said.

"Oh no," Tean groaned.

"I think it's because you're a really good guy."

"Do you know what a good guy is?" Tean asked.

"I'm looking at one."

"A good guy is a bad guy with a thin candy shell."

"God, you're dark," Jem said. "I dig it."

Groaning, Tean said, "Just get in the truck."

They headed east on North Temple toward the city and the Wasatch Mountains, which were painted with thick slashes of ochre as the sun set. The city itself was a strange mix, one that, for Jem, reflected the incongruities of Utah culture. At the heart of Salt Lake City stood a handful of skyscrapers, but most of the city was built low, spreading across the ample space of the valley. Some of the construction, like the Mormon temple and other early buildings, were ornate exhibits of craftsmanship, worked in stone, lovingly attended to. Much of the city, though, looked like it had been built cheap and fast, with ugly, streamlined designs in color palettes that made Jem think of the 70s. Old industrial buildings crowded next to upscale condominiums; a flood of new money had revitalized the downtown, including the development of City Creek Mall, but had left swaths of the city fossilized. Clean-cut men and hair-sprayed women, most of them white, most of them looking middle class in suits and conservative dresses, walked briskly past a burgeoning homeless and transient population that filled the street corners.

Tean took them first to a strip mall with a Ross, and when they went inside, he steered Jem to the circular racks at the back.

"Clearance," Tean said. "Look at this shirt. Eighty percent off."

"Uh huh," Jem said.

"You don't like it."

"Purple and green vertical stripe isn't, um, exactly my thing."

"What about this one?"

"It has a lace collar."

"It's two dollars. You can rip the collar off."

Jem didn't say anything.

"What?"

"Oh nothing. One more piece falling into place."

"You sound like Hannah," Tean grumbled as he pulled out a neon yellow bowling shirt with FREE RIDES printed on the back. "What about this?"

"Yes," Jem said. "That one. Definitely."

In the end, Jem found a three-pack of plain gray tees, a pair of jeans—not the ones with silver stitching across the ass that Tean insisted were still fashionable—and socks and underwear. He didn't like buying clothes just for the disguise, but the truth was that Jem needed to replenish some essentials, and he'd never been inside a Ross before. Tean hadn't been wrong about coming here—it was cheaper than the stuff Jem usually bought.

Back in the truck, they headed north.

"You probably shouldn't be so trusting," Tean said over the thrum of the tires. "Someone could take advantage of you."

"You're just giving me a hard time because I said you're a good guy."

"No, I'm serious. I'm not a good guy. And, more importantly, you can't be so trusting."

"That's one of my weaknesses," Jem said, flashing the gameshow smile. "I'm a little naïve."

"I could have been a serial killer."

Jem plucked at Tean's shirt. "The Khaki Killer has a nice ring to it."

"I could be planning on drugging you so I can harvest your organs."

"I don't think anybody's going to want my liver," Jem said. "I've used it pretty hard."

"Do you know how many people are killed by someone they know?"

"What kind of music do you like?"

"Over fifty percent of murder victims are killed by someone they know."

"Lucky for me," Jem said, "I just met you today. What about Taylor Swift?"

"And over a quarter of those victims are killed by a family member."

"Ok, no Taylor Swift. How about hip hop?"

"Did you know in those *Land Before Time* movies, Ducky doesn't talk after the first movie because the little girl who did her voice was killed by her father? She was ten years old."

Jem cocked his head. "You're really going dark, aren't you?"

Buzzing down the window, Tean stuck his head out for a moment, shook himself all over, and then pulled his head back inside the truck. "I don't even know what I'm talking about."

"You're talking about why you're not a good person and why I shouldn't trust people."

"Yeah. Yes."

"Because people suck."

"Exactly."

"Got it," Jem said. "Now tell me one thing you really like."

"What?"

"One thing you really, really like. I really like Zack from *Saved by the Bell*. Give me five minutes with that blond dreamboat and I'd make him forget all about Kelly Kapowski."

Tean drove for almost two minutes before he said, "What?"

Laughing, Jem squeezed his shoulder. "Come on: one thing you absolutely like. Nothing negative."

Tean tried to slide away from the touch, but Jem held on lightly.
"This is dumb."

"One thing."

"There are plenty of things I like."

"Great; this'll be easy. Let's hear one."

Tean's gaze shifted from the road to the rearview mirror to the radio, settling on Jem furtively before stealing back to the road.

"I can probably guess a few things you love," Jem said. "Bubblegum pink knee-high socks, the WNBA, department meetings—"

"Rancherito's breakfast burrito."

Jem burst out laughing. "What?"

"Their breakfast burrito. It's . . . surprisingly good."

An electric-blue Mustang shot past them on the left, its engine roaring.

Jem squeezed Tean's shoulder again. "All right, I've got to hear this."

"Well, the pork is definitely not organic or free-range—"

"Nope. No negative stuff."

"I think they use frozen potatoes that are probably ten years old—"

"Nope."

"The staff earns minimum wage, and that corporation is definitely taking advantage—"

Jem gave him a little shake. "Last chance, or things get serious."

For the next thirty seconds, Tean fiddled with the vents. Then he burst out, "It's just really, really good. The eggs are fluffy. It's got the right amount of cheese—real cheese, that has flavor. The bacon is crisp, the sausage is just the right degree of fatty. And they put something in the potatoes that makes the whole thing taste like crack."

"Wow."

"Well, this was your stupid idea. I sound like I'm obsessed with this burrito."

"No, I was just honestly waiting for some bleak story about an entire family that got food poisoning and died of a wasting sickness and they had almost discovered the cure for cancer but now it's lost forever."

Tean's face froze. Then, as though he were losing a battle, the corner of his mouth twitched.

"It's a really good burrito," Jem said. "You've got nothing to be ashamed of."

"They've got Rancherito's in California?" Tean said, twisting to glance at Jem.

"Uh, you know, I actually haven't seen one out there. But I grew up here, remember? Foster brothers, all that."

"Oh." But Tean glanced at him again. "Right. Where did you say—"

Movement in the rearview mirror caught Jem's eye, and he shouted, "Watch out!"

A red Chevy in the next lane roared up alongside them, easily going a hundred when everybody else was humming along at fifty-five. Jem barely had time to shout his warning before the Chevy swung into their lane. The Chevy connected with the side of Tean's truck. Sparks flew. Metal shrieked. The force of the impact knocked Jem's head against the glass.

Tean shouted wordlessly, yanking the wheel to the right, and then they were clear of the Chevy. The red truck shot past them. Jem's head was still ringing, but he could still think clearly enough to try to catch the plate number. Like the black SUV, though, the truck didn't have a license plate. It cut off at the next turn.

While that was happening, Tean brought their vehicle to a stop on the shoulder. The dark-haired man was breathing hard, but his hands were steady, and the first thing he did was look over and ask, "Are you ok?"

"Am I ok? Are you ok? Jesus. What the fuck was that?"

Tean shook his head.

"You were fucking fantastic," Jem said.

Tean shook his head again.

"Holy fucking shit," Jem said, vaguely aware of the adrenaline heating his blood to its flash point. "What the fuck was that?"

Once more, Tean shook his head. "I don't know," he said, "but one thing's for sure: no way are you spending the night at a motel."

15

The police came, and after they'd finished taking statements and documenting everything, Tean called his insurance and left a message with someone in HR, explaining what had happened. Jem just watched, his brain racing. It seemed impossible that someone could want to kill the doc — he was just a vet, after all. But it also seemed impossible that anyone would want to hurt Benny. But Jem had seen the SUV pick up Benny. And he'd seen the SUV outside Tean's office. And he'd just experienced, firsthand, almost getting run off the road by that goddamn Chevy. And so, impossible or not, it was starting to look like Tean was right: somehow, Tean and Jem were stuck in this mess together.

When Tean was finished making calls, they headed for Tean's apartment. The doc lived in Central City, a neighborhood Jem had been to plenty of times. In fact, he'd done a couple of deals in Tean's building, which was one of the holdouts against the neighborhood's gentrification. It was a three-story walk-up with mustard-colored brick and exterior corridors. In many places, the mansard roof had lost shingles, and around the windows, paint had peeled to expose wood that needed to be cut out and replaced. About the only good thing that could be said about the place was that it was cheap — some of the rents fluctuated in the four hundreds, which was one of the reasons the people Jem knew had chosen this place.

"You're kidding," Jem said.

Tean's shoulders hunched slightly as he pulled under a free-standing parking structure. At some point, unit numbers must have been painted over each stall, but the paint was gone, and several of the support posts were splintered and leaning, doubtless hit by careless drivers.

"God, that came out totally wrong," Jem said. "I'm sorry."

"No, it's all right," Tean said, coughing a little laugh. "I kind of feel that way too. It's better inside."

But better inside didn't explain why the doc was living in the same apartment building as Footsie, a girl who played a sick baby game on the corner of Temple Square, or Joe J., a pickpocket who spent most of his time riding Trax, Salt Lake City's light rail system.

The doc was right: his apartment was better inside. Outdated sure, with yellowing laminate countertops and walls painted the same mustard color as the brick outside. But the doc had hung several landscape paintings, many of them showing the Wasatch and Oquirrh ranges from different spots inside the valley, and his balcony had a great view looking east. Everything was clean and tidy. Everything was pleasant, actually. Everything except the dog, of course.

The black Lab bounded into them, crashing against Tean's legs with enough affection to kneecap the doc and then bracing himself, legs stiff, to bark at Jem. Jem backed up until he hit the doorjamb, hands in the pockets of his windbreaker. In one hand, he clutched the paracord; in the other, the antenna.

"Stop it," Tean was saying, kneeing Scipio gently before scratching his ears. "He's a friend. Go say hi."

The Lab whined, slunk down, and came toward Jem.

Jem tried to back up again.

"Gosh," Tean said. "Sorry. Are you afraid of dogs?"

"Nope," Jem said, frozen against the jamb, nails biting into his palms.

"Ok," Tean said. Squatting next to the Lab, Tean stroked a hand down the dog's back; Scipio was now snuffling at Jem's sneakers. "Well, full information: Scipio is all bark and no bite. He's crazy about people. He particularly likes hard salami, which I'm not supposed to give him. And if you give him a piece, he'll be your friend for life."

"Great," Jem said, bunching more of the paracord in his grip until his fingers closed over the nut at the end. "Perfect."

"I can't promise he'll leave you alone," Tean said, "but I bet you can make friends really quickly. Want to give him a treat? If you do, he might stop headbutting you."

"Uh huh."

Tean retrieved a piece of salami from the refrigerator and pressed it into Jem's hand. "Like this. Just hold it in your hand at your side and let him take it. Perfect. Exactly. Now if you want to scratch his chest—ok, there you go. Buddies for life. He really wants to smell your breath, but we're working on no jumping."

"Great," Jem said again, hearing, from a distance, the frazzled edge to the word. But he managed to release the antenna. A cold, wet nose pressed against him, snuffling some more, and then a tongue. Jem flinched.

"I'll take him out," Tean said. "Will you be ok for a bit?"

"I can go with you."

"Your call. We need to get a walk; it'll be half an hour."

"Ok. Well. Like you said: we probably shouldn't separate."

Laughing, Tean said, "Your face. No, just stay here. Help yourself to whatever you want."

"But if somebody—"

"We're in the middle of the city, there will be plenty of people around, and unlike Benny, I know what I should watch out for. I'll be fine. Besides, I don't want Scipio to traumatize you any further."

Before Jem could think of a decent argument, Tean had put a harness on the dog and led him outside, and the door was shut, and Jem was alone. Jem sagged against the counter, trying to slow his heartbeat, and then he started opening drawers, checking the fridge, pulling books from the shelves. He found the doc's checkbook on the desk in the living room. He snapped a picture of the most recent entries and sent it to Tinajas. In the single bedroom, he lifted the mattress, rifled the closet, and searched the dresser. No cash, but he found a really nice watch in the doc's underwear drawer—the doc owned a lot of expensive-looking jocks, and the rest was black briefs—which he decided to leave for now. In a couple of weeks, when all this was settled, Jem could pay a daytime visit, while the doc was at work. Then he moved on to the bathroom. In the mirrored cabinet, the doc had a brown plastic bottle of what Jem thought was Xanax—he thought he recognized the shape and color of the pills—and Jem found a plastic baggie in the kitchen and helped himself to half of the pills, holding one under his tongue until it dissolved. He took a picture of the bottle and sent that to Tinajas too.

She called him.

"That's a generic for Xanax," she said.

"That's what it feels like."

"What about the checkbook?" she said.

"Notice anything?"

"Well, he writes big checks to cash—a thousand, fifteen hundred, eighteen hundred—and they go out of the account pretty regularly after his paycheck gets deposited."

"Yeah. And?"

"And I'm at work."

"Call me if you think of an explanation."

"Drugs, sex workers, gambling."

"Nope," Jem said. "Not this guy. Keep thinking."

"I'll just do my real job," Tinajas said. "At least I get paid for that." Then she disconnected.

By the time Jem finished his search, the Xanax was acting on him. He was sitting on the couch when the door opened—it had been unlocked this whole time—and Tean came in. As soon as Scipio was out of his harness, the Lab bounded toward Jem, but after a few good sniffs he ambled back to Tean and headbutted him.

"He wants dinner," Tean said, opening a pantry, the dry rustle of kibble accompanying his words. "How about you?"

"You really shouldn't leave a total stranger alone in your apartment."

Grinning as he poured the dog food into a bowl, Tean said, "Are you going to steal my thirty-two-inch Hitachi?"

Maybe it was the Xanax. Maybe it was the fact that the doc could spill out a list of every horrible thing that had ever happened and still leave the door unlocked. Jem smiled in spite of himself. "Ok, no, but it's the principle of the thing."

"Is chili ok?"

"You don't have to feed me."

"We've got to eat something. Are you going to buy me a Rancherito's breakfast burrito instead?" Tean asked, smiling over his shoulder as he washed his hands at the sink.

Lots of smiles, Jem realized. Lots of eye contact. A heartbeat too long had passed, and Jem scrambled and said, "That sounds like something I should get you tomorrow morning."

"That's a little presumptuous," Tean said, those bushy eyebrows drawing together.

"Oh God. Sorry, I just—"

"I'm joking. I think you should stay the night. On the couch." He raised those bushy eyebrows.

"Thank God you're subtle."

"I'm serious about staying. We don't know if they're after you and me both. We don't know if they just want one of us. We don't know anything, I guess. I think it's smarter if you stay here."

"Thank you."

Tean cleared his throat and added in what he probably thought was a firm tone, "On the couch."

Jem grinned, and it had nothing to do with mirroring body language, nothing to do with building trust. It was just a grin. Then it faded as Jem realized that at some point during the day, sometime after stealing the doc's keys and breaking into his office, sometime after he'd had his first meltdown when he'd seen Benny get into the SUV, the game had stopped being a game, and everything had gone sideways. Jem wasn't in control of what was happening here anymore; he'd learned the hard way how dangerous that was.

"Thanks," Jem said, "but I should go."

"What?" Tean was pulling a covered pot out of the refrigerator, and he set it on the range, fiddling with one of the burners. "You're going to talk to Ammon, right? He'll be here in another hour or so. And we just agreed it's safer if you stay here."

"Yeah, but—" Jem could feel all of it slipping away: the gameshow smiles, the riffing, the knowledge of do this and he'll do that. He needed to get out. He decided to go with a tried and true escape plan—he'd say he'd gotten a phone call while Tean was walking the dog. New information. Had to look into it.

But when he opened his mouth, he said, "I feel so helpless. I just—I should be doing something, right? I should be out looking for Benny. And instead, I'm sitting here, and you're being nice to me, and your dog might not even eat me alive after he finishes dinner."

Scipio did some extra loud crunching, as though to remind them that he wasn't quite done yet.

"Well," Tean said, "do you know where you want to look?"

Jem shook his head.

"Do you have someone you haven't talked to? Any ideas about who you could call?"

Jem shook his head. He could feel it again, the rising waters that had sunk him twice already: once, in the security office, and then again in the stairwell. The game was the game was the game; he knew that, and he knew not to fuck it up. But this was Benny, who was in trouble, some kind of trouble that Jem didn't even understand yet. For almost thirty years, nobody had helped Jem, nobody had given one single fuck about him, and he'd managed things just fine. Right then, though, he wasn't managing anything. Benny was gone, and Jem didn't know what to do; he was sinking. All the locks and dams that Jem had built for himself were overflowing. Even the Xanax couldn't stop this flood. He pressed fists against his eyes.

Couch springs squeaked next to him, and a leg pressed against his, warm. Then an arm was around his shoulder. Jem shook once. He took one wet breath. And then he coughed a few times and took another, clearer breath this time. "I'm ok," he said.

"You don't have to be ok," Tean said.

"I am. Really." But he didn't pull his fists away, and he didn't trust himself to say anything else.

"I can't imagine how awful this is for you," Tean said. "I'm sorry; I wish I could do something else."

Jem cleared his throat, wiped his face, and imagined outer space. This was what it was like, he guessed: you've got one thing tethering you, and if that thing snaps, suddenly you're spinning off into space, all the things you thought you had a handle on now totally out of control. Like that movie, the one with Sandra Bullock.

"Ok," Jem said, "I'm totally fine. I'm just going to use the bathroom, and we're going to pretend this didn't happen, and I will, um, be right back."

"You don't have to be ok," Tean said again. "You can be upset. Do you want to break something? I've got cheap stuff; you can break something if you want."

"I'm going to go to the bathroom, and I'm going to come back, and I'll be a normal human being again."

Tean just frowned and shook his head.

In the bathroom, Jem held another Xanax under his tongue. His eyes were red and felt raw. He stared at himself in the mirror, letting the Xanax dissolve, feeling the barbed wire in his gut slowly untangle. The game was the game was the game. No mistakes. No exceptions. No room for anything as stupid as feelings. Then he let himself out of the bathroom — he was putting himself on parole, and if there were any more fuckups like the ones he'd had today, he was going to take himself out of this game and just try to find Benny on his own.

"Help me make this edible," Tean said from the kitchen.

"Chili?" Jem said. He sniffed the air and smelled tomatoes and ground beef. Tean was at the range again, stirring the pot. Steam billowed up.

"Take a look," Tean said, waving at a cabinet. "See what would make this taste better."

"What did you put in there already?"

"Ground beef. Tomatoes. Salt."

Opening the cabinet, Jem stared at the rows and rows of spices. "Isn't chili supposed to cook for a long time?"

"Oh yeah. I made it the other day. It simmered for a long time."

"And you didn't put any spices in it?"

"I was just kind of winging it."

"What about chili powder since, you know, it's chili?"

"Ok, let's try that."

Blinking, Jem scanned the bottles. He'd made this mistake before, grabbing paprika instead of chili powder, one time mistaking the seasoned salt for it.

"It's right there," Tean said.

A hot, prickling flush ran through Jem.

Tean reached past him and grabbed a bottle from the front row. "If it was a snake, it would have bitten you."

With a laugh, Jem said, "Sorry. My brain is fried."

"Ok, what else?" Tean said.

"I don't know. I'm not really a cook."

"That's ok," Tean said with a small smile. "I'm just trying to distract you. How about you be the DJ instead?"

"I think I can do that."

Jem scrolled through pictures of album covers on his phone, found one that he liked, and started it. Something chill. Something to help take the edge off.

"You don't have any beer, right?" Jem asked.

Tean shook his head, still adding spices to the pot.

"Mormon?"

"Uh, no."

"Raised Mormon?"

Tean shrugged.

"Some of my foster parents took me to church," Jem said. "Sometimes, anyway."

"I guess dinner's ready," Tean said, banging the spoon against the side of the pot. They ate — it wasn't the worst thing Jem had ever had — and Tean did the dishes in spite of Jem's offers to help. Wiping his hands on a towel, he came over to stand by Jem when he finished. The music on Jem's phone was still playing. Their eyes met, and Tean's slid away. Then those soft, dark eyes came back, lingering.

"What song is this?" Tean asked.

"It's called 'Superstar,'" Jem said.

Jem's hand moved before he let himself think about it, settling on Tean's hip, tugging him a few steps back into the living room. Lupe Fiasco sang in the background. Jem's other hand took its place at Tean's waist, and they rocked together, not quite dancing. With a nervous smile, Tean pushed his glasses back into place. He leaned forward, and Jem lowered his head so their foreheads met.

"You're really white," Tean whispered.

Jem laughed.

"Here," Tean said, still in that whisper, moving Jem's arms up to loop around his neck. Then his hands rested on Jem's hips, stilling him, and then guiding him into the rhythm. He stepped forward, their bodies brushing each other, not quite grinding but a shadow of it. Sweat broke out in stinging drops across Jem's chest; he was in outer space again, untethered, tumbling in the galactic spin.

Part of Jem knew it was all still the game. He was Jem Guthall, from California. And Jem Guthall could meet cute, smart, educated guys, and Jem Guthall could freak out when he was overwhelmed, and Jem Guthall could trust somebody else would help him handle it when things got to be too much, and Jem Guthall could dance with a guy who smelled like sagebrush and pine, their bodies barely touching, every point of contact popping with static. Jem Guthall could think about taking this guy out for breakfast, going on walks, sharing popcorn at the movies. Jem Guthall could think about waking up again and again next to him.

But Jem Guthall was just part of the game. Jem Berger wasn't from California; he squatted in a West Valley apartment without electricity. Jem Berger didn't have a job; he ran games. Jem Berger didn't meet guys who were cute and smart and educated. Jem Berger couldn't expect anyone, anywhere, to help him. Jem Berger had learned a long time ago that he could only count on himself.

For one song, though, he could be Jem Guthall.

The knock at the door shattered the spell. Tean flinched, stumbling clear of Jem, and Jem grabbed his phone and cut the song. The only sound was the chili bubbling on the stove.

The knock came again.

Tean opened the door. "Hey, Ammon. Thanks for coming."

Jem opened his mouth to introduce himself and then stopped, staring.

Ammon Young, Tean's childhood friend, the detective who made house calls, was the guy Jem had cruised in the Apollonia's bar.

16

After that initial moment of shock, Jem managed to get his gameshow smile back on. He held out his hand.

The guy who had introduced himself as Patrick, the guy who had gotten a hotel room and taken Jem upstairs and fucked his lights out and then split with a weak excuse about an early flight, just stared back at him. The wedding band on his finger caught the light; he was holding a brown paper bag that obviously contained a bottle. Had the doc's pet detective brought over a bottle of wine?

"Don't just stare at him," Tean said, cuffing the detective's shoulder and dragging him into the apartment. "Jem, Ammon. Ammon, Jem." Scipio had braced his legs again, growling at Ammon, and Tean gave him another gentle knee to the ribs. "Stop it," he ordered the dog. "Be nice." With a whimper, Scipio slunk back to — of all places — Jem, pressing against his leg.

The detective — Ammon — didn't make a move to take Jem's hand. Jem kept that gameshow smile plastered across his face.

"What the fuck do you want?" Ammon said.

Shooting a look at Tean, Jem said, "I'm trying to find my brother."

On the street below them, air brakes screeched over the rattle of a heavy chassis.

"Ok," Tean said, touching Ammon's arm again. "You're acting weird. What's going on?"

Ammon's gaze lingered on Jem. The detective was good looking: blond, clean cut, an athlete on his way to a dad bod.

"Sorry," Ammon finally said. "Bad day. Daniel is having a lot of problems at school. A lot."

"Sook?"

Shaking his head, Ammon said, "Why don't you tell me what's going on?"

"Sit down," Tean said. "I made chili."

"We made chili," Jem said, the words popping out before he could stop them.

Ammon shot him a hard look.

Tean was herding Ammon to a seat at the dinette table. He took the bag without opening it and put it away in one of the cabinets.

"It's not as bad as that ceviche you tried to make, is it?" Ammon finally asked.

"It's pretty bad," Tean said with a laugh.

"It's good," Jem said. "It's really good."

"Don't listen to him," Tean said, laughing again. "He hasn't even tried it."

"First thing you need to learn about Tean," Ammon said, directing the words to Jem with another flat look, "if you're going to hang around him: you're better off eating whatever Scipio has."

"I bet his cooking is really good," Jem said. "I bet it tastes great."

Tean laughed again; he was standing behind Ammon, his hand on Ammon's shoulder. "No, he's right. I'm terrible."

Ammon held Jem's eyes. He wasn't smirking. He didn't arch an eyebrow. He just reached up, wrapped one tan hand around Tean's wrist, and squeezed. The detective's eyes never left Jem's face.

Jem broke first, glancing down to pet Scipio.

"So," Ammon said, "you're here from Montana to find your brother?"

"From California," Tean said. "Where'd you get Montana?"

"Someone definitely told me Montana."

Jem ran his hand along Scipio's flank, concentrating on the short, silky fur, dense muscle, hard bone. The dog was still staring at Ammon, and through his leg, Jem could feel a sub-audible growl still rumbling inside the dog's chest.

"It's a lot of weird stuff, actually," Tean said, and then he explained the whole thing: the weird phone calls, the black SUV following him, Benny leaving the DWR building and getting into a black SUV, the abandoned gear in the dumpster, Benny not answering phone calls, the red Chevy trying to run them off the road.

"I can tell you one thing," Ammon said when he finished. "Nobody's said a word about a black SUV with the Hyeon investigation."

"But it's weird, right?"

"It's not an impossible coincidence," Ammon said. "Lots of weird coincidences happen," his eyes flicked to Jem, "and the first thing you have to do is figure out if they're really coincidences. If they're not, if somebody's doing something stupid, that's when you have to decide if you're going to send them a really clear message that any future coincidences are going to be a problem."

"What?" Tean said. He was still standing behind the chair; his hand had drifted up to curl along the back of Ammon's neck. "What are you talking about?"

"I want to see those papers," Ammon said. "The ones you were talking about."

"Oh, right. Jem?"

Jem got Benny's papers and passed them to Ammon. The detective flipped through them rapidly once and then looked at Jem. "Did you already read these?"

"Yeah."

"And?"

"I don't know. I wanted a second opinion."

"You might know how serious this stuff is," Ammon said to Tean, pulling out another dinette chair. "Look over this with me."

They sat together at the table, reading through Benny's notes; Jem retreated to the couch, and Scipio climbed up next to him and put his head in Jem's lap. For maybe half an hour, Ammon and Tean worked through the papers together. Once or twice, Ammon murmured a question, and Tean said something back. Both times, Ammon laughed. The second time, his hand rested on Tean's thigh. If the married detective was at all worried about getting outed, he didn't seem to consider Jem a threat. But Jem had met guys like Ammon before. They went through the Apollonia like they were on a conveyor belt: guys who figured the rules didn't apply to them, guys who were always the exception.

Night came down the mountains in a flood of blue shadows, deepening to purple in the folds of stone, washing over the city. The final transformation happened in a matter of moments: for a final few heartbeats, the Wasatch were stamped against the sky, just an impression of sawtooth ridges. Then they were gone, and the apartment building floated in a bubble of orange light.

"Ok," Ammon said after turning the last page. "What do you think?"

Jem shook his head. "You two are the experts. You first."

Ammon looked at Tean.

"It's hard to say without talking to any of these people directly," Tean said. "If we're going to go full conspiracy theory, with the phone calls and the black SUV and the truck running me off the road, all the weird stuff that's been happening, then I think we need to look really closely at Dellengbauh."

Jem blinked. "The copper mine?"

"Yeah," Tean said, "Benny's got pages and pages about it. A big argument with some woman called Julie Nash."

"Did you even read this?" Ammon said.

"Some," Jem said. "I had a hard time focusing; my brain is all over the place right now."

"Well, he talks about them a lot," Tean said. "If Dellengbauh is dumping illegally, or if one of the tailings ponds is leaching toxic waste, we could be talking about hundreds of millions of dollars in lawsuits and fines. That's the kind of motivation that could send somebody out in a black SUV to get rid of somebody who was bringing undue attention on them."

"Which is total conjecture at this point," Ammon said. "All we know is that this kid, Benny, he hasn't answered his phone for a day and he got in a car that you didn't recognize. But you're his brother from Montana—"

"California," Tean said.

"Right, California. So I don't know why it's such a big deal that you don't recognize this one car. Maybe a buddy just gave him a ride."

"He doesn't have buddies," Jem said.

"You live in Montana."

"Ok," Tean said, "cut it out, Ammon."

"You have no idea if he has buddies."

"I know he doesn't have friends," Jem said. "And what about his gear hidden in the dumpster?"

"Maybe he got sick of it. He was done camping, so he tossed it. No need to imagine something tragic."

"Jesus Christ," Jem said, shooting up from the couch. "You have no idea what you're talking about. If you don't believe me, just say you don't believe me."

"I don't believe you have any idea what's going on," Ammon said. "I think you're making a big deal out of nothing. And I want to know why."

"Because, you miserable fuck—" Jem began.

"Because he's worried," Tean said, cutting him off. "And he's scared. Everybody just calm down."

"Nash," Jem said. "That's what you said? She's the one at the mine?"

"Yes. Then Benny's got extensive descriptions of three people around Tooele, along with all the bad stuff he says they've been doing. If he's right, well, some of them might have their own reasons to want Benny to stop nosing into their business."

Jem had to lean against the couch to steady himself. He took a slow breath, tried to control his voice, and asked, "What about Tooele?"

"You're white as a sheet," Tean said. "Are you ok?"

"LouElla. Does it say anything about LouElla?"

"Why are you—"

"LouElla Arnold? God damn it, does it say anything about her?"

"No."

"What about the Jenkins?"

"No."

"What the fuck is going on?" Ammon said.

"Nothing," Jem said. Scipio licked his hand, and he suddenly felt dizzy and exhausted; he slumped onto the couch, with Scipio still lapping at his hand.

"That didn't look like nothing," Ammon said.

Jem squeezed his eyes shut.

"Who's LouElla? And why'd you get so worked up about Tooele? And just what the fuck are you not telling us?"

"He's upset," Tean said quietly. "Leave him alone for a minute."

"No," Ammon said. "It's time for him to go."

"It's my apartment," Tean said. "He doesn't have to go."

Blinking to clear his vision, Jem got to his feet. "Yeah, um, I'll go."

"Hold on," Tean said. "You're sleeping here."

"He's what?" Ammon asked. "Fuck no."

"I just need some air," Jem said. "I'll be back in a little bit."

"Wait a minute," Tean said. "You really don't look good —"

"No," Ammon said. "Let him go."

Jem threw open the door, the mountain breeze wicking along his skin, mixing the smells of pine and car exhaust with the fragrance of the chili. Jem wasn't sure if he said something as he stumbled out onto the exterior corridor, but the door closed behind him. He was halfway to the stairs when he heard the door open again, and heavy, quick steps came after him. Jem spun around, hands going into his pockets again, the paracord, the tube sock, the antenna.

Ammon was faster than he expected, though, and the detective crossed the final yards with the speed and ease of a natural athlete. He caught Jem by the shirt, hauled him a few feet, and slammed him against a wall.

"Just what the fuck do you think you're doing?" Ammon asked in a harsh whisper.

"Nothing."

"You'd better be damn fucking right that it's nothing. Stay away from Tean. Did you hear me?"

In spite of all the shit from that day, Jem laughed.

"You think this is funny?" Ammon said, slamming him against the wall again. Jem's head rocked back against brick. "You think this is a big joke?"

"Oh my God," Jem said, laughing so hard that his eyes stung. "You are so fucking stupid. Does this macho jealousy routine work? Does it get Tean all hot and bothered for you?"

The next time Ammon slammed him against the wall, Jem was ready, and he rebounded hard, crashing into the detective, and then both of them separating. Ammon looked wild, almost deranged, his collar loose, his tie askew, his breathing jagged.

"Come around him again," Ammon said. "And I'll put your ass in a cell, and I'll keep you there."

"Go play with your pussy boy," Jem said. "You're running out of time before wifey wonders where you are."

Ammon shouted something wordless and charged. Jem didn't bother with any of his weapons; bastard or not, Ammon was still a cop, and if Jem escalated things, it would only get worse for him. Instead, he just landed a solid right on Ammon's jaw. It snapped the big man's head to the side, but he didn't slow down. Crashing into Jem, he landed two hard blows, knocking the wind out of him, and then he shoved Jem toward the stairs. Jem stumbled, off balance, and he fell, rolling down to the first landing.

When Jem came to a stop, he had to take a few shuddering breaths to make sure nothing was broken. Above him, he could hear Ammon's savage breathing out of sync with his own. A security light blinked on overhead, and a moth battered itself against the thick glass.

"Fuck a cell," Ammon said through those harsh breaths. "Come around him again, and I'll kill you."

Jem rolled onto his knees. His arm was really hurting, particularly his elbow, and when he put weight on his ankle, a flash of heat shot all the way to his groin. Ammon was still at the top of the stairs, hands on knees, watching. Limping, Jem made his way to the end of the landing and eased his weight down again. When he reached the cement pad at the bottom, he heard Ammon's steps moving back toward Tean's apartment.

Let it go, Jem told himself. You played the game as far as you could play it, and you got away with some good info. The doc wouldn't be any more use. Better to clear out now. He'd go back to the DWR, get his bike, and head home. He'd buy some ice from the Latus, take some Tylenol, and spend the night feeling sorry for himself. Tomorrow, he'd go to the Jenkins and see what they could tell him.

He was still reciting this plan to himself as he walked around to the back of the apartment building. The ground-floor units had walkout patios with wooden privacy fences. In one of the units, Jem could see a man and a woman making Rice-a-Roni while a little boy watched *Toy Story 3*. In another, a woman wearing a bathrobe was running her Cocomotion machine. In another, young guys who looked like brothers were playing catch across the length of the apartment; Jem was watching when one of them biffed it and the baseball smashed a ceramic pitcher on the counter. The fourth unit was dark. Ignoring the flash of pain in his elbow, and the secondary flash of pain in his ankle, Jem hauled himself up the fence, balanced on the top, and caught hold of the railing on the second-story balcony above him. He repeated the trick, hauling himself up, and then he was looking through the sliding glass door into Tean's apartment.

Part of his brain was telling him a story about the way Ammon had squeezed Tean's wrist. Part of his brain was reminding him about Scipio, the way the dog had braced himself and growled at Ammon. Part of him was replaying the ribbon of light on a gold band, thinking about the kind of guy who didn't even take off his wedding ring when he showed up for a fuck.

Inside the apartment, things were already in motion. Ammon had taken off his jacket and dress shirt and tie; he was standing in his trousers, shoeless, and wearing the white undershirt that was half of the Mormon religious undergarment—casually referred to as garments. Tean was still wearing his all-khaki ensemble. What was going on inside the apartment had the appearance of a scene that had been scripted and rehearsed and played out so many times that everybody knew their cues, everybody hit their marks. Scipio was in the corner, curled up on a dog bed, head on his paws. Ammon had retrieved the brown-paper bag from the cabinet. When he drew out the bottle, Jem just shook his head. Everclear fucked you up; that was one of the universe's fundamental laws. But Jem figured that getting fucked up was the whole point right now.

Ammon poured what looked like the equivalent of a shot of the grain spirit, and he set the mug halfway between him and Tean. Tean shook his head and said something that the glass muffled. Ammon shrugged. Below Jem, the sliding glass door of the ground-floor unit opened, and a young man said, "Well, I'm going to tell Mom you had a girl in your room," and then angry steps crossed the cement pad. Then the steps moved back, and the slider shut, and the only noise was the distant sound of traffic.

On the other side of the glass, Tean picked up the mug and threw back the drink. He had barely finished setting down the mug when Ammon stepped in, hooking his fingers under the hem of Tean's polo and dragging it up and off in a single movement. Tean seemed to expect this, or at least understand his part; he held up his arms and wiggled enough to help Ammon remove the shirt. Ammon stood between Tean's legs, tossing the polo onto the couch, running one hand up Tean's flat stomach, up his chest, up his neck. Tean melted into the touch, and Ammon kissed him—on the cheek, on the jaw, on the ear, on the neck. Not on the lips.

That went on for a while, and then Ammon stepped back and poured another shot's worth of Everclear in the mug, bumping the ceramic toward Tean with his knuckles. This time, Tean picked up the mug and drank it down without hesitating. Ammon moved in again, his fingers sliding behind Tean's waistband, unbuttoning the khakis, sliding them down. The blond fucker didn't even pull them off all the way with his hands; when they were low enough, he just stepped on them to force them clear of Tean's ankles and feet. Tean sat there, obviously aroused in his black briefs. He ran a hand over Ammon's chest, but Ammon ignored him, dragging his hands up Tean's thighs, kissing his neck and shoulders and pecs.

When Tean shook his head at the third shot of the grain alcohol, Ammon played the game exactly right. And now Jem understood the rules of this game. They spoke for a few minutes, Tean's head hanging down, Ammon strong and tall over him. Ammon talked quietly. Ammon stroked Tean's hair. He kissed him. He talked some more. Jem could have written the script: *It's ok, baby. You don't have to do anything you don't want to do.*

Jem's head was hurting, his elbow was hurting, his ankle was hurting, and he was scudding along on Xanax, but he forgot about all of that as he studied the lean, taut lines of the doc: the stripe of dark hair down the center of his chest, the delicate wing of his collarbone, the valleys of his ribs when he reached across the counter to take the mug. He sipped at the third shot, slid it away, and then he had to stop. He held his head in his hands as he leaned on the counter.

Ammon ran his hand up and down Tean's bare back. The blond fucker was still mostly dressed, and while Jem watched, his hand slid below the elastic of Tean's briefs. Tean was still hunched over the counter. One knee was bouncing fast.

Ammon said something.

Tean didn't move.

Ammon said something, stroking Tean's wild hair, and then he said it again.

Eyes on the floor, Tean mumbled something.

Ammon kissed the side of his head. Tean's eyes were glazed. Whatever Ammon was saying, he repeated it again.

This time, when Tean spoke, the words vibrated through the glass: "Fuck, I want your cock so bad."

Ammon smoothed Tean's hair, stroking the wild tufts, speaking calm and low now, his other hand stroking Tean's shoulder, ribs, thigh. Tean turned into his hand, nuzzling into Ammon's palm. He looked wasted. Gripping Tean by the arm, Ammon helped him off the stool and shepherded him toward the bedroom. Then the door shut, and they were gone.

October nights in Utah were cool but not frigid, so part of Jem's brain wondered why he expected to see his breath steaming. From his pocket, he pulled out the wallet he had lifted when he and Ammon had crashed into each other at the top of the stairs. He took out the license, studied the picture of the detective: bad lighting revealed how his blond hair was thinning on top, and his eyes looked hollow, his cheeks puffy. He snapped a picture of the license with his phone and returned it to the wallet. He took twenty-seven bucks in cash, folded them, and stuffed them into a pocket of the windbreaker. Inside the wallet, he found a prepackaged rubber, a foil packet of lube, a picture of a wife and four kids — three boys and a little girl. Jem took the rubber and the lube because it never hurt to be prepared, and then looked over his shoulder. A privacy fence separated the apartment building from the next lot, which was a drycleaner. He chucked the wallet as hard as he could; it cleared the fence and slapped down on the cracked asphalt. Then he lit up the blunt he'd taken from Tommy and got himself high as fuck.

After pitching the wallet, though, Jem had trouble focusing. He tried to run through the information Tean and Ammon had given him: Dellengbauh Copper; Julie Nash; people in Tooele. But then a kind of electric jolt would snap across his synapses, and he'd be thinking about crouching down in the bathtub, trying to cover Benny while LouElla lashed him with the RCA antenna. It was hard to remember what Benny's sin had been that day. Probably jerking off; Benny was perpetually jerking off, especially at twelve. Jem didn't remember a lot of things about that day. He didn't remember how they had gotten into the bathroom, for example. He didn't remember why, every goddamn time, he tried to take Benny's licks. He hadn't felt the blood running down his back until later; the whistle of the antenna through the air and the force of its impact had been terrifying enough, and then something had snapped in his head and he'd turned and pushed her. Jem tried to box up the memory.

But those synapses were misfiring like crazy. He tried to think about the fat fuck he was running the child porn scam on, tried to plan the next move, when to start squeezing him, but then the delicate bird's-wing line of Tean's shoulder would pop into his mind, obliterating the chain of thoughts. He tried to do some basic accounting, adding up his scores from the week, tallying expenses, and then the image of Tean at the counter forced its way into his brain: Tean, head in his hands, trying to hold himself together as the Everclear went through him like the devil's fire. Then Jem tried to give in, tried to say fuck it to plans and to money, and let himself think about what he'd do when he caught up with Ammon in a dark alley, but even that couldn't keep his attention. He imagined the tube sock filled with pennies. And then he'd be back at Decker, with Blake and Antonio crowding him against the bunks, Tanner watching, Blake twisting his arms behind his back, Antonio yanking on the jumpsuit's zipper, the cold air, the smell of jalapeño Cheetos on Blake's breath, a knee forcing his legs apart, hands.

Jem closed his eyes and bit his lip until he tasted blood. When he opened his eyes, he was face to face with Ammon. It took Jem a moment to realize that Ammon was just staring out the sliding glass door; he hadn't seen Jem. Ammon was naked, a bundle of clothes in his hands, and he dressed hurriedly. Jem studied him, thinking back to the Apollonia: a nice-looking guy, decent in bed, no reason he should have to do what he'd just done. Then Ammon was dressed, patting himself down, obviously trying to find his wallet. After a weak attempt at a search, Ammon hustled out of the apartment. No goodbye. The asshole didn't even lock the door. On the other side of the building, an engine roared to life.

After another ten minutes, Jem climbed down, went around to the front of the apartment, and let himself inside. Scipio stirred, looked at Jem, and then rested his head on his paws again. The apartment smelled like sex and booze and chili, and Jem guessed nobody would be making a candle with that scent combination anytime soon. He locked the door behind him and called, "Tean? Hey, it's Jem. I'm back. Sorry I left like that."

No answer.

Jem padded down the short hall. The light in the bathroom was on, and the door was half closed. He rapped lightly.

"Tean? It's Jem."

A soft groan answered him.

"I'm coming in, ok?"

Another groan.

Jem pushed into the bathroom, stopped, and swore. Tean lay near the toilet, naked, his head pillowed on his arm. He'd obviously tried to clean himself up; a few pieces of toilet paper flecked with blood floated in the toilet.

"Well," Jem said, kneeling next to Tean, "that settles one thing. I'm definitely going to kill that motherfucker."

Tean blinked up at him, missing his glasses. He reeked of alcohol—four shots of a normal liquor in quick succession would have hit most people hard; four shots of Everclear was attempted murder. Tean had a light sheen of sweat, but his skin was clammy when Jem touched him. His glassy gaze tried to fix on Jem.

"I'm sick," Tean slurred.

"You're not sick," Jem said. "That asshole poisoned you."

"Gonna puke."

"Christ," Jem said.

He managed to get Tean upright, and he looped an arm around his waist and held him there while he vomited. Tean was trembling and crying when he finished.

"You're ok," Jem said, running his fingers through Tean's hair. "You got any more?"

Apparently he did. A lot.

When Tean had finished, Jem helped him up and half carried him to the bedroom. The reek of sex was still strong; Jem cracked a window before going back to the bathroom. He got the hot water running, wetted a washcloth, and took it back to the bedroom. Tean's breathing was slow and even, but those dark eyes were still open. Jem cleaned him up as best he could.

"I'm sick," Tean mumbled again.

"You're going to be ok."

Then he said something about a whale, trying to prop himself up.

"Ok," Jem said, chuckling as he carded Tean's hair and forced him back down onto the pillow. "Tell me about the whale tomorrow."

"No," Tean said, still trying to force himself up. "I'm the whale."

"No whales tonight. Just calm down."

"I'm the whale," Tean said, but he subsided again as Jem played with his hair. "He sings at fifty-two hertz. Every other whale in the whole world sings at somewhere between fifteen and twenty-five hertz."

"Uh huh."

"He's going to be alone forever because nobody can hear him sing," Tean said, starting to cry again. "And it's not his fault."

"Roll over," Jem said, and then he scratched lightly along Tean's bare back, big arcs, then rows of little scritches. "Nobody's a whale. You're not a whale."

"I am a whale," Tean said, sounding five years old and wounded.

Jem laughed softly because the alternative was worse. His ran his nails back and forth over Tean's shoulders.

After a while, Tean fell asleep or passed out. Jem decided he'd better stay up in the event of more puking, at least for a while, so he moved around the apartment, turning out lights. In the darkness of the front room, his own ghost stared back at him, superimposed on the valley's glitter.

Well, Jem asked himself, what the fuck was I supposed to do?

He sat on the bed, resting his head against the wall, and listened to Tean breathe. He tried to figure out how he'd managed to break all his own rules in the last twenty-four hours. He tried to figure out why he'd let things get complicated.

For Jem, the world had always been simple: there were two kinds of people, predator and prey, and it was better to be the predator. Benny had been a special exception. Only now, Jem thought, he had made another exception, and he already knew it was going to bite him in the ass.

17

Tean woke with a crippling headache and the need to puke. For a moment, the shattering pain in his head kept him in bed. Then his gut heaved again, and he stumbled into the bathroom, vomited, and tried not to die. Somehow he managed to rinse his mouth at the sink, splash cold water on his face, and stumble back to bed. Dawn had already broken, and the window was cracked; maybe Ammon had done that before he left, although something about the window nagged at Tean. He pulled the sheet over his head.

Soft steps padded down the hall toward his room. A chain of thoughts ran through Tean's head:

Someone was here.

Ammon never stayed.

Oh no. Jem.

The mattress sagged under additional weight, and then Jem asked, "Are you ok?"

Tean groaned; he couldn't help himself.

"You probably need some more sleep," Jem said. "But you need water and ibuprofen first. Do you think you can keep that down?"

There were all sorts of things Tean should have said—please leave, for starters—but the hangover was just too bad. He lay still under the sheet, hoping Jem would vanish; after a moment, Jem left. When he came back, he touched Tean's shoulder. "Up, just for a minute."

After a moment, Tean pushed back the sheet. The part in Jem's hair was a little less perfect today, and his beard wasn't precisely trimmed anymore, but he was still filling out the Smith Field House t-shirt very nicely, and he'd lost his jeans somewhere and was just wearing a pair of ancient plaid boxers. He had great thighs. Killer calves.

"Eyes up here," Jem said with a soft laugh. He pressed the glass into one of Tean's hands, the ibuprofen in the other.

Tean took the pills, drank the water, and burrowed back under the bedding.

Jem was laughing quietly as he left.

For about fifteen seconds, Tean was sure he'd never get back to sleep; then darkness rolled in. When he woke again, he still had a headache, but he didn't feel like he was going to die. He gathered clothes, stumbled into the bathroom, drank several more glasses of water, and showered. By the time he'd dressed, he felt passably human again.

When he got out to the living room, Jem was dozing on the couch, his long legs hanging off the end. Somehow Scipio had wedged himself into the curve of Jem's body, and when he saw Tean, his tail went wild, whacking Jem in the face.

"Hey, hey, hey," Jem grumbled, batting at the tail. "Oh," he said, eyes coming open, "hey, you're up."

"Um. Yeah."

"Sit down. I'll make you some toast; you definitely need something in your stomach."

"No, you don't have to do that."

Jem was grinning as he nudged Scipio off the couch. Scipio came over and licked Tean's hands; normally after Ammon left, Scipio was a nervous wreck, but today he just seemed to have his normal level of manic Lab love and adoration. Jem stood, stretched, and said, "Unless you've got a butler stashed away somewhere, I think I'm the only candidate."

"No, you don't—you don't have to do anything. I'm sorry you—I didn't want anyone—you shouldn't . . ."

Jem just nodded until Tean sputtered to a stop. "I think your brain is still broken," Jem informed him. "So I'm going to just do my thing until it's working again, ok?"

Tean nodded.

"Sit."

Tean sat.

"Did you drink more water?"

Another nod.

116

"Ibuprofen?"

"Just last time you gave me some."

"Ok." Jem grabbed the bottle and passed over two more. "I already walked the dog, so you don't need to worry about that. Just lie down and feel better."

"You walked Scipio?"

"Um." Jem actually blushed; the color brought out the coppery streaks in his beard. "Well, I might have gotten a little, uh, nervous, putting the harness on him, so we just had a gentleman's agreement."

Tean swallowed the pills, thought about this, and said, "What in the world does that mean?"

"Oh, I, um, just let him outside and chased after him and shouted his name and eventually we came back."

"Oh my gosh," Tean muttered, dropping onto the couch.

"He's a really good dog," Jem said. "And I fed him breakfast. Eight scoops, right?"

"Eight?" Tean said, his head coming up.

Jem grinned and held up two fingers.

"I'm sick," Tean mumbled, curling up on the couch. Scipio immediately forced his way into a cuddle. "Don't do that."

"You're hungover," Jem said. "And you need toast and, maybe, eggs."

Tean groaned.

"Ok, just toast."

Against all odds, Tean dozed again while Jem moved around in the kitchen. He stirred again when ceramic clinked against the coffee table. He smelled toast. And dog breath.

"I think Scipio's hungry again," Jem said.

Blinking his eyes clear, Tean considered the Lab's drool. "He's always hungry."

"I could make him his own toast."

"Oh my gosh, why are you being so nice to me? Do you want money? I don't have any money. Do you want sex? You must have seen last night's aftermath, so you've probably figured out that I'm the really crazy kind of fucked up, and you don't want to get involved with that. Do you want to make my skin into wallpaper? What do you want?"

Red moved into Jem's cheeks. He sat in one of the dinette chairs.

"I'm sorry," Tean said.

"Maybe just eat your toast."

Tean broke pieces of the bread and ate them in silence. Well, as close to silence as they could get—Scipio kept licking his chops and inching closer.

"I know you're worried about your brother," Tean began.

"Are you mad that I stayed here?" Jem said. "I thought that's what we agreed. What if those guys had come back for you? Was I supposed to just leave you here, passed out on the floor in your own puke, for them to pick up?"

Tean didn't tell him all the times he'd passed out in his own puke after Ammon left.

"And you know what?" Jem said. "When Ammon left, he didn't lock the door, so you know. He just walked out."

"I'm sorry for saying what I did," Tean said. "I'm embarrassed that you saw me like that last night, you know. But I'm grateful that you stayed. Grateful for everything."

"That Ammon guy?" Jem squared off. "He shouldn't treat you like that."

"It's complicated."

"Bullshit. You don't have anything to be embarrassed about. That guy, on the other hand, he treated you like dirt and—"

"Stop," Tean said.

Jem stopped, and more of that red crept into his cheeks.

"I appreciate what you're trying to do," Tean said, "but you don't have any idea what you're talking about. Thank you for last night. And for this morning. But please don't get involved in something you don't understand."

"I've met a hundred guys like him—"

"You know what? I need to go to work. I'm already late, in fact."

Jem shook his head.

After a few steps toward the bedroom, Tean stopped. He was thinking about Jem, all those times he'd been on the verge of tears yesterday, worried to death about Benny. He was thinking about Jem saying, *Your brothers would do it for you.* But the truth was that none of his brothers had been here last night when Tean needed someone. Jem, a total stranger, had. Tean's brothers hadn't been there the night Tean came out, after his parents had kindly told him he was going to Mormon hell. Tean's brothers hadn't been there the nights Tean had sat alone, the silence of the apartment crackling in his ears. They hadn't been there any of the nights after Ammon left, when Tean needed somebody, anybody, to help him put the pieces back together. Nobody had been there, in fact, when the undertow of the universe was dragging Tean out into the night.

Tean tried to soften his voice. "If you want to wait, I can give you a ride. I'll make a few calls about Dellengbauh, see if I can get any information."

"Yeah, sure. Thanks."

With a sigh, Tean headed into the bedroom. He dressed for work, and when he emerged, Jem was in the kitchen again.

"Instant decaf?" Jem called, his voice bright and friendly again. "I didn't think they made — oh no. Not again."

"What?"

Jem pointed.

"What?" Tean checked his face for toast crumbs.

"Go put on chinos. Or jeans. Can you wear jeans to work?"

Tean checked his khakis. "These are clean. They're not the same pair as yesterday."

"Oh Lord."

"They were on sale. They fit. They're a neutral color."

It took a moment for Jem to say anything, and when he managed to speak, his voice was a little too controlled. "How many pairs did you get?"

"Seven," Tean said, which seemed like the obvious answer.

"Holy God," Jem whispered. Then, scratching his beard, he said, "Let's figure this out."

"It's really not —"

"It really is. I've got a responsibility as a human being not to allow you to walk around looking like a UPS employee."

He left the jar of instant decaf on the counter and headed into the bedroom. He stood near the bed, arms folded, and said, "Show me what you've got." Then he held up a finger. "No more of those khakis."

"That's all I have."

"Don't bullshit a bullshitter."

With a groan, Tean pulled out a pair of jeans.

"These are very, very blue," Jem said.

"They're blue jeans."

"Yeah, but, these are like the color blue that my grandfather probably wore in 1972."

"They're blue jeans," Tean said again.

"They also look several sizes too big for you."

"They were on sale," Tean said.

With a sigh, Jem said, "Shirts."

From within the closet, Tean produced a long-sleeve, hunter-green flannel shirt with DWR printed on the breast.

"Let me guess," Jem said. "You didn't buy that yourself."

"I'm starting to feel judged," Tean grumbled, slipping out of the polo and tossing it on the bed. Jem's eyes skated over him once, and Tean blushed as he pulled on the flannel.

"You didn't, though," Jem said. "Buy it yourself, I mean. Did you?"

"Nobody's ever complained about my clothes before."

"This is called avoiding the question."

"Hannah gave it to me for Christmas," Tean said. When Jem started laughing, he said, "I don't know why that's so funny."

"You look good in green," Jem said. "You should wear this one more often."

Tean flopped an arm, trying to get the sleeve right.

"God, you really are a khaki baby," Jem said, beckoning. He took Tean's sleeve and folded it neatly above the elbow. He repeated the process with the other one. "Better?"

"Uh, yeah."

Grinning, Jem smoothed his collar. "Repeat after me: more green, less khaki."

"I just don't see why khaki and khaki—"

"Doc," Jem said

Something clamped down on Tean's chest at the word.

"More green," Jem said again. "Less khaki."

"Right," Tean said.

"We'd better go," Jem said. "You're late enough already."

Sighing, Tean dug out his phone and placed a call.

"Oh my gosh," she squealed, and he had to pull the phone away. "Tell me what happened with your blond dream yesterday. Did you go to dinner? Did you get busy with him?"

"Get busy," Jem whispered.

"Hannah—" Tean tried to say.

"I know you said you don't really have a type, but I think he might be your type. And did you see how he was looking at you? Like he wanted to eat you up. Oh my gosh, please tell me you at least gave him your number."

Jem was doing something where he slouched against the wall, his eyes hooded, and he whispered, "That's right: I'll eat you up," and then he ran his tongue over his lips.

Tean dropped the phone. When he recovered it, Jem was laughing quietly, and Hannah was saying, " — I really do think you could use my cousin's cabin if — "

"Hannah, I'm not coming in to work today. I've got some stuff I need to handle outside the office."

In the other room, Scipio was barking at something. Probably a squirrel.

"Like what?" Hannah said.

"Just stuff. I'll see you tomorrow."

"Wait, wait, wait. Oh my gosh, are you with — "

Tean disconnected the call. He struggled to put the phone away; for some reason, he couldn't seem to get it in the pocket. Finally he succeeded, but then he had to look at Jem, which he couldn't bring himself to do. He settled for focusing on the hamper of dirty clothes that was behind the blond man.

"That's really kind of you," Jem said. "But you shouldn't take off a day to help me."

"It's not just to help you. I'm doing it for Benny. And I'm doing it for me. Whoever these guys are, I want to find them and tell Ammon before they can cause any more trouble."

"See?" Jem said. "You're a good guy."

"Besides, I've got a million sick days, and I'll probably get hit by a truck and die before I can use them."

Jem nodded.

"Or some bureaucrat will key something in wrong and erase all of them."

Jem nodded again.

"I'll probably get fired before then."

"Think of it as a fresh start."

"And that's if we don't all die of climate change."

"Well, yeah, obviously," Jem said, grinning as he slouched against the wall, the heavy muscles in his chest and arms drawing Tean's eyes.

"I guess we should go," Tean said.

"Is that a phone in your pocket," Jem asked, "or are you just happy to see me?"

Tean didn't exactly run to the door, but he made pretty good time.

18

Jem insisted they stop for coffee and breakfast sandwiches at McDonald's.

"I had toast," Tean said.

"The dog had toast. You had a few crumbs."

"I probably shouldn't—"

"Yes, you should. Come on, I'll buy."

"Did you know that McDonald's creates consumer-culture addicts by giving children toys in their Happy Meals?"

"Another victory for capitalism," Jem said, pointing. "There's one."

"Did you know that a new McDonald's opens every fourteen and a half hours?"

"We don't need a new one. The one that I'm pointing at will be just fine."

"And more people eat at McDonald's every day than the entire population of the UK?"

"Today, we're going to be proud to be a small part of that accomplishment. You need to get into the right-hand lane now."

Tean signaled. "And the McDonald's arches are recognized more widely than the holy cross?"

"I thought Mormons didn't use crosses."

"You're missing the point."

"You're missing the turn."

At the last possible moment, Tean swung the truck into the McDonald's lot.

"Here's a good spot," Jem said.

"No, we can just go through—"

"You've got to make phone calls," Jem said, "and I've got to eat something. And get coffee. Lots of coffee."

"I think it'd be smarter to use our time—"

"You're not one of those irresponsible people who makes phone calls while they drive, are you?" Jem said. "Did you know a billion people die every day from distracted drivers on cell phones?"

Tean frowned; it was a cute frown, furrowing his forehead. "No, there's no way—"

Jem said, "Just park the truck, please, before you calculate the statistics on any more tragedies."

When they had parked, the engine ticked softly.

"Hey, look at that," Jem said. "You're going to enjoy a delicious sausage-egg-and-cheese biscuit, and no children exploded, and no cats caught on fire, and no hospitals burned down."

"Actually, did you know more cats die of—"

Groaning, Jem slid out of the truck.

Inside, Jem tried, really tried, to let Tean order. But then Tean started asking about sodium content and animal cruelty, and he'd just gotten going about live chickens being dunked into boiling water, when Jem pushed him out of the way and ordered for both of them: coffee, sausage-egg-and-cheese biscuits, and hash browns.

They got a booth while they waited for their food, and Tean pulled out his phone and, after a few minutes of tapping, placed a call. "Fawn Esplin, please. Tean Leon from DWR. Yes, thanks. Yes. Yes, ok. Great. Thank you." Then he disconnected.

Jem raised an eyebrow.

"She's just finishing up another call; she'll call back in a minute."

"Who's Fawn Esplin?"

"She's an inspector for the Division of Oil, Gas, and Mining."

"And you think she'll tell you if Dellengbauh has had any violations lately?"

"Or complaints. And their most recent inspection. That kind of stuff."

"Is she a friend?"

"Just a colleague. This isn't that unusual, actually. Tailings are toxic, and the tailings ponds have caused problems before."

"God," Jem said, scrubbing his face. "This seems impossible. Somebody kidnapped Benny because they didn't want him to report them for a dumping violation? That's crazy."

"It's a lot of money," Tean said. "But it could be personal, too."

"What do you mean? Like a rich family that owns a lot of Dellengbauh stock?"

"Well, I don't think we should fixate on the mine yet. Benny also mentioned a few people in Tooele who might, well, have their own reasons to want him to be quiet." Tean glanced at Jem and then glanced away.

"I'm not going to come unglued if you mention Tooele. Not again, I mean."

"Is that—"

"That's where Benny and I lived together, yeah."

Their food came; the kid who brought it, smiling with perfect, white teeth, looked twelve. Jem sipped his coffee. Tean took the lid off his and started dumping in cream and sugar.

"Was that woman your foster mom?"

Jem snorted. "Foster mom is a little too nice. Yes, LouElla had a lot of foster kids. Most of them moved in and out pretty quickly, but Benny and I stuck around longer. God, that woman hates children."

"Then why does she foster?"

"Money," Jem said.

Tean laughed as he stirred his coffee. Then he stopped laughing and looked at Jem. "You're kidding, right?"

"No, a lot of people do it. They take in foster kids because the state gives them money for each kid. And the state gives more money if the kid has a disability. And some of these people, they basically ranch foster kids. It's not a ton of money, but if you feed the kids cream of wheat and rice and beans, don't buy them any new clothes, and have a single pair of bunkbeds when you've got six foster kids crammed in one room, well, you can keep a lot of it for yourself."

"Oh my gosh," Tean said. The coffee stirrer slowed. "I'm sorry."

Jem waved the words away. "Do you even like coffee? I should have asked."

"Huh?" Tean seemed to remember the stirrer. He shrugged. "I didn't grow up drinking it, but every once in a while, I'll have some."

"What was that like?"

"What?"

"Being raised Mormon."

"Oh, you know. I mean, you grew up in Utah. And you said you went to church."

"Yeah, well, going to church meant LouElla made us sit in the back row, and I'd sneak out and bum a cigarette from the bishop's son. It wasn't really a religious experience."

Unwrapping his breakfast sandwich, Tean seemed to consider the question. Then he shrugged and said, "Hard."

Jem waited, but nothing more came. He could hear the layers compressed into that syllable. After a moment, the waxed paper crinkling, he unwrapped his own sandwich and began to eat. He finished the food in about six bites, chugged his coffee, and felt a little bit closer to human. A little funky, sure, because he hadn't showered. But closer. Tean nibbled at his sandwich, took a single bite from the crispiest edge of the hash brown, and mostly drank coffee.

"You don't eat?" Jem said.

"What? Oh. Sorry. I just—I'm not much of a breakfast eater."

"Or dinner."

"Huh?"

"You didn't eat dinner last night either."

"Oh, right. I kind of lose track."

"You're not hungry?"

Tean frowned. "Um, I don't know."

"You don't know if you're hungry?"

A blush moved across Tean's face, and he shrugged.

"What do you eat?" Jem said.

"What?"

"A normal day. What do you eat?"

"For breakfast, if it's cool outside, peppermint tea, maybe a piece of fruit. Or a glass of milk in the summer."

"Lunch?"

"Sometimes I take a sandwich to work."

Jem guessed that sometimes meant almost never. "Dinner?"

"Lentils. Or beans; I have a pressure cooker. This week I got wild and tried chili, but you saw how that turned out."

Studying Tean, Jem said, "God, no wonder you're so skinny."

The blush deepened.

"Don't you like eating?" Jem said.

"I mean, it's food."

"But good food. Like really tasty stuff. It doesn't have to be fancy, but like, this biscuit. It was really good. Don't you just, you know, enjoy it?"

Tean shrugged. "Yeah, I mean, I guess so."

Which meant no.

"Anyway, I should have told you before you ordered," Tean said. "I'll pay you back."

"You're done?"

"Yeah, I guess I'll throw this stuff away, although the amount of American food waste—"

"Not a chance," Jem said, grabbing the rest of the biscuit sandwich and the hash brown and taking a huge bite of first one, then the other.

Tean looked like he might say something, but his phone buzzed, and he answered the call.

"Hi, Fawn," he said. "Yes. Yes, well, I'm about to head over to Dellengbauh Copper, and I wanted to check in with you first." He listened for a moment and said, "Well, so far, nothing, but a concerned citizen reported dead birds, and my first thought was the tailings ponds." He listened again. "Ok. Ok. You did it yourself? And? Ok, thanks, Fawn. I'll let you know what I—oh wait, actually. Do you know Julie Nash over at Dellengbauh? Really? Yep, that would be perfect. I'm headed over right now. Yep, put the fear of the Lord in her if you don't mind. You're awesome. Thank you." Then Tean blushed. "No, I don't know why Hannah is telling people that. Thanks so much, Fawn. Can't talk. Gotta go. Bye."

When he disconnected, he had sweat along his hairline.

"I'm your dirty little secret," Jem said around a mouthful of hash browns.

"Don't flatter yourself," Tean said.

They drove west from the McDonald's: I-80 to 4000 West, 4000 West to 2100 South, 2100 South to Demeter, which was a north-south freeway that paced the length of the Oquirrh Mountains. The sky was another perfect, late-fall Utah sky: crisply blue with the stretched-out cotton of cirrus clouds to the south. The muted tans and browns of the Oquirrh Mountains speared into that blue. To the east, the burgeoning suburbs of the Salt Lake Valley continued to spread out, but to the west, toward the mountains, only a few man-made structures interrupted the high steppes: a single-wide trailer, its aluminum siding the same color as the sky, with a hand-pump well and old Home Depot buckets scattered around it; then miles of Russian thistle, sagebrush, and clumps of cheatgrass; then a saltbox house that Jem guessed was a hundred years old, one side bulging as though it concealed a cancerous growth, the paint almost entirely gone to expose sun-bleached wood. This was the real Utah: brutal, deadly, high steppes and cold desert. Jem was a city boy through and through, but with the sun lighting up the mountain slopes, the vast sky and the intense radiance giving the whole world a harsh glory, he wondered what it would be like to step outside the city. Just every once in a while.

At the marker for Dellengbauh Canyon, they turned west again, and the asphalt headed straight toward the massive piles of displaced earth and stone that marked the beginning of the mine. As they approached, Jem began to realize how truly massive the mining operation was: within a matter of minutes, they were staring up at the perimeter of the mines, the mountains completely hidden behind the bulk of debris.

Tean glanced over at him, hesitated, and said, "It's one of the biggest open-pit mining operations in the world. You can see it from outer space."

"They pull all of this out of the tunnels? All that extra dirt and stuff?"

"No. What you're seeing right here, the mining waste, they call it overburden. And you're right, it's basically their garbage, and they dump it in valleys or, as you can see here, they used to dump it at the edge of the mine. But it's not an underground mine."

"What?" Jem rolled down his window to study the operation ahead of him better. He glanced north, following the slopes of the Oquirrh Mountains, where stone burned under an apron of scrub and brush. Then his eyes came back to the mines. "Jesus Christ. What do you mean it's not underground?"

"Well, a lot of people automatically think of long-wall mining: you know, like, timbers bracing the tunnels, crawling miles and miles underground, maybe a minecart on rails."

"Yeah," Jem said. "Like in *Zoolander*."

"What's *Zoolander*?"

"Oh my God."

"What?"

"No, we'll fix that gaping hole in your education later. Finish telling me about the mines."

"An open-pit mine is just what it sounds like: a pit. You'll see when we get up there, but it's a totally different operation. They basically just dig down and down and down. They throw away the overburden, and they take the minerals or the rock that they want. Here, they mine copper."

"Kind of like a quarry."

"Exactly," Tean said with a smile. "A quarry is an open-pit mine, just a special kind of one, for building materials."

"Huh," Jem said, poking his head out of the truck as the road climbed up toward the mine. "I guess that sounds better than being in a tunnel. Christ, I'd go out of my mind if I was stuck somewhere like that."

Tean frowned and looked at him again. All he said, though, was, "It might be better than being in a tunnel, but not by much. It messes up the environment in just about every way you can imagine, it's incredibly dangerous, and the miners have a lot of long-term health problems. Plus there's the tailings — that's what I'm mostly interested in today."

"Those are, like, the toxic waste?"

"Yeah, basically. It's a slurry leftover from processing the ores, and if it's not processed right — well, frankly, even if it is — it's got a lot of toxic chemicals in it. It's supposed to be pumped out to a tailings pond or a tailings dam, with the proper environmental protections in place."

"Let me guess," Jem said as they rolled to a stop at the first security gate. "Those environmental protections can have problems."

Tean just grimaced and nodded.

To Jem's surprise, the guard who came out of the booth just nodded when Tean gave his name, and then he pointed and gave directions to a second security gate higher up the mountain before waving them through.

"You must have some kind of friend," Jem said.

"Well, they definitely want to stay on the good side of inspectors."

"And you're a bigwig at the DWR."

Tean laughed. "I don't think anybody has ever thought I'm a bigwig. They probably would have hemmed and hawed and made me jump through hoops to get a meeting; Fawn cracks the whip, though, and they get hopping."

"She's a real hard-ass, huh?"

"She's four-eleven, she sings with the Mormon Tabernacle Choir, and she still does her hair and makeup straight out of a 1979 issue of *Cosmopolitan*."

"But she's a hard-ass."

"Gosh, yes, it's absolutely amazing to watch."

"What'd she tell you when you called?"

"She said the mine had passed all the recent inspections. A few minor issues, like always, but nothing with the tailings." Tean ran his thumbs inside the steering wheel. "And she told me she'd come out last week to do a surprise inspection. She said they were due one anyway, and someone had been calling her office and going on and on about toxic chemicals leaching into the groundwater. She said everything was clean."

"Fuck," Jem said. Then he pounded once on the dash. "Fuck."

"We don't know it was Benny."

Jem shook his head and looked out the window.

At the next gate, they had to wait. The guard took Tean's name and returned to his booth. With the windows down, the breeze carried the smell of broken stone and dust into the truck, along with something else, a chemical smell that made the inside of Jem's nose tingle. A flutter of movement made Jem glance up; a black-and-white bird was trying to find a place to land, but lengths of mesh hung between the girders of the security gate, as well as strips of tacks on flat surfaces, kept the bird from settling anywhere. He watched for a moment until the bird finally gave up and winged south. Jem knew what it felt like. He was tired; he wanted five minutes when he could stop flapping his wings. He felt like he'd been flapping his wings since the day they let him out of Decker.

"They're probably more worried about pigeons," Tean said. "The mesh and the tacks, that's why they put them up."

"God, it's cute when you explain things.'

"Never mind."

"No, I'm serious. What kind of bird was that?"

Tean rolled his eyes; his glasses were falling off again, and he pushed them back up.

"Come on, Doc," Jem said. "You're dying to tell me."

"I'm not dying to tell you."

"You probably know eighteen facts about how that bird is a disease carrier and how now we're probably going to die from the bubonic plague, but only if there isn't an earthquake first and we're buried alive in the mine."

Tean shoved his glasses up his nose again and crossed his arms. He was trying not to smile.

"Fine," Jem said. "I'll just call it the black-and-white-cookie bird."

"That's not what they're called. That's a ridiculous name. Nobody would call them that."

"I would. Like those black-and-white cookies on *Seinfeld*."

"Huh?"

"You've never seen the black-and-white cookie episode?"

"What's *Seinfeld*?"

"Ok, how much vacation time do you have?"

"What?"

"I'm going to put together a crash course: The Best of the 90s and the Early 2000s. You're probably going to need at least a month. Have you ever watched TV until your eyes get gummy and kind of stuck open?"

"Um."

The guard came back, but before he could speak, Jem said, "Hey, buddy, you had a black-and-white-cookie bird flying around here. They're a real nuisance; you might want to get someone to look at it."

"Sir?" the guard said.

"Black-and-white-cookie—" Jem said loudly, leaning over Tean.

"It was a magpie," Tean said, shoving Jem back into his seat. "A black-billed magpie. What did Ms. Nash say?"

"Go on up," the guard said. "That bench straight ahead. She's in the red trailer; her name's on the door."

"Scientifically, though," Jem said, leaning toward the window again, "the community is very divided over whether to call it the black-and-white-cookie bird or—"

Tean didn't exactly punch the gas, but the truck did jump forward a little too fast.

"A black-billed magpie," Jem said.

"Please stop."

"That was my second guess."

"You would make a terrible vet."

"Did you know that black-billed magpies rip out the eyeballs of children and use them to make their nests?"

"What in the world are you talking about?"

"You like trivia; I just thought you'd be interested to know some more horrifying facts."

"They don't—you don't—" He scrubbed a hand through the wild, brushed-back hair, making it ten percent wilder. "What are you talking about?"

"Facts, Doc. Try to keep up."

Tean must have decided that silence was the best course of action because he hunched over the wheel and refused to look at Jem after that.

Jem took the opportunity to study the mine. Pit was a very small word to describe the operation. As they climbed up to the next bench—vast, flat shelves of stone ringing the pit—Jem saw the full extent of the mine. It ran as far as he could see, and it was so deep that he couldn't make out the bottom level. Around the perimeter of the mine, some of the benches held heavy equipment—excavators, for example—while others held trailers that provided locations for on-site offices, storage, and essential services. A few timber buildings, painted red, stood on the eastern edge of the pit, but they were obviously much older and looked preserved in a historic way, probably a legacy of the early miners.

As they reached the top of the next bench, Jem switched his attention to the parallel rows of trailers. Two trailers were red: one was halfway down the line on his right, pit-side, and the other was at the end of the left row. Vehicles, mostly trucks and SUVs, were parked haphazardly; in front of the red trailer on the left was a silver BMW, a sporty little thing at odds with the dented panels and chipped paint of the trucks around it. Spotting the car gave Jem an idea, and he craned around to study the benches again.

Tean slowed the car as they approached the first trailer on the right.

"No, it's the one on the left," Jem said. "At the end."

"He just said a red trailer," Tean said.

Jem shrugged, still scanning the benches.

A moment later, Tean made an irritated noise.

"Told you," Jem said.

"Well, you're also the guy who thought a bird was named after a cookie, so forgive me for not trusting your judgment."

Tean parked next to the silver BMW. They got out, but before Tean could approach the door, Jem caught his arm, turning him to face the pit. The air was hot and still, although that chemical smell was stronger now, and Jem had to resist the urge to rub his nose. When he tugged Tean a few steps closer to the pit, dust eddied around their feet.

"What do you see?" Jem asked.

Tean didn't make a big show of it, but he twisted his arm, trying to get free. Jem ignored him. "A pit," Tean said. "What am I supposed to see?"

"What do you see that might be interesting to us?"

"I don't know." With his free hand, Tean gently removed Jem's grip, and then he shook out his arm like he'd been burned. "What am I supposed to see?"

"Black SUVs. Look over there. That's got to be the corporate motor pool, right? It's fenced, and there's multiples of a few similar models."

"There are a few black SUVs," Tean said. "And a lot of trucks. A lot of white trucks."

"But definitely some black SUVs. And I've spotted eight more on the benches."

"Ok," Tean said.

"Do you think that's a coincidence?"

Tean pushed his glasses up again. When he spoke, his voice was careful. "When I go in there, I think you should stay out here."

"What? Why?"

"You're very personally involved in this, and yesterday you had a hard time controlling your emotions—"

"Tean, please."

"It's not a good idea."

"Tean," Jem said, thinking to himself: repeat his name, ask questions, show flaws, mirror body language. He turned so they were face to face, trying to match the earnest openness of Tean's expression. "Tean, I know you're the expert here. I know you're really, really smart. I know—Tean, trust me, I know—you want to help me find Benny. I know I'm not as smart as you. I know I'm totally out of my depth. I know I'm totally, one-hundred percent reliant on you right now. I know it, Tean. But let me ask you just one thing: what if she says something about Benny, something that's a clue, and I'm the only one who would recognize it?"

Tean touched his glasses; Jem scratched his own nose. Tean touched his hair. Jem touched his own hair. Tean put his hands on his hips, and so did Jem.

"Like what?" Tean asked.

"I don't know. What would be a good cover story for me? What could I say that wouldn't raise any questions? What would you do if you were me?"

"U.S. Fish and Wildlife—"

"And you agree that I'm pretty good at talking to people? I mean, I don't have a lot of talents, but you'd agree with that, right?"

"Yes, but—"

"And you'd agree that I'm not dumb enough to put my foot in my mouth, right? I mean, you know I can do this, right? You know I won't mess up when it could come back on you, or when it might ruin our chances of finding Benny. You know that, right? Tean, come on. You know that, right?"

"Yes, Jem, but—"

Jem gave him puppy-dog eyes, channeling his inner Scipio, and his best shell-game smile.

"Ok," Tean finally said, "but we have to be very careful about this."

"Thank you," Jem said, squeezing Tean's arm. "Thank you, thank you, thank you. You are seriously, literally, no exaggeration, the best."

Wriggling free, Tean looked around, obviously trying to find somewhere safe to rest his gaze.

"Listen," Jem said, stepping closer, "I know this isn't the time or the place, but I want to find a way to thank you—"

"You have a weird beard hair," Tean blurted.

The best phrase Jem had to describe the look on Tean's face was total panic. Struggling to hide a grin, Jem said, "What?"

Tean touched the side of his face. "It looks infected."

"Um, ok." Fighting the grin was even harder now; Jem wasn't sure why he found Tean's discomfort so amusing—and endearing— but he did. Maybe it was the fact that Tean seemed to see the real Jem, instead of the façade. Maybe it was the fact that Tean said super weird things that nobody else would ever say to Jem. "Thanks."

"You should probably see a dermatologist."

"I will do that. As soon as we find Benny."

Below them, the dozer blade of an excavator scraped over rock, and a guy was shouting, "Up, up, up," his voice tiny in the vast emptiness of the pit.

"Ok," Jem said. "Should we go inside?"

The doc was so eager to get away that he practically ran.

At the door to the trailer, Tean knocked once. A woman's voice called, "Come in," and Jem followed Tean inside. It was a utilitarian space: unadorned resin paneling, particleboard desks, straight-backed chairs that had obviously come from an office supply store. Several maps covered a table in the center of the room. Jem spotted a few laptop computers, filing cabinets, and a water cooler. Cans of Tab stood on every available surface: desks, folding tables, filing cabinets. One of the doors at the back led into a bathroom, he guessed, and the other probably connected with a private office. A pair of muddy Timberlands stood near the door next to a chainsaw and a five-gallon can of gas.

On the other side of the map table, a woman was staring at them. She was middle-aged, blond, dressed in jeans and a plaid work shirt. Her ponytail was held in place with a rubber band. She was barefoot, and a moment later, Jem spotted wet socks hanging on the back of a chair.

"Well, I knew you weren't any of our boys," she said, "because they just plow in here like they've never met a closed door their whole lives. Dr. Leon?"

"Yes, hi. Are you Ms. Nash? Cleanup operations?"

"The title is Director of Environmental Stewardship. Just Julie is fine. And you are?"

"Fred Weeks," Jem said. "U.S. Fish and Wildlife."

"Well, well, well," Julie said. "The big guns. Fawn didn't say anything about Fish and Wildlife."

"Ms. Nash, we'll just take a minute of your time," Tean said.

With a nod, she gestured them to a pair of chairs in front of a desk. When she sat opposite them, she swung her bare feet up onto the desk, almost toppling a can of Tab. "All right, boys. Let's hear it.

What'd we do now? Step on a puppy's paw? Nick a kitten's whiskers?"

"Ms. Nash, I'm not sure what Fawn told you, but I'm a wildlife veterinarian with the Division of Wildlife Resources. I'm following up on some reports of animal deaths that might be connected to Dellengbauh Copper's mining operation."

"Oh frick," the woman said. "Benny."

"That's interesting," Jem said, leaning forward. "Who's Benny?"

"Frick," the woman said again. "Just about the most annoying twerp you'll ever meet. One of those real tree-hugger types. But not the granola kind, not this kid. He's a total blimpo. And he smells like a microwaved pork steak. He'd be up here every day if he could."

"Oh really?" Jem said, leaning forward.

"Why'd you mention him," Tean asked, "when I brought up the reports of dead animals?"

Julie shrugged. "He's the first one who comes to mind. He got past security a couple of weeks ago. Don't ask me how. He planted a bomb in this very trailer. Thank goodness our security people found it."

"Bullshit," Jem said.

"He sure did," Julie said. "I wish we'd gotten it on camera, but the twerp spray painted the lenses before he did anything. If you ask me, that's who you should be arresting. Honest people are trying to do honest work, and your type is doing everything you can to throw us in jail. The real criminals are like Benny. Dangerous, crazy, nutter types. That's who you should be arresting."

"How do you know he was the one who planted the bomb?" Jem said. "When was the last time you saw him?"

"A couple of weeks ago. And I know because he was going on and on about how we were all going to pay for—I don't know, he had a whole list of things. Why aren't you writing this down? Somebody should find that kid and arrest him. I don't even know why you're worried about me right now."

Tean was frowning. "Nobody's said anything about arrests, Ms. Nash."

"Want to check your calendar?" Jem pointed to the desk, where several printed calendar pages lay loose on top of a pile of other papers. "What about Monday? Did you see Benny on Monday?"

"What?" For the first time, a crack showed in Julie's façade. She sat forward, swinging her bare feet back to the ground, and studied both of them. "Just what exactly is going on?"

"That's really not why we're here," Tean said, giving Jem a hard look before turning his attention back to Julie. "Those reports about animal deaths—"

"Come on," Julie said. "Tell me what this is really about. I'm going to get the lawyers down here. This sounds like lawyer work."

"I don't think we need lawyers, Ms. Nash. I can't go into all the details of a DWR investigation, but we're just looking into some reports right now. Have you had a lot of trouble with environmental activists? Could you tell us a little bit more about their complaints?"

"From that human soft-boiled egg?"

"Are you referring to Benny?"

Julie nodded and tugged at her ponytail.

"From him," Tean said, "but also in general."

Then she shrugged. "Most of the nutters we get are the ordinary kind. They'll tell us we're raping the earth, destroying the environment, kind of fill-in-the-blank attacks. Every once in a while, they'll hold a protest outside with signs. Of course, none of them want to talk about all the good stuff we do: the money that goes back into the community, the conservation and preservation projects that are fully funded by Dellengbauh. We were taking down some trees near a trail this morning; it would have taken the Parks Service another two weeks to get around to it, so I just grabbed my chainsaw and did it. They don't care about that kind of stuff, the nutters; most of them, I don't even think they really care about the environment. Like most people, they're just thinking about themselves. A couple years ago, we had a lady chain herself to the security gate. Took two seconds with a pair of bolt cutters to get the chain off again, and things just went on as normal, but that lady sure was pleased with herself. That's how most of them are: they want to feel good about themselves, but they don't want to be too inconvenienced doing it."

"But you mentioned Benny in particular?"

"Benny's what I'd call an extremo nutter. They're the ones you have to worry about. Blow things up. Gun you down in the street." Her voice was rising, shrill now. "I pay my taxes. I don't know why you aren't writing this down."

"Was Benny the only one?"

"They come and go. Most of them are retarded or batshit crazy, so they'll fixate on something. For a while it'll be us, and then they'll switch to collecting aluminum cans or coming up with a plan to free Willy."

"You're not supposed to say that word," Jem said.

"What word?"

"You know what word. Don't say it again."

Through the thin walls of the trailer came the rasp of an excavator's bucket blade scraping over stone, the rumble of diesel engines, and then men's voices coming closer, arguing about *Game of Thrones*.

"What made Benny an extremo nutter?" Tean said.

"Well, the bomb," Julie said, but her eyes didn't leave Jem. "That doesn't seem a bit extreme?"

"Did you report this to the police?"

"Sure. They came out, looked around. Didn't do jack-doody."

"When was this?"

"A couple of weeks ago."

"It seems strange that nobody else saw Benny, that nobody was able to stop him. How did he make it past security?"

"I don't know. He must be a criminal mastermind."

"And you're sure he planted a bomb?" Jem said.

"Security found a box with wires sticking out of it. I saw it myself."

"Weren't you worried he might come back another time?"

"Not really," Julie said, her gaze fixed on Jem. "Like I said: he was a retard."

Jem thought he did a good job at controlling himself. He thought about Saturday mornings again, *Darkwing Duck*. But something must have crossed his face because Julie stared at him, a smirk barely showing at the corner of her mouth.

"Oops," she said with the faintest arch of her eyebrows.

"Mind if I get some water?" Jem asked.

Julie shook her head.

He walked past her to the cooler, grabbed one of the paper cones that served as cups, and filled it. Most of the water slopped over his fingers. He tried to drink what made it into the cup, but he was shaking too hard.

"Have you seen an increase in animal deaths around the mine?" Tean asked. "Maybe particularly around the tailings ponds?"

"No."

"You're sure?"

"Absolutely. We've done outstandingly well on our inspections ever since I took over; we're committed to our responsibility as stewards for the planet's natural resources."

"By dumping loose rock and dirt into valleys," Jem said, "and by building poisonous lakes."

Julie glanced over her shoulder at him, her smile close to a sneer. "I suppose everybody's entitled to their opinion."

"As part of this investigation," Tean said, the words cautiously spaced, "we're looking into some events that happened on Monday. Could you tell us where you were?"

"What happened?"

"I can't go into that, I'm afraid."

"Well, well, well. I thought you guys were just out there sniffing elk butts and petting rattlesnakes."

"Monday morning, Ms. Nash."

She glanced at the calendars, selected one, and scanned it. "I was in a meeting on-site from nine to ten. Then I had a meeting in the city from eleven to one."

"Who were you meeting with?"

"Nine to ten was with operations staff. We had a state inspection last week, a surprise one," her eyebrows made those faint, mocking arches again, "and we debriefed. Then eleven to one, I was meeting with WasatchGreen, one of the organizations we donate to. You'd like them. I bet they've sniffed every elk butt in the state."

Tean opened his mouth, but the phone on the desk rang, and Julie answered it. She paled as she listened, and bright red circles appeared in her cheeks. "All right," she snapped. "Yeah, just get your butt up here." Over her shoulder, she called, "Ruth, I need you."

The door at the far end of the trailer opened, and a girl stepped out. She was dressed in what looked like page two of the J. Crew summer catalogue: a simple blue skirt, a white button-up, and a cardigan. Expensive clothes, though; Jem could tell from a distance that she hadn't bought them at Ross. Pearl earrings that looked real. A silver medallion that Jem recognized as a Mormon Good Girl symbol. Flashbacks of June Cleaver, Jem thought. If June Cleaver were eighteen years old and beautiful.

"Yes, Ms. Nash?"

"It happened again."

Ruth glanced at Jem and Tean.

After a moment, Julie followed her gaze and said, "I think that's all the time we have today, gentlemen."

"What happened again?" Jem said.

"Just a problem with a bighorn reintroduction program we're coordinating," Julie said. "Ruth's our intern, and it's become her pet project."

Jem didn't need to look at Tean to know the doctor had also recognized the lie.

"We're going to need a space to work," Julie said to Ruth, her words still clipped and hard. "Clear off this desk and get, you know, what we need."

"Is everything all right?" Tean asked.

"Yes," Julie said. "When I need the DWR's help with a few dang sheep, I'll let you know."

The plan crystallized without Jem even really having to think about it, the way his best ideas came when he was riffing. The trailer was a simple rectangle. Ruth had already started moving toward Julie's desk. Jem started moving too, fumbling with his phone, the half-full paper cup in his other hand. Poor Ruth tried to dodge him, but Jem bulled into her, and they both stumbled. The paper cone flew out of his hand, and water arced across Julie's desk.

"Dang it," Julie said, staring at the wet mess of paper. "What the heck was that?"

"Oh no," Ruth said, hurrying over to the desk.

"I am so sorry," Jem said, racing to stand next to her. Together, they tried to control the damage. They grabbed the topmost papers, shaking off the water that hadn't already been absorbed, while Julie muttered under her breath. Tean just stayed in his chair, watching.

"I'm sorry," Jem kept saying.

"Well," Julie kept saying back, "what the heck is wrong with you?"

And in all that chaos, he shoved three sheets of paper down the back of his jeans.

"Forget it," Julie finally said, shoving him away from the desk. "Just forget it."

Jem backed off a few steps, holding his hands. "I'm really, really sorry."

"Do you need something else?" Julie snapped at Tean. "Your federal buddy just made my day a whole lot worse."

"I do want to take a look around the tailings ponds," Tean said. "I may need to collect specimens."

"Good gosh," Julie said, shoving a pile of sodden pages across the desk. "Do you have any idea how busy I am?"

"If I need to," Tean said, "I can have our conservation officers get a warrant."

"I didn't say no, gosh darn it. I'm just—" She let out a noise of frustration.

The trailer's front door opened, and a big guy stepped into the office. He was easily a couple of inches taller than Jem, and he probably carried an extra fifty pounds. His head was shaved, and he was wearing a dark suit that made Jem think this guy had been watching too many Keanu Reeves movies. He was carrying an unmarked manila envelope, and he wore disposable gloves.

"There you are," Julie said. "Phil, take these guys down to the tailings ponds, will you? Put that here; we'll deal with it when you get back."

The big guy—Phil—laid the envelope on a dry corner of the desk. Then he looked at Jem and Tean expressionlessly and jerked his head at the door.

"Thanks for your time, Ms. Nash," Tean said, extending his hand.

Julie pumped it once and went back to clearing the wet papers from her desk.

"If you think of anything—"

"Yeah, sure," Julie said.

Tean waited a moment longer, but Julie just stared at him. Jem caught Tean's eyes, and they headed for the door.

"The tailings ponds," Phil said, his voice a low rumble as he led them to Tean's truck. "Please stay close to me and don't take any detours."

"Are you in charge of security, Phil?" Jem asked.

Phil stared at him.

"Did you hear anything about a bomb threat?" Jem asked; his blood was whining in his ears.

"You'll have to talk to Ms. Nash about that," Phil said.

"You must have an important job, Phil," Jem said. "Did you have any run-ins with this Benny character?"

"He came by a few times," Phil said. "Ms. Nash met with him as a courtesy."

"Even after he planted a bomb?" Jem said.

"You'll have to talk to Ms. Nash about that," Phil said.

"Let's go to the tailings ponds," Tean said. "Then we can all get on with our day."

"Right," Jem said. "Great idea."

"Stay close," Phil said. "No detours."

When they were in the truck, Tean shifted into drive. "Are you ok?"

"Sure."

Tean just nodded, but he looked tired.

"Why are we even going to the tailings?" Jem said, working the wet papers out from the waistband of his jeans. "Benny talked about the birds at the Great Salt Lake. This stuff with Nash isn't connected."

"Because Benny claimed they were dumping toxic waste illegally," Tean said, "and I want to see if there's any sign of it. Because Benny got a lot of things right even when he was wrong about the specifics. Because somebody tried to run me off the road when I went to look at those birds. Because this is my job, and I have to at least pretend to be doing it. Pick a reason."

"Why are you angry at me?"

"I'm not." Tean stopped, obviously trying to modulate his voice, and said, "I just wish I understood what was going on."

They followed Phil, who drove a small white pickup, across several benches until they reached a winding road that led down out of the mountains. Below, a large, flat open space was dominated by several bluish-gray ponds. They looked almost recreational, with long, white beaches that were bright under the sun. Another road led east, away from the tailings ponds and back to the freeway.

"What did you steal?" Tean asked. He was scanning the mountains as they drove.

"It wasn't stealing," Jem said, smoothing the wrinkled pages on his knee.

"It's her stuff, and you took it. What's that called?"

"They're just papers. It's not like I took that Ruth girl's pearl earrings."

"It's her stuff, and you took it. That's stealing. What did you steal?"

"Just some papers. It's not stealing if it's just papers."

"Dang it, Jem. You can't do that. I know you're worried about Benny. I'm really trying to remember that. But if you pull a stunt like that again, I'm not going to be able to keep doing this. I like my job. I want to keep my job."

Jem buzzed down his window; the chemical smell was overpowering now, burning the inside of his nose, and he put the window back up. The slope was flattening out as they reached the valley, and the tailings ponds floated ahead of them like a layer of scum on the pale, broken stone that Jem had mistaken, from a distance, for a sandy beach.

"I didn't think about that," Jem said.

"Big surprise."

"I'm sorry."

Tean shook his head, still looking at the mountains.

Jem didn't press the apology. He just shuffled the stolen pages, glancing out at the desert ablaze with the October sun, blinking when the glare on the tailings ponds intensified to deep troughs of light.

Phil let them through a security fence, and then through another, and then he parked and got out of the truck. Tean parked too.

"What do you think about this, though?" Jem said, holding out one of the pages.

Tean glanced at it and frowned. "That's Julie's bank statement."

"And?"

"And she's going to bounce her next check." Tean narrowed his eyes. "Especially if she withdraws another five thousand dollars in cash."

"That doesn't seem strange to you?"

"I wish I had five thousand dollars in cash."

Jem shook the page. "Focus."

"I don't know. It's a lot of money, but she could have pulled it out for a down payment on a car, for another big purchase, I don't know."

"Or drugs."

"Ok."

"Or hush money."

"Oh boy."

"Take a look at this one," Jem said.

Phil honked impatiently, and Tean held up a hand. He scanned the document in Jem's hand.

"Credit card bill," Tean said. "Jeez, she spent four hundred dollars for a hotel in Park City? She could have just slept in the back of her car for free. This one's a jewelry store—I've seen their billboard—and I think that's a spa. Well, it says spa in the name, so I know it's a spa."

"Expensive tastes," Jem said.

"Let me see that again," Tean said, taking the page and holding it closer. "This isn't her credit card. It's Ruth's."

"Ruth-the-Intern wears pearls and J. Crew and stays at a Park City hotel that costs four hundred dollars a night?"

"She looked like she came from money," Tean said.

"Why did she leave her credit card bill on her boss's desk?"

"I don't know."

"Because they're doing the hokey-pokey."

"I think you're jumping to conclusions," Tean said.

"Something is weird here. Something is weird with all this money. And I know for a fact that Julie lied to our faces. Benny never built a bomb in his life. He wouldn't hurt someone."

"Ok, I agree with that. The money is weird, but that could be totally unrelated. And I agree about Benny too, but why would Julie lie?"

"Because he's a threat, and she's trying to erode his credibility."

"That's what I meant by jumping to conclusions." He pointed a finger at Jem. "Let's talk about what's going to happen right now."

"I know, I know," Jem said. "I'm staying. Can you at least put the window down?"

"You're not a dog. I'll leave the truck running."

"You're a sweetheart."

Tean rolled his eyes.

"You're a prince," Jem said.

Tean threw open the door.

"You're the greatest, kindest human being in existence, and you deserve a mug that says that."

"Get it all out of your system while I'm gone, please."

But he was smiling a little as he pushed his glasses back up.

Jem watched for a while as Phil led Tean around the tailings ponds. After maybe half an hour, they came back, and Tean shook his head as he buckled his seat belt.

"Nothing?"

"Nope," Tean said. "Fawn said they passed the inspection, and I don't see anything here that suggests they've got a problem."

"They're covering it up," Jem said.

Yanking on his shirttails to straighten them, Tean was silent for a moment. Then he said, "I think we should at least consider other options."

"Of course."

"You're really annoying when you're being condescending."

"I'm being patronizing," Jem said, "not condescending."

Tean mumbled something.

"Did you just use a swear word?" Jem said with a grin.

"Benny wrote about Dellengbauh the most," Tean said, "but he spent almost as many pages on this other guy, a rancher. I think it makes sense to see him next; I guess he was number two on Benny's list."

"What'd the rancher do?"

"Benny claims he was poaching."

"All right," Jem said. "Let's go meet our poacher and see how he felt about my baby brother."

"If he doesn't shoot us on sight."

"Hey, that could be a good thing, right? Like, it would be a sign we were on the right track."

Tean grimaced. "Fat lot of good it'll do us if he feeds us to feral pigs and our bodies are never discovered."

"It's the circle of life."

"Or he could keep us prisoner in his basement for thirty years."

"You know what they say," Jem said, squeezing Tean's shoulder. "You can put up with anything if you've got a good friend."

Tean ran both hands through his hair, yanking wildly.

"I know," Jem said. "Sometimes the world just seems too perfect."

19

As they drove north and then east, looping around to the back of the Oquirrh Mountains, Tean tried to figure out what exactly was going on. Ninety percent of the time, Jem was unflappable: smiling, funny, easygoing, and totally in control. Whenever Benny came up, though—especially if they hit an obstacle in the search—Jem seemed to fall apart completely. And while Tean could understand Jem being upset by what looked like his brother being kidnapped, he couldn't quite make the two versions fit. And he didn't like the sense that sometimes he was seeing a mask. What had happened in Julie Nash's trailer, with Jem losing his cool and then stealing documents, made Tean worry that the real Jem didn't have things under control at all. It made Tean worry that the real Jem was hurting a lot more than he normally let on, and sometimes, when that hurt built up to an intolerable level, Jem did something to let it out. And that didn't sound like a California businessman who was tracking down his foster brother.

More troublesome, though, was the other suspicion that had been growing in Tean's gut since the night before. All the touching at the DWR offices. The dancing, if you could call it that, at Tean's apartment. The crazy things Jem said. Tean wasn't exactly an expert at this kind of thing, but he was getting very worried by the possibility that Jem might be flirting with him.

For the first half of their drive, Salt Lake City was northeast of them, buildings that were brown and faded blue and glass that turned violet when the sun hit the right angle, all of it looking like Russian sage bristling out of the high steppe. When they turned, though, the desert waited for them: pale and cracked earth that ran west in a broken sheet, with greasewood and clumps of blue grama giving way to tumbleweed and soapweed.

Tean's phone buzzed. He checked the screen, saw Ammon's name, and glanced at Jem.

"It's your truck," Jem said.

"Hi," Tean said.

"Hi," Ammon said. There was no noise in the background of the call; he was probably sitting in his car on an early lunch break. "How are you?"

"Ok."

"How's your head?"

"Better."

"Did you puke?"

"I think so."

Ammon took a deep breath, but all he said was, "Did you sleep?"

"Yeah."

"Did you take acetaminophen?"

"Yeah."

"Did you drink water?"

"Yeah."

"I sound like the Inquisition," Ammon said with a nervous chuckle. He was always like this after they'd been together, always closest to the real Ammon, the one Tean had known when they'd been boys. This was the Ammon who'd been his companion in Peru, the one who'd walked into their bathroom while Tean had been showering, the breeze off the Pacific blowing in behind him, cool and salty and stinging, and pressed Tean against the tile and kissed him while the hot water pounded down and steamed where it met the cold ocean air. "Did you eat?"

"Oh yeah."

"Are you at the office? Can I order you lunch?"

"No, I'm out—" Tean's gaze cut to Jem and then back to the road. "—working."

Another of those deep breaths. "Thank you for last night. I know that's not easy for you."

"Thank you," Tean said. "I know it's not easy for you either."

"It's not going to be like this forever."

"I know."

"Do you have any idea how much you mean to me?"

Tean laughed. Jem was watching him now, not even pretending he wasn't, and Tean switched the phone to his other hand.

"I'm serious," Ammon said. "You're everything to me. You're the only person in my life who knows me, the real me. You're this perfect, amazing guy, and I'm so lucky you care about me at all."

Jem was still watching, scratching his neatly trimmed beard, his normal smile gone. In fact, if Tean had been pressed, he might have said Jem looked pissed.

Maybe that was why Tean said next, "Why didn't you lock the door?"

"What?"

"You knew some weird stuff has been happening to me. You knew I was scared."

"You weren't scared. You're the bravest person I know."

"Well, I was worried. And you didn't lock the door."

"Frick," Ammon said. "Really? I'm sorry. I was in a rush. Lucy had called a few times. Daniel wouldn't come out of his room, wouldn't talk to anyone. He's really struggling right now."

"You know how I am after you leave."

"I know. I'm sorry. I thought your friend was coming back; didn't you tell me he was staying there that night?"

"Yeah."

"That's all. I just thought he was coming back." A pause. "Did he come back?"

"Yes."

They had cleared the Oquirrh Mountains, and now Tean guided the truck off of I-80 and onto Route 36, heading south along the back of the mountains. Scrub oak, Rocky Mountain juniper, and stunted pines wove a patchy covering up the slopes. Fields that would have held brome, buffalo grass, and blue grama now held only stubble, with rolled bales at irregular intervals.

"Where did he sleep?" Ammon asked quietly.

"Excuse me?"

"I think it's a pretty clear question."

"The question is plenty clear, but I don't know why you think you'd need to ask me that."

"Never mind. It's none of my business."

"I can't do this with you right now," Tean said. "An eighteen-wheeler just about turned me into a pancake, and I'm going to be lucky if I don't spend the rest of my life as a sex slave living in this guy's basement, and I think I've got an aneurysm."

"Fine," Ammon said. "You know I don't like it when you talk like that. We can have this conversation when we're both less angry."

"Sure," Tean said. "Let's have it after I have an aneurysm. Neither of us will be angry then."

"You need to cut it out with that stuff," Ammon said. "It gets old."

"And I went to a mine today," Tean shouted, "and I think I have lung cancer from the air pollution."

The call disconnected.

Tean hammered on the steering wheel with one hand. The tires hit the rumble strip, and he yanked the wheel left until they were back in their lane.

"Do you want to stop?" Jem asked.

"No."

"Do you want me to drive?"

"I'm fine." He ran a hand down his face and said again, "I'm fine."

On both sides of them, the stubble fields gave way to pasture; a few lazy cows stood under a gnarled cottonwood, swishing their tails in the shade.

"Well," Jem said, "do you want to talk about it?"

Tean shook his head.

"Why didn't he lock the door?" Jem asked.

"He was in a hurry." And then Tean couldn't stop himself from adding, "And then he said because you were coming back."

"Which one was it?"

"Good question."

"If I'm making things difficult for you, you know, by asking you to help—"

"No. This is how he always is. He's got Lucy and the kids; that trumps everything else."

"Maybe it'll do him some good to feel a little jealous."

Tean snorted.

"I could kiss you in front of him. You know, just to rile him up."

"He'd probably knock your teeth out." Tean played with the radio, not turning it on, just spinning the knob. "He said something to you last night, didn't he? He said he'd forgotten something in the car, but he went to talk to you. That's right, isn't it?"

"Yeah."

"What'd he say?"

"He was just being protective."

Tean laughed. "Great. He's protective. Until nine o'clock, when he has to get home and read the kids a bedtime story and watch the news with his wife."

"Outsider opinion: he's an asshole who doesn't treat you well."

"I told you that you don't understand what's going on. It's complicated."

"Ok."

"I asked you not to talk about it."

"You were just talking to me about it."

"Well, I don't want to."

"Ok."

"I don't need anybody judging how I live my life."

"Christ, Tean, I didn't mean anything by it. I was just trying to be supportive."

"I don't need your support. And I don't need your pity."

Jem just shook his head and looked out the window.

"And I'm really angry right now," Tean said, "and I know I'm shouting, and I'm just feeling a lot of really strong feelings right now, and I'm sorry I'm taking them out on you."

Flopping back against the seat, Jem just rolled his eyes, grinning. "God, you are really something, aren't you?"

After a moment, Tean smiled weakly.

"It's ok," Jem said, squeezing his shoulder. "Just so you know, I think he might be a vampire."

"What?"

"Ammon. I think he's a vampire."

"Vampire's aren't real."

"Oh God," Jem said, "don't embarrass yourself. Evidence: he only comes out at night."

"That is totally not true."

"I've only ever seen him at night."

"You've seen him one time. It just happened to be at night."

Jem brushed this aside. "Evidence: he's sucking the life out of you."

"Thin ice," Tean said.

With another grin, Jem said, "Evidence: he's like Spike from *Buffy*. One minute he's nice, and the next minute he's bad, and then the next minute he's nice, and Buffy has to keep forgiving him. Actually, that's kind of Angel's deal too, now that I think about it. More proof that he's a vampire. Tell me: to your knowledge, has Ammon ever been the victim of a gypsy curse that restored his immortal soul?"

"What's *Buffy*?"

"You're joking."

"Is it a movie?"

"Well, yes. But it's also a TV show. And it's one of the best things that's ever been on TV. I saw it all in reruns."

"Oh. Ok."

"No, it's not ok. We need to remedy this immediately. As soon as we find Benny, we're going to binge, like, the first three seasons. Minimum."

"I don't really watch much TV."

Jem groaned. "Of course you don't."

"What does that mean?"

"What do you do for fun?"

"I go on hikes sometimes."

"Great."

"I read. Mostly for work, actually, but sometimes for fun."

"So, nothing? You do nothing for fun?"

"I have a puzzle—"

"Stop, stop, stop. You're hurting me. Get ready for a marathon of TV watching. No excuses. No complaining."

Tean just shook his head, but after another mile, he realized he was still smiling.

Another fifteen minutes carried them through Tooele, where Route 36 temporarily became Main Street. They passed small houses of yellow brick, stone churches with unadorned steeples, plywood sheds with corrugated-metal roofs. They had to drive another fifteen minutes past the town to the turn off for Goody Ranch, where Ray Goody ran horses and cattle. A timber gate marked the entrance to the ranch, and Jem had to get out and open the gate and then close it behind them. Then they followed a long gravel drive. The ranch was on the east side of Route 36, backing up to the Oquirrh Mountains, and the Goody household sat on a bench in the foothills, overlooking the open fields.

"Ok," Tean said, inspecting the huge house: freshly painted clapboard, stained glass windows in the dormers, a wrap-around porch decorated with Adirondack chairs and rocking chairs and potted plants that, pretty soon, would need to be moved inside to survive the winter. "I didn't realize this guy was rich. Did you see how many miles of pasture we passed?"

"Not just rich," Jem said. "Old rich."

"How did Benny get out here?"

Jem was staring at the house. "Huh?"

"He didn't have a vehicle, right? And you said he didn't really have friends, although he got a ride with that guy Chaquille. Public transit doesn't come out this way. Did he get a cab?"

"No," Jem said. "He liked to come out and spend the weekend with some family friends outside Tooele. They have a ranch too, but a lot smaller. It's just north of here. The foothills have some hiking paths, or he might have borrowed an ATV; the Jenkins have some. He might have just hitched Route 36. I'm guessing if we look at the other people he complained about, they'll all be on this side of 36, all of them backing up to the mountains, where it was easy for Benny to get to them."

Tean frowned.

"What?" Jem asked.

"Dellengbauh is just on the other side of the mountains. We're about the same distance south."

"Well, Benny wasn't in great shape, but he loved nature. He could go miles and miles." Jem frowned, staring at the mountains. "I don't know about hiking across those, though."

As they pulled up to the house, a middle-aged man stepped out onto the porch. He had a handful of flat-strap tie downs, and he was sorting buckles as he came down from the porch. Off to the side of the house, a stock trailer was hitched to a new-looking Dodge Ram.

"This little piggy went to market," Jem said.

"This is why I shouldn't eat meat," Tean said. "Do you know that pigs are as smart as human toddlers?"

"Good thing for us he doesn't raise pigs."

"Every time we eat bacon, we might as well have pulled a kid off *Sesame Street*."

"I don't think toddlers have the same umami flavor," Jem said, reaching for the latch. The man, whom Tean assumed was Ray Goody, had spotted them and was approaching.

"Are you up to this?" Tean asked.

Nodding, Jem slid out of the truck. As Tean opened the door, he heard Jem saying, "Mr. Goody? Hi, nice to meet you. Fred Weeks. U.S. Fish and Wildlife. This is Dr. Leon from Utah Division of Wildlife Resources."

Tean considered smashing his head against the truck door. Instead, he moved around the Ford to shake Goody's hand, trying not to glare at Jem.

"What's going on, brethren?" Goody said. He wore bib overalls and a work shirt; where the shirt was unbuttoned, Tean could see the scooped neck of his garment top. The only affectation was a silver bracelet made of chunky links. "What can I do for you?"

"Mr. Goody," Jem said, "we're following up on a few different reports."

"That's right," Tean said. "We'd just like to ask you a few questions."

"About what?" Goody said. He'd lost interest in the tie downs, and now he studied both of them, his pale eyes cutting back and forth between them.

"Well, several people have reported complaints about a man named Benny Guthall. Benjamin Guthall. Your name came up in previous conversations, and we wanted to see what you could tell us about Mr. Guthall. Do you have a moment so we can step inside?"

"Sorry, brethren. Ranch work never stops, and I can save you some time. I don't know anybody named Benny Guthall."

"If we could have just a few minutes —" Tean began.

"Really?" Jem said. "That's interesting, because Benny told several people that he believed you were poaching."

Goody laughed. "Oh yeah? And what am I poaching?"

"We're restricting some details of this investigation, sir. Have you been doing any illegal hunting?"

"Brother Weeks, I run the biggest horse-and-cattle operation in the Tooele Valley. I'm not saying I wouldn't mind scoring an elk tag in the lottery; I enjoy hunting. But why would I do something stupid like poaching?"

"I don't know," Jem said. "Why would you?"

"Mr. Goody," Tean said, "we'll only take a few minutes —"

"Now listen," Goody said. "I told you I don't know him. I've never heard of him. What do you want to ask me beyond that?"

"He's overweight," Tean said. "Stringy blond hair. He probably would have talked your ear off about environmental concerns if he got close enough."

"I don't know him, son."

"We're looking into a DWR concern, and we're trying to track down some particulars. Can you tell us where you were Monday?"

"Sure I can, son. I was with your warrant."

"Cute," Jem said.

"Now I don't have time for this," Goody said. "Anything else, you can call ahead, understand?"

"We'd like to take a look around —" Tean said.

"Sure you would. Not gonna happen, son. You come back with a warrant, and you can tramp all over. Until then, get off my property. That's as clear as I'm going to say it."

"A good citizen wouldn't mind letting someone inspect his property," Jem said.

"A good citizen is king in his own castle, boy. Get off my land. I'm walking inside that house, and I'm going to call the sheriff. Now, I've known Sheriff McLillian since she was in diapers. I put two of her brothers through college, and I do a steak-dinner fundraiser for her every election year. You tell me how it's going to go when she finds you two yahoos poking around out here."

"That's interesting," Jem said.

"Come on," Tean said, catching his arm.

"That's really fucking interesting," Jem said.

"Let's go," Tean said, tugging harder this time. "Thanks for your time, Mr. Goody."

"Brethren," Goody said, "you take real good care of yourselves."

When they got in the truck, Jem said, "That motherfucker is lying through his teeth. Did you see how tight he was clutching those tie downs when I brought up poaching? That ass muncher is full of shit."

Tean said, "Ok."

"You think I'm wrong."

"No, I think you're right that he was upset. I just don't know what it means. Why would he lie about knowing Benny?"

"Maybe because Benny figured out what he was up to. Maybe Benny confronted him. We need to do some more digging and find out."

Tean didn't like where that train of thought was going, so he didn't respond. He backed away from the house, did a three-point turn, and headed back down the drive. In the rearview mirror, he could see Goody still watching them. Then the rancher headed into the house; maybe he had been serious about calling the sheriff. Tean rolled down his window. The valley air was still and on the verge of being hot, the sun hammering down and leaving pinpricks of light on the husks of seed heads.

They drove to the gate, and when Tean stopped, Jem hopped out again. He went around to open the gate, and then he froze. He strode to the side of the road, squatted, and then used a stick to force aside a tangle of thistles. He reached down and picked up something green, turning it in his hands. Then he came back. His steps were zombie-like, and his face was blank as he stared at what he carried. When he got into the truck again, he passed a green plastic bowl to Tean. It had been cast in a mold that left a stylized turtle shell pattern, and a turtle head poked up at the rim of the bowl. It looked like it was wearing a mask.

"What is this?" Tean asked.

For a moment, Jem sat there, digging his thumbs into the corners of his eyes. His was taking huge gulps of air. Tremors were working through him—tiny tremors, sure, but they made the cotton of his gray tee tremble.

"Hey," Tean said, putting a hand on his back, "what's wrong—"

"Don't touch me," Jem shouted, spinning in the seat and slapping away Tean's hand. They stared at each other for a moment. "Just don't fucking touch me, ok?"

"Yeah. Yes. Ok. I'm sorry."

Jem didn't move. He looked paralyzed, his only movement the frantic breathing that he couldn't seem to slow down. Then, with what looked like a lot of effort, he contracted into that hunched-over posture again, his hands hiding his face.

"That's Benny's. That's his Teenage Mutant Ninja Turtles bowl. He never went camping without it."

20

With the truck rumbling beneath him, Tean tried to decide what to do. He looked at Benny's Teenage Mutant Ninja Turtles bowl. He studied Jem's slumped shoulders. Then he shifted into reverse, made another three-point turn, and headed back up to Goody's house. At the top of the hill, he turned hard until the truck blocked the driveway. He opened his door and got out.

"Are you going to be ok for a minute?"

Jem didn't answer.

Tean shut the door and eyed the house, looking for some sign that Goody had spotted him and was coming out, probably with an old shotgun. But the door stayed closed, and nothing moved behind the windows. After another moment, Tean walked toward the barn. Two minutes earlier, Jem's suspicions about Goody had sounded like a desperate man trying to find an answer. Now, though, Tean wasn't so sure. The plastic bowl didn't look like it was common; Tean had never seen one like it before, and it seemed impossible that Jem would just happen to find an identical bowl on the property of a man Benny had threatened to expose for poaching.

Halfway to the barn, though, Tean heard a coughing sound from inside the trailer and then the clip of hooves. Changing course, Tean moved around to the back of the stock trailer. He didn't need to open the door to see inside; a section of the trailer's walls consisted of bars instead of solid paneling to allow for air flow. He studied the animals: dusty brown coats, stocky bodies, big horns. The last one was the real giveaway.

Taking out his phone, Tean began filming a video. First, he panned the property to include the barn and Goody's house as well as a brief panorama of the Tooele Valley. Then he filmed the trailer's license plate and the plate on the truck. He turned the camera back toward the trailer, angling it to capture the animals inside, and began speaking. "This is Dr. Teancum Leon, and today is Wednesday, October 11th, 2017. I'm on the property of Ray Goody. This video is of Mr. Goody's stock trailer, parked outside his house. Inside the trailer are two bighorn sheep, both males."

He ended the video, shared it with Hannah, and headed to the truck's cab. Through the window, he could see a woman's sweater in the passenger footwell. Then he went to the front of the house. He hammered on the door and waited.

"You have got to be stupid, son," Goody said when he opened the door. His pale eyes cut from Tean to the truck parked across the driveway. "The sheriff is going to burn your buns when she gets here."

"I don't think you called the sheriff," Tean said. "And I don't think you're going to call her."

"Son, you're making a big mistake. I'm going make sure this costs you your job. I've got friends, and they — "

"Mr. Goody, shut up."

The rancher's pale eyes widened; color rushed into his face.

"I've been making the dumbest mistakes anybody could imagine for the last fifteen years of my life. I'm tired. I'm still kind of hungover. And this guy from California is currently making me question all the safeguards I've built into my life, and it's a really awful feeling. So shut up, and I'm going to tell you why you're not going to call the sheriff: I saw the bighorns, Mr. Goody."

"Those are mine," Goody said.

"Really? Utah statute 23-20-3 prohibits collecting, possessing, or transporting protected wildlife without a valid license, permit, tag, or certificate of registration. So, Mr. Goody, let's see you get one of those documents."

"I don't have to do anything," Goody said. "You're trespassing on my land. You don't have a warrant. Doesn't matter if you saw shit; it won't be worth anything."

"Maybe," Tean said. "We came onto your land to have a conversation, and the bighorns were right out in plain sight. Don't really need a warrant for that. But we can let the courts decide. Now, the fine for poaching bighorn is thirty thousand dollars a head, and you've got two, so that puts you at sixty thousand dollars."

"I didn't poach them."

"That's another point we'll have to argue. You know what I think? I think Benny got it half right, the way he usually does. I think you might even be telling the truth—part of it, anyway. How much do you charge those guys to hunt the sheep you collect? Ten thousand dollars? Fifteen? Twenty? Some guys will pay a lot of money for the hunt."

Goody ran one trembling hand through his wiry hair.

"Just so you know," Tean said, "that first statute, that's a class B misdemeanor. But the one I'm really interested in, and the one I'd have a lot more fun with is Statute 23-20-4, which designates the capture of protected wildlife as third-degree felony. Ouch, Mr. Goody. Ouch. Even if you're right, even if we get to trial and they throw out my evidence because I got it without a warrant, how many customers do you think you'll have next season? How many of those important friends will want to be involved with a man who got dragged into court on a felony charge, even if the charge eventually gets dropped?"

"You can't—"

"Here's what we're going to do. First, you're going to tell me about Benny. Then you're going to tell me where you were on Monday. Then you're going to tell me where your employees were on Monday. Then you're going to walk me through your garage and your barn. And then I'm going to do a little reconnaissance. If things go smoothly, maybe our conversation stops here. How are we doing so far, Mr. Goody? Are we clear?"

"This is blackmail."

Tean rolled a finger.

"Oh hell," Goody said. "Fine. That fat kid is always poking around out here. He's a goddamn nuisance. One time, he tried to get the horses into a stampede. He said he was just trying to help them escape, but the darn fool could have gotten a lot of them injured or killed. Another time I caught him cutting the fence. Had these darn tin snips and he was just going crazy cutting the wires. Another time, he got a big chain and put it on the trailer. It took me half a day to cut the darn thing off. Makes my life hell, that's what he does. Every time I go after him, he scoots on up into the mountains."

"He didn't confront you about the poaching?"

Goody spat to the side. "He might have said something."

"And?"

"And what? I shouted at him, and he ran off like he always does."

"What about Monday?"

"I was in Cheyenne for a stock auction. I stayed an extra day to look at some . . . special merchandise. I have a few guys who work for me. One of them, Cisco, he was up in Cheyenne with me. Then Albino and Abram, they're brothers, they were here keeping things running." He frowned and ran a shaky hand through his hair again. "What's this all about?"

"Benny went missing on Monday."

"Now come on. You don't think I had anything to do with that."

"Let's go take a look at your garage."

Tools hung neatly on pegboards; the smell of hay and gasoline hung in the air. But there wasn't another car. No black SUV. No Chevy with a scraped-up panel.

When Tean looked at Goody, the rancher said, "Only have the truck."

"No wife?"

"Not anymore."

"Nobody else lives here?" Tean was thinking about the woman's sweater in the passenger footwell.

Goody shook his head.

"You don't have any other vehicles?"

"I told you, didn't I?"

When they got to the barn, the familiar smells of manure and leather greeted them. Several of the stalls were open to the pasture, and a skittish bay, what Tean thought was a quarter horse, lurked at one of the openings. No black SUV. No Chevy with a scraped-up panel. Nothing. Tean made Goody climb up into the loft and then followed him, but all he saw was hay. Sneezing from the dust, Tean went back down.

"This is your last chance," Tean said. "If you know anything about it, now's the time to say it."

"I haven't seen that kid in a couple of weeks. Hell, you're sure he's missing? He never came around real regular. Maybe he's just mucking around somewhere else now."

Tean studied the interior of the barn once more, saw nothing that gave him any ideas, and said, "I think it's time for me to do a little walking, Mr. Goody."

Goody shifted his weight. "Listen, I told you everything you asked, and I've got an appointment—"

"No, you don't," Tean said. "I'm not moving that truck, and you're not taking those bighorns. I'm sure you've got some oil executive or snot-nosed Silicon Valley wunderkind who's going to be really disappointed, but that's life."

"Listen, son, you don't have any idea—get your butt back here."

But Tean was already halfway to his Ford. Jem was still sitting with his head in his hands. Tean tapped on the glass of the passenger window, and Jem's head came up. His eyes were red, and he seemed to be trying to orient himself. He opened the door.

"Sorry about that," he said.

Shaking his head, Tean said, "No need."

"I'm ok."

"You don't need to be ok. I just wanted to let you know that I'm going to walk up into the mountains a little bit. If Benny liked to use the trails that run through the foothills, I might see if there's any sign he's been through here."

"He's dead," Jem said.

"Slow down," Tean said. "We don't know that."

Jem just nodded, but his face was bleak.

"I'm going to give myself an hour," Tean said. "I'd better give you my number. If I'm not back in an hour, call me. I might still have service."

Jem nodded and, when Tean recited the number, tapped it into his phone. Then he slid out of the truck. He was still carrying the plastic bowl.

"Why don't you stay here?" Tean said.

Jem shook his head.

"I think it would be better—"

"Please?" Jem said.

So they headed up the hill together. Goody stood near the trailer, hands in his pockets, watching them. The bighorns did a little more coughing; that was a nervous behavior, and Tean felt like he and the sheep were on the same page. After a few hundred yards of climbing the slope, they reached the edge of Goody's property. A simple rail fence, the wood bleached and brittle from the sun, marked the end of his land. They let themselves through the gate and followed a dirt path up into scrub sage and juniper. Here and there, a lodgepole broke out of the brush, or sometimes a poplar.

The trail led them into a fold of the mountains. A red cedar grew here, and then another. Then aspens, their leaves bright yellow in autumn and trembling. Fifty yards ahead of them, a creek, barely more than a trickle, cut down the side of the mountain. A mule deer, a doe, lapped at the water. The sun traced her outline like a halo. Tean touched Jem's arm, remembering too late the way Jem had reacted in the truck. Jem didn't shout this time, though; he stopped at the touch, and Tean pointed. To Tean's surprise, Jem smiled when he saw the doe. It wasn't the gameshow smile, either. It was soft and sad and wondering.

Tean knew that feeling, knew that it could come even during heartbreak. He knew what it was like when the sun was right, when the air smelled like juniper, when your mouth tasted like trail dust, and then something happened. It could be like this: a doe lapping from a creek, the waters shining like someone had knitted them out of silver. Or it could be a patch of cool shade, where you stood staring up at the canyon walls, orange and pale gray. It could be a moose forcing its way clear from an elderberry brake. It was never the same thing twice, whatever it was. It touched you, and your skin tightened, and your breath sharpened, and something inside, something that might be the soul, caught fire and flared for an instant. And then it went out, and the world was back at arm's length.

A cottontail broke out of a clump of cheatgrass, shooting across the path, and the doe sprang away from the creek, disappearing into the stunted trees below them. Jem let out a soft breath, and he glanced at Tean. Then his gaze came back and lingered.

"What?" Tean said.

Jem just shook his head, pushed the glasses back up Tean's nose, and shook his head again.

When they followed the path around a Douglas fir, Tean caught Jem's arm again. He grabbed an aluminum plate from the side of the path and held it up.

Squeezing his eyes shut, Jem nodded.

"You can go back—"

"No," Jem said, and he opened his eyes and started forward again.

After another hundred yards, Tean spotted something black up the slope to their right, beneath a granite overhang.

"Stay here," Tean said, and he started up the mountain.

Footsteps crunched through autumn-dry weeds behind him.

Tean sighed and kept going. Then he stopped.

"Jem, go back."

"No, I—"

"Jem, get back on the trail. Right now."

Jem stopped walking, but he didn't turn around. His breathing was shallow and rapid.

"It's him," Jem said.

"Please go back on the trail. I don't want you to see this."

"Oh my God," Jem said, and then he started toward the overhang.

"Jem, scavengers have gotten to the body. You shouldn't see him—"

Jem scrambled up the slope. Tean turned, tried to catch him, and instead got shoved out of the way. Tean landed on his butt, slid down the slope a few feet, and frantically got to his feet.

But it was too late. Jem knelt next to Benny's body: the face shredded, the eyes plucked out, the throat ripped open, the chest violated, heart and lungs and liver and kidneys long since devoured. Jem wasn't crying. He just rocked back and forth, one hand on Benny's leg, breathing those shrill, frantic breaths.

21

Somehow, Tean got Jem away from Benny. Somehow, Tean got him back to the truck.

Goody was gone; marks in the buffalo grass showed where Goody had driven his truck and the stock trailer around the Ford.

Jem refused to get into the truck; he finally sat at the edge of the drive, his butt on the blacktop, his feet in the grass, staring off into the distance. Tean made phone calls: first, the Tooele County sheriff; then, DWR conservation officers.

Sheriff McLillian got there first. She was a stout woman with her dark hair cut short and a way of curling her lip when she spoke that Tean at first took for contempt and then decided was nerves. Tean gave her a sanitized version of events. She made Tean run through all of it a couple of times, but she came back to one question again and again.

"And where's Brother Goody?"

Tean told her all of it, starting with the bighorns. A few Tooele deputies showed up, and then Jamal Harris and Maddie Beck arrived, conservation officers Tean knew personally. Jamal was black, tall and rangy, and he wore a crusher hat. Maddie was white, almost as tall as Jamal and big boned. She wore a rainbow bandana on her arm.

"I saw scat," Tean said. "It looked like a cougar dragged him up there."

The relief on the sheriff's face was embarrassing. "Well, that solves it," she said. "Animal attack."

"Not necessarily," Tean said. He looked at Jamal and Maddie.

Jamal said, "We'll see if we can find a kill site."

"And the cougar," Maddie said.

Tean nodded. "We need the cougar. The ME will have to make the decision about cause and manner of death, but I want to be able to give them all the information we can."

After a brief conversation, Maddie and Jamal headed up the mountain with the deputies. The sheriff stayed where she was.

"Do you need us to stay?" Tean asked.

"I've got your information," McLillian said. "I'll call you if I have any follow-up questions."

"Sheriff, this wasn't an animal attack. You need to start looking for someone dangerous and clever. Benny's list—"

"You told me all about the list, Mr. Leon. I don't need to hear about the list again. From what I can tell, that poor boy got a ride out here with his friends, did some camping and hiking just like he always did, and had a terrible accident. I'm sure that's how the ME will see it too."

"Have you been paying attention? We found half his gear in a DWR dumpster. Why would he leave half his gear, including his backpack and tent, and then head up here to camp?"

"He was hiking, then."

"Carrying an aluminum mess kit?"

"I don't know how that boy's mind worked."

"And the bowl down at Goody's gate?"

"You tell me," the sheriff said. "What'd he do? Leave a trail of breadcrumbs all the way up the driveway?"

"I don't know, but Goody had plenty of reason to—"

"I've heard just about enough about Brother Goody," McLillian said. "Now, listen: the DWR has officers here, and I've got my deputies here, and everything's pretty well in hand. You told your story. I think it's time for you to head on out."

"What kind of two-bit operation are you running here? A boy was killed. You're not trying to help an old lady find Mittens. This is a murder investigation, and I'm telling you that Benny left a list of suspects. If you'd take a look—"

"Mr. Leon, this becomes a murder investigation when the ME tells me it's a murder investigation. Until then, it's a suspicious death, and we're treating it as such. I've got fine deputies, and—"

"I watched those dumb fucks," Tean said, his voice slipping into a shout. "One of them couldn't even tell if his radio was on!"

McLillian's mouth pursed, and red blotched her face.

Before she could speak, though, a hand came to rest at the small of Tean's back. Tean glanced over, surprised to see Jem, so pale he looked bloodless, standing next to him.

"Come on," Jem said.

"Not until I explain a few more things to the sheriff."

Jem applied pressure until Tean let himself be guided away. They got in the truck, and Tean started down the hill. The gate was still open, and they merged out onto Route 36, heading north. For the first mile, the only sound was the thrum of tires on pavement.

"Jem, I'm so sorry."

Jem waved the statement away and said, "You can just drop me anywhere."

"I don't think that's a good idea."

"Thanks for doing this. Thanks for helping me. You're a really good guy." His breath hitched. "Just—just drop me anywhere."

Tean shook his head.

"I'm ok," Jem said. He had that horrible gameshow smile again.

"No," Tean said, "you're not."

He drove home. When he parked, Jem unclipped his seat belt and said, "Thanks again."

"Come upstairs."

"No, I should go. We found Benny, and I should go."

"Do you have a flight booked?"

"What?"

"Your flight? When's your flight home? Or do you still need to book one?"

Jem started to laugh. Wiping his eyes, he managed to say in between fits of laughter, "No flight."

Tean went around, opened the passenger door, and said, "Let's go upstairs."

This time, Jem nodded, but he was still laughing in fits and wiping his eyes. Scipio bounded off the sofa to greet them, crashing into Tean first. Jem leaned up against the doorway, his body rigid, while Scipio licked his hands and nosed his leg. Jem barely seemed to be breathing.

"I'm sorry," Tean said. "He just needs a walk."

"It's ok."

"Leave him alone," Tean said to Scipio. "Let's get your harness."

At the word, Scipio started leaping and bucking, his paws slipping on the linoleum, every movement communicating instant, uncontrollable happiness. Some of the tension seemed to go out of Jem, and the blond man wiped his face again.

"Are you ok if I take him out right now?"

"Yes," Jem said. "I'm ok. I am. I'm really ok."

Tean considered the unhealthy shine in Jem's eyes and said, "Maybe you should come with us."

So they walked south to Liberty Park, which had nice old oaks and cottonwoods, thick grass, and long walking paths. A pair of middle-aged men jogged past. On the basketball court, a group of girls was playing three on three. A young family — there were so many young families — was having a picnic: the parents looked like they were still in college, and they had two young kids crawling on a blanket. Near the end of the loop, a homeless man rattled a Nesquik container at them, coins clinking inside the plastic, and shouted, "There's my good buddy! How's you doing?" Jem gave him a half wave, and the homeless guy burst out laughing.

Scipio had to stop and smell everything, of course, and he was vigorously inspecting what looked to Tean like every other stretch of curb when Jem said, "Ok, I'm sorry about that earlier. I've got it under control."

On the other side of the park, someone was playing music — pop, with a girl telling off her ex-boyfriend. A kid on a bike whizzed past them, the chain on his bike a little too loose and rattling. When Scipio decided he'd had enough, Jem and Tean moved on, following the path around the south edge of the park, where a bridge crossed a pond. They took the bridge, their steps ringing out on wood, the structure vibrating faintly under them. When Tean touched the painted-black railing, it was hot.

"What if you try something?" Tean said when they were on solid ground again. "What if you try letting yourself not be ok for a little while?"

Jem opened his mouth, stopped, and scrubbed his knuckles against his beard. His eyes were full, and he shrugged.

They walked home. While Tean removed the harness, Jem stood at the sliding glass door, staring out at the mountains, burning with the autumn colors of the scrub. Then Jem turned and said, "I can still smell him."

"I'm sorry. I really didn't want you to see that."

"No, I needed to see it." Then he stood there, plucking at his clothes, his face blank.

"Maybe you should take a shower," Tean said.

"Yeah." But he just stood there.

"Jem," Tean said, "go take a shower."

"Yes, ok."

"Leave your clothes outside, and I'll start a load of laundry."

He nodded, already taking stiff steps toward the bathroom, peeling off the gray tee. A long scar ran diagonally across his back. Then he disappeared down the hall.

When the bathroom door shut, Tean gathered the clothes that Jem had left on the floor, and then he picked up the dirty clothes from the day before. After a moment's hesitation, he grabbed the new stuff that Jem had bought; new clothes always needed to be washed before wearing them. He ran downstairs to the apartment's laundry facility, started the load, and then walked east a couple of blocks. He stopped at Trader Joe's, got pinto beans and chicken breasts and tortillas, and then he did a second pass through the store and got lettuce and limes and carrots and onions. Then he had to go west, passing his apartment and going a couple of blocks in the other direction to the state liquor store. He bought a six-pack of Modelo Negra, and then he added a bottle of Everclear, his face hot. He paid and went home.

Scipio nosed into him as soon as he was through the door.

"No," Tean said quietly, "it's not time for dinner."

The shower was still running, so Tean started working on the food. He didn't have a recipe, but he'd seen his mom make this meal a hundred times, and he figured all food pretty much was the same, so it couldn't be that hard. He boiled the chicken breasts, sliced the onion and the carrots, washed the lettuce, and mashed the canned pinto beans with hot canola oil. Then he realized he was missing something and added salt. By that point, the chicken was done, so he shredded it, felt a burst of inspiration, and added cumin. Everything except the salad was going to be fatty and heavy. Comfort food.

It took a moment for Tean to realize that he didn't hear the shower, but there was no sign of Jem. Tean ran downstairs, switched the wet laundry into the dryer, and sprinted back up. Still no Jem. The smell of hot oil and boiled chicken filled the small apartment, and Scipio whined, so Tean filled his bowl. Scipio ignored the food and whined again.

"What?" Tean asked.

Scipio took a few steps toward the hall and looked back at Tean. "Jem?"

No answer; downstairs, the Duarte brothers must have broken something again because their dad was giving them hell.

Scipio whined again.

Tean went down the hall. The bathroom door was open; humid air, perfumed with a hint of Equate soap, rolled out, but the bathroom itself was dark. Tean nudged the door open. The mirror was still fogged.

Turning, he rapped lightly on the bedroom door.

"It's your room," Jem said. "You don't have to knock."

"I thought maybe you were asleep," Tean said, pushing open the door.

Jem lay on the bed, one of Tean's thin blue towels around his waist. He was muscular; Tean had already known that, but now he could see his shoulders and arms, the developed chest, the hint of abs, the powerful thighs and calves. Those muscles had come from good genes and from periods of hard labor in Jem's life; they weren't gym muscles. A hint of dark blond hair showed just above the towel, and Tean yanked his eyes back up to Jem's face.

But Jem wasn't looking at him; he was flipping through *Gilead*. Tean had left the book on his nightstand. Jem would flip pages, scan the text, and flip pages.

"Do you like Marilynne Robinson?"

A smile flashed behind the beard and then vanished. Jem lowered the book. "I'm more of a TV and movies guy."

"That's one of my favorites."

Jem scooted sideways on the mattress, the towel pulling open to reveal several more inches of his thigh, the dark blond hair thick over muscle. Then he patted the bed.

"I'm making dinner," Tean said. "I know you might not feel hungry, but you need to eat something."

Jem patted the mattress again.

"I made refried beans and a salad, and I'm going to fry up flautas right before we eat."

This time, Jem just propped himself on his elbow and ran a hand through his hair.

"Just for a minute," Tean said, kicking off his shoes and dropping onto the bed. But Jem didn't say anything, and Tean had no idea what to say, and the silence cocooned him, drew tighter and tighter until his chest felt like it was being crushed. Jem was still staring at the book, but he reached out now, laying one hand flat on Tean's stomach. The weight and heat of his hand made Tean close his eyes for a moment. Then he reached up, fingers closing around Jem's wrist.

Jem clicked his tongue without looking up from the book.

Tean hesitated. Then his grip relaxed, his fingers still curling around Jem's wrist but no longer trying to move his hand.

"Why do you like this book?" Jem asked.

"It's beautiful."

Lowering the novel, Jem studied him.

That same constricting thrill tightened around Tean again, and he found himself talking. "It's about a Calvinist preacher in Iowa."

"Sounds like a Michael Bay movie," Jem said.

"Who's Michael Bay?"

"Oh God," Jem said. "We have so much work to do."

"I don't know how to explain it, I guess. It's about God, finding God, I guess. And it's about predestination."

"What's predestination?"

"Some Christian religions believe that you're either already saved by grace or not, no matter what you do. Predestined, you know? You've got a ticket to heaven or a ticket to hell, and nothing's going to change that. It's based on some passages in Paul's epistles, and it's more complicated than that. I'm not explaining it very well."

"You explained it well." Jem's hand moved now in a light circle on Tean's stomach. The ring of heat coiled inside Tean. His face was hot; he thought about grabbing a pillow, using his hand, anything to cover himself down there. Jem didn't notice, or at least he acted as if he didn't; he just said, "I thought you were done with being Mormon."

"I don't think anyone's ever done with it."

"What does that mean?"

"I don't believe it, I don't practice it, I don't want anything to do with it. But that's how my brain was wired for twenty years, and you can't get rid of that kind of programming. All you can do is deal with it."

"Why are you reading a book about God and predestination if you're an atheist?"

"I don't know what I am," Tean said. The friction of Jem's hand had started a fire that burned everywhere, every inch of him blazing. "But I think there's something bigger than me. Something transcendent. I want to find it."

"Why?"

Tean shook his head.

Jem stopped rubbing, but his hand stayed where it was, heavy, pinning Tean to the bed. "The drinking, the stuff with Ammon," Jem said. "Is that because you feel bad? Guilty?"

"That's a pretty personal question."

"You told me not to talk about stuff I don't understand. Maybe I want to understand."

Tean hesitated. The fact was that nobody had asked. Nobody had wondered. Ammon had said things. Ammon had explained things. But Ammon had never asked.

"No," Tean said.

"No, you don't feel guilty?"

"No."

"Then why?"

"Ammon—" Tean's eyes prickled, and he had to shut them. "He just likes certain things. And I'm weird and have all these inhibitions. Hang-ups. I don't know what you'd call them. So if I get blasted, presto change-o, all of a sudden it's easy to do the stuff he wants."

Tean waited for the worst of it, for Jem to ask what Ammon wanted.

Instead, the mattress shifted as Jem moved, and a fingertip traced the hot line of tears from the corner of Tean's eye.

"Can I kiss you?" Jem asked.

Tean took a wet breath and nodded.

Gently, Jem removed Tean's glasses and kissed him. His lips were dry and chapped, and he tasted like spearmint mouthwash and something else, something that was just Jem. When the kiss broke, Tean could hear himself, his breath whistling in his lungs. He opened his eyes.

Jem had ditched the towel. The hand that had rested on Tean's belly drifted down and squeezed, and Tean squeaked and blushed.

"I don't—" Tean mumbled. "I don't know if I should—"

"He goes home to his wife and kids."

"I know."

"Did he make you promise to be exclusive?"

"No."

Jem ran his hand lightly between Tean's legs. "Then you've got to decide. What do you want?"

"You're not thinking clearly," Tean whispered. "You're grieving, and you want to feel better."

"Yes and yes." Jem's pupils were huge. "You told me it was ok not to be ok for a while. This is me not being ok. But that doesn't mean I don't also want this, really want this. Want you."

"You're going to hate me for taking advantage of you."

Laughing, Jem swung one leg over Tean's body, sitting astride his legs. "I don't think you understand who's taking advantage of whom here."

"I'm terrible at sex. You're going to be disappointed, and I'm going to be embarrassed, and it's going to ruin everything."

"Well," Jem said with a smirk, "lucky for you, you're about to enroll in a fast-track program."

"I—"

Jem kissed him again and sat back. His blue-gray eyes reminded Tean of that last point of sky where it blended into the Great Salt Lake.

"Just let me have a couple of drinks," Tean said, struggling to sit up.

Jem flattened him to the bed with one hand. He kissed him again, and the kissing went on for a while, one of Jem's hands sliding up under Tean's shirt, the other cupping his head or playing with his ears or stroking his neck. For the first few minutes, Tean did nothing. Then he ran his hands up and down Jem's thighs, feeling the tight muscles there. One hand slid around Jem's back.

"Would you please play with my dick already?" Jem whispered between kisses.

Tean did, and he found Jem to be very responsive and very vocal. In fact, Jem seemed to do a lot of talking during sex, which Tean couldn't help comparing to Ammon. Jem told Tean what he liked, he told Tean how to touch him, he offered suggestions, and he was very loud when he got what he wanted. He told Tean sweet, silly things that were obviously untrue.

"God, you're so hot . . . God, you're so good at this . . . Fuck yeah, fuck, you are fucking fantastic."

And Tean knew what was expected of him.

"Oh fuck," Tean said. "Yes, fuck yeah." He struggled for a moment and then managed to say, "Give me that big cock."

Jem started laughing.

"What?" Tean said.

Still laughing, Jem buried his face in Tean's shoulder.

"I told you," Tean said, his cheeks hot as he shoved Jem, trying to dislodge him. "I told you this was a mistake."

"No, no, no," Jem said, grinning, obviously trying hard not to laugh.

"Get off," Tean said.

They wrestled for a minute, and it ended with Jem pinning Tean's wrists over his head.

"Get off me," Tean said.

"I'm sorry I laughed," Jem said, but the smile was still dancing at the edge of his lips. "You just . . . you sounded like one of those computer-generated voices."

"This is so embarrassing. Please just let me go."

"No, wait, please. One more chance."

Tean rolled his eyes, but it was so gratifying to have someone else be the one to ask that he found himself relenting.

Jem kissed his neck and whispered, "I don't need to hear you say anything unless you want to say it. And I don't need you to do anything unless you want to do it. Ok?"

Tean nodded.

"Can we take this off?" Jem asked, plucking at the green flannel shirt.

Tean nodded again, reaching for the buttons, but Jem pushed his hands away. He undid the buttons quickly, and Tean arched his back to help Jem tug the shirt free. Jem's mouth was hot and wet across Tean's chest, biting and nipping and kissing. The resistance of his beard dragging across sensitive skin was like fire. After a few more minutes, his hands tensed at Tean's waistband, and he looked up.

"Yes," Tean whispered and bit his lip. "Please."

"God," Jem said, "you have no fucking idea how hot you are."

Jem kissed his way down Tean's legs, sliding down so that Tean couldn't reach him. His beard burned the tender skin on the inside of Tean's thighs. One hand stroked Tean lightly through black briefs. Tean tried to reach down, rubbing Jem's shoulders, until Jem looked up with a small smile.

"Relax," he said. "Put your hands behind your head and just relax. I told you: I don't need you to do anything for me." Then he hooked his thumbs through the leg openings in the briefs and raised an eyebrow.

Tean nodded.

"Hands behind your head."

Tean put his hands behind his head.

Smirking, Jem yanked the briefs down. The combination of wet fabric and cool air made Tean gasp. The feel of Jem's hand made him gasp again.

"Just so you know," Jem said, still smirking, his hand moving slow and then fast and then slow, and Tean unable to control the series of shuddering noises, "those sounds you're making right now are just about the hottest fucking thing in the universe." Then he bent and took Tean in his mouth.

Tean lasted only a few seconds. He tried to warn Jem. He managed to say his name, and then a long, groaning oh escaped him, and he came.

With an almost aggressive look of self-satisfaction, Jem came up. He brought himself off in a few quick jerks, coming on the bed, and then he sagged forward, his face resting against Tean's leg. He roused himself, climbed up, and then hesitated.

Tean looped an arm around his neck and kissed him.

"I should —" Jem said, sliding toward the edge of the bed. He looked at Tean and must have caught something on Tean's face. He stopped. Some emotion Tean didn't understand moved through Jem's eyes, and he squirmed back toward Tean. "Do you like to be big spoon or little spoon?"

"I don't know," Tean said.

Jem smiled softly. He curved himself around Tean, laid an arm across his chest, and kissed the side of his neck.

Tean's last thought before sleep was that, regardless of his general dislike of being touched, being little spoon was pretty fucking awesome.

22

Jem slept, and when he woke, the apartment was dark, and his arm was asleep. He shifted, trying to get some feeling back in his fingers, and a tail whopped him across the back. Then a tongue was in his ear, on his cheek, in his eye. The rush of panic came first, and he shoved Scipio away. Then, after a few breaths, he managed to say, "Good boy, good boy," and stroke Scipio's ears. The Lab accepted this with dignified approval.

Jem cleaned up in the bathroom, noticed his clothes were all still missing, and went back to the bed for the towel. Tean lay on his back, his eyes open. The doc smiled shyly.

"Hi," Jem said.

Tean stretched, showing off all that wiry muscle, his ribs, the stripe of fur down the center of his chest. "Hungry?" he asked.

"Definitely," Jem said, licking his lips.

"Perv."

Jem laughed.

"Is this—" Tean said and then stopped.

"Is it what?"

Tean's dark eyes drifted across Jem's face, and he shrugged.

"It's whatever we want it to be," Jem said. "It can just be fun. I'm not trying to make your life more complicated. I like you. How's that?"

"Good," Tean said. "I think."

"And I know you're already desperately in love with me, so you don't need to say it out loud."

The pillow hit Jem in the face.

"Go ahead and wash up," Jem said, laughing. "I'll warm up dinner."

In the kitchen, Jem turned on the heat under the beans and tossed the salad with oil and lime juice and salt. He poured a little oil in a skillet, warmed the corn tortillas, and ran filling down the center of each one. He rolled the flautas and fried them a second time until the tortillas were crispy.

"I didn't know you were a cook," Tean said. He leaned against the counter, toweling his hair, the end result messier than ever. Those huge, ugly black glasses were sliding down his nose again, and he barely caught them in time. "I should be doing that. I was trying to do something nice for you."

"This is very nice," Jem said. "And I don't mind helping. I'm actually not much of a cook, by the way. But I kind of had to figure out the basics, you know? Sometimes LouElla would be gone for a day or two, and she didn't keep a lot of easy meals around the house. I'd steal donuts and breakfast cereal—the kind full of sugar, the good stuff—from Walmart, but we'd all get sick of it after a while. Sometimes I'd get one of those rotisserie chickens too, and that helped, but eventually I figured out my life would be easier if I just learned how to make a few cheap, basic meals." He smiled as he stirred the refried beans. "Lots of beans and rice."

Scipio had made his way to the slider, and he was barking at a squirrel who was trespassing on the privacy fence. At the sink, Jem rinsed his hands, glancing over his shoulder to ask where the plates were. He stopped when he saw Tean's face.

"That's horrible," Tean said. "I didn't know—I mean, I knew from your reaction that you hadn't been treated well, and you said she only did it for the money, but I had no idea . . ." His gaze moved down from Jem's face.

Shaking water from his hands, Jem said, "Yes."

"What?"

"She gave me that scar. The one on my back."

"Oh my gosh." Tean looked like he might cry. "Oh my gosh."

"Spoiler alert," Jem said, smiling, "I survived."

Tean wiped his eyes.

"Sorry," Jem said, "I didn't mean to—"

"I just had no idea." He wiped his eyes again. And again.

"Ok," Jem said, laughing quietly as he passed him the towel. "It's ok."

"It's not ok. It's not anywhere close to ok."

"Well, I'm here, and I'm alive, and I'm reasonably functional. What do you say to eating?" Tean was still mopping his eyes with the towel, so Jem found the plates, served the food, and carried it to the dinette table. Steering Tean over to the table, he said, "I shouldn't have told you; I'm sorry. It's weird to tell people things like that."

"No, it's not weird," Tean said as he sat. "And I can't believe I'm the one who's falling apart. I should be helping you."

"You're helping," Jem said. "Just having someone to talk to so I don't, you know, dwell on it, that's helping." He sat, took a bite of the refried beans, and froze. It took a lot of willpower to swallow and then slowly set down the fork.

"Are they ok?"

"Yeah," Jem croaked, staggering to the sink for water. "They're great."

"There's beer in the refrigerator," Tean said.

After a glass of water, Jem was pretty sure he wasn't going to die from the lethal dose of salt he'd just ingested, so he grabbed a beer—Modelo Negra, a good choice—and said, "You want one?"

"Um."

"Let me guess," Jem said with a grin. "You mostly drink water."

"It's healthy."

So he filled a clean glass and brought it over, and then he opened his beer. "You don't drink because of how you were raised?"

A blush spread under Tean's light brown skin, and he shook his head. "No, I don't drink because I think beer tastes gross."

"What about wine?"

"I tried something I bought at Trader Joe's." He made a face.

"What about a cocktail?"

"Oh, sometimes I'll mix Everclear with Kool-Aid."

"Jesus Christ."

"What?"

"I'm just planning all the things you need to experience. Good food, good booze, good TV, preferably from the 90s. And more good sex."

"Too bad you have to go back to California," Tean said, adjusting the silverware and looking at his plate. "I guess this'll be another crash course."

Jem sipped the Modelo, enjoying the beer's dark, caramel notes. He figured death by salty beans was probably not going to get him a medal, so he tried the salad next. It was great: fresh, crisp, the lime juice providing just enough flavor. Then a taquito. It was perfectly crispy and crunchy, but the filling tasted like . . . chicken and cumin.

"The beans are a little salty," Tean mumbled.

Jem choked on his beer and managed a strangled, "No, they're great." When he'd cleared his airway, he said, "Try this." He smeared some of the beans on a piece of flauta, and the combination was actually surprisingly good.

"Huh," Tean said.

"We'd do that when LouElla made home fries."

Tean cut up his flauta, mixing it with the beans.

"You can ask me," Jem said. "I only freaked out the other day because I was already so worried about Benny."

"Did you live with her a long time?"

"Actually, no. Not quite two years."

"I thought foster care was, you know, supposed to be temporary."

Jem smiled.

"I sound like such an idiot," Tean said.

"No, you're just a really good guy," Jem said, "and reality sucks. So, here's the short version. I've got no idea what my dad's deal was. As far as I know, I never met him. My mom was on meth by the time I was five. I didn't know that, actually. I just knew she'd be gone for a long time, and when she'd come back, she'd smell funny; a social worker accidentally told me what she'd been doing, actually, the first time I got busted with weed. Anyway, somebody called in a report on my mom, and Child and Family Services put me in foster care. I was in six or seven homes."

"You don't remember?"

"One of them was only for half a day," Jem said, "so I don't know if I should count it. This guy tried to break into the bathroom while I was in there. I was, um, nine, I think. I bit his arm down to the bone."

Tean dropped his fork.

"Ok," Jem said. "In hindsight, I should not have told you that."

"No," Tean said. "You can tell me. I want to know."

"I wasn't a very good kid," Jem said. "That's why I bounced around a lot."

"Six homes over thirteen years," Tean said. "That's about two years at each one on average."

"Well," Tean said. "I didn't exactly spend all that time in foster care." He carefully prepared another piece of flauta, balancing it on the fork. "I met Benny at LouElla's. I was thirteen, and Benny was twelve. For some reason, we just kind of clicked. He was carrying around a stuffed animal the day he showed up at LouElla's, and he was really skinny because they hadn't diagnosed him with diabetes yet—and they hadn't put him on clozapine either. And Benny was never really in the same world with the rest of us. One day, he'd done something to piss off LouElla; honestly, I can't even remember what. But when she was really mad, she had this antenna from an old RCA TV, and she'd tie a piece of cloth around it and, well, you know. It didn't leave marks—not very clear ones, anyway—but it hurt like hell. It scared Benny to death." Jem had to stop and set down his fork. He wrapped his hands around his knees. Outside, music came on: Ed Sheeran, "Shape of You." Someone was singing along, a woman who was a little off key. "I was really protective of Benny, even back then." Jem had to stop again, his fingers aching as he clutched his knees. Scipio's nail clicked on the linoleum, and then a wet nose pressed against the side of his hand. Jem let out a harsh breath.

"Leave him alone," Tean whispered.

"No, it's ok," Jem said, and he forced himself to ruffle Scipio's ears. In return, he got a wet tongue across his palm. "Anyway, LouElla got really mad at Benny that day, and for some reason I was just done. I couldn't stand it anymore. So I grabbed Benny and tried to run, but it was like trying to get a log moving. LouElla was just laughing about it. She came after us like it was a game. We ended up in the bathroom, and I pushed Benny down into the tub and tried to cover him." He grabbed the Modelo, fumbled the bottle, and it fell sideways, spilling beer. "Shit."

Tean still had the towel across his lap, and he righted the bottle and mopped up the beer. Jem put his finger in a droplet of beer near the edge of his plate, and he traced a pattern on the tabletop.

"So, that's how I got the scar," he said. "And the whole point of this story was that I got so mad that I pushed her. She fell and hit her head on the vanity, broke a tooth. She told everybody who'd listen that I'd tried to kill her. Nobody asked about why I needed stitches from shoulder to hip. People will believe anything if they want to believe it. Or if they're afraid it's true." He shook his head. "I think things are different now; I think people are a lot more willing to listen to kids. But back then, that wasn't the case. So I spent the rest of the time, until I was eighteen, at Decker Lake." Tean's face was blank, so Jem added, "Juvie."

"Geez."

"I'll admit, I made it worse for myself. I was really upset. Really angry. And when I got out of control, I just made more trouble for myself." Jem laughed, heard the shakiness in his own voice, and said, "I think I need more beer."

Tean got it for him, and when he set it down, he laid a hand on Jem's shoulder. Jem took a long drink, counting to ten before he removed Tean's hand, squeezed it once, and let it fall.

"So, now you know," Jem said. "You just had sex with and made dinner for a notoriously violent criminal."

Shaking his head, Tean shuffled his flatware again.

"What about you, Doc? Any dark secrets?"

"My big, dark secret was that I was gay."

"You are?"

A smile broke free for a moment, and Tean rolled his eyes.

"I started to guess when I had your dick in my mouth," Jem said.

"Ok."

"But it's nice to clear the air."

Tean just shook his head, still smiling a little. Then the smile faded. "I've had this great life. Both my parents are alive and well. They made sure I always had healthy food, got me to do my homework, took me to church every week. I honestly don't even know how you can be who you are, be this amazing, successful, happy person, after everything you've been through."

"Yeah?" Jem said. "When I asked you what it was like growing up Mormon, you said it was hard."

"It was. But it wasn't anything special. Having to hide who I was, always pretending. That messed with my head. But a lot of gay guys go through that—it's more about being closeted than particular to being raised Mormon. Honestly, I've had it super easy."

"You're not being fair to yourself," Jem said. "You wouldn't be talking this way if I were telling you a story about growing up closeted and repressed and being taught directly and indirectly to hate myself. You'd be a lot more compassionate to someone else."

Tean shrugged.

"What about—" Jem said and then caught himself; he blamed the beer for even that much of the question slipping out.

"What about Ammon?"

"I know, I know. None of my business."

"I actually haven't ever talked to anyone about him. That's really weird, right?"

"It is what it is," Jem said. "You can talk about it when you're ready to talk about it."

"But us, after we just—"

"After I just swallowed your cum?"

Tean blushed and threw a piece of flauta at him.

"God," Jem said, smirking. "So innocent. Just a tender little rosebud."

"Oh my gosh, please don't say rosebud."

Jem's smirk got bigger.

Poking at the salad with his fork, Tean said, "We grew up together. You know how Mormon churches are organized?"

"Wards, stakes, something like that."

"Yeah. Wards are the smallest unit—the congregation. They're geographically assigned, and in Utah, that means really small geographic units. Sometimes just a few blocks. He lived two streets behind me; it doesn't sound like much, but it was a huge difference economically. My parents have always been scraping to get by. Ammon's dad is a cop, but his mom is a real estate agent who's made a fortune. We went to the ward, went to the same high school. We knew each other—we're the same age, and so we went to the same Sunday School class, we were in the same grade at school, sometimes in the same classes. We were friends, too. Ammon played football, basketball, and baseball."

"Let me guess," Jem said. "You were the quarterback."

"Ha ha."

"And you played center."

Tean sat back, folding his arms.

"And you pitched a wicked knuckleball."

"Are you done?"

"Thank you for indulging me," Jem said with a grin.

"It was nice, having a friend like Ammon. Everyone loved him. I mean, he was this perfect kid: held all the youth leadership positions, Eagle Scout, amazing athlete, great grades, polite, and, you know, handsome. And my parents bought a lot of our clothes at DI, which is kind of like Goodwill—"

"I did grow up here," Jem said.

"Right. Well, anyway, obviously I was also in love with him. But I knew that was impossible because as far as I could tell, I was a nice, straight Mormon kid just waiting to meet the right girl. And there wasn't a lot of pressure; Mormon kids are encouraged not to date seriously as teenagers, so it was easy to convince myself that things would click when I met the right girl after my mission. And then I went on my mission and—" Tean's voice shifted, taking on a note of wonder. "And Ammon was there. That seemed impossible. I mean, it does happen, but it's incredibly rare. Supposedly, the assignment for your mission is divinely given. And here Ammon was again. Like God had thrown us together. And then, a year into the mission, we were companions. Another thing that seemed impossible. We were in Lima. We had this apartment that fronted the Pacific. Every day, what I felt for him got bigger and stronger. I thought I was doing a good job of hiding it. And then one day he walked into the bathroom while I was taking a shower, and—and everything just happened. Perfectly. The way it was supposed to."

Jem pushed his plate away; he wasn't hungry anymore. "And what happened after, when you weren't wet and horny anymore?"

"Nothing. It was perfect. I didn't feel guilty. I didn't feel ashamed. I loved him, and finally everything in my life felt simple and clear and right. And then he got transferred to another part of Lima, and I was supposed to stay where I was."

"Supposed to?"

"They assigned me this new guy, fresh from the States, an Idaho farm boy. I lasted a couple of days, and then I got on a plane and came home. I knew who I was, and I knew I couldn't stay down there, couldn't keep pretending to be something I wasn't anymore."

"I guess that didn't go well with your parents."

"No, it didn't. They didn't disown me, but they came pretty close. I think the fact that I'm gay is the biggest tragedy, disappointment, whatever you want to call it, of their entire lives. I'd saved up the money to pay for it myself, so at least I didn't have to hear them whine about that."

"That's so fucking messed up," Jem said. "And Ammon?"

"He finished his mission," Tean said with a hard smile. "When he came home, we started up again. The night he got home, he snuck in through my back door, and he fucked me with one hand over my mouth to keep me quiet."

"Jesus."

"His situation was complicated. Is complicated. He's dealing with a lot of pressure. I honestly think his dad would kill him."

"He's a grown-ass man," Jem said. "He's in his fucking thirties."

"And he's got a wife now and kids. He's got responsibilities. His job—"

"Those were his choices."

"Maybe," Tean said. "He was going to come out. We'd talked it out. We'd figured out the whole thing. He was going to do it: divorce Lucy, quit his job, and move in with me." Tean gathered up the towel, now sodden with beer, and stood. "Lucy beat him to the punch and told him she was pregnant." Then he stood there, the wet towel dangling from one hand, staring around blankly. "I didn't think of dessert. I didn't plan anything for dessert."

Taking a long drink of Modelo, Jem pictured it: a dark alley, Ammon strolling along unaware, and then slamming a brick into the side of his head.

"I'm not trying to make any assumptions," Tean said, "but I wanted you to know you can stay here as long as you need to. If you're going to stay and make arrangements for Benny, I mean."

"Thank you." Jem took another drink and asked, "You agree with me, right? You believe Benny was murdered?"

"It's been a few intense days."

"I just need you to say yes or no."

"I think, based on what we saw on the video, and based on how Benny was found—I think it's unlikely he was attacked by a cougar while camping."

"Yes or no," Jem said, his eyes suddenly burning. "Please."

"It's not that easy," Tean said.

Jem swallowed and nodded.

"Let's wait and see what the ME can tell us. If the ME suspects an animal attack, he'll probably ask me to take a look. And if they can find the cougar, that would help too."

"Can I just say one thing?" Jem said. "You didn't imagine those weird phone calls. You didn't imagine that black SUV following you.

And neither of us imagined that Chevy running us off the road. This wasn't just about Benny, Doc. They're after you too."

"Let's hope not," Tean said, trying to smile.

Jem just nodded. He let it drop; no point in worrying Tean about it. The world had three clear categories: wolves, sheep, and that strange, uncertain ground where Benny and the doc fell. Jem had failed Benny. He didn't plan on failing again, so he had to stick around long enough to square things with Benny's killer and make sure the doc stayed safe.

23

The next days passed in a blur. For Jem, they had a strangely divided quality. At night, he was Jem Guthall. He could pack away his grief for Benny — still feeling it, but managing it, letting it out carefully in increments he could handle. He went for walks with Tean and Scipio, enjoying the mountain breeze, the October nights getting cold enough now that he could wrap an arm around Tean as they walked and Tean didn't protest. He made dinner — he insisted on making dinner — and although Tean still ate like a bird, he said thank you a lot, and he smiled this huge, unguarded smile when Jem put a plate full of food in front of him. Jem Guthall spent his nights sprawled on the couch, with Tean's legs across his lap, as he indoctrinated Tean in *Buffy the Vampire Slayer*.

"Did you know that there are people who really believe they're vampires?" Tean said during season two, episode twenty-one, "Becoming (Part 1)," right when Willow was learning the truth about the curse that gave Angel his soul.

"This is a really important part," Jem said.

"Most of them are probably just slightly delusional people," Tean said, "but some pretty horrific crimes have been committed by people who are convinced they need blood to survive. For example, in Oklahoma — "

Jem put a hand over Tean's mouth, pulled him against his chest, and let his chin rest on Tean's shoulder.

"This is for your own good," Jem whispered, and then he rewound the episode and started it again. Tean snuggled into him and, for a change, didn't have a single, terrifyingly bleak anecdote to share.

At night, Jem Guthall shared a bed with the man who was quickly becoming an important part of his life.

At night, lying in bed with Tean's body in the curve of his own — the doc always squirming away and then, once he was deeply asleep, snuggling back against Jem — he was most sensitive to the pain of losing Benny, and he could feel most clearly the frayed edges of the stories he was telling himself. But it was nice to believe he could be Jem Guthall for a while. And, as Jem had learned a long time ago, people would believe anything if they wanted it to be true. He knew he wasn't an exception.

During the day, though, he was Jem Berger, and Benny's loss was a wild thing that went through him with teeth and claws, the pain almost unbearable. On Thursday, he left Tean's apartment at the same time as the doc, walked a couple blocks south to where he'd stashed his Kawasaki, and called Chaquille. Jem didn't have a lot of resources for a situation like this, and Sammi was too young to drive. He negotiated with Chaquille for a few minutes, and they settled on Chaquille watching Goody's ranch for two hundred dollars a day. It wasn't like Chaquille needed to go to classes; he was apparently some kind of genius. After that, Jem called Tinajas.

"There's this really weird concept," Tinajas said, "called a job. You go in every day. You do the same thing. And you get paid."

"Sounds fucking awful," Jem said.

"What?"

"Can you put up a KSL ad for me? And Craigslist too? Put it under Announcements — Legal, Charity, and Lost & Found. Anywhere else you think makes sense."

"No."

"Please?"

"No. I'm tired of getting tangled up in your scams."

"I'll set you up with a nice guy."

"You're making this worse for yourself."

"I'll get you Jazz tickets."

Tinajas hesitated.

The morning was cool; the sun was cresting the Wasatch Mountains, the light in the streets was still blue and deep. Across the way, what Jem guessed was a repair store for small appliances was opening for the day. The sign overhead was yellow with red lettering, and it looked about thirty years old. The owner was probably eighty.

He was carrying an ancient curling iron in one hand as he pushed open the gate in front of the door. Who needed a curling iron repaired, Jem wondered, when you could buy a new one for ten bucks?

"Decent seats this time," Tinajas said.

"The best."

"I'm not talking some cheap-ass upper balcony where I need binoculars to see my boys."

"You'll be so close you'll need a towel for all the sweat."

"God, you're gross. Fine. What does the ad say?"

"You can tweak it, but I need it to sound old, confused, and vulnerable. Maybe something like, 'I am a patriarch in need of legal assistance. I am ninety-two years old, and the government is threatening to take away my license because I sideswiped a truck. I have to drive to buy groceries for my wife, who is blind and in a wheelchair. Please help me settle this matter out of court. If you know someone with a red Chevy with damage to the passenger side panel, please contact me and provide a picture. I will pay five hundred dollars for the right information.' And then you can fill in the rest."

Tinajas clicked and typed for a moment. Somewhere down the street, a bakery was putting out the smell of rising dough and cinnamon; today's breakfast had been cooked by Tean, which meant charcoal-briquette toast and scrambled eggs that were still runny. Jem's stomach rumbled.

"I kept the wording mostly the same," Tinajas said. "But I put it in all caps, with a few irregular lower-case letters just to mess things up. And I took out some of the punctuation. Oh, and I repeated a few words, you know, so it looks like his mind has turned to oatmeal."

"Perfect."

"Burner email is . . ." She hemmed. "patriarchdan25."

"Could you share it in a few places? Just to get it out in front of people?"

"Sure, boss. Anything else, boss?"

"A little less attitude, if it's not too much trouble."

"Remember who's going to be checking that burner email address."

Jem grinned. "Let me know as soon as you get something, please?"

"Where have you been? Kike said he went by twice to hook up, and you haven't been home."

"I've got something going right now," Jem said. He counted himself down from three and added, "Benny's dead."

"Jesus Christ. What?"

"Somebody killed him."

"That sweet kid." She was already crying; he could hear it in her voice. "Are you ok?"

"I will be."

"I want you to come over. I want to see you. You shouldn't be by yourself right now."

"I'm ok. Thanks, though."

"I want to see you."

"In a few days, after I have this settled."

"If you need anything, you call me. No matter what time it is."

"Thanks."

"Jem, you sound like you're going to do something stupid. Don't do something stupid."

"It might be stupid," Jem said, "but it needs doing."

Then Jem rode out to the mine. He watched from the shoulder of the freeway, waiting for Julie to emerge. He had patience and a lot of willpower, even if he didn't have much else, and it was easy to spot the silver BMW when it came down the access road at half past four. He followed her home to a house high on the bluffs in Draper, the damn thing probably worth a couple of million dollars, gray stucco and a slate roof and large windows that let him see almost every square inch inside. The only real surprise was that Julie wasn't the only one who got out of the BMW. Phil, the tough guy who looked like he worked security for the mine, emerged from the passenger side, carrying Julie's bags and following her into the house. As daylight failed and lamps went on inside the house, Jem could see all of it clearly: Phil opening a bottle of wine, Phil kissing Julie, Phil's hands sliding up under her plaid work shirt.

He called Chaquille and got the update: Goody was back at the ranch, and from what Chaquille could tell, he'd been telling the truth about employing three men to help him. Chaquille had followed two of them, who were probably brothers, back to an apartment on the north side of Tooele. He was going to track the third guy tomorrow. Jem reminded him to look for a red Chevy and a black SUV.

The next day was Friday, and instead of watching the mine from the freeway, he changed plans. He went back to his apartment in West Valley, climbed the fire escape, and rummaged through his closet. He found a mechanic's shirt with a name patch, and he found a trucker cap that had the iconic mud flap girl silhouette embroidered on the front. He swapped out his jeans for a less reputable pair, and then he grabbed one of those Priority Mail boxes you can grab for free at the post office—he had a whole stack of them—taped it shut, wrapped it in brown paper, and taped the paper. He added fresh clothes to a backpack—paying Chaquille was going to wipe out his slush fund, and he couldn't keep buying new clothes—and put the box on top of the clothes. Then he checked the clock on his phone and saw that he had two hours until he needed to be at the mines. He called Toro and asked him if he wanted to play Stranded Motorist.

"I'm tired of thirty percent," Toro said. He was Filipino, and he still had some of the accent. "I'm doing half the work; I should get half the score."

"You do thirty percent of the work," Jem said. "Barely. And you start giggling at the worst times."

"I want half."

"Have a great day, Toro. Don't spend too much time jerking off in between oil changes."

"Fine," Toro snapped. "Thirty."

Jem drove over to South Temple. On the north side of the street was Temple Square, the Mormon Mecca, which drew millions of visitors from across the world. Local Mormons also came to worship. Panhandlers and protesters mixed with neatly groomed men and women in conservative clothes. Some of the people who worked this block, Jem had heard, could make close to a hundred thousand dollars a year. No better way to pat yourself on the back after a nice face-to-face with God than by giving five bucks to the homeless lady with a newborn. Penny ran that schtick nine months a year—Jem could see her up ahead, wearing an enormous Opie t-shirt and holding Robbie on her shoulder. Robbie wasn't crying, but if Penny saw a good mark, sometimes she'd pinch the inside of his leg to get him going. Once, Jem had confronted her about it and threatened to get Child and Family Services on her. She'd been a lot faster than he expected, and the utility knife had opened a five-inch cut, almost perfectly straight, down his ribs.

Jem pulled up to a red curb, ignoring the signs, and parked. A few passersby gave him the evil eye, and he ignored them. Squatting next to the bike, he pretended to give it a once-over, as though trying to figure out what was wrong. In the process, he loosened the spark plug connector. Then he got on the bike again and tried to start it. Nothing. At that point, Jem got out his phone and had a loud conversation with nobody, expressing his frustration, doing his best to get worked up. A lot of it was in the voice, and he had learned early on not to do too much swearing—that brought disapproval instead of sympathy. He messed up his hair a few times, though, and he paced. When he disconnected the phone call, a young couple— they looked like they were twenty-one, maybe twenty-two, young and thin and white and shining with good-natured eagerness. They reminded Jem a little of Scipio.

"Sounds like you're having some trouble," the guy said, glancing at the girl. No rings, Jem noticed, so this was a date, and this guy was trying to impress.

They talked for a while. Jem was from out of town, California, and had been having bike trouble the whole way. He added a little spin: he'd gotten in trouble, just wanted a fresh start, his buddy had a job for him in North Dakota.

"You know anything about bikes?" Jem said.

As Jem had expected, the kid didn't, but he refused to say that outright. He was wearing a cheap suit, but he got down on his knees and looked at the bike and made a lot of manly, considering noises, and finally he shook his head.

"Sorry, man," the kid said. "I don't know what to tell you. Listen, I could ask my dad—"

At which point, Toro pulled up in his big red wrecker. Toro was a big guy with a big belly, and he climbed down from the truck, already swearing up a storm. He didn't even look at Jem. He just got to work, getting ready to load the bike and tow it.

"Hey," Jem said. "Hey, what do you think you're doing?"

Toro was pretty good at this part. He just pointed to the NO PARKING / VIOLATORS WILL BE TOWED sign.

"Just hold on," Jem said. "I called a friend. He's on his way right now."

Toro just grunted.

"You can't do that," Jem said. "That's my bike. My friend is coming right now."

"Look," Toro said. "I get two hundred dollars for every tow. If you can beat that, go for it."

Jem grabbed a small bundle of bills from his pocket. He counted them out. "I've got sixty-seven bucks right here. Come on, man. That's everything I've got. Please don't take my bike."

The guy and the girl were whispering.

"Sorry, buddy," Toro said, wheeling the bike toward the wrecker.

"Hold on," the kid said. He and the girl had put together a hundred and ninety bucks. "Look, I know it's not two hundred, but—"

Toro snatched it from them. He jabbed a finger at Jem. "You're really fucking lucky, buddy, that there are good people in this world. Get a fucking job, deadbeat."

Then he was gone.

The last part of the act was always kind of pleasant: lots of Christian well-wishing and hugging and handshakes. The girl even cried a little when Jem asked if they'd come visit him in North Dakota. He gave them a fake number, and he begged them to write down their address so he could mail them the money back when he had a job. They refused. By the time it had wrapped up, the guy and the girl leaving while Jem waited for his imaginary friend, they had left him with a mint-condition copy of the Book of Mormon, which Jem thought was number ninety-seven for him, but he wasn't sure because he hadn't counted the first few he'd been given.

He and Toro played it four more times before Jem had to go; Toro took home over three hundred bucks for less than two hours of work; Jem had a fresh six hundred and seventeen dollars in his pocket. He loved Salt Lake City.

Still wearing a little grin, he drove toward the mine, arriving a little after noon.

At the gate, the guard checked a clipboard and looked at the box Jem had prepared back at his apartment.

"You're not one of our regulars," he said.

"Tell me about it," Jem said. "You guys are in the middle of bumfuck nowhere."

"I can't let you in unless you're on the list."

"Not my problem, man. I'll drive back and tell them you dicked me. But I'm not coming out here again, and somebody needs this part bad — that's about the only reason they'd send me out here. I'm a goddamn mechanic, not some fucking courier."

The guard frowned. He was one of those guys who turned red and stayed red, like a tomato.

"All right," Jem said, turning the bike. He was pleased to see several trucks lined up behind him.

"Hold on, hold on."

"Call over there if you're not sure."

So the guard called over, and Jem's luck held: no answer.

"They're at lunch," the guard said.

"I can't waste my whole day doing this," Jem said, turning the bike again.

"Look," the guard said. "Just head straight over to the motor pool and drop it off."

"I need somebody to sign for it."

"Somebody'll be there to sign for it. I'll get somebody over there."

"God," Jem said, "this is the last time I do Mark a favor."

He eased the bike past the gate and headed to the motor pool. As he had noticed on his first visit, Dellengbauh had invested heavily in black SUVs, and a handful of them were parked in a fenced lot, either out of service or not needed today. The fence had a gate, but it was unlocked, and Jem let himself in. He walked carefully around each of the SUVs, checking the doors and body for signs of damage, in case Benny had struggled and might have left some sort of evidence. The windows were tinted, but from the right angle, he could see into each vehicle. They all had dirt and pebbles in the footwells, and the seats were stained, the upholstery worn in places. He didn't see any sign, though, that Benny had been in any of these SUVs.

Nobody had showed up yet, so Jem let himself into the motor-pool building. It smelled like automotive grease, cheap tobacco, and kitty litter. A beaten-up white Ram was up on a pneumatic lift, and Jem scored an iPad that somebody had left just sitting on a workbench. It was locked, but he figured he could still unload it for a hundred bucks. He shoved it in the backpack, took one last look around the shop, and left. He drove the benches for a while, still looking for the red Chevy, but he didn't see a truck that matched the one that had run him and Tean off the road.

He was about to leave when he heard a woman's voice.

"That's not what I'm upset about, and you know it," the woman said. Jem recognized the voice; it was Ruth-the-Intern. She must have been speaking on the phone because she paused as though listening and then spoke again. "I'm sick of that apartment. I'm sick of that car. I'm sick of having to squeeze every penny. You said things were going to be different."

Then a car door shut and an engine started. One of the black SUVs pulled out of the motor pool, and Jem studied it, waiting for it to turn. The tinted windows hid the driver, and he wondered if he'd been right recognizing Ruth's voice—and if she'd had anyone else with her. He ran back to his bike, but it took too long, and by the time he was headed out of the mine, he had lost her.

On Saturday, he prowled around the tailings ponds, looking for any evidence that Benny had been there. When he saw a dust plume and a black SUV coming out of the mine toward him, he jumped on his bike and left.

Chaquille had tracked the third ranch hand to his home, a tract house in Magna, and still hadn't spotted the red Chevy. Tinajas reported in with several emails responding to the online plea for help, and she forwarded the pictures, but none of them was a match.

That night, Jem got another call from Myers Bruce. He'd been ignoring the calls for days now, not yet willing to deal with the human shithole who had tried to buy child pornography off of him. But Chaquille was costing a fucking fortune, and Jem could only risk running the Stranded Motorist every so often. So he excused himself, stepped out onto the balcony, and shut the glass slider behind him. Then he texted a picture to Bruce. And then he called him.

"What the fuck is that?" Bruce shouted.

"That," Jem said, "is a picture of a prepubescent girl that you paid to have sex with.'

"I didn't—" The horror sapped Bruce's voice of its strength. "I never—"

"No," Jem said. "But I have an audio recording of you asking in specific detail for the type of kid you like. And my little friend helped me stage a photo op with you. So, as far as the police are concerned, you're now guilty of, God, I don't even know all the charges.

Solicitation of a minor, I think, although that's probably just the cherry on top."

"You can't do this," Bruce whined. "You sold me magazine scraps. You didn't even, I mean, I never would have done this."

"But you did do it, Bruce. You just were too fucking greedy and too fucking stupid to get what you wanted. That's on you."

"I would never — I never, never, never — "

"Here's what we're going to do, Bruce. Tomorrow, we're going to meet at City Creek, and you're going to give me a thousand dollars in cash. And you're not going to have any friends waiting to help you out. And you're not going to try to arrange any accidents for me. Do you know why you're not going to do that?"

Bruce was silent; in the lot of the dry cleaner that backed up to Tean's apartment, five teenagers were drinking Genesee and listening to Kendrick Lamar, a couple of them grinding against each other, the others just playing on their phones.

"You're not going to do anything stupid like that," Jem said, "because if you do, my friend is going to send all this stuff to the police with your name and phone number. Do you understand?"

One of the teenagers was howling at the moon like a wolf; another one had gotten on his knees and was pretending to perform cunnilingus. Today's damn kids, Jem thought with a hard grin. Weren't they all supposed to be wearing knee socks and Scouting bandanas?

"Speak up, Bruce," Jem said.

"Yes."

"Tomorrow. One thousand dollars. Same time, same place."

Jem disconnected, and then he shook off Jem Berger and let Jem Guthall go back inside with a guy he really wanted to be his boyfriend.

On Sunday, Tean asked where he was going.

"To visit a family friend," Jem said.

"I thought you did that yesterday."

"It's a different one."

Tean was currently scraping the burnt part off a piece of a toast. He frowned. "Do you want a ride?"

"No, thanks," Jem said. Pretending to check his phone, he added, "They're downstairs."

"Do you want — "

194

Jem kissed his cheek, and Tean blushed and dropped the toast. Scipio, patiently waiting, snagged it and carried it to his dog bed.

"When will you be back?"

"Tonight," Jem said. "I'll bring something for dinner," because Tean had been talking about making spaghetti, and Jem could only imagine how that would go wrong.

He jogged south, grabbed his bike, and rode over to City Creek. After he stashed the bike in an underground lot, he made his way upstairs and emerged next to a Nike store. Because it was the Lord's day, the mall was closed, although a few pilgrims in poorly fitted suits and calf-length skirts strolled arm in arm. The October sun was warm on the back of Jem's neck; the air smelled like mulch and perfume and, when a breeze kicked up, seared meat. Jem was pretty sure he was smelling a Big Mac.

Taking a seat on the bench where he had met Bruce last time, Jem checked the windbreaker's pockets: the paracord, the tube sock, the telescoping antenna, the barrette. Sometimes guys got angry. Even the meekest guy, if he felt cornered, could suddenly grow balls. Better to not let things get out of hand. Jem took out the tube sock, hunkered down next to the creek, and loaded loose river stones into the white cotton until it was a nice weight. Then, tying a knot at the top, he set it next to him on the bench.

Then all Jem could do was wait. He scanned the people who were taking advantage of the beautiful day. The ripple of water was soothing, mixing pleasantly with low voices and the tittering laugh of an older woman in a black-and-white polka dot dress. The sun glazed everything, turning the pale stone white, flicking little white crests onto the water. On Jem's next glance up and down the mall, he spotted Bruce, who was wearing a bucket hat pulled low and a khaki polo with rings of sweat under the arms. The polo made Jem smile; he decided he was going to take Tean shopping and make the doc buy a few outfits that weren't branded with the DWR—and maybe included a few colors beyond green and khaki.

He was still smiling when he glanced the other way and saw Ammon. The detective was leaning against the wall of the Nike store, near the entrance to the parking garage, in a shallow pool of shade. The smile dropped off Jem's face. Ammon was watching him, his gaze unwavering. He didn't nod or acknowledge Jem in any way. He just stood there, partially obscured by the corner of the building, observing.

"You can't do this," Bruce said as he dropped onto the bench. "You can't. I didn't do anything wrong. I didn't."

Jem wrenched his attention away from Ammon and turned to look at Bruce. The guy was a wreck: dark circles under his eyes, his face pasty and shiny with sweat, lips raw where he'd chewed them. He stunk too, a stale, flop-sweat reek that made Jem guessed that terror had kept Bruce from even basic hygiene. Today, he'd forgotten his huge sunglasses; this little sheep was so scared that he had forgotten the extreme caution he had practiced last time.

"Well," Jem said, "you thought you were doing something bad, and you still did it. That's all that counts."

"I never would have—"

"We already did this on the phone," Jem said. "Do you have the thousand dollars?"

"Please, you don't understand. This isn't fair. I'm a good guy, I don't deserve this."

"Let me guess," Jem said. "You're a bishop or a stake president or a high councilor. Is that right? And you got up early this morning for meetings, and you prayed with everybody, had a nice time, probably got a huge old boner for the Lord. Am I close?"

Bruce covered his eyes and began to cry.

"All right," Jem said, standing. "You can expect that picture and the audio recording to go to your wife first. Unless you're living in your mom's basement; then I'll send it to her. If you don't pay after that, I'll send it—"

"No," Bruce said, grabbing Jem's arm.

Jem twisted free. "Don't touch me. Do you have the money?"

At the west end of the mall, two kids, probably four and six, were playing tag. They wore child-sized black suits, and their polished dress shoes clicked out against the stone, their excited laughs echoing back through the empty mall.

Nodding, Bruce handed over an envelope.

"What am I going to do if there's not a thousand dollars in here?" Jem asked.

"You're going to send that picture and the recording to my wife," Bruce whispered.

"No, Bruce. If you screwed me, I'm going to send this stuff to the police. Do you understand me?"

Bruce nodded again.

"I'll see you next month, Bruce."

"No," Bruce shouted, trying to rise. Jem shoved him back onto the bench, and Bruce stared up at him, his face flushed in ugly patches of color now, his eyes blinking furiously. "You can't! I paid you, that's it. That's the end."

"It's the end when I say it's the end," Jem said.

"I don't deserve this! I'm a good guy!"

"You stupid motherfucker," Jem said. "You wanted pictures of little girls getting raped. You're a degenerate fucking monster. Paying a thousand bucks every month? That's getting off easy. And if I even get a whiff that you went near a kid, hell, if I suspect you've even been playing pocket pool and surfing some of those sites you like so much, I'll make sure you get locked up. Do you know what guys in prison do to guys like you?"

Bruce made a little throwing-up noise; his raw, chewed lips sealed tightly, and his eyes were full of panic.

"Go find a trash can, finish puking, and get the hell out of here," Jem said. "I'll contact you next month."

Wobbling, Bruce staggered to the closest trash can and was noisily sick.

Jem waited until Bruce was gone. Then he looked at Ammon again. The detective was still in that narrow patch of shade, still partially hidden by the building, still watching. Squatting near the creek again, Jem made a big show of untying the tube sock, dumping the small stones onto the creek bed, and folding up the sock. If Ammon thought he was unarmed, he might make a mistake. A deserted mall wasn't nearly as good as a dark alley, but maybe if they went down into the parking garage, maybe if they found a nice, private corner, Jem could teach Ammon a couple of lessons that the detective had coming.

"Who's your friend?" Ammon asked when Jem got close enough.

"College roommate," Jem said.

"He looked pretty upset."

"He's on chemo."

"What'd he give you in that envelope?"

"His last will and testament," Jem said. "I'm the responsible type."

"I think I told you something," Ammon said, "about staying away from Tean."

"In one ear," Jem said with a smile, his hand closing over the paracord in his pocket, "and out the other."

"Tean's a good guy," Ammon said. "If you hurt him, I'll murder you."

"You already threatened to kill me," Jem said, "and you didn't follow through. I'm starting to think you're a lot of hot air."

The detective arched blond eyebrows. He was wearing a suit that looked nicer than what he'd been wearing the night he'd come over to Tean's apartment; Jem wondered if he was skipping church.

"Let's go for a ride," Ammon said.

Jem smiled again and shook his head.

"Yeah," Ammon said. "I think we need to have a different kind of conversation."

"Let me guess," Jem said. "Tean hasn't been answering your calls, so you decided to lurk outside like a stalker. When I came out, you followed me."

"Don't make this harder than it needs to be."

"I guess it's easy to get away whenever you need some dick," Jem said. "You just tell the wifey you've got an emergency at work."

"You ever been to Vegas?" Ammon said. "I think you're going to like Vegas. It's a six-hour drive, but we'll make a couple of stops along the way, really get to know each other. And when I drop you off, you're going to be really happy to stay in Vegas. I might even let you try to convince me that it was your idea. That you want to stay there. You might be begging me to let you stay in Vegas by the time we get there. Do you understand me?"

"I wonder how she'd like a phone call telling her to check the credit card bill. I wonder what she'd say when she saw those charges at the Apollonia."

"Buddy," Ammon said, smiling with perfect white teeth. "Oh buddy. You are making a big mistake."

"You'd better get back to church. Hate to think of you missing the sacrament."

Ammon held his pose for a moment longer: the clean-cut cop, the hard ass, taking no shit. But then he stabbed a finger at Jem and said, "I'm warning you one last time to stay away from Tean."

"I don't know how you mindfucked him so badly, but Christ, honestly, it's actually impressive. I think I'm going to enjoy helping him see that you're the biggest shit on two legs. By the time I'm done, he'll know exactly what you are, and you can go back to trawling for dick under the overpasses."

This time, something changed in Ammon's expression. The bluster evaporated, and something hard and cold and shrunken was left behind. It was the look of a guy who'd fight to the death because he only had one thing left. Jem's hands tightened even more around the paracord and the antenna; his knuckles ached.

"Bad news about your friend," Ammon said.

"What are you talking about?"

"The medical examiner ruled it an accidental death. Bad luck, right? He's just out camping, and a cougar gets him. Really bad luck."

Jem shook his head. The sound of the creek was suddenly much louder in his ears.

"You've got nothing keeping you here," Ammon said. "Last chance. I'll even buy you a bus ticket, wherever you want to go."

"Fuck off," Jem said.

Ammon was grinning as he turned away, but that icy, contracted hatred in his eyes hadn't changed. Jem waited until he was gone, and then he pried his fingers loose, flexing them to ease the ache in the joints. And then he went down into the dark chill of the parking garage, into the smell of antifreeze and motor oil and damp concrete.

24

For Tean, the last four days had been uncannily good. He spent Thursday and Friday at work, catching up on reports he needed to finish and looking at some numbers that Norbert had put together about elk tags for next year. On Saturday, he ran errands and caught up on some time with Scipio, taking a long hike while Jem visited a friend. At night, he came home to Jem, who laughed, who asked him about his day, who elbowed him away from the stove and made a really good hamburger in the cast iron skillet. At night, for the first time in his life, he felt like he was glimpsing something he hadn't even known he'd been missing. Even though half the time he wanted to wriggle away from all the touching, he was drawn back again and again to the heat of Jem's body around his, the whisper of breath on his ear, the even keel of their sex, with Tean finding it a little easier every time to relax. And pain, of course: the ache of knowing how much Jem was hurting, seeing it in his face when Jem forgot to hide it, hearing it in his breathing at night when he pretended to sleep, once his tears falling on the side of Tean's neck like flashes of hot oil.

That was why Monday morning, he was in a panic. He let himself into Hannah's office, closed the door behind him, and leaned against it.

"What's going on?" Hannah asked. "Are the bookies here to break my leg?"

"What?"

"Because I've been laying some major bets that you've been boinking your California boy for the last five days."

Tean squeezed his eyes shut and then opened them again. "What?"

Hannah's office always looked like it had recently suffered a high-magnitude earthquake. Things had clearly been organized once: shelves with reference books, framed pictures, the skeletonized jaw of a June sucker, and, of course, somewhere close to a hundred tiny figurines of teacup Yorkies, all chosen because their coloring was similar to Divorcee's. The earthquake, however, had happened over the course of years, and now books were everywhere. A jumble of something like fifteen Yorkie figurines filled one of the chairs, and a stack of print-outs almost as high as Tean's knee was slowly spilling onto its side. She had her diffuser going; today's essence was vanilla and coffee.

"Come on," Hannah said with a grin. "Is he still in town? What did you guys do this weekend?"

"Did you know that the odds of winning the lottery are about one in a 175 million?"

"Oh my gosh," Hannah said with a little catch. "That's so romantic." She started opening drawers.

"And did you know that in one study, over seventy percent of lottery winners had spent all of their winnings within five years?"

Hannah had succeeded in extracting a tissue from the clutter in one drawer, and now she froze, staring at him. "No. Don't do this. Whatever you're doing, stop."

"And did you know that a high number of lottery winners end up going to jail for violent behavior, often linked to drug use, which is an attempt to counter the depression that comes from existential despair when you no longer have to work for money?"

"I hate you," Hannah said. "I was ready for a good, romantic cry, and now I hate you."

"And the suicide rate for lottery winners—"

The balled-up tissue hit him in the face.

"Hey!" Tean said.

"Let's have some tea," Hannah said, "and you can tell me why it's so scary that you really like him."

She made lavender tea for both of them, and Tean told her most of it. He left out the fact that Jem was sleeping over, but he told her about Benny, told her about the nights and days together, and then he went into detail about Sunday night.

"He was really agitated. He kept asking me if I'd heard anything about the manner of death, if Benny's death was going to be investigated, on and on like that." Tean shrugged. "I told him that the medical examiner isn't that fast, and we probably need to find the cougar that dragged him up to its den before we can determine the manner of death."

"The ME isn't just slow," Hannah said through the steam rising over her mug. "The office is backed up like crazy. Did you know they've got a lawsuit pending? They're being sued for not completing autopsies efficiently or something like that."

"Rand mentioned that," Tean said. "And something about stolen belongings."

"I don't know about that," Hannah said, "but they've definitely got a backlog. Is Jem really going to stay here for months while he waits for them to determine cause and manner of death?"

"I don't know," Tean said.

"Can he work remotely?"

"I don't know."

"What does he do?"

"I don't know."

"Well," Hannah said, "what do you know about him?"

"I mean, it's not like we spend all this time talking."

Hannah's eyes widened.

"No," Tean said. "That's not what I meant."

"Oh my gosh."

"Stop it. You're a good Mormon girl, so just stop it."

"This is so cute. I bet you spend all your time running your fingers through his beard. You love guys with beards."

"I don't—"

"And I bet you giggle when his beard tickles your neck."

"Goodbye," Tean said, shooting for the door.

"Come back!"

"I have a work emergency," Tean shouted over his shoulder.

"No, you don't. We work in the same—"

He pulled the door closed.

When he got to his office, though, the phone was ringing.

"It's ok to feel nervous," Hannah said. "And even a little bit scared. You really like him, and he came into your life suddenly, and you went through something awful together. It's a lot. It's overwhelming. But you're happy, right?"

"I'm cutting the phone line."

"You are, aren't you?"

"Yeah," Tean said, a huge, sloppy grin breaking out despite his best efforts. He finally packed it away and said, "Don't call me again." And then he hung up.

The phone rang immediately.

"I said —"

"Dr. Leon?"

"Yes, hi. Is this Jamal?"

"Yeah. Listen, we just got out to Tooele. That rancher, Goody, he's got a dead cougar on his hands."

"What?"

"Well, Maddie and I have been tracking it, trying to find it, but he called this morning. When we got here, the cougar was hanging up in the barn."

"Are you kidding me?"

"I wish. He says he killed it yesterday. He claims it was trying to get one of his cows."

Tean stared at the poster opposite him: it showed a 50s-era housewife in pearls and heels cooking at a stove, while a child cried in a playpen. The caption said HAVING A BAD DAY? JUST REMEMBER: ONE DAY, YOUR MOM PUT YOU DOWN AND NEVER PICKED YOU UP AGAIN.

"Is he telling the truth?" Tean finally managed to ask.

"Hard to say," Jamal said. "We asked to see the cow, but Goody says he shot the cougar before it could actually get the cow. He claims it was an accident; he was just trying to scare it off."

"Ok," Tean said. "Can you have Maddie bring it in, and you poke around and see if you can come up with a better explanation?"

"Sounds like a plan."

"Jamal, look for casings, tracks, scat, fur."

"Well, Dr. Leon, that's just such a good idea."

"Ok."

"Let me jot that down."

"Point taken."

"You said I should look for physical evidence? Or I shouldn't? Hold on, I'm still getting a pencil."

"Goodbye, Jamal."

The next step was to call the medical examiner. A young man answered, and Tean introduced himself and asked if he could speak to the medical examiner.

"And who are you again?" the young man asked.

So Tean gave his credentials again.

"I'm sorry," the young man said. "Dr. Seamount isn't available right now."

"Do you know when he will be available?"

"What is this in regard to?"

"Well, Dr. Seamount has a dead man in a refrigerator, and one of the questions around his death is whether or not he was killed by an animal. I thought he might want to know that we have a cougar coming in that might have been involved in either killing that man or scavenging the body."

In the silence, the line sounded staticky.

"Well?" Tean said.

"I'll let him know."

"Great," Tean said. "And you can let him know that if he wants an expert to take a look at any of the lesions, punctures, or bite marks, he can call my secretary."

When Tean hung up the phone, Hannah was standing in the doorway. She tucked chestnut hair behind her ears, studying him.

"You don't have a secretary," she said.

"That kid sounded like he was twenty years old, and he acted like I was calling to take a survey on urinary tract infections."

"What's going on?"

He told her, and Hannah frowned. "I have a friend in the lab who does a lot of the trace evidence analysis, and she said Seamount is . . . erratic."

"You've got a friend over there?"

Hannah sighed, pulled a chair up to his desk, and placed a call from his desk phone. She put the call on speaker. A moment later, a young woman said, "Mousa."

"Kashida, it's Hannah."

"Oh, hi, Hannah! Hey, what happened with that cute doc and the California guy. Did you ever find out if they were—"

"Um, yeah, yes, listen," Hannah said, her face bright red. "I've got a question for you. Do you know anything about a possible animal attack case, a young man who was brought in last week?"

"Do I know anything about it?" Kashida said. "That was my whole weekend."

"What?"

"Dr. Seamount bumped him to the top of the list. Made a skeleton crew come in over the weekend. Somebody really lit a fire under him, because he doesn't miss eighteen holes on Saturday for just about anything. Anyway, at least it's over. And thank goodness it was last weekend, because I'm taking off Friday and heading down to Vegas."

"Wait a minute," Hannah said. "You're saying you finished."

"Yeah. I guess it was pretty straightforward. I'm not even really sure why I had to stay the whole time. Once I'd confirmed that many of the collected hairs were animal and not human, Dr. Seamount didn't really want to hear anything else."

"Did he determine manner of death?"

Kashida hesitated. "Hannah, what's going on?"

"Well," Hannah said with a frown, looking at Tean, "I'm not sure."

"Kashida," Tean said, "this is Tean Leon; I'm a wildlife vet over at DWR. One of our conservation officers is bringing in a cougar that we think might be responsible for the attack. If I get some samples over to you, could you take a look and see if they match."

"Yes," Kashida said slowly. "But the report and death certificate have already been issued."

Hannah and Tean exchanged a look. "What did Dr. Seamount decide?" Tean asked.

Silence.

"If the report and certificate have been finalized," Hannah said, "there's no harm in telling us, right?"

"And I'm sure Dr. Seamount's office will be sending us a copy of the autopsy report," Tean said, "for our own investigation into the animal attack. I'd rather know now, though, than wait for the bureaucracy to unravel."

"Just a second," Kashida said. Sounds of clicking and typing made their way across the call, and then Kashida said, "Cause of death is listed as 'injuries consistent with an animal attack,' and manner of death is 'accidental.'"

"What did he find that made him decide that it was an animal attack?" Tean asked.

"Well," Kashida said, "I told you about the animal fur."

"And that's it?"

"I haven't read the report. I'm not sure what he found in the autopsy or if there was other evidence that he considered."

"Did you find any fibers that might have come from the upholstery in a vehicle?"

"Yes, actually."

"Are you sure?" Hannah asked. "It couldn't have come from something else."

"Well, I found several fibers that were synthetic, polyester. It's not unique, so no, it doesn't necessarily mean it came from car upholstery. But the deceased wasn't wearing anything made from polyester. It's possible he picked it up somewhere else; I could compare it against a specific vehicle, I suppose."

Tean shook his head slowly.

For a moment, Hannah watched him. Then she said, "Kashida, can you send us a digital copy of that report. Pictures too, please. Everything you've got."

"I don't know —"

"Too late for that," Hannah said. "Besides, it'll make its way over here eventually. You're just speeding things up."

Silence.

"And I'll watch Kubla Khan for you this weekend while you're in Vegas," Hannah added. To Tean, she mouthed, "Bernese Mountain Dog."

"Only because my mom refuses to dog sit," Kashida said.

"You're the best," Hannah said and disconnected.

"Thank you," Tean said.

"Don't thank me yet," Hannah said, standing and heading for the door. "You owe me, and I'm going to collect."

"I don't —"

"Double date: you and your surfer boy, Caleb and I. I haven't had a date night in a million years."

As she stepped out into the hall, Tean shouted after her, "He's not my surfer boy."

Norbert Smith was standing in the hall, shoulders stooped, his pate shining through thinning hair.

"He's not even a surfer," Tean said in a more even tone.

Norbert nodded.

Tean's face was getting hot. "And he's not my boy."

Norbert sucked his teeth.

"Would you close my door, please?" Tean said.

Norbert did, and Tean wondered if that whole exchange might constitute sexual harassment.

The autopsy report arrived in his inbox a moment later, and Tean scanned through it. It was patchy at best, obviously rushed, and Tean wondered who had put pressure on the ME to deal with Benny's death. The two obvious answers were either Goody or Julie. Either one might have been able to do it: Goody was a wealthy rancher who claimed to have political friends; Julie was an executive at one of the most important industries in the state. A few discreet calls, a few favors promised, and somebody might have twisted Seamount's arm to get the autopsy pushed through, even though the ME's office was facing a backlog and a lawsuit.

The decision to cite an animal attack as the cause and the manner of death as accidental, though, was what puzzled Tean. At a superficial level, that decision seemed obvious. Benny had died sometime on Monday, according to the report. The autopsy photos showed typical animal-attack injuries consistent with a big cat like a cougar: v-shaped puncture wounds in the abdomen, chest, and shoulder; slashes from claws; splintered bones. Cougars and other big cats were not above scavenging, and in typical fashion, the cougar—if it had been a cougar—had eaten the internal organs first, eviscerating Benny.

But what troubled Tean was that any experienced medical examiner or forensic pathologist should have known that post-mortem damage caused by animals was easy to mistake, at first glance, for ante-mortem injuries. And he didn't see anywhere in the autopsy report that Seamount had conducted any sort of histological, histochemical, and immunohistochemical test to see if the wound had been delivered before Benny had died or after. If that was an oversight, it was criminally neglectful. And if it wasn't an oversight .
. .

Seamount had been careful to take pictures of anything that might corroborate the animal attack narrative. The teeth of big cats like cougars often left marks on bones: pits, punctures, scores, and furrows. Punctures were the most common, because of the shape of big cat teeth, and Seamount had documented several of these.

The picture that held Tean's attention the longest, the one that made him doubt everything else, was a picture taken of Benny's shoulder at a bad angle. It was obvious that the cougar had bitten down hard on Benny's shoulder, probably in order to drag him under the rock overhang. Tean had read reports of big cats hiding scavenged prey so that they could return and feed again later, and this seemed to be a similar case. But what troubled Tean was something else. The picture had been taken at a poor angle, and why Seamount had chosen to include it escaped Tean, although he guessed it was probably because Seamount had been rushed and simply wanted the appearance of a comprehensively documented autopsy. But what the photograph showed very clearly, and doubtless unintentionally on Seamount's part, was where a long cut on Benny's back had laid bare a portion of the scapula. The bone showed a single, clear mark that Tean was pretty sure had come from a knife.

His phone rang.

"I've got the cougar down in the refrigerator of the necropsy lab," Maddie said.

"Will you move it to the table?" Tean said. "I'll be right down."

In the locker room, he changed clothes before moving into the necropsy lab. Then he put on a coverall, a rubber apron, protective gloves and boots, and a mask and face shield. Once he had set up his digital camera and the voice recorder, he completed the preliminary information on the report, labeled sample containers, and wrote out cards with the same information for the photographs.

For the preliminary part of the exam, he'd rely on Jamal's report, although if he had any doubts he would need to head out to Goody's ranch and inspect the area himself. He moved on to the external examination. The cougar was a young adult male, probably between two and three years old. Seven and a half feet long, a hundred and forty pounds. Thin, and probably hungry. This cougar might have been forced away from better hunting by an older, more experienced male. Or perhaps he had simply been unlucky. The only visible recent trauma also explained the cause of death: the cougar had taken two shots to the chest, and the fur was still matted and stiff with dried blood. Two shots to the chest made Tean doubt Goody had told the truth when he said he was just trying to scare off the big cat.

After taking several pictures and completing a few other measurements, Tean proceeded to the internal examination. With the cougar lying on its left side, Tean made incisions under the right front leg and right rear leg, removed the hide from the chest and abdominal wall, and then made an incision in the abdominal wall itself. He removed the ribs on the right side and took samples from the heart and lung. He also recovered both bullets, which he thought were from a .22. That was the most common ammunition in the world and would fit Goody's story about grabbing his rifle to stop the cougar from preying on his cattle. Tean would leave the real ballistic examination to an expert, though — if it ever came to that.

Next, he took samples from the liver, spleen, kidneys, bladder, and samples of blood and urine. When he opened the stomach, he paused. Then he began picking out pieces of black fabric that he was pretty sure had come from Benny's shirt. He finished the necropsy with several samples of the intestine, and then he removed the head and took samples of the tongue and brain. He paused again, considering the young cat's teeth, and took a few more pictures. There was nothing remarkable on first glance, but better safe than sorry.

Tean stored the specimens, cleaned and disinfected the necropsy lab, and then disinfected himself, showered, and changed back into his street clothes. Then he went upstairs, reviewed the autopsy report a final time, and called the ME's office again.

"I said I would leave him a message," the young man told him.

Tean didn't bother to reply; he disconnected and placed two more calls, one to Jem and one to Ammon, and then he started writing notes about everything that was wrong.

25

When Jem got to the DWR building, the sun was low in the west, huge and red and angry. Tractor trailers kicked up dust and leaves and a yellow McDonald's wrapper that flattened itself against Jem's leg. When he parked the Kawasaki at the back of the building, he could feel the grit on his neck and under his arms. The day had been cool, and the night would be colder, but something about the sun, about the smell of exhaust, about the long shadows made him feel like summer was hanging on.

This time, Antonia let him into the building without any objections, although she eyed him like she was waiting for him to try to steal a pen or make off with a clipboard or exhibit some other deviant behavior. Jem barely noticed. He had spent the day in Tooele, hiking the trail through the foothills. He had started at the Jenkins' ranch, and he had gone south toward Goody's, following the route that Benny would have used. During the search, he had been thinking about the Teenage Mutant Ninja Turtles bowl near Goody's gate, and the aluminum plate, and what had felt like a breadcrumb trail of Benny's belongings leading them to the body. But he hadn't found anything north of where they had found Benny, nothing that indicated that Benny might have walked south from the Jenkins's ranch. He hadn't expected to, but he had needed to be certain.

When he got to Tean's office, the doc was sitting behind his desk. Ammon was sitting next to him. Tean looked worried: his hair was even wilder than usual, brushed back from all the times he had run his hands through it, and his glasses were on the verge of sliding straight off his face. The detective, in contrast, was unreadable. He was in one of his cheap suits again, the jacket over one knee, his sleeves rolled up. The only remaining seat was on the other side of the desk. Two on one, Jem thought as he sat.

"This looks bad," Jem said.

"It's not good," Tean said, glancing at Ammon.

"Go ahead," Ammon said quietly, resting one hand on Tean's back, his eyes sliding toward Jem. "It's your show."

"I don't know about that," Tean said. "I guess I'll start like this: I don't think Benny was killed by the cougar. Or by any animal, for that matter. I think he was killed with a knife, and I think the killer moved the body into the mountains hoping that scavengers would make it difficult to tell what had happened to him."

"And I'm going to point out," Ammon said, "as the only law-enforcement officer in the room, that you're not a forensic pathologist, and you're not trained to make those kinds of determinations."

"Fuck off," Jem said.

Ammon had a tiny smile that vanished almost immediately.

"No," Tean said, "Ammon's right. I'm not—"

"No, he needs to fuck off," Jem said. "In fact, he needs to leave. Right now."

Somewhere down the hall, someone was running a cleaning machine. A floor buffer, Jem guessed. And then the machine hiccupped and whined like the brushes had gotten caught on something, and somebody swore.

"Ammon is right," Tean said again. "I think—"

"You think there's some big conspiracy," Ammon said. "You think someone manipulated Seamount into conducting the autopsy and declaring it an animal attack. Next thing, you're going to be wearing a tin-foil hat."

"Don't you think it's strange that the ME's office is backed up on autopsies, is facing a lawsuit for not handling them in a timely manner, and for some reason Benny gets bumped to the front of the queue?"

"Yeah," Ammon said. "It's strange. But it could have been a lot of things. A fluke with the paperwork."

"He pulled a skeleton crew in over the weekend for a paperwork fluke?"

"Or maybe Seamount just got a wild hair and wanted to look at an animal attack instead of the usual cases." Ammon sat back, folding his arms. "Or a million other possible reasons."

"He—" Tean began.

"Just tell me why you don't think it was a cougar," Jem said quietly.

"Cougar attacks aren't exactly common," Tean said. "And when a cougar does attack, it usually targets children—"

"Not exclusively," Ammon snapped.

"Although not exclusively," Tean said. "More important is that Benny's body doesn't show any of the signs of a classic cougar attack."

"I saw his body," Jem said, and then he swallowed. "Something did him up pretty bad."

Tean nodded; his dark eyes were soft. "Yes," he said, "but when cougars attack to kill, they almost always do so from behind. They try to position their teeth between the vertebrae and into the spinal cord, so they can drag their prey down and kill it by snapping its neck. It's their characteristic form of attack, actually. And Benny doesn't show signs that he was attacked that way."

"Ok," Jem said.

"And while the body does show—" Tean stopped. "I'm sorry. I shouldn't be talking about this. We can just—"

"No," Jem said, breathing slowly, his vision flecked with red and white at the edges. "No, I want to hear."

"The short version," Tean said, "is that all of the wounds could have been and probably were inflicted post-mortem."

"Although you don't know that," Ammon said.

"No," Tean said, his voice tightening for the first time, "because Seamount didn't conduct even the most basic tests to determine the sequence of events."

"So it's the neck bite," Jem said. "That's why you don't think it was an animal attack?"

"And one other thing," Tean said. "On the scapula," he reached back, touching his own shoulder blade to demonstrate, "there's a mark that I think came from a knife. It has the right characteristics: it's a thin, v-shaped trough. All the other marks on the bones are consistent with the cougar's teeth. There's no way the cougar could have left this mark."

"The claws—" Ammon said.

"No," Tean said. "It did not leave this mark on the bone. This is characteristic of a knife. I think someone cut his throat from behind, hoping that the nature of the wound would be hidden by the damage to the soft tissue from scavengers, and then something happened: the killer stumbled, or Benny moved in an unexpected way, and the knife skipped along his shoulder blade hard enough to mark the bone."

"Which is a theory from someone who has absolutely no training—" Ammon began.

Jem kept seeing Benny's body the way they had found it: savaged by animals, torn apart, flesh shredded and bone splintered. In his mind, he could see Benny smiling. He could see Benny laughing. He could see the knife slicing through Benny's throat. He bent at the waist, his breathing fast and shallow, fingers over his eyes.

Voices. Arguing.

"Just get out," Tean was saying, not shouting but close. "I said I'll handle this. You're making it worse."

"You're babying him," Ammon said.

Jem lurched out of the chair.

"Jem?" Tean asked

Throwing open the door, Jem stepped out of the office. He made his way to the bathroom, grabbed a wad of paper towels from the dispenser, and wetted them at the sink. He laid them across the back of his neck and leaned on the counter, supporting himself on his elbows, hands over his face again. He could smell the wet pulp of the paper and the commercial air freshener; a drop of water ran down his spine. At the end, how long had Benny known what was happening? Five seconds? Ten? A minute? God, had he known for a full minute that he'd been about to die, a full minute of total terror? Longer? Hours? Jem grabbed the paper towels, mopped up the back of his neck, and wrung out the wadded paper over the sink. Then he tossed the clump of towels in the trash and made his way back to the office.

The shouting had intensified. Jem stopped with his hand on the door.

"Your friend?" Ammon was saying. "You honestly believe that?"

Tean's answer was too quiet to hear.

"At least tell me you're not fucking him," Ammon said.

Somewhere outside the building, a truck was backing up, its steady beep-beep marking its progress.

"You've got to be kidding me," Ammon said into Tean's silence.

"I don't think you have any right to talk to me like that."

Jem opened the door before things could get any worse. Both men glared at him: Ammon with undisguised fury, Tean with a kind of reflected anger that he didn't seem to know he was exhibiting.

"I'm ok," Jem said. "I'm sorry about that. I just needed a minute."

"You don't have to be ok," Tean said, and he sounded so grumpy about it that Jem smiled slightly.

"Why would the ME have declared this an animal attack?" Jem said.

"Because he's a trained physician and forensic pathologist," Ammon said. "Because he's an expert."

Jem looked at Tean.

"Someone at the ME's office told me that Seamount, he's the ME, was acting like he was under a lot of pressure to wrap up Benny's autopsy. Right now, the medical examiner's office is facing a lawsuit for delays in completing autopsies. That combination tells me that somebody pulled strings to get Benny's death resolved without an investigation."

"Who?" Jem said.

"If Ray Goody was telling the truth, and he really does have influential friends, he might have been the one."

"Or an executive at one of the biggest mines in the world," Jem said.

"Or that," Tean said.

"So," Jem said, "Someone wants to cover up Benny's murder."

"Not necessarily," Ammon said.

Jem looked at Tean.

Tean shrugged and nodded.

"If we go along with this batshit theory," Ammon said, "and believe someone rushed Seamount, then there are two possibilities: the rush itself was enough of a reason for Seamount to take the easy answer and wrap things up—"

"That does seem like a possibility," Tean said with another shrug. "My source at the ME's office said he basically just wanted evidence that confirmed an animal attack."

" — or the same person that rushed him did, in fact, order a cover-up. Even if we go with that possibility, the motivation might not be to hide a murder. It might be the desire to avoid negative publicity, or it might be an attempt to hide another crime that's unrelated to Benny's death but that could be uncovered by an investigation."

"Like what?" Jem said. "Somebody muling drugs up and down the Oquirrh Mountains?"

"Like poaching," Tean said quietly. "Or a million things at the mine they don't want investigators poking into."

"What about the cougar?" Jem asked. "That's weird, right, that Goody just happened to have his cattle attacked by the same cougar? He just happened to kill it, and it happened to back up the story that the cougar killed Benny?"

Leaning back in his seat, the chair squeaking, Tean said, "There are some irregularities at Goody's ranch. He claims the cougar was preying on his cattle and that he killed it to protect the livestock, but Jamal, the conservation officer who examined the site, told me it looked . . . strange. The injuries to the cougar don't match Goody's story."

"Great," Ammon said. "Our crime scene expert is the guy who couldn't make it in the National Park Service."

"He's smart and educated and competent," Tean said. "And he said he didn't see any tracks near where Goody claimed the cougar was stalking cattle. Goody claims he trampled the tracks when he walked over to examine the kill, but it's hard to believe he trampled every single track. There was some fur on a clump of sage, and Jamal said it didn't look like it had gotten there naturally. The blood didn't look right to Jamal either. He's pretty sure the cougar was killed somewhere else and transported to the pasture."

"There you go," Jem said. "That's our opening. You said he's a poacher, right? I bet he didn't have a tag for that cougar. This is how we get out there and look for more evidence."

A frustrated smile pulled at the corners of Tean's mouth. "It's not that easy, I'm afraid. In the first place, livestock owners are allowed to kill a cougar that's been attacking livestock, provided they contact the DWR and submit the carcass, which Goody did. And we issued more cougar hunting permits this year than we have in a long time; cougar populations are up, and that means the young ones are getting forced out of good hunting. His story has just enough elements of truth to keep it afloat."

"This is bullshit," Jem said. "This is fucking bullshit."

"It gets worse," Ammon said, "so keep your panties on. You probably don't have any idea how fucking lucky you are that Tean is willing to help you, so I'm going to tell you: you're out-of-this-world lucky. He's really pushed hard to get answers. That includes lighting a fire under my ass. I called the Tooele County sheriff's department and asked about the investigation into Benny's death. This was before the ME released the autopsy report. The sheriff talked to me personally once I told them I was looking into a possible missing person case that had happened in our jurisdiction. She confirmed that neither Goody nor his ranch hands owns a black SUV or a red Chevy, and she also told me she's followed up on the alibis for Goody and Julie Nash. Goody was at the stock auction in Cheyenne, just like he said, along with Cisco Hernandez, one of his ranch hands. The other two ranch hands, Albino and Abram Pereira, alibi each other — they claim they were moving cattle all day."

"Nice," Jem said. "Brothers claiming they were together all day. I don't see any trouble with that."

"Julie Nash was in meetings the whole morning. She wasn't just sitting there twiddling her thumbs, either; she was making presentations, having conversations. No chance she slipped out long enough to abduct Benny and kill him."

"Well, that mine is full of employees. She's got two of them like her fucking maid and butler. They could have done it."

"They were at those meetings too. All three of them agree."

"Great. Great work. They alibi each other. Does anybody have all three of them on camera?"

Ammon looked at Tean.

"And the fact that the Tooele sheriff is in Goody's pocket," Jem said, "that doesn't mean anything to you? It doesn't mean anything that his ranch hands alibi each other, but nobody can prove where they were?"

"You're asking for impossibilities. It'd be more suspicious if they did have an airtight alibi for a random day."

"What I don't get," Tean said, "is why Benny got in the car in the first place."

"What?"

"You saw the video," Tean said. "You saw him get in the SUV. Nobody dragged him into the car. We don't know what happened after he was inside the vehicle, but I'm just saying, why would he get into an SUV with people he claimed were destroying the environment, people he claimed were hunting him down and trying to kill him? He was paranoid, Jem. The behavior on that video doesn't make any sense."

Jem just shook his head. He was tired, and he closed his eyes and leaned against the wall.

"This isn't the end of the road," Tean said. "I know what I saw in that autopsy picture. I still think Benny was murdered, and I'm not ready to let this go."

"There's nothing you can do," Ammon said. "You can jerk each other off as much as you want, but this case is dead in the water."

"That's enough," Tean said.

"He needs to hear the truth. You're not going to get anywhere official with this unless you file a lawsuit and have a private forensic pathologist give a second opinion. Even then, you're not guaranteed anything. And if by some miracle you force the state to open an investigation, what's going to happen? Nothing. You've got a murder victim, and the only evidence is one mark that a knife left on a bone. Your suspects, if you can even call them that, have solid alibis. You can tell me to fuck off and every other curse word in the book, but I'm just telling you how it is. If you're right, then somebody got away with murder. The only thing you can do is learn how to live with that."

"Not all of them," Jem said, opening his eyes.

"What do you mean?" Tean said. "If you're thinking about other mine employees—"

"No," Jem said. "You said in those papers, Benny talked about three people. We only got to two of them: Julie Nash and Ray Goody. Who's the third one?"

Tean shook his head and looked at Ammon.

"I don't remember," Ammon said. "I looked at that stuff once."

"Someone in Tooele, though, right? Someone that could have easily planted that stuff at Goody's ranch."

"It was someone in Tooele," Tean said slowly, "but that doesn't mean—"

"We have to look," Jem said. "We have to at least look."

Tean was frozen, hands clasped.

"I'm going to tell you once more," Ammon said, "and then I'm done with this bullshit: you should not be muddling around in this. If you're right, the only thing you're doing is putting yourselves in danger. If you're wrong, you're making fools out of yourselves and wasting your time." He looked like he might say more, and then he grimaced and pulled his phone out of his pocket. "Christ. I'm late to pick up Daniel from his therapist." He pointed a finger at Tean and then pointed at Jem. "Stay out of this. Let it go. Move on with your lives."

"We'll walk out with you," Tean said, grabbing a jacket and coming around the desk. Ammon was already heading out of the office.

"I'm not letting this go," Jem said.

"I know," Tean said quietly, taking Jem's arm and urging him out of the office. "We'll talk about it later."

It took Tean an extra moment to lock the door, and by the time he'd finished, Ammon was halfway down the hall ahead of them. Tean was still holding Jem's arm, guiding him along the hall, and Jem was so exhausted that he didn't care. It was nice to let someone else take over for a few minutes. It was nice not to have to always be planning and grasping and trying to figure out how he was going to eat or where he was going to sleep. Nice not to worry about Benny, if he were honest. Nice to have someone worry about him for a change.

Jem was in a kind of daze by the time they emerged from the building. The sodium lamps in the parking lot were weak and buzzing; they made a quilt of orange light, shadow, and patches of total darkness. A lone cricket was chirping, and then a Mack truck barreled past on North Temple, and when the roar of the engine had faded, Jem couldn't hear the cricket anymore. Ammon was almost half the length of the parking lot ahead of them. Jem felt like he was moving in a dream.

That was why he reacted so slowly. The figure, dressed all in black, sprang out of a dense pocket of shadow and sprinted across the asphalt. They were holding something in their hand, and they brought it up and swung it hard and fast. Ammon had an athlete's reflexes and training, but it was also the end of a long day, and he'd been caught unawares. He turned toward the attacker, one hand dropping to his waist for the gun holstered there. The attacker was faster. The weapon, which looked like a length of pipe, caught Ammon on the forearm with a loud thwack. A second noise undercut the first: a soft pinging, like the sound of aluminum bat knocking one out of the park. Ammon shouted, the sound full of pain, and the attacker struck again, catching him on the leg. Ammon fell. The third blow caught him on the side of the head. He went still.

"Motherfucker," Jem shouted, grabbing the paracord out of one pocket and the antenna out of the other. He flicked his wrist, sending the antenna telescoping to its full length. Then he looped the paracord around his palm. At the end of the cord, the hex nut caught the sodium light in a dull smear.

The attacker looked up. Jem had just long enough to identify the weapon—it was, as he had thought, a piece of pipe, maybe three-feet long—and then the attacker rushed at Jem.

"Call the police," Jem shouted to Tean as he ran forward.

Jem had a few advantages over Ammon: first, he wasn't still in a state of surprise; second, he had watched the attacker deliver three blows, each one with a wide, sweeping arc that told Jem this person telegraphed their attacks; and third, Jem had spent his whole life fighting dirty as fuck. Neither the antenna nor the paracord could block the pipe; it had too much mass. Jem briefly entertained the idea of using the paracord to catch the pipe, but that sounded like some Indiana Jones bullshit to him. He settled for tried and true.

The antenna was long, flexible, and strong. It helped even things out, because the attacker was bigger than Jem and otherwise would have had the better reach. When the attacker took another of those grand-slam windups with the pipe, Jem didn't wait for the delivery. He cracked the antenna across the attacker's face, catching him across the nose and one eye, and the guy—Jem could tell by the voice—howled. The blow that had probably been meant to knock Jem's head off his shoulders went wide. The whistle of air from its passage carried the taste of rust. Jem felt electric and alive.

The next swing had another of those big windups; the big guy was angry now, reckless, swinging the way he'd been taught in Little League. Instead of matching him with another swing, Jem jabbed with the antenna. It was a short, hard thrust, and it caught the asshole in the throat. One of the antenna's weaknesses was that, in a situation like this, the telescoping design caused it to collapse. That didn't bother Jem too much; he hadn't intended to skewer the guy or even collapse his windpipe. He just wanted to scare him, and as the guy choked and gagged and stumbled back, Jem figured he'd pretty much gotten what he wanted. The attacker didn't even manage to deliver the swing he'd been winding up for; instead, he pressed one hand to his throat, gagging, obviously trying not to puke.

The respite only lasted a moment, but it was all Jem needed. One of the beauties of paracord was its degree of elasticity—it could stretch and elongate. It also had a minimum breaking strength of five-hundred-and-fifty pounds. The hex nut tied at the end of the cord wasn't anything special: just good, solid, American steel. Jem whipped the cord a few times. Momentum built up speed of strike, and speed of strike multiplied the impact force on the target. Jem had made Benny look it up for him once on the internet. Then Jem cracked the nut against the side of the guy's head. There was a popping sound, and the man screamed.

Throwing the pipe at Jem, the guy stumbled back. The pipe caught Jem in the chest, not hard enough to do any serious damage, but causing him to take an unsteady step. He hit an uneven patch of asphalt and fell. The attacker didn't take advantage, though; he pressed one hand to the side of his head like he might go down, staggering in a half circle. Something clattered to the asphalt. Then he took off in a shambling run. By the time Tean was kneeling next to Jem, helping him to his feet, lights flared to life on a black SUV. The vehicle pulled out of the lot with a screech.

"Are you ok?" Tean asked.

Jem nodded.

"Holy crap," Tean said, "that was incredible."

Dropping his head, Jem tried to take deep breaths; adrenaline was making him sick to his stomach.

"I've got to check on Ammon," Tean said.

Jem just nodded again. He was vaguely aware of Tean's low voice, Ammon's groans. Something glittered on the blacktop, and Jem picked it up without thinking. It was a silver bracelet made of chunky links. Jem had seen it before; Ray Goody had been wearing it the day they had found Benny's body. Jem pocketed it. He thought about seeing if he could help Tean, but his knees felt way too loose, and he thought he might fall. He sat on a curb, head between his knees, while sirens moved toward them.

26

It was sometime past midnight when Jem led Tean out of the hospital.

"I might be able to help, though," Tean said.

"I just spent close to five hours answering questions from the police, trying to explain what happened, and watching you baby Ammon. He's fine. He's a big boy. They're keeping him overnight because of the concussion, that's all."

"If he needs something," Tean said.

The parking lot seemed to float in an outgoing tide of gray light, the cars bobbing like flotsam. Jem squeezed his eyes shut; he couldn't remember if he'd eaten that day.

"Fine," Jem said. "Go back up there. You can sit with his wife. You can exchange notes."

The sound of sneakers moving over asphalt was the only answer. When Jem opened his eyes, Tean was halfway to the truck.

"I'm sorry I said that," Jem said when he caught up.

Working the key in the lock, Tean shook his head.

"It was a shitty thing to say," Jem said. "I'm tired, and I'm sorry I said it."

"Ok," Tean said.

They drove back to the apartment in silence. The night was clear, and the moon was bright, cutting crisp shadows out of the darkness. A red warning light blinked on a broadcast tower at the foot of the mountains. Neither of them got out of the truck.

"I guess I should get a motel," Jem said.

Tean took a deep breath; his hand was clenched tightly around the keys.

"I am sorry I said that," Jem said. "You're this amazing guy who's done nothing but help me. I mean, you've gone out of your way, above and beyond anything anybody could ever expect, and I turn around and talk shit to you. You're awesome, and you don't deserve that."

Tean's shoulders relaxed, and he said, "Please stop talking."

"I just want you to know I think you're—"

"I said stop."

The engine ticked as it cooled.

"You're welcome to stay," Tean finally said, and then he got out of the truck and shut the door. Jem counted to twenty and followed.

Hannah had stopped by to take care of Scipio, but the Lab was still ecstatic to see them, and Jem had to press himself into a corner, controlling his breathing, until the dog's excitement calmed down. Tean ate burnt toast; Jem had a bowl of cereal. Tean used the bathroom first; Jem went next. After brushing his teeth, he came out of the bathroom. The apartment was dark. He took a step toward the couch.

"Don't be dumb," Tean said from the bedroom.

Something eased in Jem's chest, a tightness he hadn't even realized was there, and he moved into the bedroom. He kicked off his jeans, dragged his shirt over his head, and climbed into bed next to Tean. Some of that ultra-bright moonlight made its way through the blinds, diagonal slashes of light falling across Tean's face, picking out his cheekbone, the day's stubble, the set of his full lips.

"I'm not going to defend myself for still having feelings for him," Tean said.

Jem lay on his stomach. He ran one hand over Tean's shoulder, tracing the muscle and bone.

"You knew things were complicated before you and I started, well, whatever this is."

Jem's fingers skated down Tean's pec, teasing through the stripe of hair at the center of his chest.

"I'm not going to apologize."

Cupping Tean's face, Jem lifted his head just far enough to kiss Tean. Then he pulled back, meeting his eyes.

"Just so you know," Tean said.

"I know."

"Most relationships fail because of—"

"Ok," Jem said, climbing over Tean to straddle him, bending down to kiss him again.

222

"A recent survey showed that—"

Jem kissed him longer this time. Tean's eyes were dark even bathed in moonlight. His pupils were enormous, and his skin pebbled when Jem rocked into him.

"We're alive," Jem whispered. "Fuck everything else. We're alive."

"Sexual arousal as a response to survival mode has been blamed for the high number of rapes after military operations, and—oh Jesus Christ."

Jem licked the spot on Tean's collarbone where he had bitten down.

"I—" Tean said, and then he cut off with another sharp cry.

"Oops," Jem said, licking the nipple he had savaged with his teeth.

Tean's pupils were huge. He was breathing hard, his mouth hanging open.

"Anything else you feel like sharing?" Jem whispered.

Still breathing hard, Tean gave a tiny shake of his head.

The sex was hot and frantic, and then they slept. Jem woke first, and he walked Scipio—the gentleman's agreement again, no harness, and Jem's heart in his throat when Scipio sprinted out into the road after a squirrel. When they got back to the apartment, Tean was burning more toast.

"Thank you," Tean said.

Jem shrugged.

"Are we ok?" Tean said.

"Are you feeling the urge to reveal tidbits of nightmarish statistical data?"

"Not right now."

"Then I think we're ok."

The kibble rattled against the bowl when Jem poured it out, and Scipio butted him out of the way and started chomping his breakfast.

"I looked at those papers again," Tean said. "While you were walking Scipio. I hope that's ok."

"Of course."

"Benny claims this guy, Jerry Bowling, is single-handedly bringing down a nature preserve."

Jem frowned. "Big task."

"Well, I'm guessing it's like everything else: Benny was probably right in some way that's not quite the way he put it." Tean was trying to salvage the toast, scraping off the burnt upper layer with a knife. "Do you know that family?"

"The Bowlings?" Jem shook his head. "But it's been a long time since I left Tooele. Don't you need to work?"

"Being attacked in the parking lot is a great way to get HR to give you a free day off," Tean said with a smile. "They practically begged me not to come in. I think they're worried I'm going to sue about the lack of security."

"You don't have to do this," Jem said. "If you agree with Ammon, if you think this is a waste of time —"

"I want to do this."

"God, you're a good guy."

"No," Tean said, his smile fading. "I'm not. Somebody tried to hurt me, maybe kill me. I'm doing this for me."

"Ok," Jem said.

"I am."

"Ok," Jem said. "Now can I please have permission to fix your toaster before you ruin all the bread?"

While Jem tinkered with the toaster, Tean said, "You never told me what you do."

Jem kept fiddling with the dial on the toaster and tried to keep his voice uninterested as he asked, "What?"

"Back in California. For a job. I never asked, I guess. Are you sure you can take this much time off?"

"Trying to get rid of me?"

"No, I —"

"I'm just teasing." Jem stepped back, eyed the toaster, and shrugged. "I work construction, so it's not exactly a paid vacation. More like, unpaid leave of absence, and I'll just hope they have a job for me when I get back."

"Gosh, I'm sorry."

"Let's see if we can make toast that hasn't been through the fires of hell."

As it turned out, though, they couldn't.

"I'm buying you a new toaster," Jem said as they drove toward Tooele.

Tean looked like he was trying really hard to smile.

"That one is clearly defective," Jem said.

This time, the smile slipped free.

"What's so damn funny?" Jem said.

"Nothing. It was just very butch when you tried to fix my toaster."

Jem drew back, studying Tean. Tean was pretending to focus on the road, but he was grinning now.

"No, sir," Jem said.

"What?"

"Your role is to spout off horrifying facts. Your role is not to tease handsome, helpful, sexually generous strangers."

"I liked the part where you asked if I had a flathead screwdriver."

"Well, the external control for the toasting dial wasn't engaging—stop laughing!"

"You had this little furrow," Tean said, touching the skin between his eyebrows. "And you were just concentrating so hard."

"I could have fixed it," Jem said.

"You just didn't have the right tools," Tean murmured.

"I just didn't have—ok, you need to cut it out right now."

"You know what?" Tean said. "I think you're right: I bet it's defective."

"Oh no. Don't you dare patronize me."

"Never."

Tires thrummed as they drove another mile.

"I could fix it," Jem said.

"I know," Tean said.

"Oh my God. Oh my God. Now I'm going to have to fix it or you'll never believe me."

Tean shushed him and patted his knee. "Do you want some McDonald's? Will that make you feel better?"

"I'm not five years old."

Glancing over, Tean raised an eyebrow.

"Only because I need coffee," Jem said, his face heating.

Tean nodded and pulled off at the next exit.

"This is not because my wounded ego can be soothed with a Happy Meal."

"Of course not," Tean said with another of those gentle pats on the knee.

Jem slammed his head against the window a few times.

"Are you ok?" Tean asked.

"Oh yeah," Jem said, "just checking to see if I had a screw loose."

He was halfway through his coffee and bacon, egg, and cheese McMuffin when Tean said, "Feel better?"

"I'm not going to dignify that with an answer."

Ahead of them, to the east, the wide expanse of the Great Salt Lake Desert opened up, broken by the Cedar Mountains to the south. What might have been the Bonneville Salt Flats gleamed like bars of silver at the very edge of the horizon. Sagebrush, brown and brittle this time of year, grew in dense clumps that interrupted the flat basin. On the north side of the interstate, a tumbleweed had caught up against a thistle, and it looked like the thistle was winning. Jem felt the same flicker of apprehension that he felt every time he stared out into the desert: all that emptiness waiting to swallow him up.

"About last night," Tean said as he signaled and exited onto Route 36.

"I'm sorry," Jem said. "I shouldn't have said that. I was tired, and I was worked up from the attack, and it just slipped out."

"You already apologized," Tean said. "I was talking about the attack. Whatever else, it seems like confirmation that we're looking into something that someone is trying to cover up."

"Yeah," Jem said through a savage bite of McMuffin. "Benny's murder."

"What was that?" Tean said with a grin.

"I said—"

"I know what you said. I've just never heard a grown man try to talk around an entire English muffin. And I agree, partially. I mean, I think Benny's murder is part of it. But I think Benny was right about something, something worth a lot of money to someone."

"Like the millions of dollars in fines and reparations for letting poison leach into the environment," Jem said. "I've been thinking about it. That guy last night was big. He made me think of that mine security guy, Phil."

"You think a security guy would risk multiple assault charges for his boss?"

"I think he's doing more than security for her," Jem said.

"Maybe," Tean said. "Or it could have been poaching. I'm sure we only saw a small part of Goody's operation. The guy last night, he could have been one of Goody's ranch hands. He could have been Goody himself. He's older, but he looks tough."

"And he dropped this," Jem said, producing the bracelet.

"Where did you get this?" Tean said.

"I told you: he dropped it after I whacked him on the side of the head."

"Goody was wearing this. The day we met him, he had this on his wrist."

"I know."

"And you didn't tell the police?"

Jem shook his head.

"Why?" Tean asked.

"Because Ammon is convinced we're wasting our time. I'm not going to hand over a valuable piece of evidence."

Tean just stared at him. "Jem, they're the police. You have to give this to them and explain."

"No."

"Ammon—"

"I said no."

For a few moments, Tean was silent. Then he said, "I saw a woman's sweater in Goody's truck."

"Ok."

"He said he doesn't have a wife. And he's transporting bighorns, setting people up to hunt them illegally. And we know Julie is involved in some sort of bighorn repopulation project."

"You think they're in this together? I don't know. I—" Jem stopped. "I saw Julie and Phil getting pretty hands-on with each other. I didn't tell you about it, but I followed Julie last week. After we found Benny."

Tean rubbed his face. "Anything else you're keeping from me?"

"I'm not keeping things from you. I just—it was a horrible week. And it never came up."

"Ok. Well. I don't know what's going on, but I'm just saying—it seems like a lot of strange coincidences."

"Meanwhile," Jem said, "Goody and Julie are sitting behind solid alibis, and the ME has made sure there won't be even a token investigation into Benny's death."

"And what exactly do you think we're doing?" Tean asked.

"You know what I mean."

"I know. You're frustrated, and you're right that there are a lot of dead ends. But we're just going to keep trying until we have an answer one way or another."

Jem didn't like the open meaning of that last statement, but he just nodded.

The Bowling house was east of Tooele proper, built in the foothills of the Oquirrh Mountains only a few miles from Ray Goody's ranch. Bowling's had probably been a working ranch like Goody's at one point: a barbed-wire fence ran along the edge of the property, and although the driveway no longer had a gate, they had to cross an ancient cattle guard, the steel bars singing under their tires. They drove up the gravel drive, through an acre of tangled, harvest-brown bromegrass in need of mowing. The wind combed the long stalks and set the seed heads bobbing, and the sound of the wind over the Ford's hood was a steady, low note that made Jem sit up straight, the muscles in his back tight.

"Are we close to your friends?" Tean asked.

"The Jenkins?" Jem thought. "Not far. Even if there weren't a trail, Benny could have hiked up here pretty easily. He liked doing that sometimes; he called it 'off-roading.'"

Tean just nodded.

Then the bromegrass ended, and they moved up onto a narrow bench of land where the Bowling's house stood. This side of the mountains was tawny with scrub, broken only here and there by twisted, stunted junipers and Russian olives. The house was old, the paint blistered and peeling on the clapboard, the windows slightly warped. Junk cluttered the porch: two microwaves, an easy chair with springs poking out of the cushions, an old standing cupboard with broken glass shining in the late morning light, a Twister mat hung over one railing, a rusted muffler on which someone had scrawled a giant heart with an arrow through it—on and on like that. Behind the house stood a barn, the paint long since stripped, the wood bleached gray. A boy emerged from the barn pushing a wheelbarrow. He stopped when he saw them, and then he set the wheelbarrow down and came toward them. Jem guessed he was sixteen; he was wearing jeans and a too-large Carhartt work shirt, worn-out Timberlands, and a belt buckle the size of a dinner plate. What held Jem's eye, though, was the SpongeBob SquarePants trucker hat, brim pulled to one side.

"Can I handle this?" Jem said.

"I don't know," Tean said, "can you?"

Jem tried to swat the back of his head, but the doc was squirrelly and dodged.

Buzzing down the window, Jem stuck a hand out and waved the kid over to the passenger side of the truck. He came around, stopped, his eyes going to the lettering on the panel, and then he took a few more cautious steps.

"Hi," Jem said. "Great hat."

The kid grinned; he was missing a front tooth and obviously embarrassed of it, the way he tried to keep his smile from getting too big to show it. He tugged on the bill, giving it a few twists, and then he said, "Can I help you with something, sir?"

"Actually, you can," Jem said. "I'm not from around here, and I'm kind of in a tricky situation. You look like you might know a thing or two about this part of the world."

The kid's shoulders went back, and he stood a little taller. Then he glanced at the truck's panel again. "That's a Utah truck."

"See?" Jem said. "That's what I'm talking about. I could tell you were smart. Yeah, my friend here is just helping me out, driving me around, you know?"

After a moment, the kid gave a hesitant nod.

"So," Jem said. "Can you help me?"

"Well, sure," the kid said. "I mean, I'll try."

"I'm looking for my brother," Jem said. "His name's Benny." He displayed a picture on his phone. "He comes around here, right?"

"Yeah," the kid said, and he yanked on the bill of the hat again. "He's kind of . . . I mean, yeah, he comes around."

"It's ok," Jem said. "He's sick. It's called schizophrenia."

"I know what that is," the kid said.

"What's your name?" Jem said.

"Dallin."

"Dallin, I told my friend when I drove up that you looked like a smart kid. The hat, you know. God, I love SpongeBob, and I've got to admire a kid with good taste like you, Dallin."

Name repetition, Jem thought, coaching himself because he could feel himself losing focus. And mirroring body language, and asking questions, and showing flaws. When Dallin tugged at his hat, Jem ran a hand through his own hair. When Dallin glanced up at the house and then back at the truck, Jem squared his chest and shoulders to the window so they were facing each other directly.

"When's the last time you saw my brother?" Jem asked.

"I don't know," Dallin said. "A week or two ago. He's always up here about the trail, you know. It gets him real worked up."

"What trail?" Jem asked.

Dallin looked at the house again.

"Sorry," Jem said. "I bet you have a million things to do. Do you have to milk cows? I don't even know anything about stuff like this."

"We don't milk cows," Dallin said, but he had another of those restrained grins. "You really don't know anything about stuff like this?"

"I'm totally lost."

"The tree huggers say they own part of the canyon," Dallin said. "It's our land, though, and Pa says—"

"Dallin!" The voice came from a man standing on the porch. He was wearing an unbuttoned flannel shirt, and he was wiry except for a beer belly. Over his shoulder, he was carrying a shotgun with a camo stock. His boots clumped on the porch steps as he came down. He didn't make a big show with the shotgun, but he sure as hell wanted them to see it. When the man was still ten yards out, Tean drew in a hard breath; on the right side of his head, the man had a bandage taped in place.

"That your dad?" Jem asked.

Dallin just yanked on the bill of the SpongeBob hat.

"I thought you were doing your chores," the man said. Jem recognized the tone: a pretended calm, an illusion of control, a smokescreen of patience. The tone that bullying pieces of shit put on when they were in public. "Don't you got any chores?"

"Yes, sir."

"Then get 'em."

Dallin shot a glance at Jem, his face apologetic; that was a mistake. The man saw it too, and he moved faster than Jem expected, one fist clubbing the kid on the side of the head. Dallin stumbled, caught himself, and ran for the barn. Halfway up the hill, his shoulders crumpled, and he put a hand against his ear.

Jem reached for the door, but Tean caught his other arm, nails digging into the flesh.

"What's going on out here?" the man said.

"Mr. Bowling?" Tean said.

"Who are you?"

"I'm Tean Leon, with DWR. This is Jem Guthall, U.S. Fish and Wildlife. We've got a few questions—"

"If it's about that easement," Bowling said, "you can turn around and go back to wherever you come from. My lawyer says the whole thing is ironclad. They didn't renew the easement. That's on them. That's my land, and I'm under no obligation to give a bunch of nutjobs access just so they can smoke weed and pray to Mother Nature and then turn around and spit on our boys when they come back from war."

Jem was taking slow breaths. Name repetition, he told himself. And mirroring body language, and asking questions, and showing flaws. He focused on the camo stock of the shotgun because he was afraid if he looked Bowling in the face, he'd do something he'd regret later.

"We got off to a bad start," Jem said. "What's your name?"

"Clint Bowling. Now you know my name, now you know I'm the property owner, and now I'm telling you this is private land, and this is still the United States of America, and you're not welcome here. So get off my property before I put birdshot in your butts."

"We're looking into a report of an attack," Tean said. He gestured to the side of his head and asked, "Did someone assault you?"

For a moment, Bowling said nothing. Then he pointed south to a slot canyon. "The tree huggers think they can just take their four-wheelers and their dirt bikes up there. Then they get up to all sorts of mischief. Knocked down part of my fence, wearing trails into the pasture. They cut down some trees, let 'em fall right across the path, just to spite me; they don't like me hunting up there. I was clearing them out when I got caught by a branch."

"Do you know a young man named Benny?" Jem managed to ask. He showed the picture again. "He's been around here."

"No," Bowling said; he didn't even look at the phone.

"I think you do," Jem said. "When was the last time you saw him?"

"You need to get off my land," Bowling said. "I'm not much of one for calling the sheriff; we handle things ourselves."

"Thanks for your time, Mr. Bowling," Tean said.

"That's your boy?" Jem asked.

"Leave it," Tean said as he shifted the truck into gear.

"You've got something to say about my son?"

"I sure do," Jem said. "Let me get out so I can say it in a way you'll understand just fucking perfectly."

He reached for the door, but Tean caught his arm again and eased the truck back down the hill. Bowling stayed at the edge of the gravel drive, watching them. Plumes of dust rose under the truck, filling the cab with the scent of dry stone.

At the bottom of the hill, Jem shook himself and said, "Ok."

Tean's grip eased, but he didn't release Jem's arm.

After a moment, Jem worked his hand around Tean's, loosening his fingers. He squeezed his hand once and then let go.

When they reached the cattle guard, Tean hit the brakes hard enough that the seat belt snapped tight against Jem's chest. He glanced over and was surprised to see Tean pulling wildly at his hair, staring at the numbers on the mailbox. Then the doc grabbed his phone and placed a call.

"Hannah, I need you to go into my office and look at that file I have with Sook's last call-outs and reports." He waited and then he said, "Yes, that's it. Can you see if one of those was for 447 Kemper Bluff out in Tooele? Yes. Yes. Ok, perfect. Yes, take a picture of it and send it to me, please. And Sook's address. And her parents'. Thank you."

He disconnected while she was still talking, and then he eased the truck forward again.

"What?" Jem said.

"We had a conservation officer who was murdered a couple of weeks ago," Tean said. "Sook Hyeon. The last day she was alive, she came out to investigate dead animals reported at Clint Bowling's ranch."

27

Tean drove through Salt Lake and across the valley. The Hyeons lived in Woodridge Terrace, an upper-middle-class area on the east side of the city, butting up against the Wasatch Mountains and Millcreek Canyon. It was currently undergoing an upgrade phase: old strip malls were being demolished and replaced with either new strip malls, mixed-use development, or expensive condos. Many of the new buildings mirrored construction in the rest of the valley: stucco and glass and pale stone. The older homes, however, were timber and clapboard with shingle roofs, and the residential streets were lined with yew and cottonwood and ponderosa pines.

"You think Bowling killed both of them?" Jem asked.

The sound of his voice startled Tean, who had been wrapped up in his own thoughts. He nodded slowly. "I think it's possible. We know Benny was out there; Dallin confirmed it for us. We know Sook was out there; her own reports tell us that much. We know Bowling is hostile to anyone he perceives as the environmentalist type. And the wound on the side of his head is a pretty good match for where you hit our attacker last night."

"What's his motive?"

"Sook probably saw something that she wasn't supposed to see. Maybe he's done more than just cut down a few trees to keep those people from crossing his land. She might have seen something that could have really hurt someone. Or she might have seen something else."

"Something she didn't report?" Jem said.

"She was killed the same day," Tean said. "She didn't write a report, at least, not one that she submitted. We just have the record of the complaint that she was responding to. Someone claimed there were sick animals on the property."

"That sounds like what Benny said about the birds," Jem said.

Tean nodded.

"What the fuck?" Jem said.

"That's what I want to know."

The Hyeon's house was small, with dove-colored clapboard, probably two bedrooms and one bath; it looked even smaller on its half-acre lot. The yard was neatly tended, and climbing roses grew on a trellis at the front of the house. Under an aluminum carport, a car cover had slid halfway off an ancient Ford Pinto.

Mr. Hyeon had salt-and-pepper hair in a neat part, clear brown eyes, and an argyle sweater. Mrs. Hyeon had a dark bob, wore glasses with mother-of-pearl frames, and kept trying to smile, although grief was obviously making it difficult. They ushered Tean and Jem into the home, and in a matter of minutes, they were each holding a mug of tea, and on the coffee table in front of them was a plate of Oreos. Jem took two, looked at Tean, set his jaw, and took two more.

"Mr. and Mrs. Hyeon," Tean said, "I want to tell you how sorry I am about Sook. We loved working with her; she was happy and smart and hardworking, and she cared about her job."

Mr. Hyeon nodded. Mrs. Hyeon wiped her eyes.

"Did Sook talk to you that night?"

"No," Mr. Hyeon said.

"Just a phone call," Mrs. Hyeon said. "We talked every night on the phone."

"Did she say anything about that day? Anything strange that had happened? Anything she mentioned, even in passing?"

Mrs. Hyeon shook her head.

"What about her boyfriend?" Tean asked.

"Ricky is a good boy."

"Did she talk to him?"

"No," Mrs. Hyeon said.

"We asked," Mr. Hyeon said. "The police asked. She didn't talk to him that day."

"Were there any unusual phone calls? I assume you had access to her phone records? Anything out of the ordinary in her mail? Letters?"

The Hyeons exchanged another look and both shook their heads.

Tean looked at his tea, at the faint wisps of steam curling up from it, and then he set the mug down gently. "Do you have any idea why she went out that night?"

Mr. Hyeon gave a hard shake of his head; Mrs. Hyeon started to cry. Pulling the mother-of-pearl glasses from her eyes, she made her way out of the room.

Outside, the wind shook the branches of a ponderosa. Green needles scraped the window, leaving tracks on the glass, the sound shrill and startling. Jem was munching Oreos.

"If it's all right with you," Tean said, "I'd like to look for a few work items at Sook's apartment. Would you mind —"

But he hadn't finished asking the question before Mr. Hyeon had produced a pair of keys and passed them over.

"Thank you," Tean said. "I'm sorry we had to bother you. Thank you for your time."

Mr. Hyeon followed them to the door.

But as Tean followed Jem outside, Mrs. Hyeon emerged from the hallway and said, "What about Sook's bag?"

"I'm sorry?"

"Sook's bag. We never got Sook's bag."

"I'll check at work," Tean said, but he was thinking about the lawsuit against the ME's office, the possessions that had disappeared. "And I'll ask the police."

Then Mr. Hyeon shut the door, and the late October light felt like a sunburn on the side of Tean's face.

"What's the deal there?" Jem asked as they drove toward Sook's apartment in Murray. They were leaving the mountains behind them, driving deeper into the suburban wasteland of the valley, lodgepoles and ponderosas and cottonwoods replaced by car wash advertisements and check-cashing stores.

"Nobody knows," Tean said. "She went home, called her mom, and the next thing anyone knows, the police found her dead outside a mechanic's garage in Glendale."

"Jesus."

Tean just nodded. He pulled into the parking lot of an apartment building: yellow brick, painted-shut windows, drip patterns of rust under the fire escape. At this hour much of the lot was empty, and Tean found an unmarked spot and parked. They went around front; the entrance of the door looked secure, and Tean grabbed the keys

Mr. Hyeon had given him, but Jem just gave a hard tug and the door came open.

"Lock's broken," he said. "You can see it even with the door closed."

"Show me," Tean said.

Jem let the door swing shut. Pointing to the space between the door and the jamb, he said, "The latch doesn't catch. See? On an old building like this, in a decent area, it probably hasn't been enough of a problem to get the building manager to repair it. Hell, most of the residents are probably glad they don't have to deal with the lock."

"Yeah," Tean said. "But if it were my first time here, I wouldn't have even looked. I would have just assumed it was functioning. The first thing I would have done is buzzed up to see if she could let me in."

Jem shrugged. "You aren't hanging around with enough criminals."

"I thought exterior doors opened inward," Tean said.

"What?"

Tean tugged on the door, pulling it toward them.

Jem shrugged again.

"Shouldn't you know?" Tean said. "You know, from your job."

"Oh," Jem said, grinning. "That's not really my area. Give me a cement truck or a jackhammer, you know?"

Tean nodded.

"But fire doors open out," Jem said.

"Right," Tean said. "Of course."

"Are you waiting for me to do another amazing feat of observation?" Jem said.

Tean shook his head.

"Then after you, Doc," Jem said, catching the door and ushering Jem into the building.

They took the stairs to the second floor, and when they got to Sook's apartment, Tean looked at Jem.

"Can't walk through walls," Jem said in an apologetic tone. "Yet."

So Tean tried the door, which was locked, and then tried the first key, then tried the second. He opened the door, and the smell of a closed-up space wafted out to meet them, stale air with undernotes of spoiled food. When he pushed open the door, Jem put a hand on his belly and said, "Let me take a look."

"She's been dead for weeks," Tean said. "Nobody's waiting inside."

"Then it won't hurt for me to go first."

"This is silly," Tean said.

"It wasn't silly when a guy tried to beat our brains in last night," Jem said.

"I don't think—"

"You're ruining the advantage of surprise," Jem said with a small smile.

Tean rolled his eyes, but he let Jem go first. The blond man had that length of paracord dangling from one hand, and in the other he held the collapsed antenna. Tean followed him into the apartment. While Jem moved from room to room, turning on lights, Tean tried to consider Sook's home: off-white walls; lots of framed pictures of Sook, her boyfriend Ricky, and other friends and family; a couch that looked like it was from her college days; an electric keyboard with sheet music for a piano arrangement of Morrissey's "Everyday Is Like Sunday." In the bedroom, a mountain of brightly colored pillows was arranged on the bed; in the closet, clothes were arranged first by color and then style. He wondered if the apartment had been this clean when Sook left it for the final time? He wondered if her parents had come and cleaned? Sook's lease must have extended through the end of the month; perhaps her parents simply couldn't bring themselves to remove their daughter's possessions. He had a mental image of Mrs. Hyeon coming here and arranging those pillows on the bed, and he felt like part of him was breaking.

But while Tean catalogued and questioned all of this with one part of his brain, another part of his brain was thinking. What kind of construction worker carried improvised weapons in the pockets of his windbreaker? What kind of construction worker didn't know if exterior doors opened in or out? Yes, the explanation about fire exits made sense, but it had been too late; Jem was smart, and Jem had thought of the right answer, but he hadn't known it. What kind of construction worker insisted on going first into a place he thought was dangerous? Well, that was maybe most of them—toxic masculinity probably ran rampant among those guys.

"What are you smiling about?" Jem asked.

"Just wondering who you are," Tean said.

Pocketing the weapons again, Jem rolled his eyes.

"Did you know that toxic masculinity probably explains why men die before women? Statistically, I mean."

"Oh God," Jem said, sliding past Tean, his hand skating over Tean's chest familiarly. "Statistics. I better find the toilet for when I need to throw up."

"I don't even know where to start looking," Tean said.

"What are we looking for?"

"I don't know. Anything that might explain why Sook and Benny both died after they were on Bowling's property."

"Are we worried about fingerprints?" Jem said.

"I don't think so. The police have already been through here and released it."

"Then the first place you look is everywhere you've ever tried to hide something," Jem said. "You know. Like maybe you hide a very expensive watch in your underwear drawer."

Tean's jaw dropped.

"The blue jock is really cute," Jem said. "I like the duckies on it."

"You went through my stuff?"

"You can learn a lot about a guy from his underwear," Jem said. "Besides, it was the night I was cleaning you up after Ammon left."

Tean just stared, trying to work through that.

"Although the police have probably found anything that was hidden somewhere obvious like that," Jem said, moving to the dresser and pulling open the top drawer.

"How do you know this kind of stuff?"

"Maybe I've got a history of B and Es," Jem said. "I'm a convicted felon, after all."

"Really? It was a felony?"

"No," Jem said. "Why? Would you like me more if it was?"

Tean snorted and moved back to the closet.

"The bad-boy thing," Jem said, "that does it for you, huh?"

"Did you know that leather jacket sales went up by seventeen percent after the Fonz started wearing one?"

"The Fonz? Isn't he a little old for you?"

"And Elvis was considered such a threat that he was burned in effigy after appearing on the *The Ed Sullivan Show*."

"I think I was burned in effigy once."

"And even though everybody knows from a distance that the bad-boy appeal is socially counterproductive and unlikely to lead to a successful relationship, people still fall into the same trap. That's why one in three teenagers have experienced violence in a romantic relationship."

"Yeah," Jem said, "but they were probably asking for it."

Tean was digging around at the base of the closet, and he sat up so hard that he got tangled in some of Sook's black skirts. By the time he got free, he was saying, "That's absolutely one of the most inappropriate—"

Jem was sitting on the dresser, smiling, his crooked front teeth making him look like he'd just broken a window with a slingshot.

"Oh," Tean said.

"God, you're cute."

Tean pushed his glasses back up before they could fall.

"And those little yellow duckies," Jem said.

"Ok. Can you do something productive, please?"

"I'm all finished. Checked the drawers. Checked the bottoms of the drawers. Checked for false panels. Checked inside the dresser's frame. Checked under the dresser."

"You did?"

"Gotta be fast in a B and E, Doc."

"I honestly don't understand you at all," Tean said.

Jem's smile turned into a smirk.

"Go do something useful," Tean said.

"I'll search the bed."

"Great."

"Maybe you should come over here and search it with me."

"Never mind. Go do something useful in another room where you're not going to drive me crazy."

Jem was still smirking as he saluted. Then he hopped off the dresser and stretched, his shirt rucking up to expose the faint blond hairs above the waistband of his jeans.

"Go," Tean shouted, throwing a shoe.

It caught Jem on the shoulder, and he pretended to stagger. He was still laughing at his own joke as he left the room.

After that, Tean moved methodically through the room: he opened shoeboxes, patted down jackets and coats, checked pockets, opened and examined the vacuum-packed storage cubes on the closet's upper shelf. He searched the bed, checked the mattress for any slits or openings, and he even squished each one of the brightly colored pillows. He found nothing.

When he went out to the kitchen, Jem was standing on the counter, poking around above the upper cabinets.

"Did you already check the baseboards?" Tean said.

"They're all fastened," Jem said.

"Yeah, but these are just finish nails. They pop right off. You can cut a little space out of the drywall."

"Spoken like a true criminal, Doc. Sounds like you might have some experience."

"I had to hide, um, some pictures when I was growing up."

Tean opened drawers until he found one with flatware. He was waiting for the teasing. Some sort of joke about his underwear again. Maybe jokes about sexual proclivities. He selected a butter knife. Still nothing. Finally, he couldn't take it, and he glanced up.

Jem was staring at him, his expression grim. "Hiding pornographic pictures of young men, Teanthony Leon? I'm very disappointed in you."

Tean tried to stab his foot, but Jem was surprisingly nimble.

"And it's not Teanthony," he shouted as he headed into the bedroom.

He examined the baseboards in the closet first, then the ones in the bedroom itself. None of them showed the signs of wear and tear that he would expect on a piece that was frequently removed, but he tapped on each piece with the knife. Everything sounded solid. When he moved into the living room, he started near the bedroom door and worked his way around the room. Nothing.

When he moved into the kitchen, Jem was perched on the counter, swinging his legs slowly. "Teandrew."

"Don't do that," Tean said, tapping his way along the baseboards.

"Teanastasio."

"Did you know that there are historically verifiable cases of people being killed just for being annoying?"

"Teangelo."

"Oh my gosh," Tean said, sitting back on his heels. "Teancum. Teancum. My full name is Teancum Mahonri Leon. Can you please do something instead of trying to accelerate my inevitable aneurysm?"

"Dude," Jem said, covering his mouth with one hand. "Your name literally has cum in it."

Something about the way Tean adjusted his grip on the knife must have been convincing because Jem hurried into the other room.

Tean continued to work his way along the baseboards, but he stopped when he neared the refrigerator. A strange brown spot marked the top of the baseboard. A dot. Just a speck, really. He worked the knife behind the baseboard, pried it loose, and swore.

"Did I just hear you use a bad word?" Jem called.

"Come here," Tean said.

Jem's steps were hurried. "What's wrong?"

Tean pointed to the brown stains that had been hidden by the baseboard. It must have seeped behind the wood, avoiding the cleanup efforts of whoever had removed the stains on the wall.

"That," Jem said, "looks like blood."

28

Their search inside the apartment didn't turn up anything else, but Jem didn't really expect it to. After finding the blood, Tean had fallen apart. It wasn't immediately noticeable, especially not if you didn't know the doc well, but Jem had spent pretty much every moment of the last week in close quarters with him. His face was pale, his pupils were huge, and his hands were shaking. Jem let him go for a while, hoping he'd wear himself out, but he realized pretty quickly that the doc wasn't the type who gave up easily. When Tean wanted to go door to door for interviews, Jem gently caught his wrist and pulled him toward the stairs.

"The neighbors might have—"

"The police already talked to them," Jem said.

"I know, but—"

"Doc," Jem said, "call Ammon. Tell him what you found. If it's blood, they'll test it and they can see if it's hers. Then they'll talk to the neighbors again."

"I want to do something."

"No," Jem said, "you want to run yourself into the ground because you're hurting. That's not productive." He gave another tug, and this time, Tean let him lead him out of the building.

When they got to the car, Jem said, "Keys."

"I can drive."

"I know. You've been giving me the *Driving Miss Daisy* treatment for almost a week now. Keys."

"It's a government vehicle, and you're not allowed—"

Jem reached into Tean's pocket, extracted the keys, and then steered Tean by the shoulders toward the passenger door. As he guided the truck out of the parking lot, he said again, "Call Ammon."

So Tean placed the call, and Jem had to listen while Ammon shouted about Tean being irresponsible and ignoring his explicit instructions to stop pretending he was a detective. Tean was silent for most of the conversation, his shoulders hunched, his head against the glass. When he disconnected, he held the phone in both hands and stared out the window.

"He sounds like he's feeling better," Jem said.

The Ford's tired suspension creaked and groaned as they rolled over a metal plate in a construction zone.

"And he was as charming as ever," Jem said.

"Please stop."

"I just don't think he should talk to you like that. No, fuck that. He definitely shouldn't talk to you like that."

Tean brought his head up; his gaze was cool and dark as he stared at Jem.

But Jem couldn't seem to stop. "And I bet he's really pissed he can't squeeze one out with that broken arm."

Tean pocketed his phone.

"I guess wifey will have to be on call," Jem said. "Double duty until he's out of a cast. Maybe she'll squirt some in the wrong direction and they'll have another kid, one more happy accident."

"You're a real asshole," Tean said quietly.

"Wowzah," Jem said. "A nickel-and-dime bad word."

Tean just shook his head and stared out the window again.

They drove another half mile, passing an Albertson's with a sign that said OUR PHARMACY NOW CARRIES THE HPV VACCINE. Pumpkins sat on hay bales at the edge of the parking lot. A boy with a witch's hat was climbing on the bales while his mom took pictures, although Halloween was still a couple of weeks away. Jem found himself thinking his way back along a dark alley, thoughts he usually kept chained off, as he merged onto I-15 and headed north.

He cleared his throat and asked, "What did you dress up as last Halloween?"

Tean was still staring out the window.

"I dressed up as slutty K-Fed," Jem said, "which I think is just normal K-Fed but with shaved pits."

"Get off at the next exit," Tean said, pointing ahead. "I-15 is at a total stop up ahead."

Instead, Jem merged left.

"No, you need to get off," Tean said. "We're going to get stuck, and—Jem, what are you doing?"

"Oops," Jem said as he brought the truck to a stop. Cars filled in the spaces around them, and then they were stuck in the traffic jam.

"We could be here for hours."

"Yeah," Jem said. "I-15 is always a shitshow."

"Why didn't you just get off the highway?"

"My hearing is going out. I asked you a question about Halloween, and I couldn't hear what you said."

Tean mumbled something.

"That sounded like another bad word," Jem said with a smile.

Folding his arms, Tean angled his body away from Jem and toward the door.

"Come on," Jem said. "We're stuck here. You can't ignore me forever because I'm just going to annoy you until you talk to me, and anyway, I don't like Grumpy Doc. You're supposed to be sweet and slightly befuddled and charming."

"You know what?" Tean said, turning so quickly that he caught Jem by surprise. "I am sick of being nice. I'm sick of it. It sucks."

Jem's smile faded, and he studied the doc. "Ok," Jem said. "Tell it like it is."

"And you want to know another thing? I like you. And that's really messing with my head because once we figure this out with Benny, you're going to go back to California, and you're going to realize that a long-distance relationship with an ultra-repressed and seriously confused vet is way too much work. And I'll probably die from grief. Not because I can't live without you, so don't get that big grin on your face, but because science has proven that grief can cause inflammation that can actually, literally kill you. And that would be my kind of luck."

"I just want to give you credit," Jem said, "for finding the bleakest and most depressing way I've ever heard of telling me that you like me."

"And here's one more thing," Tean said, his voice rising. "I've already got an asshole in my life who has my head spinning and makes me feel like shit about myself and about my choices. I don't need two." His face was getting red. "And I'm shouting because I'm really hurt and angry right now."

They sat that way for a few more seconds, and then Tean slumped against the seat and looked out the window again.

Jem drummed his thumbs against the steering wheel and said, "Feel better?"

"A little."

"Unofficial diagnosis: you're a really good guy, and maybe you could try being a little less good. It might take the edge off."

"I'm not good. I'm not a good guy. I'm nice, which is totally different. Being nice is a nightmare."

"I also am going to prescribe that you do some more venting and yelling, whenever you feel like you need it."

"You're going to talk to me about how to handle big emotions?" Tean said, giving Jem a hard look. "You?"

"Ok, fair. But just because I don't follow my own advice doesn't mean it's not good advice. Actually, come to think of it, you're pretty good at being honest about your emotions."

"Sure," Tean said. "Look how great I'm doing."

"And you've got a really good set of lungs."

Tean leaned his head against the glass. In a quieter voice, he said, "Can you just not talk about Ammon, please? I tried to explain it to you. I obviously didn't do a good job. You don't understand what we have."

But Jem understood. He understood it inside and out, and he'd seen twenty or thirty versions of the same show and knew how it ended every time.

All he said, though, was, "Yeah."

"And say you're sorry."

"I'm not sorry for saying he shouldn't talk to you like that."

"Jem."

"Ok, ok. I'm sorry I said the rest of it. And I'm sorry I upset you. And I'm sorry I made you use a bad word."

"Oh my gosh," Tean said, covering his eyes.

"You need a little practice. It doesn't really roll off the tongue yet."

"Oh my gosh," Tean said again, drawing out the words.

"You'll get there." Jem said, letting a grin slip out. "Now, can we please talk about your name?"

Tean groaned.

"Cum on," Jem said, but he spoiled it by laughing. "Did you hear how I said it? Cum. Like Teancum. Or like when you —"

"What? What do you need to know about my name? Anything to hurry this along."

"How in the world did your parents come up with those names?"

"They're Mormon names."

"What do they mean?"

"They're from the Book of Mormon."

"You don't want to tell me."

"Have you read the Book of Mormon?"

"No," Jem said.

"Are you interested in reading the Book of Mormon?"

"Not particularly."

Tean held out an open hand.

"But," Jem said, "that doesn't mean I don't want to hear about your names. I'm interested in you."

They inched forward in traffic. In the car next to them, someone was playing "Barbie Girl," singing along with the chorus. Tean cracked his window, and the smell of too-sweet exhaust filtered into the car, mixing with the fragrance that Jem had come to associate with Tean: sagebrush, the open range, crushed pine needles.

"Teancum is an assassin," Tean said. "Nominally, he's a good guy. He sneaks into the tents of evil kings and kills them in their sleep."

"That's a badass name."

"Well, he gets caught and executed."

"Oh. Bummer."

"And Mahonri is — gosh, it's such a long story. But the short version is that he's supposed to be one of the prophets with the most faith."

Jem nodded.

"There you go," Tean said.

"Thank you."

Playing with the glovebox latch, Tean frowned. Then he dropped his hand and said, "It's just more evidence of my parents' massive disappointment. They wanted a warrior. Well, the first time I went hunting, I was twelve, I think. With my grandpa. Even at the time, I was pretty sure we were poaching, but that wasn't the main problem."

"Little Tean," Jem said, grinning, but the verso of the grin cutting sharp, slicing him up inside. "Even back then you loved your rules."

"Huh. I never really thought about myself that way. I guess that's kind of true, although I'm pretty bad at actually obeying all the rules. Anyway, I got a turkey, and that was it. I sobbed and sobbed. Never picked up a gun again, which pissed my dad off to no end. I couldn't even pretend it was an ethical objection. I mean, I still eat meat. I'm just too much of a coward to do the killing myself."

"You're not a coward."

"And faith, well, don't get me started. I mean, by the time I realized I was more interested in what was under Ammon's shorts than what was under the girls' skirts, I was done with church."

"You went on a mission."

"I was the oldest. My parents expected it. Heck, I expected it. And I hadn't verbalized, not even to myself, a lot of the stuff I was experiencing."

"And then Ammon happened."

"And then Ammon happened," Tean agreed. "And there was no going back."

Something shifted ahead, and Jem eased the truck forward as the traffic broke up. He glanced over, wanting something to say, wondering why he felt cut to ribbons inside. Tean's face was blank, his dark eyes distant, but he was running his hands through his wild dark hair and tugging hard.

When they got back to the apartment, they sat in the truck as the engine cooled. Jem checked his phone; Tinajas had sent more pictures that people had submitted in response to his KSL ad, but none of them matched the Chevy that had almost run Jem and Tean off the road. Then Jem said, "I'm going back to the Bowlings' place tonight."

"I figured."

"I'm sorry. I know you shouldn't get dragged into this. If you don't want me to come back here after trespassing, I'll understand."

"Maybe we'll get arrested," Tean said.

"Maybe," Jem said. "And you know what they say: you never forget your first."

"And I'll probably end up getting shanked in the showers because my cellmate hates me."

"Oh, you'll definitely get poked by something."

"Hey!" Tean said, pushing his glasses back into place.

"You're just too cute."

"And I'll probably get hepatitis and AIDS and die."

"Well, if you get shanked, you'll probably die from that first."

Tean pushed his glasses up slowly again. "Ammon gets so mad when I say stuff like that. My parents try to pretend they don't hear anything. Hannah at least knows it's a joke and just ignores me. Why don't you get mad?"

"Oh, Doc," Jem said. He just shook his head and got out of the truck.

"I'm coming too," Tean said, moving around the truck.

"That's not a good idea."

"Someone killed Sook. Someone murdered her. And I don't know if they did it in her apartment or if they attacked her there and took her somewhere else, but someone killed her and tried to make it look like something else. She wasn't out driving around in a bad part of town. She didn't just make a bad mistake."

"She made a mistake," Jem said. "It just wasn't the one we thought. And you're jumping to conclusions based on some blood."

"Blood that someone tried to clean up." Tean set his jaw. "I'm going with you."

"Great," Jem said. "Now can we have a nap?"

"What?"

"Come on," Jem said. "Let's walk Scipio and take a nap."

So they did, although Scipio was extra excited to see them, and he kept jumping on Jem while Jem backed himself into a corner and pressed sweaty palms against his thighs. After the walk, they napped, and when they woke, Tean had squirmed away from Jem, moving all the way to the edge of the mattress. The sun was coming in through the window, and Jem was hot and sweating and sticky where his skin touched Tean's skin. He extracted himself, ignoring Tean's groans, and showered. When he had dressed in clean jeans and his Smith Field House shirt, gray heather and freshly washed, he found Tean in the kitchen.

"I'm boiling eggs," Tean said, and Jem could already smell the slight sulfur odor that meant they had overcooked. "I think we can mash them up and put them with butter on pasta."

"Ok," Jem said, "I think you've done just about enough."

"What?"

"I mean, that's very sweet of you. Go shower."

"I don't—"

"We're going out. Go shower."

Tean grimaced, but he left the kitchen, and Jem turned off the burners and let the extra-boiled eggs and the limp pasta cool down in the pots. He fed Scipio—the Lab kept trying to nuzzle his hand, and Jem gave him a few conciliatory pats on the head, his heart beating in his throat the whole time—and by then the shower had stopped running.

"Is this ok?" Tean said, gesturing at the outfit he'd put on.

Jem covered his mouth. "I like where your head's at," he said when he trusted himself to talk again. "Let's just do a quick second look."

"You said more green, less khaki." Tean plucked at the lime-green t-shirt that said DWR GIVES BACK and then gestured at the olive camo pants.

"I did," Jem said, nodding, and he shepherded Tean back into the bedroom. Opening the drawer with all of Tean's tops, Jem sorted through them. "You have a lot of khaki polos."

"There was a deal."

"How many do you have?"

"The last time I bought twenty."

Jem just nodded. "And do you have any t-shirts that you didn't get from a charitable 5K or a service opportunity?"

"I think there's one from a car wash."

Jem nodded again.

"Yours is from BYU," Tean said. "Did you go to BYU?"

"I did not."

"Why is it different for you to wear a BYU t-shirt and for me to wear this t-shirt?"

"Glasses," Jem said, holding out his hand.

"I need them to see."

"I'm not holding you hostage. I'll give them back in a minute." When Tean had given him his glasses, Jem passed over a t-shirt—the car wash one, which was navy and had a cute—and small—design of a smiling convertible. Then he passed over a pair of khakis.

"You said less khaki."

"Just change, please."

"I did exactly what you said," Tean grumbled as he switched out the clothes. "More green. That's what you said. Less khaki."

"You did very well. Bathroom."

"Can I have my glasses?"

"In a minute. Bathroom first."

The air was still humid and smelled like the bar of Equate soap. Jem sat Tean on the toilet and then found a comb in the mirrored cabinet. He ran it through Tean's hair, creating a simple part. The hair was long enough to tuck behind Tean's ears, and it was straight and dark and soft.

"You've got some gray, Doc."

Jem whoofed as Tean's punch connected with his gut.

"Hey," Jem said, laughing as he dropped the comb. "Don't kill the messenger."

"Let me see," Tean said.

Passing him the glasses, Jem stepped back. "We need to get you new glasses," Jem said.

"These are fine," Tean said.

"Ones that don't want to fall off your face every five minutes."

Tean was considering himself in the mirror.

Resting his chin on Tean's shoulder, Jem hugged him from behind and said, "Well?"

"I look weird."

"You look handsome."

Blushing, Tean shrugged. "I don't know how to do a lot of this stuff."

"Comb. Hair." Jem kissed the side of his neck. "Come on."

"Where are we going?"

"Just come on."

Following Jem's directions, Tean drove them to the Apollonia. When Jem indicated he should turn into the hotel's underground parking, Tean shook his head.

"I'm sorry. I can't afford a place like that."

"That's ok," Jem said. "I've got a friend here who hooks me up."

They had to circle around the block, with Jem coaxing, but on the next pass, Tean followed the ramp under the hotel and found a spot to park. They headed to the hotel restaurant. Stef was working the bar, her hair pink today, the sides of her head freshly shaved, so Jem nudged Tean toward one of the stools. It was still early, and nobody else was at the bar. When Tean's glasses slipped and almost fell, Stef raised an eyebrow, her face asking some version of a familiar question: *Really? This guy?*

"Stef," Jem said, "this is a really good friend. Tean, this is Stef, and she's a total bitch."

She whipped him with the bar rag, but her eyes were a little wider than usual. When Jem came here to work, they pretended not to know each other; tonight, Jem had broken new ground.

"You put up with this guy?" Stef asked.

Tean shrugged, but he was smiling.

"What do you want to drink? The first one is on the house because you've got to deal with his dumb ass."

"I don't really —" Tean said.

"He's going to have a Ruby."

Tean turned to look at Jem. Stef raised an eyebrow.

"Ok, both of you can turn it down a little bit," Jem said. "I'm going to have a Campfire. And we're going to have the charcuterie board, and we're going to split the ribeye and the salmon, both of them with mashed potatoes."

"What's a Ruby?" Tean said.

"It's a cider. And before you ask, yes, it has alcohol."

"I don't like that stuff."

Jem put a hand on his knee and squeezed. "Try it?"

"Ok," Tean said with a shrug.

Stef was giving Jem an unreadable look. When she left to get their drinks, Jem said, "You don't like food, you don't like booze, and we're still working on fantastic sex."

"We are?" Tean said

The question was so innocent, and his eyes were so wide that Jem laughed. "Just focus on actually enjoying things tonight. Pay attention to what you taste, how the flavors mix, how your body feels, what the food is like in your mouth."

"This sounds dirty."

"Good," Jem said, smirking. "Then I'm doing it right."

When their drinks came, Tean tried his cider and then frowned at Jem.

Jem laughed again.

"It's good."

Jem shrugged.

"Like, really good," Tean said.

"Stick with me, kid."

"You know I'm older than you, right?"

"How could I forget? I saw all that gray, remember."

When Stef brought the charcuterie board, she explained everything that was included, and then Jem made Tean try everything: the meats and cheeses, but also the house faux gras — made with mushrooms, lentils, and nuts, instead of liver — the bread, the water crackers, the peach chutney. He made him try combinations. And he made him talk about it.

"Ok," Jem finally said, "but how is it good? You've got to think about it beyond 'it's good' or 'it's bad.'"

Tean rolled his eyes and tried again.

When the salmon and ribeye came, they took turns, each of them eating a few bites of the salmon or the ribeye and then switching.

"I think I like the salmon more," Tean said. "I like the texture, and I like the bite from the capers."

"Look at you," Jem said. "Capers."

Then, a few minutes later, Tean said, "Actually, I think I like the steak more. I like how the meat is seared."

Jem raised both eyebrows.

"I guess that's more proof I have no idea what I'm talking about," Tean said with a nervous laugh.

"Nope," Jem said. "It's proof that we ordered two good meals, and you're enjoying both of them.

When they'd finished eating, Jem settled up with Stef at the end of the bar; he didn't want Tean knowing how much he paid. He peeled off a hundred and then a pair of twenties. Stef took them, tapping the bills together, lining up the edges.

"You're playing a dangerous game," Stef said.

"Come on," Jem said. "I bought him dinner. He's a sweet guy. You've seen me in here with some real dickbags."

"It's dangerous," Stef said, "because you really like him."

In the stairwell, Tean suddenly turned, grabbing Jem by the hips and forcing him against the wall, kissing him. His mouth tasted like the crisp brightness of apples. His hands were uncertain on Jem's hips.

When he pulled back, he had to blink to clear his eyes.

"I liked that," Jem said, his own eyes hooded, his chest rising and falling quickly. "I like that you did that."

Tean gave a half-nod, but he looked even more confused.

Another moment passed, and then above them, footfalls and drunken laughter rang out against the poured cement. Tean started.

Squeezing Tean's wrist, Jem moved toward the garage. "Come on. Let's do some trespassing and investigating, and then let's get back to the apartment so I can do a lot of very wicked things to you."

Over his shoulder, he caught a glimpse of Tean's bemused grin.

29

The Bowling ranch looked deserted at night, and for a moment, Tean felt wildly optimistic. The Bowlings had gone somewhere. They were at a stock auction. They were taking a family vacation. They had fled the country. Even that last option didn't dampen the surge of hope. Tean could search the place tonight with Jem, and they would find nothing, and then they could go home. Home. That sounded right.

The world was in motion: the clumps of rabbit brush and saltbrush, winterfat and sage, flickered in the headlights like the pieces of stop motion film; the shadows of rolled bales ballooned and then shrank in mowed fields of blue grama and buffalo grass; a few stalks of rye in a trampled field trembled as they passed; a jackrabbit broke from a clump of dead weeds; the stars wheeled overhead. And Tean, too, caught up in that movement, pieces of him flowing on a current he was tired of fighting.

Ancient people believed that the stars were a kind of god, Tean wanted to say. He could feel the words almost breaking free. They believed there were gods in the trees and in the rivers, in the land and in the sky. But the stars especially, and the sun and the moon, and the planets. The night sky was clear; on this side of the Oquirrh Mountains, free of the city's light pollution, the stars were painful in their clarity. The Mormons too, Tean wanted to say. They were just a few more in a tradition stretching back to a time before humans first mastered fire. Was it really that strange to believe that heaven was a place, that it had coordinates out among the stars, that if the Enterprise kept up its mission of peaceful exploration, Kirk or Picard might one day stumble across it?

"Park on the shoulder," Jem said. His body was tense; the light from the dash painted his strong features in patches of soft yellow and shadow. He wasn't smiling, not exactly, but his lips were curved, those crooked front teeth showing.

They parked, and when Tean shut off the lights, it was like the night pulling in a breath. Together they jogged across the road, jumped the drainage ditch to avoid the cattle guard, and started up the hill. Light glazed only a single window at the front of the Bowlings' house, but after a moment, Tean realized that he could see a much weaker light flickering in another room—a television, he thought, or perhaps a show being streamed on a laptop or tablet. The breeze off the Oquirrhs soughed in the overgrown brome, matting clumps of it and then letting them spring back up, the field bristling and stirring.

When they reached the bench where the Bowlings' home stood, Tean saw that the single lighted window showed a middle-aged woman sitting at the dining room table, eating something out of a bowl. Her profile was severe, and she stared at one of the kitchen walls, her hand moving mechanically to bring food to her mouth.

Jem stopped, studying the house. Tean tried to see what Jem might be seeing. They knew, now, that there were three possible occupants: Mr. and Mrs. Bowling, and their son, Dallin. Mrs. Bowling was presumably accounted for, and it was possible that Mr. Bowling and Dallin were watching television in the other room. But Tean realized that was not a safe assumption; he hadn't seen Bowling or Dallin yet; they could be anywhere. They could be coming back late from a day's work.

Tilting his head toward the barn, Jem motioned for Tean to follow. On the porch, the collected junk that Tean had noticed on their last visit threw shadows that shifted and crawled. The door of an electric oven hung open, and Tean's movement and the bobbing shadows made it look like a rictus grin. As they circled around the house, a pair of motion-detector floodlights came on, throwing a harsh, white illumination over the cement apron. Tean froze. Jem kept going, and then he glanced back, smiled, and beckoned. Tean was waiting for dogs, an alarm, maybe Mrs. Bowling to fire a shotgun over their heads. But nothing happened, and he forced himself forward. The October night was cold, especially with the breeze, but his face was hot with a flush and pinpoint drops of sweat.

Jem was already slipping inside the barn; Tean followed. He was hit with a wall of foul air. He'd been in plenty of barns in his life, personally and professionally, and he knew what he was smelling: dung, dirt, mildew, and something rancid. Jem had already turned on the lights and was moving along the row of stalls. Tean hurried ahead, passing a broken-down, spindle-legged horse that just lifted a weary head and stared at them, and checked the loft. Several of the ladder's rungs were split. The floorboards in the loft were bowed under the weight of baled hay; the clean, sweet smell of the bales was the only decent thing in the whole barn.

By the time Tean got to the floor again, Jem was waiting, an eyebrow cocked.

"This doesn't make any sense," Tean whispered, jerking a thumb to indicate their surroundings.

"Sure it does," Jem said. "Bowling is a filthy slob; you saw his house. No surprise that the barn is the exact same. That poor horse is standing in inches of its own shit."

"He's got freshly baled hay up in the loft," Tean said. "But he can't be troubled to mow and bale what he's got out in front of his house."

"So he's a lazy fucker too," Jem said. "The truck's not here; let's go."

Tean didn't press the point. They headed outside, Tean turning off the lights as he left, and this time Jem jogged straight toward the house. The floodlights sprang to life again. This time, Tean kept moving, although his heart still kicked up to about a hundred and thirty. At the garage, Jem stopped and considered the door. Then he got to his knees, worked his fingers under the disintegrating weather stripping at the bottom of the door, and pulled. With a hollow boom of metal flexing, the door rolled up a few inches.

"Go," Jem whispered.

Tean slid under the door on his belly, got to his feet, and fumbled for his phone. This was more than trespassing now. This was breaking and entering. This meant a criminal record, jail time, losing his job. Jem squirmed under the door, and by then, Tean had turned on the phone's flashlight. He swept it slowly across the garage: a black Dodge Ram that looked brand new; a lime-green VW Beetle, brand new; and in the third bay, an orange Mustang, brand new. An artificial, coconut smell filled the air, and it took Tean a moment to spot the Beetle's windows rolled down, a hula girl air freshener hanging from the rearview mirror.

"Fuck me," Jem whispered. He paced a full circuit of the garage, using his own phone for light now, and then he came back and shook his head. They squirmed under the garage door again, and Jem forced it down, the door giving another of those soft booms as it fell against the cement.

"The red truck isn't here," Tean said. "And we didn't see anything in the barn, so let's go. "We'll contact that nature group, or whoever claims they have land in the canyon, and we'll go up there and check it out tomorrow."

"Bowling won't like that."

"We won't tell Bowling. For now, though, let's go. I don't want to spend the last few years of my thirties getting used and abused by my cellmate Tiny."

"Tiny might be really gentle with you," Jem said, his head swiveling as he scanned the side of the house. When he moved again toward the back of the house, the floodlights flicked on.

"And it won't just be Tiny," Tean said. "Tiny will probably sell me for toilet wine, and I'll end up like one of those guys, and they'll make me wear a mop as a wig and use crushed up candy for makeup."

"If that happens," Jem said, waving as he spotted something around the back of the house, "just remember to try to stick as close as possible to your natural colors; you're already so damn pretty, you'll just mess it up if you go overboard."

"I'm not pretty," Tean said, jogging after him. "And when they get bored with me, which they will because I'm terrible at sex, they'll probably turn me into a mule, and I'll have to spend the rest of my time sneaking things from one part of the jail to another." Tean considered this. "Probably up my butt."

Jem had stopped at a pair of wheeled trash cans behind the house, and he motioned for Tean to open one while he searched the other. "Paperwork," Jem said. "Credit card bills, bank statements, mortgage, car payments, anything."

Tean nodded and opened his trash can, but he glanced along the side of the house: in addition to the trash cans, neatly split firewood was stacked almost as high as Tean's shoulders, and several larger sections of logs were lying there, obviously intended to be broken down when necessary. French doors connected the house with the wraparound porch, and although the space immediately on the other side of the doors was dark, Tean could see the flicker of the television. If one of the Bowling clan passed by and looked, they'd be sure to see something.

"First," Jem said as he ripped open a white plastic liner, "I'm a little offended that you think I'd spend so much time with someone who is truly terrible at sex."

"Oh, I've already thought about it," Tean said as he waved the air in front of his face, trying to clear the stench of rotting meat that had clouded up from the bag he had just opened. "You're either playing a really long game to get my kidneys, or you have one of those sensory processing disorders so you have a skewed perspective, or you're just really bad at sex too so you can't tell."

"Teanimal Mahatma Leon."

"Mahonri," Tean whispered.

Jem stared at him, his fingers clutching a black plastic liner so tightly that it had stretched, the plastic turning white along stress lines.

"Retracted," Tean said, "I definitely retract that last part about you being bad at sex."

After a moment, when Jem seemed to think he'd made his point, he went back to work. As he ripped open the next bag, he said, "Second, I think you're not giving yourself enough credit. You're tough, and you're smart. And you're a survivor."

"Yep," Tean said. "I've successfully survived being middle class in one of the most prosperous, safest nations in history."

Jem was carefully lifting one of the bags clear of the trash, obviously trying to get to the next bag. He set the ripped bag down slowly and then turned his attention to the trash can again. "Let's try that again," Jem said. "Say something nice about yourself."

"I've successfully survived having parents who didn't divorce, never abused me, always put food on the table, and helped me get a college education. They also were very supportive when I was in grad school." Tean punched his finger through another plastic membrane and was met with a slimy pile of potato peels. "Yep, I'm a survivor."

"You get one last try," Jem said. "I'm serious this time."

Tean rocked the bag from side to side, sliding the potato peels, trying to see if some valuable paperwork was mixed in with the kitchen trash.

"Five," Jem said.

"It's just a joke. Just ignore me."

"I don't mind jokes, but now let's hear something good about you. That's four, by the way."

"You don't have to get mad."

"I'm not mad. Three."

"Fine. You can yell at me when we're in the truck. You can tell me how ungrateful I sound."

"Not interested in yelling at you. I'd just like to hear you admit one good thing about yourself. That's two. If I get to zero, I'm going to knock on the Bowlings' door and ask them if you can use the bathroom."

"Frick you."

"Golly gee gosh, Doc, you almost used a swear. One." Jem turned on his heel toward the French doors.

"Fine. Fine. Fine." Tean lifted the bag, dropped it, and potato peels slid out. "I am above average at some of my responsibilities at work."

"You're fucking fantastic at your job. Say it."

"I'm well qualified and—"

"Fucking fantastic."

"—I work hard—"

"Two words. Please?"

Tean set his jaw; he was clamping down so hard that his teeth ached.

"It's ok," Jem said with a smile. "We'll keep working on it. Now tell me something deeply disturbing about microplastics."

"On average, humans ingest approximately five grams of microplastic a week. That's the equivalent of about two pennies, if you want to visualize it. Over the course of a year, it would be like eating twelve pieces of plastic the size and shape and weight of double AA batteries. And over the course of your lifetime—wait, go back."

Jem was in the processing of lifting another bag out of the trash when Tean stopped him. Tean reached past him and extricated a smaller, second trash liner from inside the larger bag. He tore open one side and said, "Look at that."

Squinting, Jem considered the papers. Then he looked at Tean.

"You said credit card statements," Tean said. "And this looks like a bank statement, right? Wells Fargo."

Nodding, Jem said, "Good job. Let's—"

From inside the house came raised voices.

"—don't care if it's just a goddamn raccoon." That was Bowling's voice. "When I tell you to do something, you do it. It's not a debate."

"I wasn't—" Dallin replied.

The sound of the blow carried clearly from within the house. Jem flinched.

"Come on," Tean whispered, touching his arm.

"Don't," Jem growled, yanking his arm away. Then, obviously trying to control himself, he added, "Don't touch me right now."

Before Tean could say anything, before he could even think of how to handle this, a shape moved in the darkness on the other side of the French doors. Then one of the doors opened, and the shape emerged from the house. Dallin. He came down the two steps off the deck and stopped when he saw them. He was holding one hand to the side of his head, breathing fast. The weak ambient light shone in his unshed tears.

"What are you—"

"Hey SpongeBob," Jem said, his voice almost normal again. "Your ride is here. Let's go."

"What?" Dallin's gaze moved to Tean. "What are you guys doing?"

"Let's go," Jem said. "You don't have to stay here with that asshole. You don't have to stick around with somebody knocking the stuffing out of you."

"Jem," Tean said, "we can't take him with us. And we need to go right now."

"There are shelters," Jem said. "Social workers."

"We can call this in and report it," Tean said, "but if we take him, we're committing a felony."

"We'll just say he was hitching," Jem said. "We'll just say we picked him up and didn't know what to do with him."

"Jem," Tean said, "you need to stop and think about this."

But Dallin had already shuffled toward the stacked firewood. He grabbed a billet and shook it at them like he was scaring off a wild dog. "Get out of here," Dallin said.

"Your dad's been doing something bad," Jem said. "Hasn't he? And that conservation officer came, and then my brother came, and your dad had to make sure nobody knew what was really happening here."

"Get — get off our property," Dallin said, his voice firming. "Get out of here before I call my dad."

"Is it you?" Jem said. "Did they see him hurting you, and he had to make sure nobody knew about it?"

"Go," Dallin said. He waved the billet of firewood at them. "Get going!"

The shout broke the stillness.

"Is it worse than that? What did they see him do to you? Give me five minutes with that son of a bitch, and he'll never come near you again," Jem said.

"We're leaving," Tean said, grabbing Jem's shirt.

Jem twisted free and took a step toward the deck, as though he were going to walk right through Dallin. Dallin's face twisted with fear and something that might have been relief. He swung the billet, bringing it up and back and then down. Tean could see the blow coming from a mile away, but somehow it seemed to catch Jem off guard. At the last minute he raised his arm, catching the firewood at an angle. Then Dallin stumbled back, and Jem went after him, swatting the wood out of his hand. Dallin braced himself on the stairs to the deck, his face pale, and said, "He's my dad. You're not doing anything to my dad."

From inside, Bowling shouted, "What's going on out there?"

"We're leaving," Tean said. He grabbed Jem's arm; in his other hand, Tean was still carrying the stolen papers. After the first two steps, Jem seemed to understand, and he stumbled along with him.

They were clearing the side of the house when the sound of the door opening reached Tean, and then he could hear Bowling saying, "What the hell is going on?"

Tean's heartbeat pounded in his ears as he and Jem approached the gravel drive.

"Just raccoons," Dallin said.

The rush of relief was so strong that Tean didn't hear anything else, and he ran, towing Jem down the hill.

30

By the time they got back to the apartment, Jem realized how badly he had fucked things up. On the drive back, Jem had been busy jamming his emotions back into place, tying them down, trying not to think about Decker, or the restraints, or the smell of jalapeño Cheetos on Blake's breath, a knee forcing his legs apart, Tanner and Antonio taking turns after Blake was spent. He had noticed that Tean was being very quiet, but he'd been too busy with his own mess to think about it.

But now, climbing the stairs to the apartment, he realized that Tean's silence had an awful depth to it. Tean wasn't looking at Jem, but he didn't seem to be looking at anything. The silence was anger, Jem decided after watching how Tean shoved the key into the lock. And that anger was because Jem had almost fucked up everything by losing control. And for what? For a kid who would take whatever licks his dad gave him because he just wanted to be loved. For a kid who wouldn't take a lifeline when somebody tossed it to him. For a dumbfuck kid. Jem had risked Tean's whole life, everything, for a kid who didn't have the balls to run and be his own man and not take shit from anybody.

Scipio was bouncing and jumping, greeting Tean with snuffles and licks. Tean scratched the dog's ears absently, barely noticing. Jem waited, his back pressed against the door, his heart thumping while Scipio inspected him with a few sniffs and then greeted him by licking his hands. Tean gave the apartment a brief glance, as though making sure it was still there. Then he threw the stolen paperwork on the counter and moved to the balcony. When he opened the sliding glass door and stepped outside, cold air rushed inside, carrying the smell of woodsmoke and the crackle of a fire. Then Tean shut the door. The city lights gave him a silhouette; at some point during the drive, he'd pushed his hair back, and it was wild again.

Scipio whined.

"I know," Jem said. "I'm trying to figure it out."

Scipio must have decided Jem hadn't gotten the message, though, because he scratched on the door and whined again.

"Oh," Jem said. Then, he said, "We've still got a deal, right?" And he opened the door and followed Scipio downstairs. The deal still seemed to be in place because Scipio did his business, sniffed around the flowerbeds for a few minutes and then let Jem call him back upstairs and into the apartment. When Jem shut the door, he saw that Tean was still out on the balcony.

The sliding door was open again, though, and eddies of cold air drifted between Jem's legs as he grabbed a blanket and stepped outside. At the sound of his footsteps, Tean glanced over. He smiled a little when he saw the blanket. When Jem held up a corner of the blanket, Tean nodded, and Jem draped it over his shoulders.

"Thank you," Tean said. His voice was very quiet. The world was very quiet; the crackle of the fire was gone. Nothing from the neighbors. No kids in the lot on the other side of the privacy fence. The distant sound of traffic was the rush of a great river.

"I want to apologize," Jem said. "For losing my shit. Again."

Tean shook his head.

"No, really," Jem said. "I'm ok. I've got it under control. It won't happen again."

"You're not ok, Jem. You aren't supposed to be ok, not with what's going on. Although, I'll admit it's not ideal to have you try to kidnap a kid while we're trespassing." He tugged the blanket up. "Did you take a look at those papers?"

"No, I let Scipio out."

With a hard laugh, Tean shook his head. "Gosh, I really can't do anything right, can I?"

Leaning on the rail, his elbow bumping Tean's, Jem stared out at the glow of electric lighting, corporate signage, a sea of hazy orange and gray with slivers of neon blues and reds. Sweat popped out on his forehead, his chest, under his arms. He wiped his mouth. He asked, "Is that bottle of Everclear still in the cabinet?"

"What? Why?"

"Because I would really rather be drunk to talk about this."

"Talk about what."

"I told you about Decker Lake, right? Juvie, or whatever you want to call it."

"You said you'd been there."

"I was so angry. Because I was scared for myself, and for Benny, who was still stuck with LouElla. Because of . . . because of some things that happened with the older boys. And I'd get out of control, fighting, trying to destroy something—which was hard because they make everything really fucking solid. Anyway, the preferred method of dealing with out-of-control kids was a full-body restraint, which is close enough to a straitjacket that you could blink and miss the difference. I had Benny do some research after I got out. The theory is that it's supposed to be comforting, kind of like a hug that your body will recognize and respond to. But it's not like that. It wasn't for me. It was like being suffocated. The worst claustrophobia I've ever had in my whole life. And nobody listens to you screaming because you were already screaming when they put the restraints on you." Jem blinked. At the edge of his line of sight, a blurred sign, neon blue, swam in and out of focus. "And when you get angry, you make stupid mistakes. Tanner and those guys were older; they already knew that. They knew I'd do something stupid, and they'd do everything they could to get me stupid angry so they could take advantage of it. Ok, I kind of forgot where I was going with this. And before that, with foster parents, the pressure was always to be good, always to be happy, don't cause trouble or you'd get kicked back into a group home or sent somewhere even worse. I think I'm rambling."

"Who were Tanner and those other boys? What did they do to you?"

Jem shook his head.

"That's why you freaked out."

"Freaked out?" Jem said.

"In the truck, when you told me not to touch you."

"Oh. Yeah. Sorry; when I get—when I get worked up, it's like flashbacks to Decker."

"I'm so sorry."

Jem shook his head again. "I'm telling you this because it's really hard for me to do what you do. You know, the way you can just say what you're feeling. The way you just feel it and then it's over."

Tean shook his head, but he turned, angling his body toward Jem, considering him. "I don't know what I'm feeling."

"You're angry at me because I almost ruined tonight."

Another slow shake of his head.

"It's ok," Jem said with a smile. "I can handle an angry doc. You're such a good guy; I'll try not to start laughing when you yell at me."

"Camus said the only serious philosophical question is suicide. When you know life has no meaning, no purpose, that we're just a cloud of molecules rocketing through space with other molecules, and one day, somebody flips the lights and it's all over, the question is why we should go on living."

Jem took a moment to try to understand the segue. "Are you thinking about killing yourself?"

"No," Tean said, and his smiling was strangely sharp and hard. "That's actually never been a problem, believe it or not. There's something in me that just wants to keep on living. Biological imperative, I guess. All those cells wanting to reproduce." He tugged on the blanket again, his slender fingers gathering the folds. "Hearing about what happened to you, seeing what Dallin lives with, and knowing that nothing means anything, that we're just trapped on this rock hurtling through a cosmic abyss, and all we do is make more suffering for each other—it's hard. It's so hard sometimes I can't breathe."

Jem bumped Tean with his hip, sliding against him. When Tean offered a corner of the blanket, Jem re-settled it over both of them and put one arm around Tean's waist. After a moment, the doc laid his head on Jem's shoulder; he smelled like sagebrush and pine resin and the night breeze.

"I know a little bit about that," Jem said. "About feeling like you can't breathe."

"I grew up with this view of the world that was so clear: black and white, very little gray. I grew up thinking that humans had this divine spark in them, that we were good by nature and chose to be evil. That we were special, unique in creation, different in quality from everything else. Growing up like that—I don't know how to explain it. You feel certain about who you are, your place in the world. You feel special. You feel good. Well, guilty as hell a lot of the time, but with a sense of your final goodness. Special. Evil and suffering, sure, they exist, but you can brush them away because, in the first place, they're just the result of people making bad choices, and in the second place, they're just these little specks that get swallowed up by eternity. Eternity makes everything all right in the end."

He was shaking now, and Jem squeezed him around the waist.

"Anyway, when you figure out none of that's true — humans aren't special, aren't different from any other animal, and that you're not special either and there's nothing particularly good or unique about you, and that evil and suffering are much more a chain of consequences than a series of discrete, rational choices; when you realize eternity isn't ever going to roll around, and all we have is here, now, and none of it means anything — that's hard to swallow. Hard to stare into the darkness, waiting for the lights to go out."

"And what does Camus say about that question? Why do you go on living?"

"In typical Camus fashion, he tells a story that doesn't quite give you the answer. Do you know who Sisyphus was?"

"The guy pushing the boulder."

"Right, condemned to spend eternity in the underworld pushing a boulder up a hill, only to have it roll back down at the end of every day. That's life, Camus said. The endless struggle of humanity is to search for some kind of meaning in life, only to come face to face again with the essential absurdity of existence."

"God," Jem whispered. "Finding Camus must have been a wet dream for little Tean Leon's black heart."

Tean burst out laughing, and when he had calmed down, he burrowed into Jem. "Ok, yes. Teenage Tean was very upset when he had to read Camus in high school. Big flaming homo Tean was ecstatic when he went back to it."

"I like big flaming homo Tean," Jem said. "Even if he does inhabit a nightmare wasteland of broken illusions. Maybe especially because he does."

He could feel Tean smiling into his chest, but when Tean spoke, his voice was hard. "That's why I don't want you telling me you think I'm a good person. I'm tired of that. I spent a lot of my life feeling good and looking down at everybody around me. I don't want to be good. I just want to be . . . I don't know. Honest about who I am, I guess. At the end, when Camus is almost done talking about

Sisyphus, he says that Sisyphus's fate belongs to him, which is a strange thing to say about someone condemned to do something fruitless for eternity. He says it's because Sisyphus's point of view has changed. He's free, and his fate belongs to him, not to the gods. The struggle is enough, Camus says. You can be happy with the struggle. I guess that's what I want."

"To push a boulder up a hill for eternity?" Jem asked.

"Yeah," Tean said. "I guess so. To know that my fate is my own; to look into the emptiness of existence and be satisfied with the struggle."

"You told me earlier that you want to find something transcendent."

"I do," Tean said. "Is that a contradiction?"

"I don't know. Is it?"

Laughing, Tean said, "I honestly don't know either. Maybe I want to find something. Maybe I want to be wrong."

The mountain breeze caught the edge of the blanket, flapping it against Jem's legs, and Jem shivered.

"I freaked you out," Tean said. "I'm sorry."

"You didn't freak me out."

"I told Ammon this stuff once. He didn't talk to me for a month."

"Ammon is an—"

Tean poked him.

"Ammon is Ammon," Jem amended his intended statement. "I'm me."

"It's ok. It's weird. I know it's weird to talk like that."

"I'm just trying to understand it. You're a lot smarter than me, and I'm still trying to figure out what you mean."

"I'm not smarter than you. And I've been thinking about this for a long time."

"I still think you're a good person." When Tean opened his mouth, Jem said, "But I won't keep telling you that if you don't want to hear it."

Tean leaned into Jem, rubbing his belly with one hand in slow, smooth circles.

"Can I tell you you're hot stuff?" Jem asked.

"Nope," Tean said. "Flattery will get you nowhere."

"It's not flattery. Can I tell you you're smoking hot?"

Tean slapped Jem's belly before resuming the slow circles.

"That's a yes," Jem said. "Can I tell you that you're brave?"

"Ok, I—"

"Because I just want to get a full list of the things I can tell you. Staring into this chasm of meaninglessness and still trying to be who you are, that's pretty fucking brave."

"That's enough."

Jem cupped Tean's face and turned it up and kissed him. Tean's lips were soft, his mouth responsive, his eyes dark and full of unshed tears.

"Are you still going to tell me horrifying statistics?"

Tean nodded; a tear spilled down his cheek.

"Like a hundred and seven percent of people have herpes?"

"I think your math is off," Tean whispered.

Jem put his hands on the doc's hips and rucked up the tee, his thumbs tracing circles over Tean's hips. "And every minute a million orphanages burn down."

Tean rolled his eyes; more tears ran down his face, but he was smiling when he wiped them away.

Jem's hands slid up, grazing Tean's wiry frame, sifting the stripe of hair at the center of his chest. The doc's skin was warm. His heartbeat was loud against Jem's palm.

"And artificial raspberry flavoring is made from the crushed-up bones of puppies," Jem whispered.

"Actually," Tean said, "the FDA labels castoreum, an anal excretion from beavers, as a natural flavoring, so it's entirely possible that—"

Jem kissed him again, a little harder this time, a little longer.

"Seven billion people just died in the time it took you to give me some tongue," Jem said.

"That's not—you're not even—"

Jem kissed him.

When they separated, Tean's breathing was uneven, his face flushed, his glasses askew.

"Did you know," Jem asked, "that scientists found that, statistically speaking, the adult male will only have one good orgasm in his entire life? All the rest of them will be mediocre."

"There's no way that's true."

"Sorry. It's a fact."

"It sounds like somebody needs to do more research," Tean said, his voice rough.

Well," Jem said with a frown, "maybe a controlled experiment. But you know that six hundred thousand monkeys are electrocuted every day in labs—"

He couldn't finish because Tean had a hand over his mouth and was steering him back into the apartment.

31

The next morning, Tean woke first. Jem still had one arm across his waist, so he scooted out from under it as smoothly as he could. He showered. He considered his hair. He tried the comb, and it didn't look as nice as when Jem had done it. After dressing, he took Scipio for a walk, fed him, and tried to replay last night, wondering if he'd made a mistake in telling Jem so much.

He couldn't answer that question, so he sat at the dinette table and studied the papers they had rescued from the Bowlings' trash. The ones that interested him the most were the bank statements and credit card bills. He read through them twice; in the background, he heard Jem yawn, pad around the apartment, shower. Tean was so lost in the documents that he was startled when Jem's hand settled on his nape.

"Oh," Tean said, glancing up. Jem was in jeans and another of those gray t-shirts, his hair perfectly parted again, his beard neatly trimmed. "Morning. Sorry, I was going to make—"

"McDonald's," Jem said a little too quickly.

Tean narrowed his eyes.

"Not that I don't appreciate the offer," Jem said, but his smile looked a little bit guilty to Tean. "One of those McGriddles just sounds really good right now."

"I can cook."

"I know."

"I can make you pancakes. I don't have any buttermilk, but I think I have powdered milk. And maybe some lime juice. Or some vinegar. Or—"

"You know what, though?" Jem said like somebody who had just remembered an important fact. "I really could go for some coffee."

"Why don't I make some of those powdered eggs, and—"

"Hey, what'd you find in there? Anything interesting?"

"That was a terrible attempt to change the topic."

"Your hair looks really nice."

"That was slightly better."

"You are, however, wearing khakis with a brown shirt again."

"This isn't brown. It's like sand. Or maybe that really light-colored soil they've got on the west side of the state."

"Sweet Jesus," Jem said, grabbing the hem of the shirt and tugging it over Tean's head. "Talk about those papers while I find you something you can wear."

Skin pebbling in the cool air, Tean followed Jem into the bedroom. "The Bowlings were massively in debt."

"Were?" Jem asked from inside the closet.

"Yep. About three weeks ago, they paid off six thousand dollars on a credit card. The week after that, they paid off another four thousand. Then two weeks ago they paid off eight thousand on a separate card. The bank statements show cash deposits for the same amounts."

"Holy shit," Jem said. "They were twenty thousand dollars in debt?"

"I think that was the tip of the iceberg," Tean said. "The bank statement shows a hefty mortgage payment, as well as withdrawals that look like minimum required payments on other credit cards. Remember the barn? And the bromegrass? They might own a ranch, but did you see any animals besides that poor horse?"

A shirt flew out of the closet. "You said they had a lot of hay."

"Yeah, and that's strange too. They're buying hay for animals they don't have, but they're not mowing or baling their own pasture."

"Come here," Jem said.

"That's not all," Tean said, crossing to stand by the closet. "Those cars."

Jem emerged from the closet with a blue chambray shirt that Tean vaguely remembered his mother giving him.

"I don't like that one," Tean said. "I'm pretty sure one of my brothers-in-law didn't want it anymore, and my mom foisted it off on me."

Holding the shirt up to Tean's torso, Jem studied him.

And the top button is too high," Tean said. "It feels like it's strangling me."

"Arm," Jem said, holding up the shirt.

"Besides, I'm pretty sure this is a fast-fashion shirt, and you know how fast fashion is destroying the environment."

"I do indeed," Jem said as he helped Tean get his other arm in its sleeve.

"So I'm basically collaborating with an industry that rapes our planet and takes advantage of the poor in order to churn out shoddy merchandise."

"Yes," Jem said, his fingers nimbly doing up the buttons, "but it's blue. And you look good in blue."

"It's an ethical stance," Tean said. "I absolutely cannot wear this shirt because then I'm a willing, knowing participant in one of late-stage capitalism's worst outrages. I might as well just go stab a dolphin in the eye or scuttle an oil tanker."

"What did that dolphin ever do to you?" Jem asked, sounding very much like he was only half paying attention.

"Exactly. And the top button makes the collar too tight."

"Then we'll undo it," Jem said, twisting the button loose.

"Now I need an undershirt," Tean said. "You can see—"

"I can literally see one inch of your chest. And it's a very nice chest. Tell me about the cars."

"I might as well be naked."

"Is that an option?" Jem asked with a raised eyebrow.

"The cars in the garage," Tean said.

"Damn it," Jem said. "That sounds like a no."

"The cars in the garage," Tean tried again, his face heating, "are obviously new. How did they buy those cars when they were in debt up to their eyeballs?"

"I don't know. Where'd they get the money to pay off those credit card bills?"

Tean shook his head. "I think they got a lot more than that. I mean, the amount of money in those deposits is consistently below the amount that banks are required to report. So my guess is that they're sitting on a stack of cash and making relatively smaller deposits as needed. The bank is probably suspicious already, but for now, nobody has looked into it. It's been less than a month, after all."

"They're taking payoffs," Jem said.

"That's one possibility."

"What's another?"

"A cash inheritance that they don't want to declare, maybe. Or drugs."

"Christ." Jem shook his head. "Remember how Julie's bank account had been emptied? There's no way this isn't connected. What do you want to do? Go back out there? See if we can rattle Bowling and get him to talk?"

"Maybe," Tean said. "But not first thing. Actually, I want to take a look at Benny's place. The fact that he and Sook were both killed after being on the Bowlings' land is really troubling, and I want to see if Benny wrote anything else about Bowling." Tean hesitated, and his face was guarded, his voice hesitant as he asked, "Unless you've already read everything in the apartment?"

"No," Jem said, feeling the old gameshow smile slide out. "I haven't even looked because I'm not as smart as you. It's a good idea."

"Let's go."

"McDonald's first," Jem said.

"I could make you—"

"No, thanks."

"I think the toaster is working better—"

"Definitely a no."

"You just want the hash browns," Tean said.

"See?" Jem said, a real smile now. "You know me already."

After they ate—well, after Tean had a few bites of a sausage biscuit and Jem devoured everything he could reach—they headed over to Benny's apartment. A brown-skinned boy was practicing a kickflip near the dumpsters, moving in and out of the cottonwoods' shadows, and he waved once. Jem waved back.

"You know him?" Tean said.

"Not really. I've seen him when I've visited Benny's before."

"And he waves to you on sight?"

"I asked him a few questions last time. I guess I made an impression."

"Did he tell you anything useful?" Tean asked as Jem led him upstairs.

"Just that he didn't remember the last time he saw Benny. Big surprise; Tommy's a major stoner."

"How'd you know that?" Tean said.

"I recognize the type." Jem stopped at an apartment door, worked a key in the lock, and let them inside.

"I thought we'd have to ask the manager to let us in," Tean said. "Why do you have keys to Benny's apartment?"

Jem stopped in the doorway and put his hands on his hips. "What's with all the questions?"

"I don't know."

"I made copies when I moved him in."

"Even though you live in California?"

"Yes, even though I live in California. And it looks like I was right to do it."

"Yeah," Tean said.

"I don't understand what's going on," Jem said.

"Nothing. Sorry. I'm just spacey."

But he didn't feel spacey. He felt the way he had when he and Ammon had run down to the beach at midnight, with Lima lit up behind them like a fallen star burning itself out. They had stood ankle deep in the Pacific, and every time the ocean retreated, the sand underfoot drained away in a million grains.

"How do you want to do this?" Jem asked.

Tean considered the apartment: the carpet matted with grease and traffic, the thrift-store couch, the bagged newspapers, the paint bubbling where water damage stained the walls. Garbage, mostly fast-food wrappers and empty soda cans, covered the floor. The place stank, a combination of smells: BO, mold, trash that needed to be taken out. Something must have shown on Tean's face because Jem blushed and scratched his beard.

"I should have found a way to make him clean up," Jem said. "But Benny never did anything he didn't want to do."

"It's not that. I just feel bad that he was living like this. I guess I knew he was probably living rough, but I just didn't know how bad it was."

"He wanted to live on his own," Jem said. "This was the only way we could manage it. He had a roof over his head. He had running water, electricity, heat in the winter. He had appliances that worked, more or less. And he was safe."

"I'm sorry. I wasn't trying to be critical."

Jem was still scratching his beard, his eyes moving around the apartment. "I stopped by when I first started looking for him." He pointed to the couch cushions, which were askew, their zippers open, and then to the television turned sideways, and then to the open cabinets in the kitchen. "I didn't realize it at the time, but I think somebody came here looking for something."

"You think the killer has been here?"

"It makes sense. Whatever they're trying to cover up, they wanted to make sure Benny didn't have any evidence lying around. Of course, the place is such a shithole that they're probably just lucky they didn't walk away with hepatitis."

"Jem, I'm sorry I made you feel like I was—"

"I'll start in here. Why don't you check the bedroom?"

"I shouldn't have said anything. It was his life, and if he was happy—"

"We should probably hurry."

Outside came the click and whir of the skateboard's wheels hitting asphalt and rolling.

Tean nodded and moved toward the bedroom. It was in an even worse state than the front room: the mattress lay halfway off the box springs; a fitted sheet showed oily body marks, and there was no sign of a flat sheet or a blanket; the nightstand had fallen and hit the wall, scraping away paint and gouging the drywall. More trash covered the floor, but mixed in with the Whopper wrappers and the clamshell take-out containers were clothes, mostly t-shirts and mesh shorts. At least the window was open, and the October morning air helped with some of the foulness in the apartment.

On his first step, Tean hit something with his foot. He used the toe of his Keens to nudge aside a pair of University of Utah shorts with a faded seat and stared at the Hamburglar novelty canteen they had been hiding. He took another step, working his way to the wall, thinking he'd start by searching the bed and then moving the mattress back into place. When he saw the leather shoulder bag, he stopped and said, "Jem, could you come here?"

The bag was a little larger than a normal purse, but it also wasn't a utilitarian piece—it had some sort of designer logo worked into the zipper and in molded ornaments that hung from the strap's D-rings. Tean had seen that bag before; it belonged to Sook.

"Holy shit," Jem said. "That's not Benny's."

"No," Tean said. "It's Sook's. Why is it here?"

"I don't know."

"Why did Benny have Sook's bag?"

"I don't know. He didn't. I don't know why it's here. It wasn't here when I—" Then he stopped, staring at the Hamburglar canteen. He squatted, and when he reached to touch it, Tean caught his shoulder.

"Fingerprints," Tean said.

Jem shook him off, but he didn't reach for the canteen again. "This is Benny's," he said. "He always took it camping with him. Why would they bring it back here? What's the point?"

"Ok, we need to call someone. We need to call Ammon."

Nodding slowly, Jem stared at the canteen; he didn't seem to have understood what Tean said. Tean placed the call, and when Ammon picked up, he explained what they had found. Or he tried to.

Ammon cut him off. "I cannot fucking believe this. I told you to stay out of this. I told you after you went to Sook's and stuck your foot right in the middle of my investigation, I said that was the end."

"Someone is trying to make it look like Benny killed Sook," Tean said. "Jem is sure that the bag wasn't here when he came the first time. I told you that both of them had been killed after going to the Bowlings' place. Now somebody wants Benny to take the fall for Sook's death, and Benny's already been written off as an accident, and that means nobody's in trouble for anything."

"Are you listening to yourself?" Ammon said. "Can you even hear how crazy you sound?"

"Will you just come over here, please?"

"I'm on medical leave, Tean. I got the shit beaten out of me trying to help you with this bullshit amateur hour you're running."

"I know," Tean said, his face hot, his eyes hot. "I know, but isn't that proof? Isn't that proof that there's something going on here?"

"It's proof that you need to drop this. Right now."

"No."

"What did you just say to me?" Ammon didn't sound angry; he sounded incredulous.

"No. I'm not going to drop it. He's Jem's brother, and someone killed him. I'd do it for you if Micah went missing."

"My brother isn't a schizo freak."

"And I'd want somebody to help me if something happened to Corom or Amos."

"I looked into that guy, Bowling. I checked him out, tried to see if he had an alibi for the time you say Benny got grabbed. He was at the C-A-L. He was ordering winter feed, and he's on camera the whole time. I've got the video sitting in my inbox right now. There's no way he was on the other side of the Oquirrh Mountains abducting that kid."

"Something happened. Something happened, Ammon, and you don't want to see it because—I don't know why. Because you want this to be over. Or because you got hurt and now you're scared. I don't know. But you're closing your eyes, and that's the wrong thing to do."

"They've all got alibis, Tean. Give me something to work with and I'll try to help, but you've got to face the fact that this might be a dead end."

"It's not. We'll just keep working. We'll find something."

"You're really pissing me off right now," Ammon said. "You're so fucking naïve, and you don't have any idea what you're talking about."

Someone in the apartment next door was laughing—huge guffaws. The breeze through the window picked up, cool against the flush in Tean's face. In the parking lot below them, a crow settled onto the asphalt in a graceful flutter.

"I think maybe we shouldn't see each other anymore," Tean said, not recognizing the sound of his own voice. "I'll call 911 and ask them to send a uniformed officer."

"Hey," Ammon said. "Hold on. Just hold on. I'm sorry I talked to you that way."

"No," Tean said. Jem was looking at him, his eyes soft and unreadable. "I can't talk to you right now."

He was pulling the phone away from his ear when Ammon said, "Jem isn't who he says he is."

Tean wanted to disconnect the call; he could feel his heartbeat in his throat. Then he asked, "What?"

"He's been lying to you this whole time. He's local. He's a grifter or a con man or something. He's a thief. He's a blackmailer. He's into some bad stuff, really bad, and he's dragging you into it. You think this is about his brother? It's not. This is about him finding a way to extort money from people so he can go on being a fucking deadbeat."

"There's no way that's true," Tean said, but his gaze shifted to Jem, and he thought about the key, about the kid waving, about all the strangeness when Jem hadn't been worried about a job, all the things that didn't add up about his life in California.

"It's true," Ammon said. "I'm sorry, but it's true. I followed him and recorded the whole thing."

"What's he saying?" Jem said, standing up from the squat. "What's he talking about?"

"Why didn't you say something?" Tean asked.

"Because you wouldn't have believed me. You still don't believe me. I'm going to send you the audio right now, and you can hear it for yourself."

"What's he telling you, Tean?" Jem asked. "Let me talk to him."

"Play the file," Ammon said, "and then call me back."

The call disconnected; the phone vibrated in Tean's hand, and he saw a message from Ammon with an audio attachment.

"What was that about?" Jem said, his voice hard. "What's going on?"

Tean tapped play.

The voice that came across the speakers was clearly Jem's: "You can expect that picture and the audio recording to go to your wife first. Unless you're living in your mom's basement; then I'll send it to her. If you don't pay after that, I'll send it—"

Then another man interrupted, shouting, "No."

Jem's voice again: "Don't touch me. Do you have the money?"

The recording ended.

"Hold on," Jem said, raising both hands. "Just hold on. That's taken completely out of context—"

"Who are you?"

"That guy—"

"Who are you?"

"Will you let me explain?"

"Who are you? What's your name? Who the fuck are you?"

"Jem. I'm Jem. You know me."

Tean shook his head and wiped tears away; he didn't feel like he was crying, but the proof was on his palm, shining silver where it caught sunlight.

"Tean—"

Tean backed toward the door. "I don't want to see you again. Don't—don't come around me ever again."

"Wait," Jem said, taking a step.

"No," Tean said. "Stay right there."

"Ok, I'm not moving. I'm not doing anything. I'm just standing here, I've got my hands where you can see them, and I'm begging you to please let me explain. I made a really big mistake, and then I didn't know how to get out of it. Please let me tell you what happened."

Tean hesitated in the doorway. His phone was buzzing again, Ammon's name flashing on the screen.

"Leave him out of this for a minute," Jem said. "He's going to mess with your head."

Tean accepted the call, but he kept it down by his side. "If you do something to me, he's going to hear. There's a witness now."

"Do something to you? Jesus Christ, Tean. I'd never hurt you."

Ammon's voice came over the phone, the words too faint for Tean to make out. "You want to explain?" Tean said. "Explain. You've got two minutes, and then I'm leaving."

"My name's Jem Berger. I'm not from California. I live here, in West Valley. That's it. Everything else I told you was true. I thought you wouldn't help me if you knew I was local; I thought you wouldn't take things seriously. And I thought—I don't know, I thought I'd just be dealing with you for a few minutes at your office. I didn't know everything else would happen."

"Like sleeping at my apartment. Like sucking my cock. Like—" There was too much from the last week, and it all got caught in Tean's throat.

"And then it was too late," Jem said. "I didn't know how to tell you."

Ammon's voice buzzed in the distance.

Tean swallowed, and the action was harder than he expected. Then he said, "I don't want to see you again. Ever. Is that clear?"

"Please don't—"

"Is that clear?"

Jem crossed his arms and stared at him. His jaw was set. Where the sunlight caught his beard, it was full of coppery embers and silver fire. "No," Jem said. "That's not clear. And it's not acceptable. And I'm not going to allow it."

Tean laughed in spite of himself. "You don't have any say in it."

"Do you want to talk about lies?" Jem said. "What do you know about Ammon?"

"I told you not to talk about him. You don't understand—"

"Stop it. Do you even hear yourself? Do you hear the bullshit you spout? You're a smart guy; how can you not figure out that you're in a relationship with an abusive asshole?"

"Ok," Tean said. "Ok. We're done."

"No, we're not done. We're done when I'm done. When I'm ready to be done."

"Goodbye."

Jem lunged, catching Tean's arm. Tean swung with his other hand, the one holding the phone. The phone connected with the side of Jem's head, rocking it to the side. The force of the blow knocked the phone from Tean's grip, and it hit the floor. Blood ran from a cut in Jem's ear, snaking down his neck and staining the collar of his shirt. Still grabbing Tean's other arm, Jem spun Tean around, twisting his wrist until he had Tean in an armlock, with Tean's face pressed against the drywall. Tean bucked once, and the pain in his shoulder and elbow was incredible.

"Stop it," Jem snapped.

Tean tried again.

This time, Jem grabbed the back of his neck and slammed him into the drywall again. "I said stop it. You're going to hurt yourself."

"Fuck you," Tean said.

"You're going to listen to me. You're going to hear every goddamn word. And then you can go."

Ammon was shouting, but the phone was far away, and Tean couldn't move.

"I hate you," Tean said. "I'm going to kill you."

"Yeah," Jem said. "Hate me. Fine. But I'm still going to do you a few favors. Here's the first one: Ammon, your dream guy, the one you're in love with? He cruises bars and pretends to be from out of town. He picks up guys. He fucks whoever he wants. You're not his one true love, and he's never going to leave his wife. You're just an easy, convenient, desperate fuck."

"You're lying."

"Really? I picked him up in the Apollonia. He paid for a room. We fucked. And you know what? He's a B-, C+. Hope that's not a blow to your self-esteem."

Tean screamed and tried to twist free again, but Jem held the armlock tight, still pressing down hard with his other hand on Tean's neck.

"You're the worst fucking scum I've ever met," Tean said. His breathing was ragged. "You're a liar. You're a thief. You're a blackmailer. And you're so fucking pathetic. You're just a sad, pathetic nothing. That's what you are."

"Here's the next favor," Jem said. "You are one messed up guy, Tean. You need about a hundred years of therapy. But I'm going to give you a shortcut and point out that you are the biggest fucking hypocrite I've met in my entire life, and that's really saying something. You mope and spout off all those depressing facts, acting like you're jaded and cynical, but you've got a cushy life and you came from a cushy home and you're so fucking trusting you're like a little kid. You think you're always looking for the worst, and then you let a piece of shit like Ammon lead you around by the nose. You claim you're not a good guy, but you're one of the kindest people I've ever met. You've got no fucking idea what the real world is like, and you don't understand a single fucking thing about yourself. Why do you have to be so fucking stupid sometimes?"

Tean had gone still. He almost felt relaxed, his muscles loose, his body limber, except for the weird, jolting energy running through him. "Get off me," he said calmly.

Jem released him and stepped back.

Bending down, Tean collected his phone and ended the call. It began to vibrate a moment later, Ammon's name on the screen again, but he ignored it and pocketed the phone.

"I went overboard," Jem said. His chest was rising and falling erratically. Spots of color marred his cheeks. "Give me a minute to get myself under control, and I'll apologize."

"No," Tean said. "You're right. I didn't know that about Ammon. I didn't—" He laughed and scrubbed his palms on his khakis. "I guess I didn't know anything. I still don't."

Jem covered his eyes, plucking at his tee with one hand as though trying to cool himself.

"You're right," Tean said. He said it slowly, savoring the edge of what was to come, the pure butchery of it. "I'm really fucking stupid."

"No, you're not—"

"But at least I can read."

Jem froze. He uncovered his eyes. His pupils were small and hard, and the color had drained from his face.

"I can read," Jem said.

Tean shook his head. He was smiling; it was easy to smile right then.

"I can," Jem said.

"Don't embarrass yourself."

"I know how to read."

Tean turned and headed back to the living room. Lined paper and colored pencils covered the coffee table. Behind him, Tean could hear Jem following. Selecting a pencil, Tean grabbed a blank piece of paper. He scrawled out a single sentence and turned around, holding out the message.

In the hall to the bedroom, Jem stood with his shoulders curved, his arms folded, his face waxen.

"Go on," Tean said. "Read it."

Jem looked at the paper. For a moment, the struggle in his face threatened to break Tean's heart. Then Jem looked away, his jaw set.

"That's what I thought," Tean said, letting the paper flutter to the ground. "Now who's fucking stupid?"

He stepped out into the late morning, the wind stirring the cottonwoods, the smell of fresh popcorn from the convenience mart on the corner, the world nothing but alkali and brush and dead water to the west.

32

In the West Valley apartment where he squatted, Jem slept in fits, waking to the memory of Tean's voice: *But at least I can read.* Each time he broached the surface of sleep, his hangover was worse: the dryness in his mouth and throat, the foul taste, the headache. He had forgotten to drag the improvised curtains into place, and when dawn came through the window, he finally quit trying to rest. For a while he lay on the mattress on the floor, staring up at the ceiling, the layers of paint crusted around the door frame, the drips frozen in time. His mind probed his fresh wounds, calling up snippets of memories that played and then dropped away, sometimes good, sometimes bad. Tean sitting on the couch next to him, hesitantly putting his arm around Jem's shoulders; Tean asking him to get the cumin, and the old shame, the old fear, swamping Jem as he stared at the bottles and couldn't tell which was which. Nights on the couch watching *Buffy*, his arm hugging Tean against him. Tean asking him if he'd already read Benny's manifesto. How long had he known? How long had he pitied Jem, felt sorry for him — maybe even felt embarrassed for him? How long had he doubted himself, thinking it was impossible, but still collecting data, still watching as Jem struggled? What had finally convinced him?

Jem rolled off the bed, clutched the jamb to keep himself upright, and closed his eyes against the sharply tilting world. He stumbled into the bathroom, drank water from the tap, and sat on the toilet while he started the shower. The hiss of falling water, the curling tongues of steam, the humidity against his skin. Leaning against the porcelain sink, he closed his eyes again, drifting until, again, he heard: *But at least I can read.* Then he sat up with a jolt, and the humidity and the heat made him nauseated. He turned the water to lukewarm, stripped, and sat under the spray, lowering the temperature by degrees until he felt like his head might not split apart.

After dressing, he let himself out the window and went down the fire escape. He couldn't eat. He couldn't sleep. It was just after seven in the morning, the air in the valley was cold and crisp, like a spoken word would send cracks spiderwebbing through it. On the flanks of the Wasatch Mountains, the autumn fire-show of red brush and yellow aspens had burned itself out; everything was ash, the whole world in shadow because the sun hadn't cleared the mountains yet.

He called Chaquille, who answered on the first ring. Music blasted in the background; it was obvious that Chaquille hadn't gone to sleep yet, which meant he was stoned and drunk and maybe loaded up with seven other special herbs and spices.

"I need you to watch that guy again," Jem said. "The one you were watching last weekend. I'll pay you the same."

"What?" Chaquille shouted.

"I need you to watch that guy again. Goody. He's got the ranch in Tooele."

"Yeah, man. Shaniqua, girl, get down from there!"

"Never mind."

"No, man. I got you."

"I don't need a stoner who's going to fall asleep on the job."

"Man, I never let you down yet, did I?"

"Then get your ass out there and see what he does today."

Jem sat on the bike, the chill, gray tide of morning making him shiver in spite of the windbreaker, trying to think. The problem was that there were too many people he needed to watch, and Jem was just one man. Even if he wanted to pay somebody to watch Bowling, he didn't think he could afford it—just like he couldn't afford for extra eyes to watch Bowlings' wife and kid, or Goody's ranch hands, or Julie's office staff. That was one of the problems in the case that seemed clearer to Jem that morning: the seemingly rock-solid alibis didn't cover everyone. Julie was in a meeting, but nobody could prove that Phil and Ruth had been with her. Goody was at a stock auction, but nobody could prove where two of his ranch hands had been. Bowling had been buying winter feed, but the wife and kid were unaccounted for. So many people to consider, and now Jem had to do this alone.

He almost called Chaquille back to tell him to watch the Bowlings' property instead, but a mixture of anger and pettiness stopped him. Jem's gut told him Bowling wasn't the killer. That had been Tean's theory, but that was because Tean wanted to tie the two cases together. It could have been a coincidence, Benny and the DWR girl both dying after they went on Bowling's land. It could have been chance. Goody, on the other hand, had Benny's property on his land—the Teenage Mutant Ninja Turtles bowl, the mess kit—and Benny had died less than a mile up the trail from Goody's house.

Kick-starting the bike, Jem pushed the questions aside. He'd tried to run down every possible lead: tracking Benny's movements, then trying to trace the black SUV, then the red Chevy, then the people Benny had been in conflict with. Everywhere he turned, he met a dead end. All he could do now was watch, wait, and hope the killer slipped up.

For how long, a little voice asked him. How long can you keep this up, spending your days doing jack shit, paying Chaquille?

As long as it takes, Jem told himself.

He drove south; I-15 was a parking lot during rush hour, but on the bike, it was easy to use the shoulder when he needed to, easy to squeeze between cars idling as they waited for the congealed traffic to start moving again. Driving like that was illegal, although the legislature had been rumbling about legalizing lane splitting—or, at least, filtering forward at red lights. Right then, though, Jem didn't care about getting pulled over. His world had narrowed down to the throbbing ache behind his eyes, the bike's rubberized hand controls, and Benny's killer.

The big house in Draper, the one high on the bluffs where he had followed Julie and Phil the weekend before, had the garage door open, and Jem saw Julie's silver BMW parked inside. He followed the street past the house to where it hugged the curve of the bluffs, and then he flipped around and parked, with the house at the edge of his field of vision. He'd be able to see the little silver car when it emerged, but he hoped she wouldn't spot him waiting for her.

By eight, the silver BMW still hadn't moved. By nine, Jem needed to pee, which he did in the drainage ditch, the long, dried-out weeds whispering against his legs. Down the road, a big old brute of a dog came outside and immediately started barking. The sound did what it always did: sent Jem's brain into high gear. LouElla had kept her dog, whose name was Antony, on a chain in the basement. Jem had been sent down to the basement a time or two before everything had happened with Benny and he'd gone to Decker. Getting sent down was about as bad as it got; Antony's chain was long enough to reach you, no matter where you went, and the dog was crazy. Now, as an adult, Jem didn't blame the poor thing; it wasn't the dog's fault. But he still had a half-moon of scars, faded almost to nothing, high on one arm.

The shadows had receded, drawing up the mountains in sooty folds; in the valley, the underlying brown of the steppes was crosshatched by irrigated green lawns and everywhere the glitter of glass, like God was just a big kid smashing bottles from high up. Jem wondered what Tean would think about that idea; he would probably have some sort of absolutely terrifying fact about cruelty in children, and he'd deliver it so seriously, his brows knitted together, like he was sorry he had to be the bearer of bad news. Then Jem heard himself thinking about Tean and shut the whole thing down.

At a quarter past nine, the BMW emerged from the garage, and Jem followed it back into the valley. Instead of heading west and north, toward Dellengbauh's operations in the Oquirrh Mountains, Julie drove into the city. Sugar House was yet another pleasantly middle-class neighborhood, although this one had the charm of having been an early settlement, with a few Victorian-style buildings from the Mormon pioneers. Like most of Utah, it still worshipped at the twin altars of strip malls and shopping malls, but unlike much of the state, it was also home to a hipsterish community of independent coffee shops, art galleries, consignment stores, and bookstores.

Julie headed straight for the closest shopping mall. She parked, and Jem let her walk halfway across the parking lot before he started after her. He followed her through Nordstrom and into the mall proper, past storefronts that were just now opening — it was barely ten o'clock, and the mall was practically empty. Jem thought his footsteps sounded unnaturally loud against the concrete floors. An Auntie Anne's pretzel shop fanned the aroma of hot butter and cinnamon into his path, and for the first time all morning, Jem's stomach grumbled. Ahead of him, Julie perched on a bench. She was wearing flannel and muddy jeans again, complete with the big boots he had seen in the mining trailer. After a minute, she kicked both feet up onto the bench, the way she had the week before at her desk.

Jem stopped and bought himself a pretzel, eating it while he pretended to look at his phone. She wasn't even looking in his direction, but he didn't want to give her any reason to pay attention to him. When he'd finished the pretzel, he decided a second was in order, and he ate that one too. He was considering getting a lemonade when he glanced down the mall and saw Ruth-the-Intern.

Something was different about Ruth. Something Jem couldn't put his finger on. She was dressed conservatively again: a navy skirt and a dressy, button-down shirt. She had on her pearls and her little silver Mormon-good-girl medallion. But something was different. Her smile, maybe. Or her eyes.

When she reached Julie, Julie stood, and the women kissed. Julie had one work-roughened hand on Ruth's side, high and to the front. Pretty close to a boob grab for a public space.

Oh, Jem thought. That's what's different.

The women were holding hands as they walked into a jewelry store. The clerk kept pace with them from behind the counter. He was asking questions, and Jem would have liked to hear the conversation; he imagined it was polite but slightly probing, the guy trying to get a read on how serious the relationship was and how much he could try to get them to spend. It looked like he didn't need to try very hard. After a few minutes, Ruth pointed to something in the case. A woman who knows what she wants, Jem thought. And she isn't afraid to ask for it. The clerk produced a diamond tennis bracelet in white gold and helped Ruth try it on. When Ruth squealed with excitement and Julie smiled, Jem could practically see the dollar signs roll up in the clerk's eyes.

It was as quick and easy as that: Julie paid for the bracelet, and Ruth wore it out of the store, the women holding hands again. Jem followed at a distance, wondering which one he should follow when they split up. He was surprised — very surprised — to see Ruth here. Jem had gotten a vibe from Julie when they'd met, but after seeing her with Phil, he'd assumed that he'd just been playing to stereotypes: the flannel, the boots, the chainsaw. The truth was obviously more complicated. But Ruth was a total surprise; Jem would have pegged the girl as the fasting-and-praying-to-stay-at-size-zero type. The type earnestly striving to get somebody to put a ring on it.

In the end, Jem didn't have to make a decision about who to follow; the women left through the Nordstrom exit, and Jem walked through the parking lot parallel with them along a separate aisle. The women stopped at a Chevy Impala with rusted-out wheel wells, an engine hood that was black when the rest of the car was silver, and a bumper hanging askew. Jem kept going, cut between a minivan and plumber's truck, and watched them in the truck's side mirror. They kissed for a while, and Julie got a little tweaky with Ruth, which, to judge by the sounds, Ruth didn't mind at all. Then Ruth got into the broken-down Impala, and Julie walked to her BMW. Jem thought maybe they'd split up, but he was wrong again; Ruth followed close behind Julie all the way back to the mine.

Instead of hanging around with the dust and the scrub sage, he turned the bike north, cut west on I-80, and then followed the back of the Oquirrh Mountains to the Bowlings' ranch. He saw cop cars parked up on the bench by the Bowlings' house, though, and so he kept driving, heading back to Route 36 and driving south through Tooele proper. On the other side of town, he drove a few miles before he saw Chaquille's van. It was parked on the shoulder a few hundred yards past the entrance to Goody's ranch, an orange cone near the van's front wheel and a length of high-vis reflective safety tape tied around the side mirror.

Jem parked in front of the van. The sun was coming down at the right angle to turn the windshield into a mirror of sky and cloud, so Jem shaded his eyes as he moved to the passenger side and rapped on the window. Chaquille, long and lanky with cornrows and a tight fade, was sprawled across both front seats. A joint was on the dash, obviously in preparation for when the boredom got a little too intense. With a grin, Chaquille sat up and unlocked the door, and Jem opened it and got in.

He coughed, left the door open, and said, "How much weed have you smoked?"

"Not enough, my man. Not enough. There's a big, wide world out there, all that pot waiting for me to try it: Hindu Kush and Kosher Kush, White Widow, Strawberry Cough, Ghost Train Haze. And that's not even getting into hash, man. They got the best hash in Turkey. The best in the world." He grabbed a book from the footwell.

"*Teach Yourself Turkish in 90 Days*," he said. "I bet I can do it in two months, though."

"You're a man with a mission," Jem said, glancing at the rearview mirror. Chaquille had chosen a good spot; nobody could come and go on Goody's main drive without being spotted. Jem didn't doubt that the ranch had plenty of other access points, but he didn't have the manpower or the funds to watch all of it. He didn't even really know what he was watching for. Just a mistake. Or something strange like what he'd seen with Ruth and Julie.

"It's like Pokémon, you know? Gotta catch 'em all."

"Any traffic so far?"

"Those Mexican boys showed up for work. And the mail lady came."

"Goody hasn't left?"

Chaquille shook his head.

"All right," Jem said. "Let's see what he does."

"What do you mean, let's see?"

"I mean let's see."

Groaning, Chaquille shook his head. "Oh no, white boy. Get out of the van, get on your bike, and go find something to do."

"You're bored. You need company."

"Go find something to do."

"I've got nothing to do."

"That's your problem," Chaquille said. "That's your whole problem right there."

"What does that mean?"

"What do you think I'm going to see, sitting out here?"

"If somebody — I mean, if Goody goes somewhere —" Jem trailed off. "Christ, I don't know. I don't know. I don't even know why I'm doing this; I just know somebody killed Benny, and I've got to find out who did it, and this is the only thing I can think of."

"Look, man, I'm cut up about Benny too. I really am. He was a sweet kid, and he bought a lot of weed. And if you want to pay me to sit here and get high and tell you that this white guy just works on his ranch all day, that's tough. But you look like shit, and you're sure as hell crazy as shit, and I don't want you messing up the chill I got going. Besides, what's somebody going to think if they see your bike out there?"

Jem just shook his head.

"Go home, man," Chaquille said. "Get laid. Get drunk. Get high. And then get yourself better. Benny's gone; there's nothing you can do about that."

Jem's jaw cracked when he swallowed. He nodded and slid out of the van.

"Hold on," Chaquille said, "let me spot you." He dug a joint out of his fanny pack, and Jem took it. Then Jem shut the van door.

The bike came to life on the first kick, and Jem headed north into Tooele. *Get laid, get drunk, get high.* He was passing the edge of town when he remembered last week, and Chaquille tracking two of Goody's ranch hands back to their apartment. He called Chaquille and got the address, and then he cut down a street on the far side of town, looking for the building.

It was a four-plex with faux wood siding and a painted cement foundation. The unit that belonged to the ranch hands was on the ground floor, at the back of the building. Jem tried the door; it was locked. He kicked back the welcome mat, but no key. He ran his fingers along the top of the door frame and got only dust.

Next, he went around to the back of the building. A single sliding window looked into the apartment; the ranch hands hadn't hung curtains, probably because the window looked out on miles and miles of sage and saltbrush. Through the glass, Jem could see the signs of bachelor living: a couch they'd probably gotten at DI, a massive TV, a PlayStation, and five cardboard boxes from Tony's microwavable pizzas.

Jem jiggled the window, and it rocked in the frame. It was a sliding window, which meant the lock was in the center. Jem bumped the glass with the heel of his hand and, at the same time, tried to slide it sideways. The window rocked again, trying to move. Jem repeated the combination. Then a third time. That time, it worked: the sash lock popped free, and the window slid open. The October sun felt hot now, and Jem was sweating as he pulled himself into the apartment.

He wasn't sure what he was looking for; he found it in less than five minutes. Benny's wallet was in the bedroom, on the floor next to a twin bed. It still had Benny's state ID, although it was empty of cash and other cards, including the plastic Honorary Power Ranger shield that Benny always carried.

After that, it was a waiting game. Jem drank the three Michelob Ultras that were in the refrigerator. He microwaved one of the remaining Tony's pizzas. While the timer ran down, he flipped both the twin beds and came up with a pack of cigarillos, a 2012 *Playboy*, and an unopened package of Red Vines. He carried it all out to the kitchen, where he could keep an eye on the front door. Just to be a shit, he got one of the cheap knives from the drawer — the blades were stamped and had about as much steel as a paperclip — and shredded the cigarillos while he ate the pizza. While he flipped through the nudie mag, he regretted the sequence of events; he should have saved two of the beers for after the pizza.

Outside, the sun fell behind Bald Mountain; the shadows that rushed down the slopes, racing toward Tooele, leached the color out of the land. Everything was black and white: the black of the shadows, the black of the rabbitbrush, the black of the Russian thistles; the white of pale soil, the white of the alkali pan. Like everything had been pared back, exposing bone. Tean would have had something to say about that, of course. Eyebrows knitted together. Worried. Always so worried.

Jem tried to turn his attention back to the skin rag, smoothing out the wrinkles in Miss July's caboose. He smoothed and smoothed until he ripped the page clean out. That undid something inside him, something he'd kept fastened down since Decker. He'd spent more than ten years trying to be ok, trying not to care, trying not to hurt. Ten years was enough.

He put the microwave through the window. He kicked the TV until one of his sneakers went through the screen. With one of the flimsy stamped knives, he slashed up the couch cushions; he got through two before the blade snapped off at the hilt. He was kicking a hole in the bathroom wall, chips of tile and clouds of plaster dust floating down to the floor, when he heard shouting.

As he came out of the bathroom, the front door opened, and he found himself staring at two men. They looked Latino, short and compact, with dark hair and dark eyes. A thin woman, blond, bags under her eyes, was standing in the hallway behind them, waving a cigarette furiously as she shouted something.

"Where'd you get this?" Jem asked, holding up Benny's wallet.

The one on the left said, "Hijo de puta."

The one on the right shook his head.

"Where'd you get this?" Jem asked. And then he borrowed a line from LouElla: "I'm not mad, I just want to know."

"I find it," the one on the right said. They might have been brothers; they looked like brothers. "It's yours?"

"Where'd you find it?"

"Pinche cabrón," the one on the left said. "Qué porquería hiciste?"

The one on the right said, "We're calling the police."

"Uh uh," Jem said. He didn't even bother with the paracord, the tube sock, the barrette, the antenna. He wanted to use his fists; that was another thing he'd learned from LouElla. "You're going to tell me exactly where you got this. Then you're going to tell me everything I want to know about Benny. And then I'll call the police when I'm good and done with you."

"Este hijo de puta—" The one on the left began.

Jem got in the first blow because he was fast and because he was angry, but mostly because of surprise. He caught the one on the left in the teeth; he felt his knuckles, which were still healing, split open again. He got in a second blow, an elbow that caught the one on the right in the ear and knocked him into the jamb. The blonde with the cigarette was screaming; Jem ignored her. He brought his knee up into the one on the right's gut, and that guy folded; his breath whooshed out with the reek of cigarillos, and Jem wanted to tell him he had bad news about the smokes.

Then a fist caught Jem at the corner of his eye. His vision turned into a sheet of crackling white as he stumbled back. The hangover headache that the Michelob Ultras had muted roared back to life. He got up an arm in time to block the next punch, but the third one he took on the jaw. For a moment, he was nowhere. Then he realized he was sitting on the floor. And he was laughing.

Someone had cut the cable from his brain to his mouth, but he wanted to say thanks. For one clear moment, he wanted to say thanks, because this was what he'd been wanting and he hadn't even known it. Then one of them kicked him in the side of the head, scrambling his channels. He tuned in and out through the beating; then it was over, and he was lying in the weeds in front of the apartment building, the stalks dry and cool against his cheek. He lay there a long time, his brain trying to catch up with his body.

When he got to his knees, he saw Benny's wallet on the cement walk. He scooped it up and pocketed it. Then, with one of his knees on fire, he lurched toward the bike. He managed to stay upright for the half-mile it took him to get to a Texaco. After dry heaving in the bathroom, he bought a bag of ice and sat on the curb, applying chunks of ice to the parts of himself that hurt the most. He ended up wet and cold; the mountain breeze made the October air sharp enough to bite. Then he sat with his head in his hands, staring at the oil-stained concrete, while the sodium lamps buzzed overhead.

33

Tean lay in bed. The window was open; it was almost midnight, and the mountain breeze had died down, but cold air still leaked into the room. He had thrown the pillow that smelled like Jem into the closet, which, he had convinced himself, had made lying in bed much easier. His eyes were still puffy and stinging. When he closed them, he saw how canyons were formed: thousands of drops of water wearing away stone.

Ammon was still knocking. He'd been standing at the apartment's front door, knocking on and off, for almost an hour. Then the knocking stopped, and footsteps moved away. Tean let out a breath. The muscles in his stomach ached.

Then a pebble dinged against the bedroom window. And another.

"Can you just tell me you're ok?" Ammon called up. "I don't care if you hate me for telling you the truth. I just want to know you're ok."

"Damn it, son," a man shouted from upstairs. "It's past eleven o'clock."

"This is an emergency," Ammon called back.

"It sure will be. You raise your voice one more time, and I'm calling the police."

Tean got up from the bed, made his way to the window, and said, "Go home, Ammon."

Then he slid the window shut.

A few minutes later, an engine started in the parking lot below, and headlights poured bright, halogen cones across the asphalt. When Ammon pulled out of the lot, Tean lowered the blinds and climbed back into bed.

But he couldn't sleep. When he drifted in a gray haze on the edge of unconsciousness, he would remember the look on Jem's face, the mixture of shame and pain. Worse than shame. Humiliation. And Tean had put that look there. Had, for a single moment, liked it there. If he were honest, as he flipped the pillow, the reverse side cool against his fevered cheeks, he still liked it. Liked knowing that for all the ways Jem had played him for a fool, Tean still had something over him.

Hearing that thought blunted the edge of Tean's anger. How was Tean better than Jem? Tean could read; Jem couldn't. Was that Jem's fault? Of course not. He'd spent his entire childhood being bounced between foster homes and schools and a juvenile detention center. If he'd ever been lucky enough to have foster parents who made him do his homework, those days had probably been few and far between. And if he had some sort of learning disorder like dyslexia, then he'd probably never had a chance.

But he was still a liar and a thief and a blackmailer, Tean told himself.

Well, Tean thought, he had done a little lying himself. By omission, if nothing else, when he'd pretended not to notice that Jem couldn't read the spices, had trouble when he hit the wrong button on Netflix, always picked McDonald's because he knew the menu and could order by number—with the exception of the Apollonia, where he could rely on his bartender friend if he ran into trouble. And Tean hadn't been above using Jem for his own ends: to feel safe, yes, especially after the Chevy had almost run them off the road, but also for sex, for companionship, for the way it felt when, in that maddening way of his, Jem put a positive spin on everything Tean said.

Tean was up before he realized what he was doing. He dressed, grabbed his best flashlight, filled a water bottle, and left before he could change his mind. He drove west, hugging the back of the Oquirrh Mountains. A thumbnail moon provided scant light, but this side of the mountains, the stars were bright and thick. He had kayaked in Montana once, in Glacier, and by day the river was high, the water's crests so bright they hurt to look at. But at night, the river had been dark, the stars suspended where the water smoothed out into untroubled sheets. He had gone alone, and with the snap and crackle of the fire dying behind him, without another living human for miles around him, he had felt something like this, hadn't he? He didn't know the word for it. A sense of proportion, maybe. Vertigo. A despair that was so intense that it bordered on ecstasy — or maybe it was exactly the opposite. It was too keen, and it cut too quickly, for him to know.

He parked on the shoulder of the road south of the Bowlings' ranch. Flashlight in one hand, water bottle in the other, he jumped the drainage ditch, hiked across the overgrown pasture, and then cut up the canyon. When he was a hundred yards into the canyon, he set a timer on his watch and turned on the light. After that, the going got worse. Someone — Bowling? — had brought down trees directly across the trail, and Tean had to climb over them to head any farther up the canyon.

What had Bowling said? An environmentalist group? A nature conservancy? Something. The canyon was public land, but the easement on Bowling's land had expired — was that it? Bowling had claimed that he had brought down the trees to discourage the tree huggers from crossing his land and entering the canyon, but in the pre-dawn twilight, Tean doubted everything. He remembered the strangeness of his first encounter with Julie Nash, finding her barefoot in her office, and her story about cutting down trees. He doubted that too. He only knew that Sook had been murdered after she had visited Bowling, and Benny had been murdered too.

The hike was rigorous but not too hard; a light sheen of sweat built on Tean's body, and after half an hour, he felt warm enough to shrug out of his jacket and tie it around his waist. A creek ran on his left, a cottonwood breaking up the rocky bank with its roots; on his right, stunted juniper, a pathetic zigzag of poplars, and where the soil was still too hard and dry, clumps of ephedra and winterfat.

When the timer went off, he had been hiking for three hours and hadn't found anything. He'd startled a buck mule deer, and the poor thing had gone bounding off like Tean had taken a shot at it, but other than that, Tean had been alone. He thought he'd made good time, and the trail had worn away almost to nothing. It didn't look like Bowling or the conservationists came this far back in the canyon.

So what had Sook and Benny seen that made them a threat?

Tean didn't know that either, and the hike had given him no answers. He played the flashlight up the canyon walls, trying to examine the land a little farther, he caught only more of the stone —

some orange, some red, some light brown. The sweat was cooling on his face and arms, and he shivered. Then he turned and headed back.

By the time he reached the truck, the sun was up, although still buried by the mountains. He drove home, showered, changed, and then headed to work. He had two days of stuff he needed to catch up on — although the truth was that he really needed to catch up on almost a week's worth of work, since he'd been so focused on trying to find out what had happened to Benny. He started by going through his emails, which ranged in importance from the ones he needed to answer right away and the ones he could delete without reading all the way to the end — Larry Gregorson, who ran the warehouse and loading dock, sent him weekly reminders that he could visit LDS Family Services for free and "be helped with his problem," which, of course, meant a predilection for dick.

When the knock came at the door, Tean had just sent off a follow-up email about the wild horse population around St. George. "Come in," he called.

Hannah stepped into the office, closing the door behind her. She opened her mouth to say something and then stopped. She looked at him for what felt like a long time, tucked the chestnut hair behind her ears, and asked, "Oh my gosh, what happened with California boy?"

"What?"

She sat, leaned forward, and put her hands on her cheeks. "Oh Tean. Oh my gosh. I'm so sorry."

"What are you talking about? Nothing happened. He's gone. That's all."

For a moment, Hannah looked like she might cry. Then she stood and said, "I'm going to make you some tea.

"I'm fine. I don't need tea."

But she took the kettle, filled it, and came back with two packets of something called Y-OOLONG BELONG! The gratuitous exclamation point was probably supposed to reinforce the optimistic message for people who were extra depressed.

"I've got a lot to do today, Hannah."

She just stood with her hands on her hips, watching him.

"I barely even knew him," Tean said. "He was just here long enough to figure out what happened with Benny."

The kettle whistled, and Hannah poured boiling water into each mug and hung the bags of tea to steep.

"It's probably for the best," Tean said. "Before I made a mistake and things got too serious."

"Oh sweetheart," Hannah said, stepping next to his chair and running her fingers through his hair.

Tean started to cry.

He managed to pull himself back together again pretty quickly, and he told her everything, all of it.

"I'm going to kill him," Hannah said. "I'm going to find him and I'm going to kill him."

"Stop," Tean said. "You're a nice Mormon girl. Don't mess that up; you've got a good thing going."

"I wasn't always a nice Mormon girl," she muttered. "I just need you to provide me with an alibi. Can you do that?"

He laughed, but the fixed expression of fury on her face didn't change.

"Don't murder him," Tean said. "I'm just embarrassed really. And he's right: I act like I'm the only one who sees the world clearly, and instead, I'm the first sucker to get hooked."

"You're not a sucker."

"It's mortifying. I mean, maybe I just need to become a hermit and live in the mountains somewhere."

"Slow down."

"I'll buy a used-up gold mine and just spend the next fifty years alone, growing a gross, mountain-man beard and panning for gold. I'll forget what human speech sounds like, and I'll probably be buried when part of the mine collapses, and it'll take weeks for me to die because I'll have this little puddle of water I can drink from. And nobody will ever find me. And then they'll build a ski resort up there, and I'll spend eternity under a Cinnabon."

"Don't be so pessimistic," Hannah said. "There are worse ways to spend the afterlife."

"That was the optimistic version."

She smiled and touched Tean's shoulder.

"I must be pretty desperate to fall for something like that," Tean said.

"You didn't fall for anything."

"I believed his whole story. Jeez, Hannah, I let him stay at my house. I fell for him. Hard."

"But—" Hannah was frowning now. "But something weird really is happening, right? Something with Benny's death. And Sook's. I mean, they were both killed after visiting the Bowlings' ranch. And you found blood at Sook's apartment, which means she didn't just drive out to the middle of nowhere and get herself shot. And you've had people following you, trying to hurt you. Oh my God. The attack the other night, the one in the parking lot—that was about the murders too, wasn't it?"

"We don't know—I mean, there was some evidence, but—"

"Of course it was. Gosh, Tean, you guys are really on to something. What are the police doing?"

"Well, Ammon is laid up with a broken arm, and he's mad at me for poking my nose into his investigation. I know he sent someone to Sook's apartment to get a sample of the blood we found, and I think he'll follow up on the Bowlings. But now they've got Sook's bag at Benny's apartment, and I'm worried he'll take the easy road and pin her death on Benny; he said they found a gun at Benny's place when they searched it, and it could be a match for the one that someone used to kill Sook." Shaking his head, Tean said, "In the absolute best-case scenario, it's all going to take time. But nobody is going to do anything about Benny; his death is still classified as accidental, and nothing short of a protracted lawsuit is going to change that."

Hannah nodded slowly. "I'm sorry, Tean. I wish I knew what to tell you. I wish I could say that somebody would set everything right. But—but people like Benny, well, it's pretty easy to sweep them under the rug. I think we should focus on Sook. We can still get justice for her."

Tean nodded. He sipped his tea.

"You'll let me know what the detectives say?" Hannah said. "And if there's anything I can do to help?"

"Sure."

"Things are going to work out, Tean."

"Sure," Tean said again. "The best of all possible worlds."

Hannah's smile was a thin line, and she touched his arm once more before leaving.

Once she was gone, Tean checked his email again and found the results from the toxicology lab: the birds he'd collected at the Great Salt Lake hadn't shown any sign of poisoning. So that was the nail in the coffin; whatever Benny had thought he had seen, he had been wrong. And he had died for it.

Tean clicked the next email and stared at the screen, unable to parse the words in front of him. And then even sitting upright seemed like too much. He laid his head on the desk, his eyes open, staring at a hardback copy of *Scientific Farm Animal Production*, which he'd kept after grad school for some reason and which now occupied valuable shelf space. He thought about doing a full purge of his office. That sounded productive.

Instead, though, he lay there. Telling Hannah everything had opened a door, and Tean didn't know how to shut it. And the worst part was that he hadn't really told her everything—not all of it, not about Jem's two slightly crooked front teeth, not about the way he was so careful with the comb, not about the convoluted retellings of *Darkwing Duck* episodes, not about what it had felt like to have Jem curled around him at night, to wake up in the morning, to see purple shadows lightening to blue, the whole world being born again.

When the door opened, Tean couldn't even lift his head; he was vaguely aware of Norbert Smith asking something in a querulous tone, and then Norbert went away. Sometime later, Maddie was standing by his desk, saying something. Tean was pretty sure he answered because she went away.

In the hall, voices dragged him out of his daze.

"I know," Hannah was saying.

"Something is seriously wrong," Maddie was saying.

"I know," Hannah said again. "I'm taking care of it."

Then the door opened, and Hannah was standing beside him, her hand taking him just above the elbow. "Let's get lunch."

Tean tried to shake his head, which was hard when he was flat on the desk.

"Up," Hannah said, jingling her keys. "You'll feel better after you eat."

Somehow she managed to bully him out to her car, which was a Ford Focus with blue paint flaking off the hood. The October day was bright and sunny. Every day seemed like it was bright and sunny.

"Maybe I should move to Seattle," Tean said as they drove.

"I don't think that's a good idea."

"I think I'd like the clouds."

"Uh huh."

"I'm totally fine, Hannah."

"That's why you were face-planted on your desk."

"I'm tired."

"Sure."

"I was up all night. I just need some sleep."

"Ok."

"I'm a grown man," Tean said. "I'm not going to fall to pieces because the first guy I've felt a real connection with since Ammon just happened to be a lying, blackmailing, thieving, conniving son of a bitch. I'm already totally over it."

"I can tell," Hannah murmured.

"What was that?"

"Nothing."

In West Valley, she parked in front of a building with a sign that said Bluebell Apartments. It was tall, yellow brick broken by narrow windows, with fire escapes on two sides. The paint was flaking away from the fire escapes, and rust ran down the bricks in red rills. Over the front door, someone had obviously tried to paint bluebells on the bricks, but they looked more like grapes.

"Come on," Hannah said. When she turned off the car, she didn't put her keys away; instead, she fumbled them until she was holding a can of pepper spray. Then she got out of the car.

"What are we doing here?" Tean asked as he followed her toward the building. "This doesn't look like lunch."

"We're going to get you some closure."

"What?"

"That jerk lives here, ok? And you're going to look him in the eye and tell him you hate him. Or punch him. I don't know, whatever you need to do."

Tean stopped, and Hannah went two more paces before she realized and looked back.

"Are you kidding?" Tean asked.

"No."

"How did you find him?"

"I asked Rand, and he called around. Salt Lake doesn't have a huge gay community; he has a friend who has a friend at the DMV, and that guy recognized the description Rand gave him."

"No way," Tean said.

"Yes."

"No. I don't want to see him."

"Well, I do. He hurt you. He broke your heart. And I want to blast him in the face with pepper spray."

"I can't believe you did this," Tean said. "This is typical Hannah."

Her eyes were red, and she was trembling.

Tean just shook his head and turned back to the car.

After a moment he heard her steps, but instead of coming after him, she was heading to the building. Fine, Tean thought. Fine. Let her. She could go inside, find Jem, and give him a couple of toots of pepper spray. And then they could go, and Tean could sweep up the rubble of his life and start over. Again.

He leaned against the Focus. The metal was warm, pleasant against his back. A breeze had kicked up, and the air smelled like Fabuloso; someone was cleaning. To one side of the apartment building stood a small playground. A handful of kids were laughing as they hung upside down from the monkey bars. A man and a woman were watching them from a bench, talking quietly. A happy family, Tean thought. That was what Ammon went home to. That was what Hannah went home to. That was what it seemed like everyone in the world went home to—even though he knew it wasn't true, even though he knew it wasn't that simple.

One of the kids got herself halfway down from the monkey bars, and then she seemed to have second thoughts. The hesitation made her lose her grip, and she hung by one leg, screaming in panic.

The guy got up and jogged over. He caught her, flipped her right side up, and set her down gently. He was a nice-looking guy. Tall, a body that looked fit from work instead of from the gym, blond hair in a hard side part, a beard that had more red than the hair on top of his head—

Jem looked up as though Tean had said his name, and their eyes met across the playground's pea-gravel fill. His face was washed out, with dark hollows under his eyes. He'd been in a fight—a nasty one, to judge by the look of him: bruises all over his face and arms, two fingers taped together, a bandage across his nose. The way he held himself made Tean think the damage extended down his body. The only sign that Jem might have felt something like surprise at seeing Tean was that he became very still. The woman next to him said something, and he didn't look at her. She said something else. He kept staring at Tean.

And Tean was staring back. He was thinking about all of it: that Jem had slept with Ammon, that Jem had lied to Tean, that Jem had taken advantage of him, winning his trust minute by minute, so that Tean would help him find Benny — and then so Tean would help him find Benny's killer. Tean thought about all the lies, spoken and unspoken, that Jem had woven for him. And he thought about how pathetically, eagerly blind he'd been — and the irony was that he'd been so easy to fool because he had wanted so badly what Jem had pretended to offer. What was Jem's little saying? *People will believe anything if they want it to be true.*

Caught up in the whirlwind of his thoughts, Tean barely realized that Hannah had returned from the apartment building and was speaking to him.

"— door's locked, and nobody's answering, but I'm going to come back and find him." Her voice faltered. "I'm sorry I brought you. I don't know why; I thought it would help."

Tean gave a tiny shake of his head.

"What are you — that son of a bitch," Hannah said, fumbling for the keyring can of pepper spray.

"Stop," Tean said.

"No, I'm going to do it. I'm going to blast him right in the face."

"Hannah, stop it."

Something in his voice made her flinch.

Jem was still staring at him. It was hard to tell from a distance, but Tean was pretty sure he hadn't even blinked yet. The woman next to him, short and muscular and dark-skinned, was standing now, pulling on Jem's arm, trying to get him to move toward the building. The two kids huddled together, picking up on the tension in the air without understanding it.

"Come on," Hannah said. "You're right: I shouldn't have done this. Let's go."

But Jem was just standing there, staring at him.

"Go away," Tean shouted across the lawn. "Will you just go away?"

A shudder went through Jem, and then he seemed to pull himself together, offering that gameshow smile. He called back, "I live here. Well, kind of."

"Then go inside," Tean shouted. "I don't want to have to look at you."

"I was here first. And to be fair, you just kind of showed up."

That was kind of a stumper, and Tean had to think about it for a moment.

"Are you ok?" Jem yelled.

"No. I'm not ok. I'm not sleeping well, and that raises the risk of heart attack by twenty-five percent. I'm going to die—"

"Don't do it," Hannah whispered.

"—alone in my apartment, and Scipio will eat my face, and they'll have to cremate me because it'll be weeks before anyone finds me."

"Maybe now isn't the time—" Hannah tried to say.

"Cremation is actually a really economical option compared to a traditional funeral," Jem said. "Think of all the money you'll be saving your loved ones."

"Money that they'll waste on the spendthrift culture of late-stage capitalism, fueling a cycle of loneliness and psychological dissatisfaction that will end in extreme emotional distress, financial insolvency, and suicide clusters. Are you happy? You just made everyone in my family die by suicide."

"Ok," Hannah said. "This isn't productive."

Jem took a step forward, the pea gravel crunching underfoot.

"Stay right there," Tean snapped.

Raising both hands, Jem stopped. He said, "Excess consumer spending is a problem, but your family will also be creating jobs for people that desperately need work because they don't have the education or skills for a different setting. They're basically putting food in the mouths of the underprivileged."

"That's just a reductive view of voodoo economics."

"Are you fighting?" Hannah whispered. "Or making up?"

Tean glared at her, and she backed toward the car.

By the time he looked over, Jem had taken a few more steps.

"I said stop," Tean shouted.

"Ok," Jem said, hands up again. "I'm stopping. But wouldn't it be easier to move a little closer so we didn't have to shout?"

"I like shouting. I've got a lot to shout about. You deserve to be shouted at."

"Definitely, definitely. So, I've taken about five steps. Why don't you take one? Is that fair?" Jem seemed to consider something and hurried to add, "Because if you keep shouting, you'll probably strain your vocal chords, and then you'll be walking through a parking lot, and a garbage truck will be backing up, and you'll try to tell him to stop but you won't be loud enough because you lost your voice, and you'll get flattened."

"Good," Tean said. "Good, I hope that happens."

"One step? I won't take up a lot of your time. I've been thinking about what I wanted to say to you, if you ever let me, and I even did some research. To apologize. And to try to explain. Well, I made Tinajas do it, actually." He gestured to the dark-skinned woman behind him, who was glowering at Tean. It took a moment for Tean to recognize the expression; Hannah was wearing the exact same one. Then Jem flushed an ugly scarlet and added, "Because, you know, I can't read."

Tean considered this, how much it had cost him. And then he thought about himself, and about where things were going. He could turn away. He could get in the Focus with Hannah and drive back to work, and that would be the end of things. His whole life, he had lived with the fear that he could trust no one, that if they knew the truth about him, they wouldn't love him anymore, and that the world was a hard and brutal place. Over time, that fear had become a kind of pride and a kind of strength as experience bore it out again and again: first with his parents, who had shuttered a part of themselves when he came out; then with his siblings, who had chalked out the areas of their lives where he was no longer admitted. Even with Ammon; whatever had existed between them was now buried under all the broken promises, all the shattered trust. And with Jem, all those fears had been true in their most extreme form. So it made sense, Tean told himself. It made sense that he should just get in the car, go back to work, and live the rest of his life with the bitter satisfaction that he'd been right: that he could trust no one, that love was an illusion contingent on need and desire and satisfaction of some unwritten set of rules, and that the world was a rock spinning in a black void.

But he remembered the heat of Jem's breath, and the way his eyes had shone at the cartoon reruns, and the intense severity of his face as he jiggled a screwdriver inside the toaster.

Instead of turning toward the car, Tean took a breath and stepped forward.

"I'm going to take another five," Jem said. "You take one?"

So they did.

"How about—"

"This is close enough." Ten yards still separated them; Tean could see sweat at Jem's hairline, the dark loops of it under his arms. "Say whatever you want to say."

"I'm sorry."

Tean waited.

"First," Jem said, "did you know that the cadaver dogs they used after 9/11, the ones that they used to find people buried in the rubble, actually developed symptoms of depression? That's how bad it was. Even the dogs were depressed. And I feel like that's been the last week for me, finding bad thing after bad thing about Benny; it was awful. But at least you were there. Until, you know, you weren't."

"That was your fault," Tean said. "You made the choices that brought us here. You lied. You manipulated. If you'd told me who you really were, I still would have helped you."

"Really? If I'd told you I was a criminal, that I was a squatter, that I made money blackmailing pervs, and that I didn't feel bad about any of it, you would have smiled and nodded and said that was all right."

Tean didn't answer.

"Did you know," Jem said, "that there are over twenty-five hundred dead languages? That means that at some point, there was a person in the world who couldn't talk to anyone in the language they'd learned from their parents; maybe they spoke another language, so they could still talk, but it wasn't the same. That means they died not able to say the things they learned as a kid, the basic things, like being afraid and loving someone and feeling regret."

"Like the whale," Tean whispered.

"Again with the whale," Hannah said.

"So, I feel like that right now," Jem said. "I feel like that a lot of the time when I'm with you, actually, because we grew up so differently, and we are so different, and I don't know if the things I want to say to you will make any sense or if they'll just come out gibberish. And I want to say I'm sorry and that I care about you, but . . . but I'm worried we don't speak the same language. The stuff I do,

I don't feel bad about it. It's a hard world; I do what I have to. The only thing I feel bad about is hurting you. You're a good guy, and you showed me a lot of kindness, and you didn't deserve what I did."

"In Japan," Tean said, "there are teenagers, some adults too, who they call hikikomori. They're totally isolated: no job, no friends. They depend entirely on parents or siblings to care for them; some of them have been doing it for over twenty years. There are over seven hundred thousand of them, and the Japanese government estimates another one-point-five million people will become hikikomori in the near future."

"No," Jem said, smiling through split lips. "You're not allowed to become hikikomori."

"But I understand it. That's what a lot of wounded animals do: they crawl into their dens and lick their wounds." Tean pushed his glasses back up. "I can't do this, Jem. I need to go."

"Can I say one more thing? Please?"

Down the street, a woman and a gaggle of four kids emerged from a duplex. The kids were arguing about ice cream, and one little girl shrieked, "I want a bong pop!"

Jem's mouth twitched.

"Fine," Tean said.

"You are not a whale, and you are not operating at some frequency that no other human operates at. You have had some shitty luck with guys—I include myself in that statement, by the way—but that's not about you. You'll find somebody really great. I'm going to make sure of it."

Blood hammered in Tean's ears. He bit his lip. Then he said, "On Mars—"

Hannah groaned and whispered, "Just kiss him."

"On Mars," Tean said again, his face burning, "when NASA decided to land two rovers, Spirit and Opportunity, they landed them on opposite sides of the planet. And then they were out there, alone, until they died."

"They couldn't be alone if there were two of them," Jem said. "I know you probably won't ever trust me again, and you deserve someone you can trust. But I'd like to at least be your friend." He grinned, the real Jem grin that showed his crooked front teeth, and said, "I'd like to be your space rover buddy, if you'll let me. We can just drive around on opposite sides of the planet and send each other beeps to make sure the other one is ok."

"That makes absolutely no sense. Rovers don't send each other beeps."

Jem's grin got bigger if that were possible. "I think you should be Spirit, though. I'll be Opportunity."

"That sounds about right," Tean said, and he was surprised to realize he was smiling too.

34

"Take the rest of the day," Hannah said to Tean near the front of the DWR building. Jem could hear her as he parked the bike. "Actually, maybe we should both take the rest of the day. I don't like the idea of you being alone with him."

"I'll be fine."

"He's going to try to get inside your head again."

"It's going to be ok."

"I don't like him," Hannah said, glaring across the parking lot.

"Noted," Tean said. He squeezed her arm and said, "Thank you."

Instead of going inside, though, Hannah waited by the building's front doors, staring at Jem. Tean moved toward his truck, and Jem loped to meet him; the bike was parked in the shade at the back of the building.

"She is really giving me a death stare," Jem said.

"You're lucky you didn't get a face full of pepper spray."

Jem winced.

"I'm watching you," Hannah shouted.

"What did I do?" Jem said.

"The lying," Tean said, "the blackmailing, the stealing, the manipulating, the betrayal."

"She's still mad about that stuff?" Jem said.

"Maybe we should go."

"I've got my eye on you," Hannah shouted as they headed out of the parking lot in Tean's truck. "I see everything!"

"Good Lord," Jem muttered.

"Lunch?"

"Yes, please. Let's go find you an unsalted bread crumb."

"Oh, I don't want to gorge myself."

Jem grinned, the tension in his body unwinding, sprawling against the door of the truck to watch Tean. "Does the doc have jokes?"

"Maybe I'm having a stroke."

"What about Rancherito's?"

"We don't have to go there. I just like the breakfast burrito."

"I've actually never been."

"Wait," Tean said. They were approaching a red light, and he hit the brakes too hard, stopping well short of the car ahead of them. "What?"

"You heard me."

"You've never been there?"

"No."

"But you said you liked it. You said you'd had it when you were growing up here?"

"Yeah, well," Jem pointed to himself, "liar, remember? It's kind of hard to stop."

"You've really never had Rancherito's?"

"I'm going to say it one more time," Jem said. His face was hot, and he was taking deep breaths. "And if you ask me again, I'm going to think you're making fun of me."

"Not making fun," Tean said. "I just can't believe it."

"Here we go, for the last time: I have never had Rancherito's."

"Wow. Seriously?"

Jem tried to swat him, and Tean leaned away, laughing.

"Ok," Tean said. "I just didn't realize anybody could grow up in Utah and not try it at least once."

"It's the menu," Jem said, rolling down the window and turning into the cool air that whipped through the truck.

"What?"

"The pictures of the combination plates aren't very good; it's hard to tell what's what. And the rest of the menu is just a wall of text. They've got like fifty different options."

"Oh," Tean said. "I didn't—"

"We're going to have a hard time being friends if you feel sorry for me."

"I don't feel sorry—ok, ok. I guess I can hear the tone I was using. But tell me what I'm supposed to do. Or say."

"It's not a big deal for me; don't let it be a big deal for you. If I need help, I can ask you now, thank God. If I don't ask, but it's important, you can just tell me. But don't get all awkward and sad every time you remember I'm an illiterate dumbass."

"That's not what I think."

"I know."

"It's not."

"Tean, I'm just being defensive. Let me be prickly for a few minutes."

"Oh. Ok." Tean drummed on the steering wheel and said, "It's really helpful when you do that. Tell me what's going on, I mean."

"I know," Jem said, sprawling in the seat. "But sometimes it's fun to watch you squirm."

The doc had fast hands and a vicious right jab; Jem groaned and wrapped his arms around himself.

"Don't be a baby," Tean said.

"You're not the one with three broken ribs," Jem said.

"Oh my gosh. I didn't know. Are you ok?"

"Well, I think the number just went up to four."

"I'm so sorry. I didn't even think. I just—"

"Ok, ok," Jem said. "I just wanted to make you squirm some more; I don't have any broken ribs."

They drove half a mile and then Tean said, "You are an awful person."

"And a liar."

"And you're a liar. I felt horrible."

"I know."

"You can't do that to people."

"Apparently, I can," Jem said. "You shouldn't make it so easy, though."

The closest Rancherito's location was a small building with two-toned, brown stucco. It had obviously once been a Taco Bell; the front windows were soaped with words that probably spelled out a deal, although some of the writing had been scraped away.

"Three for six dollars," Tean said. "But it doesn't say what because someone already wiped that part off."

"See? That wasn't hard. Nice and casual."

It was noon, and the lunch rush backed up the drive-through. The sun came in through the truck's windows, warm against Jem's arm where the air was crisp. He could smell seared meat and frying onions coming from the kitchen, and his stomach grumbled.

"I do have some bad news," Tean said.

"Bad news? From you?"

"Ok."

"I don't believe it."

"Very funny."

"I can't believe it."

Tean sighed and looked out the window.

"You are the physical embodiment of a rainbow mixed with a ray of sunshine," Jem said.

"Are you done?"

"Almost. I added the rainbow part because you're super gay."

"The tox reports came back," Tean said. "There's no sign that any of the birds were poisoned. I think we're just going to have to face the fact that Benny was wrong this time."

"He was murdered, Tean."

"I know."

"You're the one who told me he was murdered. You told me about the knife mark on the bone."

"I know. But I'm telling you right now, I don't know why someone would have killed him. The mine passed their inspections. Goody would have faced some bad fines for the poaching, but it wouldn't have been worth killing over; his government friends probably could have made it go away. And I went up the canyon by Bowling's land; I couldn't find anything that would explain why Bowling might want to kill Sook or Benny for going up there."

"Fuck," Jem said. "Fuck, fuck, fuck."

"I think—"

"Just stop. Just stop for a minute." Jem closed his eyes; his heart was hammering in his throat, and the dangerous sense of slipping, of hanging on the edge of a crumbling cliff, took all his focus.

"The harder you fight it," Tean said quietly, "the more it's going to hurt."

Jem's eyes flicked open. "I said just stop for one fucking minute. Is there something hard for you to understand about that?"

Tean shoved his glasses back into place and shook his head.

Jem closed his eyes again, let his head drop back against the seat, and held on to the crumbling edge of the cliff. He felt the truck roll forward a few times, and then a voice buzzed on the intercom. Tean ordered something—Jem couldn't focus on the words—and the truck rolled forward. Then they stopped, and the engine cut off. Something hot and heavy landed across Jem's legs.

Rolling his head to the side, Jem opened his eyes and looked at Tean and said, "Is that a burrito in my lap, or are you just happy to see me?"

"You need to apologize."

"God, yes, please. Get stern."

"I'm serious, Jem. If we're going to be friends, you can't just schmooze your way out of problems. You can yell at me if you get upset, but now you need to apologize."

"I'm sorry."

"Thanks."

"I feel like I've been saying that a lot today."

"Practice makes perfect," Tean said.

They ate in silence for a few minutes; Tean had gotten them each a breakfast burrito, with little cups of salsa verde on the side, and Jem had to admit the doc had good taste: the burrito was amazing. Chewing hurt like hell, though, and Jem only made it through a few bites before he had to take a break.

"Do you know," Jem said, "that this is the best breakfast burrito of my entire life?"

"Obviously."

"How many people do you think have seen me cry in the last ten years?"

"A hundred."

"Wait, you do statistics for a living?"

Tean smiled and ate some more burrito.

"I think zero. Maybe Tinajas, but she didn't actually see it. She probably heard it on the phone; we were talking about Benny a couple of years ago, and he'd gone off his meds again, and I was so frustrated that I broke down."

Tean took a few more bites, rationing out his salsa verde, chewing slowly, wiping his mouth after each bite. He might actually finish the burrito, Jem realized. Then the doc folded his napkin and said, "Not zero. At least one."

"Yeah," Jem said slowly. "I guess that's my point. One person: you."

"You're allowed to cry," Tean said, his dark eyes very soft as he looked across the cab. "You don't have to be embarrassed of it."

"I'm not embarrassed."

Two bushy eyebrows went up.

"Ok," Jem said, "I'm embarrassed. But mostly—I don't know how to say this. Do you know what I do for a living?"

"Steal?"

"Ouch." Jem shifted; the door's armrest was digging into his back, but he liked how the cool air tickled the back of his neck. "Yes, I mean, I guess. But that's a really ugly way of putting it. Sometimes I've got a broken-down car. Sometimes I've just been robbed. Sometimes I maneuver them into causing an accident," he rubbed his back, "although I think I'm getting too old for that. People will give up a lot of cash if they think they're helping somebody because people want to believe they're helping somebody. They want to believe they're good people."

The doc polished off his burrito in two huge bites; his eyes never left Jem's face.

"So I'm nice. Sometimes I'm upset, but I'm always kind and polite and grateful. And in control. That's the key part. It doesn't matter if I just found out Benny flushed his meds that morning. It doesn't matter if the guy I was hooking up with just got a real boyfriend. It doesn't matter if I've got a cold, or I didn't eat, or I'm just in a bad mood because I've been thinking about Decker or LouElla or all the shit that's gone wrong in my life. When I'm working, I'm working, and I stay in control."

Tean wadded up the waxed paper from his burrito; his gaze dropped to his hands. "That sounds like a very hard way to live."

Jem tried to smile; instead, he wiped his eyes. "God, this is what I'm talking about. I don't know why I cannot keep my shit locked down when I'm around you, but it is really fucking frustrating."

"Jem—"

"Also, everybody else thinks I'm cute and adorable and charming and good. People are just so pleased to help me because I'm such a good guy. Everybody except a certain doc who thinks the absolute worst of me."

"It helps to remember that you're covered in over a thousand species of bacteria and fungi. Your skin microbiome, I mean. Plus your teeth are a little crooked."

Jem bit his lower lip "Anything else?"

"You spend too much time on your hair and beard."

"I should just hold my head behind a Mack truck's exhaust pipe every morning like you?"

Tean nodded and said, "Are you going to finish that?"

"Jesus Christ," Jem whispered, shaking his head as he passed over the half-eaten burrito. "You might actually get enough calories today to sustain a small child."

"I know," Tean said with a shrug. "I'll skip breakfast tomorrow." And then he proceeded to go through the burrito like a backhoe. Between two massive bites, he looked up and said, "Want to tell me how you got knocked around?"

So Jem told him about following Julie, about the police at the Bowlings' ranch, about Chaquille watching Goody, and about breaking into the apartment.

"I know we keep hitting dead end after dead end," Jem said, "but it's got to be Goody. I mean, the ranch hands had Benny's wallet. I think Goody paid those guys extra to pick up Benny, kill him, and leave the body for scavengers. They don't have an alibi; the only one the police looked at was Goody himself, and he made sure he was at the stock auction. Then Goody attacked us in the DWR parking lot—"

"We don't know it was Goody."

"He was wearing Goody's bracelet."

"Jem, if someone planted Benny's stuff on Goody's land, the ranch hands could have picked up the wallet and decided it was a lucky find. The bracelet could have been stolen, and—"

"I know. And I know you can't help me anymore. And I don't want you to. I just needed to tell somebody: I'm not going to let it go. I'm going to figure out how to prove it."

Crumpling up a second ball of waxed paper, Tean seemed to think about this. He had a dab of salsa verde at the corner of his mouth, and Jem reached up to thumb it away. Tean stared at him, startled, and then his tongue darted out to check the spot.

"You're good," Jem said, cleaning his hand on a napkin.

"You can't do that."

"You'd rather wander around all day with food on your face?"

"You just can't do that. Now that we're not—I mean, now that we're just, you know, rover buddies—"

"Oh, grow up," Jem said.

Tean started saying something else, but Jem's phone buzzed. He took it out, and when he swiped open the message from Tinajas, he said, "Hot damn."

"What?"

"That's the truck," Jem said, showing Tean the picture on his phone. His mind was racing all over the place, trying to put together a plan, what to do next. "That's the Chevy that tried to run us off the road."

"Yeah," Tean said. "Yeah, I guess it is."

The phone buzzed again, and a wall of text came through. Jem made a face and held it out toward Tean. "Would you do the honors?"

"It says, 'Hey, is this the truck you're looking for? Saw it in my neighbor's garage. Cash first and then I'll give you the address.' Cash first? What is he talking about? How did you find this?"

"God damn. Do you have five hundred dollars? I'll pay you back."

"Uh huh," Tean said. "Why do you need five hundred dollars?"

"Because I offered a reward for help finding the truck. Now we've got it, but I spent most of my money paying Chaquille to watch Goody." Jem touched his ribs and winced. "And at a CVS after those guys worked me over."

Tean was quiet for a few moments. "I can scrape together five hundred, but I really need it back, Jem."

"You'll get it back," Jem said. "I'm not that kind of thief. Can we get the money right now? I want to find out where this truck is stashed before the killer moves it again."

"Ok," Tean said, keying the truck to life. Then he stopped. "Let me see that picture again. Hold on. I'll call Ammon, although he is furious with me right now, so I don't know if he'll help."

"Call Ammon?"

"The dummy who sent you that picture didn't think of the fact that the owner put the license plates back on. Ammon can run the plates and tell us who it belongs to. Although, I guess that's a stupid idea. If the killer really did hide the truck, it's not going to be sitting in his garage, and from what I can see of that house, it doesn't look like any of the places we've visited."

"No," Jem said. "It's a good idea. You can see the house numbers here," he tapped the screen, "and once Ammon gives us the street, we can at least verify if it's at the registered owner's address."

Tean tapped his phone a few times, held it to his ear, and said, "I know you're angry—" Dusky color moved into his cheeks. "Please don't yell at me." After a few more seconds, he angled his body away from Jem, staring out the window. "I know you were worried. I know I shouldn't have ignored you."

Jem let his head rock back; the sun coming in was too hot now, a flush climbing his chest and neck, his stomach curdling. He stared at the scrollwork clouds that had drifted in front of the sun, the light so intense it made his eyes water.

After about fourteen more rounds of "I'm sorry," Tean finally managed to explain why he was calling. Ammon cut him off, shouting so loudly that Jem could hear his voice distorted over the phone's speaker. Then it all cut off. Tean dropped the phone in his lap.

Jem thought about what it would feel like to have to explain all that to somebody else. To have to justify it.

"You know what?" Jem said. "Let me try."

He called Tinajas.

"If that stupid little bitch hurt you—" she began.

"No, things are fine. I just need a little help." He explained, and on the other end of the call, Tinajas was already typing.

"Yeah, it's in Tooele. Are you ready?"

"Ready."

She gave him the address; the numbers matched the ones on the house.

"Do you have a phone number?"

"God, you are really needy sometimes."

"That's part of my charm," Jem said.

"No. It's not. Here's the number."

After she gave it, Jem said, "Thank you."

"Good seats, Jem. You promised me good seats."

"The ones right where the guy comes out to sell popcorn."

"You son of a bitch—"

Jem disconnected. "Are you ok?" he asked. "Do you want me to drive?"

"No, I'm fine."

"Let's head to Tooele; I've got a street and an address, but I'm going to call over first and see if I recognize a voice."

Tean nodded mechanically; he shifted into drive and headed out of the lot.

While the phone rang against Jem's ear, he said, "Do you want to talk about how you're feeling?"

"Yes," Tean growled.

"Ok."

"I feel like I want to murder that self-righteous, self-important, self-absorbed, unfeeling, arrogant—" He cut off, obviously struggling with something. Then he burst out with, "Fuckwipe!"

Jem had to fight really hard not to giggle. Then the phone stopped ringing, and an unfamiliar man's voice said, "Hello?"

"Yes, I'm calling about the red Chevy registered to your name. My name's Johnny, and I'm with Omaha Mutual. We have an insurance claim filed for damage to the side of the truck. Could I verify the name of the person I'm speaking with?"

"Yeah," the man said. "You're speaking with the father of a kid who is in a lot of trouble. Hold on."

For a moment, there was silence, and then in the background, Jem heard the man saying, "It's your insurance policy and you're the one who got in an accident. You need to handle this."

Then a much younger voice came on the line, obviously already on the brink of tears. "Hello?"

"Yes, this is Johnny from Omaha Mutual. Can I verify your name, please?"

"Zach Elder. Zachary. Oh my God, did someone get hurt?"

To Tean, Jem mouthed, *Zachary Elder*. Tean frowned and shook his head.

"Mr. Elder, we're following up on a claim for damage that one of our drivers made. They claim you tried to force them off the road in a red Chevy—"

"It wasn't me," Zach said, a sob threatening to slip loose. "I just lent him the truck, and he said he turned too close to a dumpster. He said he was going to pay for it."

The sun glanced across the windshield at the next turn, dazzling Jem. As he blinked his eyes, he asked, "And who was driving the vehicle, Mr. Elder?"

"Dallin," Zach said. "Dallin Bowling."

35

When they got to the Bowlings' ranch, Jem was having trouble with his thoughts. Once, when they'd been on beans and brown rice for a week straight at LouElla's, he and the kids had decided to even the score. LouElla kept a display case full of glass figurines, all of them religiously inspired. They'd taken the largest piece, a Jesus as tall as Jem's forearm was long, and they'd taken the stainless-steel meat tenderizer from the kitchen, and they'd gone up into the foothills, where they knew LouElla never went because of her gout. It had been a hot August day; the sun had been like sandpaper on the back of Jem's neck. On a granite outcrop clear of brush, they had set the figurine down, and they'd taken turns at it with the tenderizer. Jem had gotten the first go, and a shard of glass had gone straight into his calf; after that, the others were more careful. What he remembered most clearly, when they were sweaty and exhausted, the wind plastering dust against exposed skin, was his sense of wonder that something so painstakingly crafted could be reduced to a million splinters, all of them shimmering with kaleidoscope colors where the sun touched their edges.

His thoughts were like that now, and every time he tried to seize onto a plan, every time he tried to construct a chain of events, every time he tried to explain how Dallin Bowling had been involved and what had led to Benny's death, he felt a tremendous force smash into him, and he was left with a few shimmering splinters that he couldn't fit back together again.

"I think we need to be careful," Tean said, as the truck rocked unsteadily up the gravel drive. "I think we shouldn't leap to any conclusions."

"But he's involved. And he knows something. He knew Benny."

"Yes," Tean said. "But let's not get ahead of ourselves."

"Of course," Jem said, tasting blood in his mouth, wondering when and how he'd bitten the inside of his cheek. "I'm cool. I'm totally cool. I'm an Ice Age over here."

Tean sighed.

When they got up to the Bowlings' house, they were met by the sagging clapboard, the blistered paint, and the accumulated junk. Since their last visit, the Bowlings had added what Jem thought was an ancient milking machine, complete with a tarnished brass hand pump. The garage door stood open. The orange Mustang was still in its bay, but the VW Beetle and the Ram were both gone. Dallin was home alone, Jem guessed, which was perfect for what needed to happen next. The wind raked tall grass, drawing neat lines through the mess, whistling against the truck's window. Then, out of the barn, Dallin emerged carrying an ancient saddle over one shoulder, and Jem felt his thoughts splinter again. He reached for the door.

"Jem—"

But he was already dropping out of the truck. Behind him, he heard Tean shift into park and the engine die, and then a door opened and Tean was saying, "Jem, wait a second."

"Hello," Dallin said, drawing to a stop, adjusting the saddle on his shoulder. "My parents aren't home, so you should probably—"

"You killed my brother," Jem said.

"Jem!" Racing footsteps came from behind.

Jem had already grabbed Dallin by the too-large Carhartt shirt, and he marched him backwards. The saddle spilled off Dallin's shoulders, threatening to trip both of them, but Jem just kept going.

"Hey," Dallin was shouting, grabbing at Jem's hands to pry him loose, "get off of me!"

"You killed my brother, you stupid, greedy son of a bitch," Jem shouted, and then he slammed the kid against the barn.

"Enough," Tean said, forcing his way between Jem and Dallin. He shoved Jem back a step, and when Jem came forward, he shoved him again.

"Get out of my way," Jem said calmly. His whole world was calm. He didn't need to think anymore. He just listened to the wind, remembered the way sunlight slid along glass, playing rainbows on the broken edges.

"You're frightening him," Tean said. "Stop it."

"I didn't kill anyone," Dallin said. "I didn't kill anyone."

"You knew him," Jem said. "You knew Benny, you knew he wasn't a threat to anyone, and you still killed him."

"I didn't—"

"We know about the truck, dumbass," Jem shouted. He almost got to the kid that time, but Tean was stronger than he looked, and he kept fending off Jem's approach.

Dallin paled and went still. He was wearing a Mayflower trucker's hat, and his mouth was open, exposing the missing front tooth. He had a fresh black eye.

"I scraped up against a dumpster," Dallin whispered.

"You're a bad fucking liar, kid. You think you know how to take a lick because of your dad? I'm going to give you a taste of the big bad world, just a fucking taste, and when I'm done—"

The move came so quickly, and the surprise was so great, that Jem couldn't stop it: Tean hooked a foot behind his ankle and shoved, and Jem fell on his ass.

"You're done," Tean said. "You're finished. Go wait in the truck."

Then, arm around Dallin's shoulders, Tean led the kid toward the house.

Jem walked the length of the barn in the other direction, the bromegrass whispering at his waist and filling his nose with its dusty, grain smell. He stopped at the far end of the barn to punch the old clapboard until a length of brittle wood snapped. Then he let his hands hang at his side, blood running from split knuckles, the drops weighing down the grass and bending the heavy stalks. When he could breathe normally again, he found the first aid kit in Tean's truck and wiped his hands clean. Then he went around the back of the house.

Tean and Dallin were sitting on the deck railing, the doc's skinny legs hooked around one of the supports, the glasses at the tip of his nose and in danger of falling. Dallin was answering questions in broken phrases too quiet for Jem to hear.

At the sound of Jem's steps, Tean whispered something to Dallin, slid down from the railing and crossed the deck.

"I'm really sorry about that," Jem began. "I'm ok—"

"You're not ok. That's got to be our baseline, or we're done here."

"Ok, I'm not all right. I'm so fucking far from all right that I feel like I'm drowning, and I can't handle that."

"What are you going to do if you find Benny's killer?"

"When."

"What are you going to do when you find Benny's killer?"

Jem put his hands on his hips and looked over his shoulder.

"I'll tell you," Tean said, taking one of Jem's hands and examining it, then taking the other. "If you keep this up, you're going to lose your mind. And then he — or she — will have the upper hand."

"I'll have a plan—"

"No, Jem. You won't. You just assaulted an abused teenage boy because you found out he borrowed a friend's truck." He probed one of the deeper cuts. "You're at the end of your rope."

"Ow," Jem said.

"Well, you need to learn to hit things that are softer. I can bandage these if you bring me the kit."

"Maybe in a minute," Jem said.

"How are these two?" Tean tested the taped fingers.

Jem hissed.

"Worse than they were before?" Tean asked.

"Quit doing that!"

Tean released his hand. "I understand, a little, why you don't trust yourself to feel what you need to feel. But this other way isn't helping either. Do you understand that?"

Jem understood. But the thing waiting for him was a flood of dead waters, black-blue and briny, as vast as the Great Salt Lake. He understood that too, and Tean didn't.

"What's he told you so far?" Jem said, gently extracting his hands from Tean's grip.

"He's told me that he's going to be a NASCAR driver when he grows up," Tean said, "and that he doesn't have time for girls because they're a distraction."

"Did you tell him that's your excuse too?"

"I just raised an internal eyebrow. And maybe an external one too. Jem, he's scared."

"Of course he's scared; he tried to run us off the road, and he's about to get his ass busted for it."

"No, he's not scared for himself. He's protecting someone. If he'd been the one to run us off the road, he would have recognized us the first time we came out here. I think he borrowed the truck from a friend, but he was doing it for someone else; someone else was driving."

Farther up the mountain, rocks clicked together, and a chunk of stone rattled down slope of scree.

"You know who he's protecting," Jem said.

"Not completely."

"Yes, you do," Jem said. "We both do."

Dallin tensed as Jem approached; the boy was sitting with his heels on one of the lower rails, and now he looked like he was ready to jump off the deck just to get a head start. Jem held up his hands.

"Sorry about earlier. I'm losing my mind; the doc has had a front-row seat to the whole thing, so he can tell you about it. Did I hurt you?"

Dallin shook his head.

"Good. I'm still sorry."

Shifting on the rail, Dallin said, "Takes a lot more than that."

"I bet. I bet you've been through worse. I know all about that." Jem tapped his back. "The best scar is right here, but the really bad stuff, it didn't leave a mark where anyone could see."

Dallin angled his body away.

"I'm going to tell you something I wish someone had told me," Jem said. "When you're eighteen, you walk out of here, and you're free."

Dallin's fingers curled along the top rail; the old wood, weak from dry rot, flexed under his grip.

"But if you don't get your head straight," Jem said, "there's just somebody else down the line waiting to give you more of the same. Do you understand what I'm saying?"

"You two ought to go. I've got chores."

"Kid—"

"I'm not a kid."

"We know you're not a kid," Tean said.

"He's bigger than you," Jem said. "And he's older than you. And you've got nothing to be ashamed of except this: keeping quiet when you know you ought to say something."

"I want you off our land." He ruined it by running his wrist under his nose. "Right now."

"Somebody killed my brother," Jem said. "You want to know what weak and helpless feels like? That's it, right there, all of it. And it'll never go away because he's never coming back."

Dallin made a wet noise in his throat, his hands, big for a kid, wrapping around his knees.

"What happened with your friend's truck?" Tean asked.

"He asked me to borrow it. He said there was something wrong with the Ram and he needed to move a few bales. But there wasn't anything wrong with the Ram; I started it up after he left."

"Your dad," Jem said.

After a nod, Dallin said, "He brought Zach's truck back all scraped up. I asked him what happened, and he knocked me down the stairs. Then, at dinner, he said he'd pay to get it fixed up. He told me not to worry about it. I thought that was it, but then people started calling about that lady, and then you guys came out here, and—I don't know. I don't know what he did. I don't want to know. Then you called the house, and he got even more upset. He said he thought you'd gotten the message. He thought, you know, you'd stop. I walked in on him once, and he was on the phone, talking weird, telling someone to leave it alone. He's been acting so weird lately."

Jem glanced at Tean, who said, "A few phone calls, actually. Your dad was trying to scare me off, Dallin. Is that it?"

Dallin nodded.

"What happened with the lady?" Tean asked. "Which lady?"

"The Asian girl that came out here."

"Her name was Sook," Tean said, slowly pushing his glasses back into place. "What happened?

"She asked me if I'd seen anything strange, and I had. I'd followed that fat guy—your brother. I'd followed him one time. He was always trespassing, and one time I thought maybe I'd scare him so he wouldn't come back, so I followed him up into the canyon. He knew a path I didn't, and I followed him straight to the animals. When that lady asked, I thought that's what she was talking about. I showed her where he went. I showed her all the animals."

"What animals?" Tean asked.

"All the dead ones. The ones they keep hauling up there."

36

It took some convincing, but Dallin finally agreed to show them, and they drove along a dirt track on the Bowlings' ranch until they reached the mouth of the canyon. When Tean parked the truck, Dallin craned around to stare back at the house. The kid let out a shaky breath.

"Oh hell," he whispered.

Behind them, a black truck was pulling up at the Bowlings' house; Jem knew if they could see Bowling, he could see them.

"Oh hell," Dallin said. "He is going to kill me."

"No, he's not," Jem said. "Because you didn't want to bring us here, did you? You didn't tell us anything."

"I—"

"I had a gun on you," Jem said, holding out his hand in the shape of a gun. "I told you if you didn't show us the trail, I'd kill you. That's what you say to him."

Tean was shaking his head, frowning, but he didn't say anything.

"Is the trail difficult?" Jem said. "Maybe you point us to it and then run back to the house, pretend like you got away."

Dallin was breathing fast, his hands wrapped around his knees again. Then he shook his head.

"It'll be easier on you—" Jem said.

"No. No, I don't care about none of that anymore. He did something wrong, didn't he? Did he kill that lady? Did he kill your brother?"

"We don't know," Tean said. "We're trying to figure that out."

"If I'd known he was going to do that, I would have stopped him."

"Dallin," Tean said, "just help us find the path Benny used, and then you should—"

"I'm showing you, aren't I? I would, anyway, if we weren't all sitting in this truck."

So they got out of the truck and headed up the canyon. The trail was steep, and loose earth slid away underfoot, tumbling down to knock up against the roots of cottonwoods and the clumps of weeds that grew along the creek. High up the canyon walls, where scrub and brush pulled back, the rock was orangish-red in the sun. The air smelled like cool water and, when the air shifted, like cedar.

They'd gone maybe a mile when Dallin stopped, turned off the path, and scrambled up a rocky slope. Tean followed, making it look easy in his boots, his lean form loping up after Dallin. Jem slid and scraped his palms and cursed his sneakers until he finally reached the stony spine where they stood. He swore, wiping his raw palms on his jeans, and then he swore a few more times. Dallin and Tean exchanged smiles.

"It's not funny," Jem said. "Not all of us are half mountain goat."

"Some us aren't even ten percent," Tean murmured, and for some reason that made Dallin laugh.

"Can we get going?" Jem said. "Before a rattlesnake bites my dick off?"

Dallin was actually grinning, seemingly forgetting the missing front tooth, and pointed up the side of the canyon. "It's a straight shot. You see it?"

"Jeez," Tean said. "How'd Benny ever figure that out?"

Jeez was, in Jem's opinion, an understatement. The path wasn't really a path—it was a faint depression in the side of the canyon, so shallow someone might as well have put it there with an eraser. In a few places, outcroppings offered wider platforms to stop and rest, but for most of the way, it was steep and narrow.

"I'm going to slide right off that thing and break my neck," Jem said. "And then I'll be lucky if a bear doesn't come along and rip my face off while I'm lying there."

"That's the best thing I've ever heard you say," Tean whispered.

"Your brother did it all right," Dallin said. Then a little smirk pulled at the corner of his mouth. "Course, he could get up the hill without looking like he was in ice skates."

"I have bad shoes," Jem said.

"It's a poor carpenter," Tean murmured.

"What was that?"

"Nothing."

Dallin was grinning again, but it faded more quickly. His gaze slid past them to the mouth of the canyon.

"Go on," Tean said. "You've got to be smart about this. Thank you for what you've done."

"Remember," Jem said. "Tell him I've got a gun, and I was going to shoot you."

"No," Dallin said slowly. "No, I'll see it through. If he hurt that lady—"

"Dumbass," Jem said, swatting his arm. "Go, before I push you down there and leave you for the bear."

Overhead, a hawk circled, its shadow a blob that elongated as the bird banked. A warm breeze came up from the valley, dust drifting around Jem's sneakers.

"You just keep going," Dallin said, "and you'll find them."

Then he half slid, half ran down the slope, headed back to the mouth of the canyon. Jem watched him go, his heart beating in his chest.

"He'll be ok," Tean said, touching Jem's arm.

"Story or no story," Jem said, "he's going to get his ass beat."

"Then let's do something about this, so we can do something about that."

They started up the barely visible path. It was easier going than Jem had expected, although he'd been right about the treacherous nature of the trail; pebbles and loose stones shifted under his weight, and more than once he had to grapple with the canyon's rock walls to keep from sliding. Tean, God damn him, looked like he was half cat and half goat.

"Cool," the doc said, studying Jem when they stopped at the next shelf to catch their breath. "I didn't know someone's hands could bleed so much."

Instead of following the canyon deeper into the mountains, though, the path cut up to the canyon's rim, where a shallow pass led Jem and Tean out of the canyon proper and onto the south face of the mountain. The footing here wasn't much better—a mixture of scree and pale, crumbling earth that wound between sapling lodgepoles and thinning brush. It was harder for Jem to gauge distance here, but he thought they might have gone that way for a quarter mile or so before they reached another pass and the trail descended into a canyon.

Tean stopped him and said, "Which way are we facing?"

"You're the nature expert."

"I'm asking for your benefit."

"The sun's behind us, so west. Oh my God, your face. East. We're facing east."

"And the canyon runs which way?"

"East?"

"Which means?"

"It means I wish I'd brought water."

"It means Benny's trail took us across the mountain. This is the Salt Lake Valley side of the Oquirrh."

"Ok."

"It means this is the Dellengbauh side of the mountains."

"Oh. Shit."

Tean nodded, his mouth a grim line, and started the descent. This side was much easier; after a few hundred yards of pushing through scrubby cedars and a clump of dead aspens, they hit a series of natural switchbacks, the outcroppings angled to provide a clear, easy way down into the canyon. As they went lower, the rush of running water reached Jem, which sounded like a dream with the October sun high and hot on the back of his neck. The air still smelled like cedar, sweat, and trampled sage. Then warm air from the valley wafted up, and the stink of death rolled over them.

"Fuh," Jem muttered.

"This is bad," Tean said. He dug out his phone. "And, of course, I've got no service."

"I'm going to check it out," Jem said.

"I know," Tean said. He studied the canyon ahead of them, sighed, and said, "I know you are."

Then they started down again and, near the creek, hit a trail that was wide enough for a small pickup or an ATV. They found the first dead animals two hundred feet later, six mule deer carcasses dumped on a wide stretch of lichen-speckled granite. They were bloated, the flesh ripped in some places, their heads twisted around, their legs curled up. Jem made the mistake of taking a deep breath, and then he stumbled into a clump of brush and puked.

Tean didn't look much better when Jem got back, but all the doc said was, "You ok?"

Jem nodded, and they kept going. Jem was starting to realize this canyon was much bigger than the one they had entered. He had already noticed the wide dirt track, but now he realized that instead of a creek, a small river ran below them, the water white where it leapt over multicolored stone. The upper parts of the canyon walls were still bald, but lower down, thick stands of pine, maple, ash, and spruce offered shade. Cottonwoods paraded along the river, with knee-high weeds and grass climbing the banks until the soil grew too hard and dry.

They found the birds next, a pile of them, their bodies contorted and bloated, their feathers a dirty avalanche that drifted when the breeze picked up. Maggots crawled; flies buzzed. A fox sprinted away from the pile of carcasses, and Jem struggled not to be sick again.

"Birds don't just die in a pile like this," Jem said. "Do they?"

"No," Tean said. "They do not."

"So someone is dumping them."

"That's right."

"Who?"

"Someone from the mines, I think. The animals are being poisoned wherever the tailings ponds are leaking, probably somewhere they might be noticed, and someone is dragging the carcasses up here to keep that from happening."

The whine of an engine answered, rapidly moving closer from the east.

"Shit," Jem said. "Back. We've got to go back."

They made it a hundred yards before an ATV whipped around a bend in the canyon. The driver wore a helmet. A woman, Jem guessed, because she was small and wearing a blur of pink. Then the figure rose up, steadying herself against the ATV's bouncing, and leveled a gun at them.

Jem grabbed the doc and threw them both down the canyon, following the grade toward the river, as the driver fired.

The gunshot echoed up and down the canyon. Jem rolled for twenty yards, the bruises on his body igniting in a blaze of pain. In an instant of clarity, he felt grateful that most of his progress was through the thick grasses and weeds growing along the bank, and then he slid to a stop against a cottonwood. One sneaker was in the river, and the cold shocked him back to himself. Another gunshot rang out, and he heard a ping that sounded like the bullet ricocheting from the canyon wall. Then a third shot broke the water ten feet from where Jem lay, and he flopped onto his belly.

"Here," Tean whispered, motioning from where he was crouching under a rocky overhang. Blood ran from his temple, and the rough passage down the canyon had left an abrasion that ran along the side of his neck, but otherwise he looked intact. Jem squirmed up the bank until he reached Tean. The shadows were cool. The rock was cool. His face was hot, and everything smelled like river water. A few midges, the ones that had lasted into October, droned in his ear.

"Are you ok?" Tean whispered

Jem put a finger to his lips and tried to listen. The last shot had made him think that their attacker had known where he was, but now Jem wasn't sure; another shot hadn't followed, and he couldn't hear anything that sounded like movement.

Then a woman spoke, the voice young, the words tight with what sounded like excitement. "Boys, boys, boys," she said. "Where are you hiding?"

Jem recognized the voice.

Tean whispered, "Ruth."

Jem nodded. It was Julie's intern, the girl who wore pearls and conservative skirts and that little Mormon medallion around her neck. The girl who had picked out a diamond tennis bracelet without batting an eye. He tried to run through a logical sequence of events, but all he could come up with was two facts: Bowling had known they were headed up the canyon, and now Ruth was here. Bowling must have called to warn her that someone else was about to find the dead animals. He thought of all that new money Bowling was throwing around.

Why, Jem wanted to know. What could prompt a girl with her whole life ahead of her to kill? Because Jem was certain this girl had killed Benny and Sook. Greed, maybe. He thought of the phone call he had overheard, Ruth's rage about—what were the words?— *having to squeeze every penny.* He remembered how quickly she had snatched up the tennis bracelet. But how did covering up the deaths of these animals profit Ruth? And why was she willing to kill for it?

The questions sparked and died out before Jem could focus on them. Benny. This girl had killed Benny. And then the grief was there, eating him from the inside out, and Jem rolled onto his knees and squirmed toward the edge of the overhang, not caring about the gun, not caring about anything except not having to feel this way anymore.

"What are you doing?" Tean whispered, grabbing Jem's arm.

"I'm going to kill that bitch."

"Jem, stop."

Jem tried to shake the doc free, but Tean hung on.

"You're going to get yourself killed," Tean whispered. "Stop. I know it hurts, but you have to just stop and think for a minute. You don't have to do anything with all that pain. You just have to stop fighting it, and then it won't be such a big part of you."

For a moment, Jem was in the bathtub again, with the whiplash crack of the antenna as it sliced into his back. He was in the dormitory at Decker, with Blake and Antonio crowding him against the bunk, with Tanner's honey-colored eyes watching him above a smile, with the cold air on bare skin as they stripped him and bent him over the bed, the reek of Blake's Cheetos breath something Jem could focus on so he didn't go crazy. He was in Decker, the staff putting him in restraints after he'd kicked a hole in the vending machine's plastic front, and he couldn't breathe.

"You don't have to do it alone," Tean whispered.

It was hard. It was maybe the hardest thing Jem had ever had to do as an adult, to pull back from the constant struggle for control, to let the pain and anger and humiliation, all the helplessness and hurting, rise up like a black tide to crash down on him. But he did. And after a moment of digging his fingers into the rocky soil under them, he was still alive, still himself, and thinking clearly. The pain was there, God, a poisoned lake of it. But it was just a part of him, and the other parts could function again.

His fingers were bloody when he worked them free from the ground. He pulled out the tube sock and handed it to Tean.

"Are you—" Tean whispered.

"Run down to the river," Jem said. "Fill this with rocks. Then keep going to the mouth of the canyon and call the police. I'll make sure she uses up all her bullets, so if she comes after you, don't hesitate to get up close and hit her as hard as you can. Do you understand?"

"Yes, but—"

"I'm going to keep her talking. Stay here until you've got an opening; you'll know when it's time to move."

Without waiting for an answer, Jem pulled out his phone, opened an app, and turned the volume all the way up. He angled the phone out from under the projecting stone, aiming it in the direction he thought he had heard Ruth's voice. LouElla had been the one who had really helped him to understand the truth about the world: people would believe anything if they wanted it to be true, or if they were afraid it was. Jem had told Dallin to tell his dad that he had a gun. Bowling had called Ruth. It was time to find out if he'd included that important detail.

Jem tapped an icon on the screen, and the phone blared a realistic gunshot.

Frantic movement and a shout announced Ruth's reaction. Jem was already moving, racing up the bank, sprinting across the trail, and diving into the thick brush and trees on the other side. Another shot rang out. Jem didn't even look. He worked his way into the thickest parts of the brush, keeping close to the trail, not wanting to climb too high where the cover thinned as he moved toward the back of the canyon.

"You're trapped," Ruth said, but she sounded out of breath now, and the excitement in her voice was gone. "You're not going anywhere. So you've got two choices: we can do this the easy way or the hard way."

Jem tried not to roll his eyes too hard as he called back, "Why'd you kill them?"

The rustle of steps through scrub was the only answer.

"Whoever's pulling your strings," Jem said, "they're going to let you take all the heat for this. You know that, right?"

"Pulling my strings," Ruth said. "Give me a break."

"You?" Jem laughed. "You're telling me you're behind all this?"

"Men. You think if it doesn't happen between our legs, we don't have any idea what's going on. I'm the one that made nice with that fat kid after he talked to Julie. I'm the one that got him to get into the car. I'm the one that went to the Asian girl. I played it perfectly. Can you believe the same thing worked on both of them?" Her voice became mockingly girlish. "Oh, please, I'm just so worried about my boss. I think she's doing something terrible, and I really need to talk to someone." Then her voice dropped back to normal. "She walked me right inside her apartment. And that fat kid couldn't wait to climb up in the seat next to me. It didn't hurt that the dumbshit thought I was his girlfriend."

Jem crouched behind a brake of dead elderberries, the thin, brown branches, rasping lightly against his jeans. The stink of his sweat, of adrenaline, made him take thin, papery breaths. Bird shit between his feet made him think of the doc; the doc would probably know what kind of birds used to come here for the berries. He wiped his hands on his jeans, waiting.

Through the screen of trees and brush, he saw Ruth move forward along the trail. She had ditched the helmet, and she was wearing a polka-dot skirt that came to her knees and a fuzzy pink cardigan over a white blouse. She even had on her pearls. The next level would have been tennis whites, Jem thought. When her gaze moved away from him, he hunkered lower and tapped the icon on his phone again.

Her head whipped around faster than he had expected. This time, the shot came so close that the elderberry brake was quivering from the bullet's passage, and Jem let out a slow, shaky breath. Where he had scraped his fingers earlier, clawing at the dirt, blood ran down to his nails and beaded and fell to the ground. Ruth was staring in his direction. She was still holding up the gun, as though considering another shot. It was a revolver. Most revolvers could hold six cartridges. Most, Jem thought. But not all. And she'd shot five times so far. One more shot. She had one more shot, and then she'd have to reload, and that would be his chance. Unless, of course, the cylinder held eight cartridges.

"I see you," she said.

It was a bluff. Jem held himself still. But the revolver swung in his direction, and Ruth smiled a bright, pink smile.

"You made a big mistake," Jem said.

"Stand up and walk down here and I'll do it right: once in the back of the head. Otherwise I'll probably get you in the gut, and you'll be up here a long time dying."

"When you dealt with Benny, he trusted you. And when you dealt with Sook, she trusted you."

"Stand up."

"But I'm not the trusting kind."

"All right," Ruth said. "I'll just see if I can get you from here."

"Now," Jem shouted. "Get her!"

It was pure bluster, but Ruth was, in spite of the murders and the greed, still young, still inexperienced. She whirled around, already assuming that Jem had lured her into a trap. Jem was just about to launch himself deeper into the canyon when he saw Tean leap out from behind a boulder. The doc's glasses were on the tip of his nose, and his hair looked like he'd stuck his head in a whirlwind, but he held the weighted sock at waist level, obviously ready to use it.

Jem tapped the app again and changed course.

Flinching, Ruth spun toward the sound of the gunshot. Jem was racing straight at her. She brought the gun up, leveling it at him, when Tean hit her with the tube sock at the small of the back. She stumbled, her arm carrying the gun wide as she tried to recover her balance, and by then Jem had closed in. He slashed with the antenna, cracking it hard against her hand, and she cried out and released the revolver. It hit soft earth; Jem didn't even hear it land. Ruth was still stumbling, still dealing with pain and shock, when Jem got the barrette's edge against her throat.

"You killed Benny," Jem said. He was shaking; the filed edge of the barrette's clip had already sliced through skin, and blood trickled down Ruth's throat.

"Ok," Tean said. The doc's hand was warm and soft on Jem's wrist, and he gently applied pressure. For a moment, Jem resisted. Then Tean said, "We're both ok. We're ok, Jem. Let's end this the right way."

A breeze stirred the cottonwoods, tearing a few final leaves free and scattering them on the river. The rush of the water filled Jem's ears. A bird—the doc would know what kind—broke out of a pine and struggled up into the air.

"We're both ok," Tean whispered.

Jem let him guide the weapon away from Ruth's throat.

"Tie her," Jem said, shaking so hard that he could barely press the length of paracord into Tean's hands. "And then let's march her out of here."

Tean made quick work of the job, and they started walking.

They had made it a quarter mile before Jem said, "You were supposed to run and call the police."

"I was too busy recording her confession," Tean said, and a huge, very un-doctor-like smile broke out across his face. "Besides, I wasn't going to leave you alone."

37

"I cannot believe how fucking stupid you are," Ammon said, pacing back and forth in the interview room. "I just honestly cannot believe it."

It was sometime past midnight; after escorting Ruth out of the canyon, Tean had finally been able to place the call to the police. After that, everything had taken time: time for the police to arrive, time to explain their story, time for the police to drive them to the department's main building, an amoeba-like structure of glass and steel that looked like the Salt Palace's kid sister. Then more time in this room that smelled like microwaved curry and a CVS knockoff of Acqua di Gio. On the two-way glass, someone had taped a printed sign that said PROCEEDINGS ARE ALWAYS MONITORED AND RECORDED; one edge was torn, and someone had repaired it with masking tape.

"I think we're past the part of this conversation that's productive," Tean said. "I understand that you're upset—"

"Upset? You haven't begun to see me fucking upset. Do you understand—" He laid mocking emphasis on the word. "—that you could have been killed? Did you even think about it? Did you even think about what that would mean for one fucking second?"

This was the dance. Neither of them saying what really needed to be said because they were in the stationhouse, because this was Ammon's job, and because PROCEEDINGS ARE ALWAYS MONITORED AND RECORDED.

Rubbing grainy eyes, Tean said, "I'd like to go home."

It wasn't quite that straightforward, but eventually Ammon shouted himself out. He really did look like a wreck: his face was drawn and sallow, his collar was undone, his tie loose. But it was more than that. It was something in his energy that manifested once or twice as a tic near his eye. If Tean were in another situation, with an animal he knew, he might have thought Ammon was on the verge of full-blown panic.

Ammon finally walked him out, a hand on Tean's upper arm like Tean was a flight risk. They left the squad room, made their way along an empty corridor that was painfully bright with fluorescents. A third of the way down the hall, Ammon glanced behind him, checking that the coast was clear, and threw open a door. He shoved Tean into what turned out to be a custodial supply closet, and then he stepped in after him and pulled the door shut.

"If you want to yell at me off camera—" Tean began.

Even with a broken arm, Ammon had no trouble throwing him against the wall and kissing him. His good hand was tight on Tean's waist, biting into the flesh there, and the kisses were hard and desperate. For a few moments, Tean stiff-armed him, trying to force him away. But this was Ammon, and those were Ammon's kisses, Ammon's hand on his waist, Ammon's leg between his, his knee coming up to apply light pressure.

"Oh Christ," Ammon whispered when he finally pulled back. "Tean, you could have died. I could have lost you. You're my whole life, and I could have lost you."

The fluorescents hummed. The smell of ammonia hung in the air. Tean tried to look away, but Ammon turned his face back with one finger. Ammon's eyes were wet, and he blinked rapidly.

"I'm done lying," Ammon whispered. "I'm done. If I'd lost you, I would have gone out of my fucking mind. Give me a few days to square things with Lucy, and then let's go away. I'll go wherever you want. I'll do whatever you want. When we come back—if we come back—I want to be together."

Tean closed his eyes and let his head rock back.

"Say something, please," Ammon said, his voice cracking once.

"Ok," Tean said.

"I'm serious."

"I know you are."

Ammon kissed the side of Tean's neck. Stubble from a long day burned pleasantly there. "Please."

"We're both tired, and we're both upset—"

Ammon kissed him, softly, tenderly, almost as hesitantly as that first kiss in a steam-filled shower, where the breeze off the Pacific wicked over bare skin like a razor.

"I am one-hundred percent serious," Ammon said. "I wish you could feel what I'm feeling right now. I wish you knew what the thought of losing you, really losing you, was doing to me. God, if anything had happened to you —" He started to cry, pressing his face into Tean's neck, his tears hot and flowing.

"Ok," Tean whispered. "It's ok. I'm ok."

"Say you'll go with me," Ammon whispered, his face still pressed to Tean's neck. "Say you won't let me do this alone."

Closing his eyes against the sting of tears, Tean remembered high school, sitting at Ammon's table, watching him laugh at a dumb joke Nora had made, knowing for the first time what it meant to love someone. He remembered the feeling of a clockwork universe, every gear engaging, when Ammon had walked into the apartment in Lima for the first time. He remembered the steam of the shower, the feeling of slick skin, playful bites, laughter, weightlessness, and what it meant not just to love someone but to make love. He remembered all the times they had played this scene before: in college, when Ammon had promised to run away together; before Daniel was born, when Ammon had promised again; the first time Tean had threatened to break things off, when Ammon had laid out a clear, three-month plan, begging Tean to be patient.

"Ok," Tean said. "Ok."

"Sunday at the latest," Ammon said, pulling away from Tean, grinning through his tears. "Today's Friday, and I'll have everything worked out by Sunday. Let's go to Tahiti. Or Maui. Or Lima. Would you like Lima after, you know, everything?"

Tean swallowed and nodded.

"Lima," Ammon said. "Lima." He laughed. "We're going to Lima."

There were more tears, more kisses, more apologies, but after that, things wound themselves down, and Tean emerged onto the cement plaza outside the station. He walked toward the lot — Ammon had sent a uniformed officer to pick up the truck from Bowling's property — and then stopped when he saw someone leaning against the white Ford.

Jem scratched his beard; in the dusty apron of light from the sodium lamp, he was mostly shadow, just a glimmer of blond hair in a hard side part.

"You look like this is weird," Jem finally said.

"No," Tean said. "Not at all. I just didn't know if they'd finished talking to you."

"Almost an hour ago," Jem said. "They told me you were done too."

"Ammon wanted to yell at me," Tean said, not quite meeting Jem's shadowed gaze as he dug out his keys.

"I just wanted to say goodbye."

Down the street, a car accelerated, and the soft pump of Britney Spears, "I'm Not A Girl," ghosted through the parking lot.

"Thanks," Jem said. "For everything."

Tean thought it could end here. Tean thought about letting it end here. And then he thought about Sook, who had opened her door and trusted Ruth and been murdered.

"She said, 'next to me,'" Tean said.

"What?"

"Next to me. When she was talking about Benny getting in the car, she said he couldn't wait to get in the seat next to her. But we saw the video, Tean. Benny got in the back seat."

In the darkness, the blue of Jem's eyes was almost black. "Probably just a slip."

"You know it wasn't."

"Probably just a bad description."

"Someone else was driving that SUV, Jem. You know it. I know it. But I don't know who it was."

"Let's talk about it later."

"You want to handle the rest of this on your own; you're cutting me out."

"I think you've done enough. Besides, I think your boyfriend will hunt me down and put a bullet in my brain if I get you in trouble again."

Tean held Jem's gaze. The side of his neck burned where Ammon's stubble had scraped him.

"What?" Jem said. "You're not going to tell me he's not your boyfriend?"

But Jem was the first to look away.

"They killed Sook," Tean said. "I want both of them to pay for that."

"We don't know who she was working with. We don't know anything."

"It could have been Phil," Tean said. "He's the right size to be the man who attacked us outside the DWR."

"What's his motive?"

"It could have been Goody," Tean said. "That was Ruth's sweater in the front seat of his truck. The attacker wore his bracelet. He probably met her through the bighorn repopulation plan. He's obviously having some kind of relationship with her, and people will do stupid things for love."

"Pretty weak."

"Or Bowling. It could have been Bowling, too. He had that injury on his head, just like the one you gave the attacker. We know he was taking money from Ruth, keeping an eye on the canyon, making sure no one used the back trail to find those animals. He cut down all those trees. He reported anytime someone went up there."

"That's not the same thing as murder."

"Don't do that," Tean said, his voice slipping with frustration. "Don't try to box me out."

"I'm not boxing you out. I'm trying to keep you safe."

"Bullshit. You want revenge, and you want to do this on your own. And I won't let you. I'll confront each of them myself. I'll do it. And I'll be convincing enough and threatening enough that the real killer will have to act. He won't let me drag him down; he'll have to stop me."

Jem ran his fingers over the Ford's hood. "That's your plan?"

"That's the start of it."

"That's a terrible plan."

"Well, I like it. And I'm going to do it. Even if it does mean I'll probably end up with my head bashed in, dying over a course of days from bleeding on the brain, half buried in overburden up one of the canyons. Before coyotes eat my face. And ants eat my eyes. While I'm still alive. And no one can hear me screaming."

"God, you're adorable. Fine. You convinced me."

"I wasn't trying to—"

"But let's go make a decent plan." Jem jiggled the Ford's latch. "Come on, I don't have all night."

"Then you do know who was helping her?"

"Obviously," Jem said, his crooked front teeth showing in a huge smile.

So they drove back to Tean's apartment and planned.

38

When they got to Dellengbauh the next day, Tean gave his name to the guard at the gate. The sun was barely clearing the Wasatch Mountains behind them, and streamers of shadow curled up into the Oquirrh Range. The stone was pale in the early light, and the Russian thistles next to the gate looked extra murderous as the shadows multiplied their thorns. Tean ran his hands around the steering wheel.

"Not on here," the guard said after examining the clipboard.

"Could you call up and check?"

The guard ambled back up to the gatehouse.

"Ok," Jem said, grabbing Tean's wrist to still his hand. "You're driving me crazy."

"This isn't going to work."

"Of course it will."

"We're both going to end up dead. And not just normal dead. Probably chopped up into pieces and dissolved in the tailings ponds. And we'll break down into molecules and then they'll probably sell the slurry from the ponds to a manufacturer and we'll be processed into some sort of toilet clog cleaner and that's it, that's our afterlife, clearing out clumps of hair and shit."

Jem covered his face with both hands.

"What?" Tean said.

"I'm just trying to take it all in."

"What?"

"I honestly don't think you'd understand if I explained."

The guard was coming back, but Tean still said, "That's really condescending."

"I know," Jem said, dropping his hands and smiling at him.

"Go on up," the guard said. "She said you've been there before?"

"Yep," Jem said. "We got it."

The guard waved them through, and Tean eased the truck forward. The mine opened up below them, the benches busy with trucks and equipment. The sounds of heavy machinery ran through the morning air: sometimes the grinding of gears, sometimes the whine of a hydraulic pump, once the stuttering percussion of what Tean imagined was an industrial scale hammer drill. Tean found himself considering the black SUVs in the mine's motor pool, wondering what had happened to the one that Ruth had used to abduct and murder Benny. Was it in one of the canyons, already entombed by overburden?

"Your boyfriend is going to kill you," Jem said. Then he tapped the box on his lap and said, "This is not what he would consider a smart idea."

"Ammon just wants things to be done. I know what he'd say if I told him about this. He'd say it was one word. He'd say I was making something out of nothing, or that she was caught up in the moment. He'd sweep it under the rug because he's already got his conviction lined up; he doesn't need any complications." Tean tried to hold back the rest, but it slipped out: "His whole life has been choosing to avoid complications."

Jem studied him, those squalling blue eyes soft now.

"Anyway," Tean said.

"Maybe he'll get abducted by a gang of clowns, and they'll sodomize him for days in their tiny clown car, and then they'll blast him in the face with bad seltzer and it'll have flesh-eating bacteria in it and he'll literally be eaten alive."

Tean considered this. "That seems a bit extreme."

"Oh my God," Jem whispered, and then he bit his lower lip and shook his head.

"And why clowns?"

For some reason that made Jem laugh all the way to their destination.

This time, Tean didn't knock; he walked into the trailer that served as Julie's office without announcing himself. It looked more or less as he remembered: papers covering every surface, cans of Tab on tables and desks, the smell of wet boots. Julie was in flannel and dirty jeans again, although she was wearing shoes this time. She was talking to a pair of executive types, a man and a woman in suits. Both of them looked like they'd been squeezed out of an MBA program

"If you could wait outside, please," Julie said. "We're not finished here, and I don't remember scheduling—"

Jem just tapped the box.

"I don't have any idea what that means," Julie said.

"It means we're going to talk now, Ms. Nash," Tean said. "This is in regard to certain discoveries made yesterday in a local canyon."

Julie didn't flinch, but she looked a little green as she excused herself to the executive types and walked them out of the trailer. Both the man and the woman looked unhealthily interested in what might be about to happen—chum in the water, Tean thought. Thank God he'd never worked in a corporation.

When she shut the door, Julie grabbed her phone, placed a call, and said, "Get up here." To Tean and Jem, she said, "What the heck do you think you're doing, coming in here, threatening me? You say what you came to say, and then you get your butts out of here. I don't care if this is an official investigation; I won't be talking to you without a lawyer and without advance notice."

"Busy day?" Jem said.

"We've got double the work to do now that Ruth is gone, not to mention the sheer hell that she dragged me and this company into." Julie crossed the trailer to her desk, dropped into the chair, and put her feet up. "Do you know they're trying to hang this around my neck? Can you even believe that?"

Tean and Jem sat opposite her, and Tean said, "We know that you knew about the tailings ponds leaking. We know that you were involved in the cover-up."

"All right," Julie said. "That's the end of this conversation. Anything else, you can say it through lawyers. Goodbye, gentlemen."

At that moment, the door opened, and Phil moved into the room. He was carrying a manila envelope identical to the one Tean had seen him carrying on their last visit, and he displayed it to Julie as he entered.

"Again?" Julie said, seeming to forget Tean and Jem for a moment, her eyes bulging as she stared at the envelope. "Haven't they heard the expression 'blood from a stone'?"

Tean studied the security guard. He had forgotten that Phil was big, taller than Jem, built heavier, much of the weight muscle. But what struck him right then, staring at the man, was the bandage on the side of his head. Right where Jem had hit him with the hex nut on the end of the paracord. That was the confirmation Tean needed.

"Sit down," Jem said. "We're going to have a conversation."

"Do you want me to throw them out of here?" Phil said.

"Buddy," Jem tapped the box again, "don't push me."

"Just say whatever you've got to say," Julie snapped. "Phil, quit hanging around the door like a goon."

After a moment, Phil moved to sit next to Julie.

"You knew about the tailings pond leak—the seepage, whatever you want to call it," Tean said to Julie. "You knew that animals were being poisoned and dying. The contamination must have been hard to spot at first, which was why you passed your inspections, but then all those dead animals started turning up, and you were afraid someone was going to notice. The fines and the bad PR would have been bad enough, but I think you were mostly worried about losing your job. You needed to buy yourselves time, so you hid the carcasses on Dellengbauh property, in one of the canyons you use for overburden, where you figured hunters and hikers wouldn't stumble onto them."

"No," Julie said. "I'm telling you categorically, no. And that's the end of this conversation."

Phil said nothing.

"You thought you had it under control. You were going to find a way to stop the leakage, and nobody would have to know that anything had ever happened. That is, until Benny showed up and said he knew the mines were poisoning animals. I bet he didn't have the details right. I bet he was confused. But you were still worried. You argued."

"That's what this is about? That fat kid that got killed?" Julie's jaw hung open for a moment. "Jeez, you think I had something to do with that. Ruth confessed—that's what I heard. Ruth did that."

"Ruth couldn't drag Sook's dead body out of that apartment and across town," Jem said. "Not on her own. Same thing with Benny: somebody helped her move his body up into the foothills."

"I didn't—"

"Had they already started blackmailing you when Benny came to see you?" Tean asked.

The shock on Julie's face wiped out everything else.

"Phil and Ruth are the ones blackmailing you," Tean said, "just so you know. That's why Phil's always the one who comes in with those manila envelopes, always the one bringing you the next set of demands. That was their big plan. They knew you had money — your own, of course, but also access to a lot of discretionary funds for environmental programs, charitable donations, all the rest. They wanted that money. Of course, they were greedy and stupid, so they made some mistakes. Whose idea was it, Phil? Yours or Ruth's?"

"Fuck you," Phil said.

"It was Ruth's," Jem said.

"Blackmail? Blackmail me for what?"

"For covering up the damage from the tailings ponds," Jem said. "And then, later, when it was convenient, they added Benny's murder."

"That's ridiculous. I didn't have anything to do with that." She licked her lips; her face was pasty. "There is no cover-up. I don't even know what you're talking about."

"It's hard to know how long they'd been planning this, or when they put certain parts into play. But we saw your bank statement, all the money you've paid out. I bet the police will find the blackmail letters once they start going through your office and your house. And of course you didn't suspect Phil and Ruth because you were fucking both of them."

Julie leaned back as though the words had been a slap.

"One of them," Tean said, "Ruth or Phil, had the foresight to pay Bowling to watch the canyon. They knew that if anybody stumbled across those animals, if word got out about the tailings pond leak, their blackmail would be worthless. They wouldn't be able to hold it over your head because it would be public knowledge, so they had to keep anyone from stumbling into that canyon. They might have even realized that some of the poisoned birds could have made their way to Bowling's side of the mountains, but Ruth and Phil really aren't very smart, so I'm not sure they actually thought it through that carefully. They even got you to do some of the work for them. The day we first met you, you'd been over there cutting down trees, helping Bowling bring them down right across the trail. Did you know why? It was one more way to keep people from exploring."

Julie's face was a mixture of horror and confusion. Phil's face was a death mask.

"Phil and Ruth had to kill Sook," Jem said, "when Bowling called and told them she'd been poking around, because she'd seen the dead animals; they were lucky that she didn't have time to write an official report and didn't mention it to anyone that first day. She'd been on private land without a warrant—she'd crossed into one of Dellengbauh's canyons—and they couldn't risk her coming back."

"No," Julie said, "There's no way they would—"

"Be quiet," Phil snapped.

Julie's head swiveled, the rest of her body frozen, and she stared at him as though seeing him for the first time.

"And then, when Benny kept poking around in the canyon, when Bowling called and told Ruth and Phil about that, that's when they realized he had to go too. Ruth told us how easily she was able to kill Sook and Benny; they both made the mistake of trusting her." A specter of a sad smile appeared on Jem's lips and then vanished. "Benny thought she was his girlfriend."

"This is insane," Julie said, swinging her feet off the desk and standing. Her voice rose into a shout. "Even if I—I mean, I would never agree to having someone killed. Jeez, get real. I wouldn't be part of this. Not at all. It's like you said, this is Ruth and Phil."

"Maybe," Tean said.

"Maybe," Jem said. "But that didn't matter. You said something really foolish when you got into an argument with Benny. You threatened him. And Ruth and Phil had been recording you for a long time, gathering material to blackmail you. Originally, they probably planned for blackmail on the cover-up of the tailings pond. Then you threatened Benny, and they had Benny killed to keep their whole operation from collapsing. It was like you'd handed them the golden ticket."

"I want a lawyer," Julie said. "Phil, I need my lawyer."

"Phil's your whole problem," Jem said. "Haven't you been listening? He's not going to help you now."

Phil was coiled like a spring at the edge of his seat.

"Do you remember," Jem said, playing with the flaps of the box in his lap, "when you told us Benny had planted a bomb in your trailer?"

Julie stared at him.

"Call for more guys from security," Phil said. "Get them out of here."

"Only, you never really saw Benny, did you? Not with your own eyes. You stopped by the trailer late. You weren't supposed to be here; nobody was expecting you. And you found Phil holding a device. And he told you he'd caught Benny trying to plant a bomb, and all the bullshit about the camera lenses spray-painted black, about how nobody else had seen him. He told you he'd already reported it to the police. Well, Julie, here's a lesson for you: don't take anything at face value. You stumbled onto Phil when he was retrieving that day's audio recordings, and he had to say something or else you'd figure out what he was up to. The idea of Benny planting a bomb would have been laughable, but you've got an ego, and you've got your own opinions about nutters, so it worked. You fell for it."

"Call the police," Phil said. "They can't prove any of this."

"Phil," Julie said, her voice shaky. "Phil. Oh my gosh. Oh my gosh."

"They're full of shit," Phil said. "They're—"

"Phil, buddy," Jem said, opening the box, "you've really got to learn how to cover your tracks better, especially if you want to be the big, bad wolf in with all the sheep. It wasn't hard at all to find the device—"

In all their planning, Tean and Jem had never expected Phil to make a move so early or so quickly. He sprang out of the seat, a folding knife snapping open as he lunged at Jem. Jem tumbled back, the empty box—another bluff—falling to the floor. The knife might have caught him anyway because Phil was so tall and had a long reach, but Tean shoved Jem clear, sending the blond man to the floor. The chair went with him, and Jem's legs tangled with the furniture. For a moment, he was out of the fight.

Phil turned on Tean.

Julie was screaming.

Tean shot out of the chair, kicking it into Phil's path as the bigger man came around the desk. Phil batted it away and kept coming. His arm whipped out again, the knife swiping through the air inches from Tean's face, and Tean threw himself back again. His hip connected with one of the desks that filled the trailer, and a flicker of despair lit him up: he was cornered.

He worked the tube sock, the same one Jem had given him, out of his pocket. He'd thought that Phil might try to fight his way free, or maybe that Phil would threaten Julie, but he hadn't expected the brutal direct attack. He should have, he understood now. He was dealing with a killer, one who felt no remorse or hesitation. The irony, Tean glimpsed darkly, was that he was going to die for not being cynical enough.

Tean groped the desk behind him. He chucked a stapler and caught Phil under the eye, and the big man roared, but he kept coming. He found a tape dispenser, a tin of tacks, a pencil. He threw all of them. Phil kept coming. Then his hand closed on one of the cans of Tab that littered the office. This one was still full. He grabbed it and tried to force it into the tube sock, the same way he had used the stones from the river the day before, but his fingers were stiff, and he couldn't make the can fit.

Phil lunged.

Then Jem was there, still on the floor, still tangled in the chair, but grabbing Phil's leg. Phil slashed once with the knife, catching Jem's forearm when Jem shielded his head. Then Phil turned, kicking Jem hard in the face, then pivoting and stomping down on his head. Jem fell, his body limp and unresponsive.

A switch flicked in Tean. The whole world was clear, crystalline, cold. His fingers responded, and the can of Tab slid into the tube sock. Tean tested the weight, swung the sock once to build up momentum, and then struck. Phil was still turning around when the improvised sap caught him on the side of the head, in the exact same spot Jem had hit him with the hex nut earlier that week.

The cracking noise was awful, and Phil did a jittery, two-step dance before collapsing, blood at his nose and mouth.

Julie was still screaming.

Tean dialed 911 and then dropped to his knees next to Jem, bloody and still and unresponsive.

39

Tean was sitting in a hallway at LDS Hospital when Ammon found him. For a while, after the police had first brought them there, a frantic energy had driven questioning by both the police and the doctors and nurses. Then Tean had been shunted aside. For a while, a uniformed officer had stood watch over him, but then the officer's radio had squawked and he'd left Tean alone.

A lull had come over the hospital in the late afternoon, with a greasy smell that floated up from the cafeteria; Tean imagined it was meat loaf. From time to time, a machine hummed, and at the next intersection, a nurse typed manically on a computer. The legs of the chair scraped the vinyl flooring as Ammon dragged it next to Tean's.

"If you're going to yell at me, we should probably go somewhere else. I think they're still doing Jem's X-rays."

Ammon didn't answer. Then he stretched out, sliding down until his head rested against the back of the chair, and closed his eyes. The fluorescents exposed fine lines around his eyes and mouth that Tean hadn't noticed before. Lines in his forehead too. He was wearing the same wrinkled suit and shirt that Tean had seen him in the night before.

"I'm sorry," Tean said.

"Ok."

"I am."

"At least you didn't get hurt. I guess that's something."

A middle-aged man limped past them, hauling a rolling IV pole with him, the casters whining.

"Ammon, I really am—"

"I don't think I can listen to another apology from you right now. Why don't you just tell me what happened?"

So Tean told him: Ruth's slip, revealing that she had been working with someone else; the strangeness of Julie's original story about Benny planting a bomb; the logistical challenges that meant Ruth couldn't have acted alone in the killings.

"We knew all that," Ammon said. "We knew she had help. She's vicious and self-interested. She was going to cut a deal and give us her partner. She already admitted to stealing Goody's bracelet to throw suspicion on him; apparently, he was playing the part of sugar daddy, buying her gifts, giving her cash. They met through the bighorn repopulation project that Dellengbauh is funding. She sent him after the cougar. He's the one who rushed the autopsy; Ruth twisted his arm until he called in a few favors. She also sold out Bowling almost immediately, and we're charging him as an accessory."

"You could have told me that. You could have told me any of that, and things would have been different."

Ammon sat up slowly, his blue eyes fixing on Tean.

"Ok," Tean said, shifting in his seat. "Fair enough."

"I know this guy is a bad influence on you—"

"Excuse me?"

"—but I cannot believe you didn't come to me with this."

A part of Tean couldn't believe it either. A part of Tean felt strangely wild, strangely free, as though he'd clipped a tether he hadn't even been aware of before. And a part of him, of course, felt like shit.

"I just thought we were going to have a conversation," was what he said, though. "I thought maybe I'd have more evidence for you after we talked to them."

Ammon grunted. He wiped his eyes, where he always got crusties when he was tired, and then he looked like he was fighting a smile. "But Jesus Christ, Tean, you bluffed this guy with an empty box?"

Tean shrugged. "We didn't really know where he'd hidden the recordings, but we thought he'd be panicking after Ruth got picked up."

The smile broke free. "And he fell for it?"

"You should have seen his face."

"Yeah, thanks, I've seen it. Well, the good news is that we got a warrant, and the dumbass didn't hide the recordings well at all. They were on microcassettes under his bed. Don't laugh; I'm serious."

But Tean just laughed harder.

"I've only listened to bits and pieces, but we found the tape where Julie Nash fights with Benny, and a few of the other ones have conversations where Julie is organizing the cover-up of the tailings-pond leak. Still no sign of the SUV they used to pick up Benny, but he had a pair of boots at the back of his closet that we sent to the lab. He tried to clean them up, but the techs think there's blood on them. It was enough to get him to flip. Plus, you should have seen Phil's face when he learned that Ruth was two-timing him with an old man and a woman. Poor guy's never had it so hard. He really thought she loved him." Ammon shook his head. "He told us that he was the one who first found the dead animals near the tailings pond seepage; he was doing a security sweep on Dellengbauh's perimeter. He took it to Julie, and Ruth was right there — love at first sight. After they killed Benny, he followed you because he and Ruth couldn't find Benny's notes. They figured Benny had given them to you, which he had. Of course, Phil botched it and got made because he's dumber than a bag of rocks."

"Ruth played all of them, not just Phil; she made Julie and Goody believe that she loved them too."

"Money, money, money. It's always about money."

A door opened, and Jem emerged in a wheelchair being pushed by a tech. Jem's nose was broken, both eyes starting to blacken, and he had a bandage on his cheek and arm. His head was lolling from whatever they'd doped him with, and he didn't seem to register Tean or Ammon. The tech, a big guy who might have been Samoan, nodded at them as he took Jem down the hall. Tean stood to follow.

When Ammon grabbed his wrist, Tean looked down and was surprised to see tears in Ammon's eyes. The detective blinked them away and asked in a hoarse voice, "Do you want to tell me what's going on, or do I have to put the puzzle together myself?"

"What do you mean?"

"You're still spending time with him. You're going after him like you're joined at the hip."

"He doesn't have anybody else, Ammon. Literally. I'm going to make sure he gets through this ok; that's all."

"I bought two tickets to Lima, Tean. I'm talking to Lucy tomorrow. Are you going to tell me right now that I'm making a fucking fool of myself, or am I going to have to find out the hard way? Is that what you want? You want me to throw my whole life away so you can laugh at me?"

"You're hurting me," Tean said quietly.

Ammon released him; pale crescents marked where his nails had bitten into Tean's wrist.

"You know I love you," Tean said. "I've loved you my whole life, and I've waited my whole life for you."

Biting the inside of his cheek, Ammon shook his head and looked away.

"You're talking to Lucy tomorrow?"

"Yes. I'm done with this. I'm done with having half a life."

"Maybe I can be down there. In the area, you know, not at your house. In case you need someone after."

Ammon just nodded.

"We'll have our bags packed. We'll stay at a hotel that last night, go to the airport the next day, and head to Lima."

"I just need you to tell me now if—"

"I'm telling you right now: I love you."

Ammon wiped his eyes again. "You're the best thing in my life," he said.

For a heartbeat, Tean thought there might be more.

Then nothing.

Nodding, Tean hurried after Jem, his eyes stinging, barely making it around a corner before an invisible hand crushed his chest.

40

"I love you," Jem sang from the couch. "I love you, I love you, I love you."

"The neighbors can hear you," Tean said, pointing to the sliding door. It stood open, admitting cool air into the apartment, and the sounds of kids laughing came from the dry cleaner's lot behind the privacy fence. "You've got to be quieter."

"You brought me fried chicken," Jem sang between pauses to rip meat from a thigh. It was a tuneless, painfully unmusical song, but it was a song. "You brought me RC Cola. You brought me a McDonald's apple pie."

"Volume down," Tean whispered, miming turning a dial.

"I love you!"

Tean was starting to think he had made a mistake, but all he said was, "Good Lord, what did they put you on?"

Whatever it was, Jem seemed thrilled with it, and he claimed that eating didn't hurt at all. Scipio was thrilled too; a lot of the Colonel's original recipe was falling to the floor, and Scipio snatched up the scraps before Tean could stop him—not that Tean was trying too hard. Outside, the day's last light painted the slopes gold, the tips of the mountains like incandescent filaments against the purpling sky.

"I love you, I love you, I love you."

"Ok," Tean said, "this was definitely a mistake."

But he smiled as Jem explained, for a solid five minutes, why he loved McDonald's apple pies—something to do with the cinnamon. And he was still smiling as Jem moved on to the eleven herbs and spices. And he was still smiling, his face hurting from it, when he came back from the kitchen with a hard cider and saw Jem letting

Scipio lick his hands clean — and wincing, obviously still half afraid, as he did it.

"That's enough," Tean said, and he came back with a warm washcloth and wiped Jem's hands. "You're going to make him sick."

"He likes me."

"Of course he does; he likes everyone."

"He doesn't like Ammon."

Tean focused on cleaning Jem's fingers. He had nice hands, his fingers blunt, a scattering of gold hair on the knuckles.

"LouElla had a dog," Jem said. And then he went into a story that was hard to follow, something about a basement and stairs and a dog — Tean was pretty sure it was a dog — named Antony, and then something about scars. He was struggling to turn himself out of his shirt, still talking about the scars, as Tean pulled the shirt back down, laughing, and inside not laughing at all as his hands grazed the tight frame of Jem's torso: hard muscle, warm skin, the scattering of golden hair across his chest and stomach.

"Ok, ok, ok," Tean said. "I saw it. I saw the scar. Just stop trying to take off your shirt."

"No, not that one, the one from Antony — "

"Yes, I saw. I saw the one from the dog."

"From Antony."

"From Antony."

Jem thought about that, his shirt halfway over his head, and then he let Tean pull his shirt back into place.

Opening the cider, Tean sat on the coffee table, inches separating him from where Jem was stretched out on the couch. He was surprised to find that he still liked the cider, that it hadn't been a fluke that one night with Jem at the Apollonia. Not that Tean needed to drink. Not usually, anyway. Tonight, though, he needed something, and he didn't want to make himself sick.

Jem had fallen silent, those stormy blue eyes drifting from spot to spot in the apartment. Tean rolled the cider in his mouth, the taste of apples, the slight bite of the alcohol, the sweat on his breastbone, the apartment too hot now, and the breeze from the balcony the only thing that kept Tean from bursting into flames.

Rolling onto his side, Jem put his hand on Tean's knee. Then his hand slid up. And up.

Tean pulled his hand away and said, "You're on a lot of medication."

"I want to kiss you."

"Let's talk about it tomorrow."

"I want to kiss you right now," Jem said, raising himself up on one elbow, catching Tean's shirt, trying to pull him forward.

"Jem, no."

"Why not?" He frowned, eyes glassy. "We already kissed. We're good at kissing."

"We agreed that we were better as friends. Anyway, you need to rest."

"Ammon. It's because of Ammon."

"You need sleep."

But Jem just waited, still propped up on one elbow, his other hand still clutching Tean's shirt.

"Yes," Tean finally said. "Ammon."

"He treats you like—" Jem struggled for words. "He treats you like—" His eyes fell on Scipio, who was sleeping on his side, his world in order after scraps of fried chicken. "He treats you like dog shit."

"I don't want to talk about it. Not right now. Not when you're like this."

"I don't care if you—" Jem tried to get up, but he got tangled in the blanket around his feet. "I don't care if you don't want—" Somehow he managed to get himself tangled even further. "Mother Mary fucking son of a bitch piece of shit!" He threw up his hands and dropped back onto the couch.

Tean removed the blanket, spread it out again, tucked Jem in, and said, "I think we both need sleep."

"Do you really want him?" Jem asked, his voice hazy. He was plummeting toward sleep, the final outburst seeming to have exhausted him. "Do you really still want him?"

Then his eyes closed, and Tean was glad he didn't have to answer.

The next morning, Tean woke to the smell of bacon, and he pulled on a tee and stumbled out to investigate.

"Morning," Jem said, his voice a little rough, his eyes much clearer. The bruises and swelling on his face were worse, and from time to time as he turned the bacon, his hand came up to probe his jaw, his nose, a black eye. Scipio was waiting patiently, and to judge by the drool, had already been rewarded with a few crispy bits while Tean was still asleep.

"Morning," Tean said. "I can do that."

"I needed to be up and doing something. But Scipio needs a walk."

So Tean dressed, walked Scipio, and when he came back, Jem was plating bacon and eggs and only slightly burned toast.

"I've almost got it," Jem said with a smile that was a little rough around the edges. "Give me sixteen more hours with a screwdriver, and I'll really fix that son of a bitch."

They ate, Jem only flinched once when Scipio shoved a cold nose into his arm.

"Are you feeling better?"

"Well, I'm not flying Air Fentanyl, so I guess the answer is no."

"I'm sorry."

"I'll be out of your hair today, though. Sorry you had to put up with me."

"I wasn't putting up with you. I like you. And you're my friend."

Jem scraped his fork across his plate, studying something on the table.

"Jem?"

"Right. Rover buddies, opposite sides of the planet, beep-beep-boop, just checking in. Like that?"

"Does that mean we're friends?"

"I don't know," he said, and then he pushed back from the table so hard that Scipio startled and ran to the other side of the apartment. "Yes. We're friends."

"Good." Tean dropped a burnt crust on his plate and dusted his hands. "Because I care about you. I want you to be my friend."

Jem leaned over the sink, probing the injuries on his face, and then he whirled around. "Can I just say one thing?"

"I really don't think—"

"You deserve way better than that asshole."

"Ok."

"You do. And I know you don't believe it for some reason, but you do."

"I've asked you not to talk about this. I've told you that you don't understand."

Out on the street, air brakes blasted the silence.

"You're right," Jem said. "You're absolutely right."

"Thank you."

"I don't understand."

"Jem."

"Ok, ok. I know that I really messed things up by lying to you. I know you'll never really be able to trust me again. But this is it, all in, everything on the table: is there any way we can start with a fresh slate?"

The sun was just breaking the crest of the mountains, sunlight coming between the blinds in dusty slats. Tean wanted to close his eyes, but he was too much of a coward, so he stared at the curling corner of the linoleum, where dust bunnies were trapped in old adhesive.

"One chance," Jem said. "Please. That's all I'm asking. Let me take you out once, just once, for real: Jeremiah Berger, Teancum Leon, on an honest-to-God date. And then, if you don't want to see me again, at least I'll feel like I had a chance."

"I'm never going to want that—not to see you again, I mean."

Jem was gripping the countertop behind him, his knuckles blanched.

"Ammon and I—" Tean tried.

"Please."

"I don't want to mess up our friendship."

"Please."

Tean didn't know if he believed in fate, but he knew when he'd been beaten, although it had never felt as strangely liberating as this. "It has to be today. We're going to Lima tomorrow, so it has to be today."

"Perfect."

"Jem, I feel like I need to be honest: Ammon and I have so much history together, and I've waited my whole life for this, to be with him. I don't want you to waste your time. And I don't want you to get your feelings hurt."

"Just don't make your decision yet," Jem said, grinning, and the crooked front teeth and the split lip and the black-and-blue bruises couldn't hide any of the cockiness. "I can be very persuasive."

"You've got egg on you face," Tean informed him. "Literally. It's on your nose."

41

Jem caught a ride with Tean to the DWR building and then barely made it back to the West Valley apartment on his bike. Getting up the fire escape was a fiasco, but he made it, and he showered and cleaned up as best he could. He took a couple of hydrocodone, rolled a joint, and smoked half of it before he felt up to the rest of the day. The sun was high and golden, the sky huge and blue arching over the valley.

He decided to do the rest of his errands walking. The Walmart was a mile and a half west, which wasn't too bad, especially with the air cool and still. When he got there, the hydrocodone and the joint were really starting to land, and he leaned on the cart to steady himself as he went up and down the aisles. He bought candles, matches, real plates, real flatware, a tablecloth, two filets, asparagus, and deli mashed potatoes. He bought Smith & Forge, a hard cider that was a little stronger, for Tean to try this time. He hit the state liquor store on the way back and bought a bottle of Campfire for himself. By the time he got home, he realized he had forgotten glasses.

He went to the Latus' apartment first. Sammi's mom, Amelika, answered the door; she was wearing a floral-print housedress and patent-leather mules, her gray hair in a long braid down her back.

"I forgot glasses," Jem said.

"We have glasses."

"And ice."

"We have ice."

"God, you're the absolute best. Can you keep this in your fridge while I get ready?"

Amelika smiled, accepted the bag with the food, and said, "What's his name?"

"Tean."

"You're blushing," Amelika said and then cackled. "You like him."

"No, I don't," Jem said, and then his face felt like a supernova. "Oh my God, I sound like I'm fifteen."

"Who does Jem like?" Sammi called from the other room.

"Nobody," Jem shouted back.

"He's got a new pretty boy," Amelika said.

"He's not pretty. He's got this hair that's, like, ka-chow. And these eyebrows—" Jem heard himself and managed to clamp his jaw shut. "Don't smile like that. You know what? I hate this family."

"Who's his pretty boy?" Kaelo asked, the big man filling a doorway down the hall. "What about his eyebrows? Are they nice?"

"They're ka-chow," Sammi called from deeper in the apartment.

"No," Amelika said, "that was his hair."

Jem ran away as fast as he could, given his injuries.

He made his way up the fire escape, sat on the windowsill and panted for a while, and then climbed inside the apartment. He unlocked the front door, something he almost never did, and then he set about getting the place ready: pushing the mattress into one corner, so it couldn't be seen from the living room; hanging the tablecloth from the shower curtain rod and running the shower at full steam to get the wrinkles out; picking up the old Hostess wrappers and the Banquet frozen meal trays. He shoved the garbage in an empty Walmart bag and tied it from the fire escape.

When he thought the tablecloth might be ready, he pulled it down from the rod, carried it into the living room, and spread it out on the floor. It was like a picnic. An indoor picnic. He kept repeating that as he weighted down the tablecloth's corners with tealight candles and then set more candles around the room. Hopping on one foot as he stripped, he held his phone to his ear and called Tean.

"I would like to take you on a date," Jem said when the doc answered.

"I thought we already talked about this."

"But now I'm calling you. Now I'm asking officially."

"Oh. Ok."

"Is that a yes?"

"Sure."

"You have to drive yourself."

"I can handle that."

"And you're just coming to my place; we're not actually going out to a restaurant or anything."

"Probably better that we don't go to a restaurant. I was just reading about the probability of contracting hepatitis—"

"Let's say six?"

"You sound out of breath."

"Do you remember where I live? Can you get here by yourself?"

"I think so. Why do you sound a little crazy?"

"See you at six," Jem said, disconnected, and realized he was naked and covered in sweat.

He showered. He wiped steam from the mirror. He didn't have muscles like a gym rat, and for some reason, the scar on his upper arm, the half-moon left by Antony's teeth, seemed very noticeable. Jem turned and looked over his shoulder, examining the long, white line that ran diagonally from shoulder to hip. Would it have killed him to do some pushups? Some pullups? Some fucking squats?

He put on a clean pair of jeans and a button-up printed with palm trees. In front of the mirror, he combed his hair and wondered when he'd let himself get so shaggy. When he checked the time—a few minutes past five—he actually groaned, and then he ran downstairs barefoot.

Amelika's eyes widened when she saw him.

Out of breath, Jem pointed to his hair.

"Looking good, man," Kaelo said as he passed through the hall. "I like how you're letting it grow out."

Jem groaned again.

"Ok," Amelika said. "It'll take five minutes."

They were the longest five minutes of Jem's life. The Latus' home smelled like fried pork and warm rice, with the slightest hint of a tang—maybe the homemade yogurt Kaelo kept trying to perfect. Every inch of space was filled with something that either might be usable, valuable, or usable or valuable in the future: armchairs stacked one upside down on the other; lithograph prints of Jesus fanned out like playing cards; the guts of an ancient radio, including vacuum tubes; a rolling rack of donated clothing, with a yellow polyester zoot suit at the front. Amelika cleared a chair, set it on the linoleum in the kitchen, and shook out the cape before tying it around Jem's shoulders.

"It's really not that long," Amelika said as she fitted the guard onto the clippers. "You look very handsome."

"I look like a wildebeest," Jem said.

"You know who you look like?" Kaelo said, grabbing a bowl of fried rice and a fork and considering Jem.

"Leave him alone," Amelika said.

"That guy in 6C," Kaelo said.

Jem made a strangled noise. "He's old."

"It's the hair," Kaelo said, gesturing with the fork. "He lets the sides get all long and bushy like that too."

"Stop teasing him," Amelika said.

Kaelo might have been grinning as he left; it was hard to tell with the big guy.

"This date is going to be a disaster," Sammi said as she stood in the opening that connected to the living room. "It's going to be like one of those things the History channel makes a special about."

"Stop it!" Amelika said. "You're both being terrible to him."

"People don't even go on dates anymore," she said, leaning against the wall. "Old people go on dates. Normal people just hang out. Or hook up. Why don't you just hook up with him?"

Amelika paused long enough to point the clippers at Sammi, and Sammi mumbled, "Um, not that, you should, you know, do that kind of stuff."

Jem rolled his eyes and said, "Amelika, I'm running out of time."

"I bet you're going to be such a dork," Sammi said, "and wear a suit and give him flowers and chocolates."

"Oh my God. Should I be wearing a suit?"

"You look very nice," Amelika said, switching off the clippers and patting his shoulder. "And you're good to go."

"But flowers. I should have flowers, right? And chocolates?"

"Don't listen to her. She's just like her father."

"I'll get flowers for you," Sammi said.

"Thank you," Jem breathed.

"Forty bucks."

From the other room came the sound of canned laughter, and then Kaelo's bellowing laugh joining in.

"Time's running out," Sammi said with a shrug.

"Amelika," Jem said.

"Oh no. I stay out of business."

"You're a war profiteer," Jem said as he pulled off the cape and counted out the cash. "These flowers better be worth forty dollars."

"Things are worth what people are willing to pay for them, bitch," Sammi said.

"Samantha," Amelika snapped. "Just for that, you're sweeping up."

Collecting the food and ice from the Latus, as well as borrowing jelly glasses and a frying pan for the steaks, Jem left. Back upstairs, Jem combed his hair again. And again. And again. And it was better after the haircut, but it was also the stupidest hair anyone had ever had on their head.

When he heard that thought, he dropped the comb. Bracing himself on the sink, the porcelain cool under his hands, he took a breath and met his own gaze. "You are losing your shit," he told himself. Himself agreed.

Sammi knocked at ten to six, and she was holding a bouquet of red roses.

"Where'd you get these?"

"Don't worry about it."

"How much did they cost?"

"They cost you forty bucks," she said with a smirk. As she left, she threw back, "Have fun on your date."

She said it the way she might have said *buggy ride*, and Jem was suddenly aware that he was in his late twenties and had absolutely no idea what teenagers thought anymore.

At six, he had the frying pan on the stove, the filets on the counter, and the ice in the jelly glasses. The tealights burned with tiny flames.

At six-ten, the ice was still ice, but little puddles had formed at the bottom of the jelly glasses.

At six-thirty, he called and got Tean's voicemail. "I just want to make sure you're ok," Jem said, hearing the raveled edges of his words. "I don't care if you're late; I just want to make sure you didn't get in an accident."

By seven the ice was melted, his phone was still dark, and the steaks were oozing blood. He carried everything downstairs. When he knocked, Amelika opened the door, and her eyes were dark and soft.

"You guys can, you know, have this," he said.

"Is your date over already?" Kaelo asked from somewhere in the apartment. "What happened? Did you blow it?"

"Jem, I'm so sorry," Amelika said.

He nodded and headed back upstairs. He locked the front door, smelling the hot wax of the candles, the burning wicks. He considered the cans of hard cider. Then he considered a little more seriously the bottle of whiskey. He sat on the tablecloth, legs stretched out, considering until it was a little past eight, and the only illumination in the apartment came from the wink and flutter of the tealights.

Two hydrocodone helped. A little.

His phone rang at three minutes after nine.

"I'm so sorry," Tean said. "I'm really, really sorry."

"Are you ok?"

"Yes. Yeah, I'm fine." Tean took a breath and said, "Ammon's oldest son tried to kill himself tonight. Daniel. Ammon thinks it's because Daniel's gay, but honestly, nobody knows anything yet, and . . . anyway, I had to come."

"You're with Ammon."

"I know we had plans, but this was an emergency, and Ammon really needed me."

"Yeah. Not like he had parents or siblings or neighbors or a wife."

"You don't understand—"

"I understand," Jem said and disconnected.

He rolled a joint, lit it, and crawled out onto the fire escape. Sitting there, the rusting iron cold under his ass, he could feel the hydrocodone like the roar of a twin prop, and it felt better than what lay beneath it. When he exhaled, the smoke drifted up toward the stars for just a moment before the wind slapped it back down into the valley.

42

It was November, and the mornings were too cold now to sit outside, but Tean did it anyway. His breath steamed in the darkness before dawn. For a while, Scipio lay beside him, and then he went back inside to the warmth and comfort of his doggie bed. Prayer might not have been the right word, but there was still that sense of bending, of straining toward something that might be hidden in the mountains, in the aspens, in the stillness of the river, in the trail a fox followed beside an elderberry bush. For answers, maybe. Or simply for a sense of something greater than everything else. The ancients had believed that the divine lay inside everything, just under its surface, as though the world were only a skin for transcendence. Was it really so strange, then, to believe a planet could have a soul?

He heard the occasional engine, a motorcycle pulling into the parking lot—someone getting off third shift, coming home to sleep away Saturday before doing it all again tonight. Tean blew on his hands and headed inside to make peppermint tea.

When the knock came at the door, Scipio went crazy barking, and Tean had a flash of premonition: something terrible had happened to his parents. No, to Ammon. Only that didn't make any sense; the police wouldn't send a uniformed officer to politely inform him that Ammon had been gunned down on a routine investigation. They would tell his wife. It was early, and he was still trying to think through things when he opened the door.

Jem stood there in a leather bomber jacket, a helmet under his arm.

"Oh," Tean said, which was perhaps the worst form of greeting/apology in the history of the universe. He was about to give it a second try when Scipio lunged past him, barreling into Jem's legs.

Jem stumbled back, his face pale, but already trying to regain control of the situation. Laughing—a little forced, it sounded to Tean—he ruffled Scipio's ears and stroked his head until the dog seemed satisfied. Then Scipio seemed to think investigating the stairs was a good idea, but Jem caught his collar and steered him back toward the apartment.

"Sorry," Tean said.

"At least he likes me," Jem said with a smile that, on anyone else, Tean would have called nervous. "I hate to think what he'd do if I made him mad."

"I'm sorry about all of it," Tean said. "This probably isn't the right way to do it, but I'm sorry, Jem. I'm really, really sorry."

"It's ok."

"No, it's not—" Tean cut off when Jem tossed the helmet to him, catching it by reflex. "What—"

"Get a heavy coat. Some blankets. Are you making your tea?"

"Yes, but—"

"Put it in a thermos."

Tean rolled the helmet in his hands.

"Hurry, dummy," Jem said, pushing him into the apartment.

Fifteen minutes later, Tean was on the back of Jem's motorcycle as they headed up into the mountains. The wind sharpened as they followed the canyon, and the heat of Jem's body, the smell of the leather, they were a welcome contrast to the cold. The darkness was thicker between the steep rock walls, and the headlight on Jem's bike provided only a watery, yellow spill over the asphalt. The roar of the engine swallowed everything else, rumbling up the canyon with its echo.

They followed I-80 until they cleared the canyon and exits for Park City appeared; Jem turned, following the valley south, but instead of heading for Park City, he turned west again, heading up the back of the Wasatch Mountains again. Utah's Olympic Park opened ahead of them, a maze of buildings and structures nestled in the mountains, most of it obliterated by the pre-dawn dark.

Jem coasted to the end of the parking lot and stopped the bike. Without a word, Jem led Tean to a bench that faced east, looking out across a brown swath of lawn and then, beyond the park's manicured grounds, the valley's wilderness of nettles, thistles, and the brush of the cold steppes. Together, they wrapped themselves in blankets and sat on the bench, shivering, as the sky to the east turned gray.

After a few minutes, Tean rested his head on Jem's shoulder.

"That bad, huh?" Jem said.

"Pretty bad."

"Do you want to talk about it?"

"Not really." But a moment later, Tean said, "We didn't go to Lima. He didn't say anything to Lucy. He's never going to say anything to Lucy, and he's never going to leave her. This time, it was because Daniel's too fragile, Ammon says he can't risk making things worse. It's always something. There's always a reason. I don't know why I let myself fall for it every time."

A Canada goose poked its dark head up from a tangle of weeds near the edge of the parking lot, and Tean realized he could see a little farther.

"And I really messed things up with you," Tean said. "Why did you come back? Why are you doing this?"

"Well, I seem to remember you saying something about friends and apologies. And you're my friend, and you already apologized, so I think we're ok." Jem pulled something out of his pocket. A piece of paper. He unfolded it, and Tean remembered that horrible day in Benny's apartment, the words he had scribbled across the page.

I needed to trust you.

"Tinajas read it to me," Jem said.

"I shouldn't have done that. Any of that. I'm sorry again."

"But you meant it. What you wrote. You needed someone you could trust. I know I messed up, but I want to be that person."

Tean tried to shrug, but he was so swaddled in blankets that he didn't know if the gesture came across.

"Besides," Jem said, "I think we're better as rover buddies anyway. I think we both need a rover buddy right now more than we need something else."

Tean started to cry, and he couldn't get his hands free from the blanket, so he just blinked as rapidly as he could.

"Beep-beep-boop?" Jem said, the inflection at the end a question.

With a wet laugh, Tean shook his head.

"That's me as a rover," Jem said. "And I'm all the way on this side of Mars, and you're all the way on the other side, and I'm just checking in, you know? Beep-beep-boop?"

Tean struggled free and wiped his face. "Boop," he finally said.

Jem put an arm around him, and that was better than the blanket. "It's going to get better."

"I know. It always does."

"And until it does, you're going to be too busy to wallow in it."

"I am?"

Jem worked something out of his bomber jacket and passed it over. It was a rolled-up book; when Tean flattened it against his knee, he could read the title: *Adult Literacy Workbook I*. He looked up at Jem.

"If it's not too much trouble," Jem said, the color high in his cheeks—Tean could see that too, now. "I don't have a lot of people I can ask."

"It's not too much trouble," Tean said.

"You don't have to."

"I want to."

"It's going to be really fucking annoying because I'm so dumb, but—"

"You're not dumb. You might be the smartest person I've ever met."

Something Tean couldn't read flickered in Jem's face, and the blond man blinked once and looked away and cleared his throat. Then he said, "Yeah, well, I mean, I'm pretty smart. I already know all seven vowels." He glanced over and burst out laughing. "I'm joking, Doc. I know there are only six."

"Umm, actually, there are only five."

"And y," Jem said. "Y can sometimes be a vowel."

Tean smiled the first real smile in weeks. "The student has become the master."

"I remembered that from school."

They sat there with the sagebrush and the smell of juniper, the cool darkness turning purple and then blue. The sun hadn't quite cleared the eastern rim of the valley when Jem spoke again.

"You remember what you said, about how life is a joke because we're going to die, and nothing we do means anything, and the only thing close to purpose we can find in life is to struggle with our own purposelessness?"

"That doesn't sound like me," Tean said.

Jem pinched him.

"Ow, ok. Yes. I remember. Vaguely."

"I guess I think that's bullshit. We do mean something. To ourselves, to each other. And we did something really good together. We changed the world in this teeny, tiny way, and made it better. And we did something good for Benny and Sook. And all of that means something. Even if we'd died, it would have meant something."

Silence weighed down the timothy, the wild rose, the soapweed, the bitterbrush. The whole world was still. And then, in the east, the sun cleared the mountains, and day came into the valley.

THE SAME PLACE

Keep reading for a sneak preview of *The Same Place,* book two
of The Lamb and the Lion.

1

Teancum Leon was sitting on his balcony in the morning dark, staring across the Salt Lake Valley, when the knock came. The May air was cool. Dawn had just outlined the spine of the Wasatch Mountains. The peppermint tea trembled in his hand as he jolted upright and stumbled inside. Scipio, his black Lab was barking furiously — probably with the expectation that whoever was standing in the hallway had treats and was desperate to give them to him, if only that damn door weren't in the way.

When Tean answered the door, Mrs. Wish was standing there. His neighbor from down the hall, she was normally a specimen of starch and hairspray. Right then, though, she looked like a ball of yarn after her army of cats — nicknamed the Irreconcilables — had really gotten going: her long white hair stood out in a million directions, and her housecoat was misbuttoned, exposing a length of white calf and blue veins.

"It's one of the babies," Mrs. Wish said and began to sob.

Tean stared at her for a moment. Then, pressing the mug of peppermint tea into her hands, he said, "Let's go take a look."

As a wildlife veterinarian for Utah's Division of Wildlife Resources, Tean had to be an expert on a wide variety of animals. More than that, he had to be capable of learning what he needed to know quickly so that he could understand and address problems in the state's diverse ecosystem. On any given day, he might have to deal with elk poaching, complaints about the steelhead population, or a California condor struggling to hatch her eggs. Maybe all three, in fact. To date, nothing had come anywhere close to the challenge that Mrs. Wish presented.

When they got to the end of the hall, Mrs. Wish fumbled with the mug of tea, still sobbing, and tried to open the door. Tean gently nudged her aside, took her keys, and let them both inside. The apartment was sixty-percent cat dander, thirty-percent potpourri, and ten-percent livable space. From one wall, a larger-than-life President Woodrow Wilson stared down at them from his portrait. He looked just as worried about the Irreconcilables as Mrs. Wish.

After settling Mrs. Wish at her small dining table and making sure she took a long drink of the peppermint tea, Tean headed for the closet where they had set up Senator George H. Moses's birthing box. Tean had been here for several hours in the middle of the night, doing what Mrs. Wish insisted on calling 'supervisorial vigilance,' although Tean hadn't really done anything except eat store-brand chocolate chip cookies straight out of the package, listen to Mrs. Wish's rambling invectives against Teddy Roosevelt's mustache, and let Senator George H. Moses handle her own business. Barring an emergency, the cat knew better than Tean how to deliver her litter; she was biologically programmed to do it. And she'd done it just fine. Once Senator George H. Moses and the kits were settled in the birthing box in the closet, Tean had given a few basic instructions and caught a few hours of sleep.

"Not in there," Mrs. Wish said through her tears, waving him away from the closet. "I moved them."

Tean frowned. "I told you to leave them alone, keep your distance, and keep an eye on the other Irreconcilables."

Coloring faintly, Mrs. Wish said, "I had to make sure the babies were all right through the night. And it's a good thing, too. I woke up to the most horrible noises. By the time I'd gathered the courage to get out of bed and turn on the light, one of the kits was gone. You have to help me find her."

"Why don't you wait here?" Tean said. "I'll take a look. The birthing box is in your bedroom?"

Mrs. Wish took a sip of tea and nodded. Through more tears, she said, "This is very weak, you know. You're not brewing it correctly."

At the end of the hall, Tean paused at the door to Mrs. Wish's bedroom. Senator Poindexter, a nasty, brutish Siamese who started pretty much every scrap in the apartment, was lurking in the doorway across the hall. He hissed when Tean looked over.

"Watch out," Tean said. "If she says the word, I've got a pair of nail scissors that'll go through your balls like they're butter."

"What's that?" Mrs. Wish shouted.

"Nothing," Tean called back.

He let himself into the bedroom, barely closing it in time to prevent Senator Poindexter from squeezing past him. Lace, especially lace doilies, were a prominent part of Mrs. Wish's overall decorating scheme, but she had taken it to a new level in the bedroom. Waterfalls of lace. Huge, ruffled explosions of lace. Tean wondered if psychologists already had a name for a phobia of lace. They'd have one for sure after they institutionalized him.

At the side of the bed he found the birthing box. He approached carefully and looked in from a distance. Then he sighed. Moving the box hadn't been enough for Mrs. Wish. She'd washed the kittens, in spite of Tean's instructions to leave them alone, and she'd cluttered the nest with tiny toys. She'd even added treats, although she must have known that the kittens weren't weaned yet. Senator George I I. Moses was crouched between Tean and the kits, and when she saw him, she hissed. Blood stained her whiskers.

Tean checked the food and water in the box and then let himself out of the room. He made his way down the hall. When Mrs. Wish saw his face, she started to cry again.

"Mrs. Wish—"

"Oh, she's dead, isn't she?"

"I think so."

"What happened? I didn't step on her, did I? Or do something in my sleep?"

"No."

"Well, what happened? I made absolutely sure that the door was closed. I told Senator Poindexter quite clearly that he couldn't sleep with me. He was very upset. I suppose I'll have to get everyone together and hold a funeral." Tean wasn't sure if everyone meant Mrs. Wish and the Irreconcilables or Mrs. Wish and her enormous extended family—with her, either one was possible, or both. "Where did you put her poor little body?"

"I don't think you understand. Sometimes, when a kit is sick or already dead, the mother disposes of it."

"She couldn't have buried the poor thing. She hasn't been outside."

Tean drew a deep breath. "Many animals will eat their young in extreme conditions."

It took a moment, and then Mrs. Wish's cheeks pinkened. "I should think not."

"It does happen."

"I don't believe it. Senator George H. Moses is their mother. She has a mother's instinct. She never, never would have hurt her own kittens." With a kind of exalted certainty, Mrs. Wish raised her chin. "I know it in my heart."

"Well," Tean said, "right now, my recommendation is to leave the kittens with their mother, but if you see any sort of behavior—"

"Certainly," Mrs. Wish said, standing, shoving the mug along the table so hard that it skittered. "Certainly. She's their mother, Dr. Leon. To think I would allow anything else . . . I just honestly can't believe what I'm hearing from you. I can't believe this constitutes your professional, medical opinion. Is this what they teach you in schools these days?"

"I think I should go."

"You said if the kitten was sick, but earlier, you told me they all looked healthy. Did you make some kind of mistake? Is that what this is? You're trying to cover up your own shoddy work."

"Good night, Mrs. Wish."

He reached for the mug, and she slapped his hand. A horrified look flitted across her face, as though she couldn't quite believe what she'd done, and then it was gone, and her expression was hard.

Tean thought about telling her why it had happened: stress, stress, stress. The stress of the birthing box being moved. The stress of having the kittens taken away one by one, bathed, and handled. The stress—Tean imagined—of Mrs. Wish rising in the middle of the night to check on the kittens again and again.

Instead, though, he kept his mouth shut and headed for the door.

"I can't believe I thought you'd be an acceptable match for Violet," Mrs. Wish said to his back. "She might be a bit gimpy, and she's got a droopy mouth, and she's older than dirt, but at least she has the milk of human kindness. She's not a heartless beast like you, imagining the absolute worst, most impossible things. As though one of God's own creations could do what you've just suggested. As though a mother could do such a thing, Dr. Leon. Their own mother."

From the hallway, with his hand on the doorknob, Tean said, "Mrs. Wish, the best thing you can do right now is keep your bedroom door shut, sleep in the guest bedroom, and only check on Senator George H. Moses to fill her food and water and clean out the litter box."

"I certainly don't need any more instructions from you, you . . . you Communist pig."

"It was a flyer from the socialist party," Tean muttered as he dragged the door shut. "And someone just put it under my windshield wiper."

2

Tean had to hurry to dress and walk Scipio before work. Their walk was pretty standard; today, it included Scipio chasing a squirrel when Jem let him off the leash at Liberty Park, and then, a few minutes later, Tean rescuing Scipio when a goose cornered him. The black Lab had been pressed up against an old oak, barking wildly at the goose until Tean reattached the leash and led him away. As soon as they'd put a few yards between themselves and the bird, Scipio started bounding and frolicking, his tail going like mad. He obviously considered himself the winner of that particular skirmish and was unbearably proud of himself.

When Tean got to work, he found himself immediately caught up in a fresh conflict. Norbert Smith, eighty years old, who frequently forgot to shave and—even more noticeably—to bathe, had worked for DWR for over forty years. He'd handled a lot of the state's poaching complaints, especially from the northwest quadrant, and he'd done a good job of it until a bad fall and a broken leg in December. Everyone, Tean included, had expected that to loosen Norbert's death grip on his job, but instead of retiring, Norbert had clung on. Now he was back, using a walker to navigate the DWR building, unable to drive long distances let alone hike into the back country to catch poachers. And from the hints he had dropped, he was obviously hoping someone would try to fire him so he could sue.

Instead, Tean had put him in a clerical job, digitizing old records. It was work that needed to be done—although from what Tean could tell on his initial review, all Norbert had managed to do was scan the blank backs of hundreds of pages and include them all in the same file. More importantly, it kept Norbert clear of DWR's daily operations.

Except for this morning. And ten other mornings just like it over the last two months.

"I know you think I'm a bitch," Hannah was saying. She was Tean's colleague and friend, a biologist specializing in native aquatics. Her chestnut hair had a million flyaways today, and her face was splotchy. "Just say it, Norbert. You think I'm a bitch. But I don't care. I don't know how that phone call got routed to you, but you have absolutely no right fielding calls from the public and authorizing them to do whatever they want to do."

Norbert sank down in his chair, an eighty-year-old sullen child. "Can I go now? Got work to do."

"She's right," Tean said. "Your job isn't to handle calls from the public."

"I've done this job longer than either of you's been alive," Norbert said, his sunken eyes cutting back and forth as though he couldn't quite fix on Tean. "It was a simple question. I know my years of experience don't mean bullplucky to either of you, but they ought to count for something."

"Well, that's fair," Tean said, darting a look at Hannah. "I do value your experience, and I know that many times, people call in with the same questions, so I'm sure you felt comfortable answering—"

"The man wanted to go fishing with dynamite," Hannah shouted. "And Norbert said yes."

"It's those damn burbot," he said, referring to an invasive species of fish. "Let him blow them all to hell if he wants."

"That's illegal and unethical—"

"Ok," Tean said. "Norbert, it's not your job to answer the phone. If you do, and if you're fielding questions from the public, you need to give answers in line with DWR policy. Is that clear?"

"Wasn't like this back in the day," Norbert said, slouching even lower in the chair.

"Is that clear?"

"Yes."

"And talk to him about the paperwork," Hannah said.

"The paperwork?" Tean said.

"He's not doing any of the clerical work he's supposed to be doing. He's supposed to be processing surrendered turkey tags, and—"

"Young lady," Norbert said, "if they got a tag, and if they didn't get a darn turkey, why should I care what happens to the tag after?"

"Because it's your job."

"All right," Tean said. "Hannah, thank you for raising your concerns. Norbert, even if you don't think the task is important, it still needs to get done."

"I don't have time for this," Norbert said, easing himself up from the seat and grabbing his walker.

"That's right," Hannah said, "you need to hurry back to your desk and look at those Japanese *Playboys* you keep in the top drawer."

Tean covered his eyes.

Norbert huffed, and it sounded like he might say something, but then the door opened, and the walker creaked away. He slammed the door behind him.

"Well, you were a lot of help," Hannah said.

Dropping his hand, Tean said, "Don't start with me."

"He ought to be fired. I wasn't joking about those pornos, either. He really does have them in his desk."

"He wants to be fired, Hannah. And then he's going to sue for ageism or who knows what."

"He was only ever good for one thing, and that was rousting poachers, and he was only good at it because he did half the poaching himself. He's a nightmare with public calls. He's a disaster with clerical work. The Division has perfectly legitimate grounds to fire him."

"You know it's not that simple."

"He's creating a hostile work environment," Hannah said. "He objectifies women, especially with those magazines. I feel sexually harassed. I'm going to sue."

"Look, I will make him get rid of the magazines. I didn't even know about the magazines. And I had no idea you felt like this was a hostile work environment. We're going to—"

Hannah screamed as she got up from the chair. "I get so sick of being the only one around here with a pair of balls."

She slammed the door even harder than Norbert had.

When the ringing in his ears died down, Tean got back to work on his most recent project: controlling an outbreak of canine distemper that was affecting populations of coyotes and feral dogs around Heber City. It was starting to get into the domestic populations, and there would be hell to pay if the virus worked its way north into Park City and someone's designer Chihuahua caught it. He was just digging into the research around controlling outbreaks when his door flew open again.

Hannah stood there, her face even more splotchy than before, her hair looking like she'd been building up a static charge. She just stood there, breathing hard, arms folded across her chest. Tean braced himself. He and Hannah had worked together for years, and until recently, they'd gotten along well. She was smart, capable, dependable, and funny. Something had changed, though, and over the last weeks and months, she'd displayed a temper—not always unjustified, as the case with Norbert had shown—that was nevertheless out of character. She had dark rings under her eyes, and although Tean felt like a bad person for thinking this, she'd put on a little weight.

Then Hannah stepped into the office, shutting the door behind her, and started to cry.

Lurching out of his seat, Tean made his way around the desk and hugged her. She cried for a long time, sobbing against his shoulder while he patted her back. His whole body was locking up at the sheer amount of contact with another person; he summoned up memories of the Darwin Awards to keep himself from climbing out of his skin. The guy who had tried to build his own rocket car. The guy who had performed experimental surgery on himself. The guy who had tried to chew through an overhead power line to prove that squirrels weren't any better than humans.

Finally, Hannah squeezed his arm and pulled back. "I'm fine," she said thickly, wiping her face. "I'm really fine. I just hate that I fell apart like that."

"It's ok."

"It's not ok. It's this horrible female stereotype, and I hate playing into it."

"I cried the other night when Jem made me watch the same episode of *The Simpsons* for the fourth time in a row."

Hannah laughed, and then she coughed, and then she laughed some more.

"Want to sit down?" Tean asked. "Have some tea?"

Hannah nodded and said, "Not that horrible homemade nettle tea."

"I'll just go borrow some from your office then."

So he sprinted to her office, stole two foil-wrapped bags of Morning Jazz, and sprinted back. He filled the electric kettle. While the water heated, he got the mugs and unwrapped the tea bags.

"How is Jem?" Hannah asked, obviously trying and not quite succeeding to keep the disapproving note from her voice.

"He's the same as always. He breaks into my apartment whenever he wants, and I come home to find him and Scipio napping on the couch together. He makes me spend money I don't have on clothes I don't want, and then he proceeds to tell me I have no butt and gives me ridiculous orders about how many squats I should be doing. Oh, and he eats like he's fourteen. I think if I took a blood sample, I'd see Big Mac special sauce running in his veins."

Her eyes narrowed. "Why is he talking about your butt? Is that a gay thing? Is he making a move?"

Tean rolled his eyes. "We're just friends."

"As my grandmother used to say, 'You can fool yourself, and you can fool your mother, but you can't fool me.'"

"We're just friends."

The kettle whistled, and it was a nice excuse for Tean to turn away from the look in Hannah's eyes. After pouring the hot water so the tea could steep, Tean sat and said, "Is this about Norbert?"

"No. I mean, not really. I hate that old bag of bones, and I think he's doing a terrible job at something I care about. He's this awful reminder of how things used to be—a good-old-boys club where all you had to do was ride around in your truck and bust people who weren't your friends. But it's not enough to get worked up over."

Tean chose not to mention the screaming that had taken place fifteen minutes earlier.

Fiddling with the tag at the end of the tea bag's string, Hannah stared off into space for a moment. When she spoke again, she said, "I honestly feel like I'm going crazy, Tean."

"You have seemed upset for a while now."

Hannah laughed. "You're too nice. I've been a bitch for months. I know I have. I've had a lot going on. That's not really an excuse, no reason to treat people badly. But it's the truth. No, this is something else. It's just been the last little while."

"What?"

"I think someone's following me."

3

Jem was stocking men's shirts in Snow's Department Store, in the men's section, under the watchful eye of Mr. Kroll.

"No, no, no," Mr. Kroll snapped. He stood with perfect posture, hands clasped schoolboy style at his waist, his graying hair shiny with pomade. "Mr. Berger, have you been paying attention at all?"

"Yes, Mr. Kroll," Jem said. "I've definitely been paying attention." He'd been paying attention, for example, to the way Mr. Kroll watched his ass when he bent over to arrange the shirts on the display table's lower shelves.

"Well, it's very hard to tell from the sloppiness of this work. Can you please try a little harder?"

"Of course, Mr. Kroll."

Jem was hoping that would settle the matter—sometimes Mr. Kroll just liked to poke his nose in long enough to remind everyone that he was the manager of men's wear at Snow's Department Store, which was apparently the retail equivalent of being the king of England. Instead, though, Mr. Kroll just stood there, smelling like baby powder and gardenia, until Jem started to sweat. His back was itching like crazy, and he couldn't breathe in a shirt and tie and jacket.

"For heaven's sake," Mr. Kroll said, pushing past Jem to grab a shirt that was still wrapped in its plastic. He shook it in front of Jem. "What does this say?"

"Giroux," Jem said. He'd memorized that one quickly. "And the rest of these are Giroux too."

"Not the brand, ignoramus," Mr. Kroll said, moving closer until his body pinned Jem against the display table. Jem had front-row seats to the broken capillaries in Mr. Kroll's nose, to the faint wrinkles around his mouth, to the way he ran his tongue inside his upper lip when he raked his eyes up and down Jem. Mr. Kroll tapped a finger against the packaging. "This. What does this say?"

Jem's face heated. He was learning—with Tean's help—but it was still hard, and he was slow. He still had to work out the sounds in his head most of the time. Decoding, Tean called it. And it was extra hard because Tean also insisted that Jem was dyslexic, although Jem didn't think that was the case. Nobody had ever told him before that he was dyslexic, anyway.

Mr. Kroll was still staring.

Sweat prickled under Jem's arms. He resorted to his usual tactic in these situations—his number one, charm-the-shit-out-of-a-bear smile.

"LinenTouch," Mr. Kroll said. "And what about this one?"

That one was easy because Tean made Jem read everything at the grocery store. "Cream."

"And is LinenTouch the same as Cream?"

Jem had something smart to say about that, something about Tean, who probably would have worn LinenTouch pants with a cream-colored shirt and ivory loafers, but he just smiled and shook his head. Now that Mr. Kroll had pointed out the difference, Jem could see the slight variation in the colors of the—what he'd thought of, until now, as white—dress shirts he'd been stocking.

"And I don't suppose reading each shirt's color and then putting it in the right pile, I don't suppose that's too much."

"No, Mr. Kroll."

"And it's not too much to assume you can read, is it?"

Jem's face was on fire, but he still smiled. "No, Mr. Kroll."

"And it's not too much to hope you can finish this job in an efficient, timely manner, without my standing over you to make sure you do it properly, is it?"

The old perv would have loved that, Jem knew: standing there, mooning over Jem's ass, snapping out orders that Jem had to obey. Once, he had made Jem pick up pins after another girl had knocked them on the floor. Mr. Kroll had stayed to observe the whole thing. He hadn't picked up a damn pin himself; he'd just stood there, swallowing obscenely whenever Jem looked up from where he knelt on the floor.

All Jem said, though, was, "No, Mr. Kroll."

"Then see that you do it."

With a snappy little spin—about a half-inch shy of clicking his heels together like a good Nazi—Mr. Kroll headed over to ties, where he was already ripping into Sydney. "If our patrons choose to buy a poorly manufactured tie from a margarita-swilling, beach-bum crooner, that's their own business—and their own poor taste in judgment," Mr. Kroll was saying. "But the Snow's Department Store men's wear will go up in flames before we display those ties next to the Stefano Riccis."

"What got in his garter?" a voice asked behind Jem. Mckenna was barely twenty, Tongan, with glossy black hair that came to her waist. She was also stunningly gorgeous, which seemed to be Snow's Department Store's primary requirement for female employees. Distantly related to Jem's neighbors, the Latus, Mckenna had helped Jem get the job at Snow's in spite of his lack of a job history—he had never had a job before. He was starting to figure out why.

"It's just a phase," Jem said. "He's just going through that forty-year-long, involuntary celibacy phase. You know. When creeps like him are awful assholes because they can't get anybody to look at their junk."

"I think he wants you to do more than look at it."

Jem gagged.

"Oh shit, he's looking over here," Mckenna said. And, true, Mr. Kroll was glaring at them and already abandoning Sydney, who was sobbing into a rack of Margaritaville neckwear.

"Pretend you're whispering something," Jem said.

"Why?"

"Because I told you to."

"No, I mean, why pretend? I can just whisper something for real."

Mr. Kroll was getting closer.

"Then whisper something for real," Jem growled.

Mckenna leaned in and spoke softly into his ear: "I swear to God he's getting a boner just thinking about yelling at you."

"You're the devil," Jem said, fighting a smile as Mckenna slipped away.

"I'm sorry," Mr. Kroll said as he approached. "Did I miss something? Did I overlook a staff notification that this time is meant to be used for idle conversation and fraternization? This is Snow's Department Store," invoking it like the name of God, "and that might not mean anything to you, Mr. Berger, but it certainly does to me. Your behavior reflects on the men's wear department as a whole and on me personally, and I'm starting to believe I made a grave error—"

Jem let the rest of the words float past on a cloud of baby powder and gardenia. He might not be able to read LinenTouch—not yet, anyway—but he could read people, and Mr. Kroll couldn't have bluffed his way past a middle schooler.

"I'm sorry," Jem said, lowering his voice and laying a hand on Mr. Kroll's arm. It was painful, really, the sudden flush in Mr. Kroll's wrinkled cheeks. "I'm really sorry. I just heard, though, and I thought you should know. Everybody else wanted to let them catch you with your pants down—oops, I mean, you know, unawares; sorry for the vulgarity—but I just don't think that's right. You take care of us; we ought to be taking care of you too."

The cocktail of flattery, physical touch, and conspiracy hit most people hard; Jem had used it plenty of times before. It hit Mr. Kroll harder than most, practically flattening him.

"Yes, well, I don't—you'll have to—it's not entirely clear—"

"Surprise inspection."

Mr. Kroll's eyes shot open.

"Mckenna thinks it's only a sixty-percent chance. She didn't want to freak you out. But I think the only responsible thing to do is to get ready."

"Good heavens," Mr. Kroll breathed, fanning himself. "Merciful heavens."

"It's too bad we don't have much time," Jem said, "because I was talking to the CEO's secretary—we bumped into each other when I was filing my HR paperwork—and she told me how much he loves See's caramels. I'd run over and get some, but—"

Jem threw a dispirited look at the display table with the dress shirts.

"Go," Mr. Kroll whispered fiercely. "Hurry. And get two boxes. No, three."

"My credit card—"

"Go." Mr. Kroll was strangling on the word as he shoved cash into Jem's hands and pushed him toward the door. "Mr. Snow himself," he breathed, the Messiah coming again. "Hurry!"

Jem jogged toward the door. He waved the cash at Mckenna as he passed men's active wear and winked.

She rolled her eyes.

Acknowledgments

My deepest thanks go out to the following people (in alphabetical order):

Austin Gwin, for giving me collectible presidential ashtrays, helping me think about all the ways a gay Mormon boy can be a disappointment, teaching me that it's Nordstrom and not Nordstrom's, and reminding me that *Playboy* has serious articles too! For a whole lot of encouragement, too, when I sorely needed it.

Steve Leonard, for keeping track of margaritas, reassuring me that these guys have chemistry, researching dog fur, thinking about timelines and Ponderosa pines, counting assholes, reminding me that this is not a first-person story (somehow that slipped past everyone else!).

Anne Justice-Allen, without whom, this book wouldn't exist, for taking the time to talk about the life and career of a wildlife veterinarian, describing her office and lab, talking me through a necropsy, researching avian cholera, providing the germ for this murder, and for her general willingness to lend her expertise!

Cheryl Oakley, for helping me think so critically about the Mrs. Wish chapter, discussing the implications of cleaning up bloodstains, reading the manuscript twice, helping me track the pacing in the beginning, and spotting the moment things started to come together—and too many other things to list!

Tray Stephenson, for encouraging me to think about how these characters develop, for his careful attention to plural names, for catching so many of my typos and errors, and for his unfailingly positive and upbeat emails.

Dianne Thies, for reminding me to use salami, pointing out that Corona bottles are clear, teaching me more about dogs (and there will be definitely be more of that in the future!), helping me think about those three magic words, spotting so many of my mistakes, and most of all for her encouragement when I was at a low point in revisions.

Jo Wegstein, for so many things that I'll fall short listing them: ventral and dorsal abdomens, Sook's place in the plot, questions of pacing, the logistics of driving around an open-pit mine, clarity and specificity in my prose, consistency in characterization, Tean as a scientist — and for so much more.

About the Author

Learn more about Gregory Ashe and forthcoming works at
www.gregoryashe.com.

For advanced access, exclusive content, limited-time promotions,
and insider information, please sign up for my mailing list at
http://bit.ly/ashemailinglist.

www.ingramcontent.com/pod-product-compliance
Lightning Source LLC
Chambersburg PA
CBHW051938240626
47153CB00005B/1543